What readers are saying about
Old Wounds to the Heart

"Secrets, passion, love, and violence: they're not for the weak of heart or body, which is what makes the septua- and octogenarians in Ken Oder's latest Whippoorwill Hollow novel so intriguing. The characters are endearing and eccentric, and the setting at once brutal and brooding. I couldn't put it down, and I can't wait for the next one."

- Pamela Fagan Hutchins, Brenham, TX;

USA Best Book Award winning author of *Heaven to Betsy* and the Katie & Annalise mysteries

". . . a work of art, or poetry, or beauty and all of the above. Oder takes you back in time to a place in a rural Virginia town and gently reveals parts and pieces of its topography and people. The story is not a gentle one . . . but it is simply beautiful."

- Rebecca Nolen, Houston, TX;
author of *Deadly Thyme* and *The Dry*

". . . masterfully crafted, brimming with the sort of spellbinding wisdom that takes your breath away. Cast from characters who could easily be our friends and family, this story confronts the darker side of human nature with unflinching precision. It reveals that the line dividing right from wrong isn't always clearly defined, that an undeniable symbiosis exists between joy and heartache."

- Daniel Wimberley, Collinsville, OK;
author of *The Pedestal*

"A fascinating yet simple story that grabs you immediately. . . . I loved the way the scenes were set and yet left room for your imagination. Given the advanced age of the characters, I was surprised to find how well I related to their feelings. This story was beautifully told, and I very much enjoyed it."

- Jason Holmes, St. Louis, MO

"…fantastic. I love romance-based books. Having lived in the Blue Ridge Mountains all my life, I thought the author couldn't have picked a better setting. The whole story is wonderful."

- Justin Lambe, Fancy Gap, VA

OLD WOUNDS
TO THE HEART

A NOVEL BY
KEN ODER

SkipJack Publishing

Oder, Ken.
Old wounds to the heart : a novel / by Ken Oder. -- First edition.
pages cm. -- (The Whippoorwill Hollow novels ; 2)
ISBN 978-1-939889-29-4 (first edition : paperback)
ISBN 978-150897033-0 (advanced review edition)
ISBN 978-1-939889-28-7 (e-book)

1. Appalachians (People)--Fiction. 2. Appalachian Region, Southern--Fiction.   I. Title. II. Series: Oder, Ken. Whippoorwill Hollow novels ; 2.

PS3615.D4657O43 2015   813'.6
                              QBI15-600128

978-1-939889-29-4 paperback
978-1-939889-28-7 e-book
First Edition: July 2015

Editor: Meghan Pinson

Cover photo: *Eugene in the Fog* by Debby Oder, enhanced by Devon Oder, and adapted for the cover by Hannah Hawker

***

SkipJack Publishing
Houston

To Cindy

Contents

PART I

THANKSGIVING

Chapter 1

The Abduction

Thanksgiving Day, 1967

Whippoorwill Hollow, Virginia

A red pickup truck crested a knoll on Whiskey Road two hours before dawn. Its driver cut off its lights and engine and the truck drifted down a hill, rolled across a one-lane bridge, and came to rest in a clearing beside the road. The door creaked open and a tall, stout man wearing a red ball cap, a hunting jacket, and bib overalls stepped off the running board into the pale glow of a silver-ringed moon. He blew a stream of vapor into the cold night air and leaned inside the truck cab. He withdrew leg irons and manacles and shoved them in the side pockets of his jacket, lifted a rifle from a rack over the back window, pulled its strap over his shoulder, and walked across the clearing to a split-rail fence. He unlatched a gate and closed it behind him.

A rust-red barn stood fifty yards in front of him. To his right, Little Bear River snaked through pastureland. A hill rose up steeply on his left and a two-story white farmhouse with a green tin roof stood on its summit. The house was dark and quiet and he saw no movement inside. He took off his hat, pulled a black ski mask over his head, and lifted the rifle off his shoulder to switch off the safety latch before he walked to the base of the hill.

In the house, Billy Kirby lay in bed thinking about the mess he had made of his life. He had passed his eightieth birthday in August. In September, his wife succumbed to cancer. They were estranged when she passed and she died hating him; his serial infidelity had broken her heart and wrecked their marriage. They had separated and reconciled many times, but even when they were together, they fought. Their only child was the worse for it all. He grew up to become a cruel drunk and an angry brawler. Billy had paid off Blakey's victims and managed to keep him out of jail for most of his adult life, but in Blakey's early forties he assaulted the boyfriend of a woman who had jilted him and held her at gunpoint in her bedroom for four hours. He was convicted of assault and kidnapping and was sentenced to ten years in the state penitentiary in Richmond. Billy blamed himself in part for the way Blakey turned out. Blakey blamed him for all of it.

Thanksgiving morning Billy was alone and miserable and saw no prospect of happiness in his future. He lay on his back in bed with his arm draped over his brow and stared at moon-shadows on the ceiling. Mary Jo's death had pitched him into a deep well of grief and hopelessness. Since her passing he had become obsessed with the many mistakes he'd made that had ruined their lives: the trysts, the affairs, the scores of women who lined the long hallway of his memory. Most of them had meant nothing to him at the time beyond the pleasure and excitement of the moment, but for the past few weeks, his thoughts kept returning to a summer afternoon many years ago, before he married Mary Jo, when he lay on a blanket with a young beauty under a maple tree beside Little Bear River. She told him she loved him that day, and he turned away from her. In the winter of his life when it was too late to make a difference, he was convinced that rejecting her was his biggest mistake. He thought he could have lived a good life with her, but in his youth he was too foolish to understand that. He made the wrong choice and rejected her love. Now, in his old age, he was alone; no one loved him; and he loved no one.

Billy rolled over on his side and looked out the window at the barren limbs of a sweetgum tree swaying in the wind and thought about the pistol that lay in a bureau drawer fifteen paces from his bed. For three nights running, the specter of the revolver, its smooth blue barrel and its wooden grip, had haunted him. It offered the best way out, he thought. If his hand was steady, he would feel nothing. Death would be instantaneous, and the eight decades of mistakes that rode in the bottom of his heart like a sack of cold stones would die with him.

He was still thinking about the pistol when a scraping sound downstairs broke his concentration. The noise seemed to have come from the dining room window below his bedroom. He sat up in bed and listened. The dining room floor creaked near the window and then groaned farther into the room.

He got out of bed, crossed the bedroom, and withdrew the pistol from the bureau drawer. He stood looking down at it, cold and heavy in his hand, his thoughts of ending his misery still fresh in his mind. The faint popping and cracking of the staircase drew his attention back to the problem at hand. He took a step toward the hallway and listened. He could barely hear the light tread of someone creeping down the hall. He tiptoed to the bedroom closet, stepped inside, and peeked through the crack between the door and the frame. A man wearing a black ski mask and carrying a rifle stepped into the moonlit room and went to the foot of the bed.

Billy stepped out of the closet and trained his pistol on the man's back. "Drop it."

The man turned and faced Billy.

"Drop the rifle," Billy said, "or I'll shoot you down in your tracks." The man hesitated and then took a step toward Billy. Billy squeezed the trigger. There was a click, but no explosion. The man in the ski mask flinched. Billy squeezed the trigger again, but there was no report. Again. Still nothing. The man closed the distance between them and brought the barrel of his rifle down on Billy's head.

Billy lay on a blanket under a maple tree by Little Bear River. A young woman lay beside him, sleeping. A soft wind rustled the leaves and leopard spots of shade and sunlight quivered on her smooth skin. He traced his fingertips from the curve of her hip up her back to her shoulders and caressed the silky blonde curl at the nape of her neck.

She stirred and rolled over, covering her breasts with her arm. A lock of golden hair fell across her eyes, and she smiled. "I love you, Billy."

His gut tightened, but he forced a smile. "Come on now, darlin. Don't spoil the fun with that foolishness. You don't love me. You love the good times we've had. That's what you love, the good times."

The hurt took a while to gather in her eyes, but it soon came on strong. She rolled over and pressed her face into the folds of the blanket and her shoulders shuddered with quiet sobs.

When he reached out to touch her, the blanket beneath them began to move and he fell backwards, confused. Night had fallen suddenly and she was gone and he was on his back. He raised a hand to his throbbing head and his other hand dragged strangely along beside it. He held his hands up to the moonlight. They were handcuffed together and there was blood on them.

He groaned and looked around. He was sliding across frozen ground on his back. His ankles were bound by leg irons and a ski-masked man with a rifle strapped over his shoulder was pulling him across the yard by the chains of his leg manacles. He pulled Billy through a break in the boxwood bushes that lined the driveway and Billy's nightshirt rode up his back and gravel raked his flesh. The man stopped, leaned over, and propped his hands on his knees, breathing heavily. Billy wanted to get to his feet to try to overwhelm him, but the blow to his head had robbed him of his strength and his will.

Billy's assailant seemed to recover his wind. He picked up the leg irons and pulled Billy on across the yard to a split-rail fence. He grabbed Billy's handcuffs and pulled him up to a standing position. Then he shoved Billy against the fence, forced him to bend over the top rail, and pushed him over it. Billy slid down to the ground on the other side and lay helplessly on his back while the man climbed over the fence. His trailing leg hung on the top rail and he almost fell, but he righted himself as he pitched forward and he landed on his feet. He bent over and grasped his knee, groaning. After a short while, he straightened up, grabbed the leg irons, and dragged Billy down the hill toward the barn.

Grit and rocks sliced Billy's back and he wanted to scream, but he could not; a farmer had crushed the life out of his voice during a fight in a saloon in 1938. After that brawl, Billy's voice sounded like a file dragging across a piece of iron. Thirty years later, his cries were rasping hisses that didn't carry across the cold night air.

The man stopped at the bottom of the hill and propped his hands on his knees again to catch his wind. Billy tried again to muster the strength to resist his attacker. He rolled over and slowly got up on his hands and knees, but the man kicked him in the side and he fell over on his back. The man grabbed the leg irons and dragged Billy through the gate to the rear of a pickup truck parked in a clearing by Whiskey Road. He leaned against the truck, gasped for breath for a few seconds, and then lowered the tailgate and pulled Billy up to a standing position. He motioned with his rifle for Billy to climb up on the truck, and Billy crawled into the truck bed on his hands and knees. His assailant climbed up to stand beside him, put his boot on Billy's back, and pushed him down to lie flat on his belly.

Billy rolled over on his side. "Who are you?" he said. "Why have you attacked me?"

The man cried out, a guttural sound like the cry of an animal caught in a trap, and kicked Billy in the gut. Billy curled into the fetal position and retched. His attacker stood over him, pointing the rifle at him. Billy stared at the mouth of the barrel, his heart pounding. After a few seconds, the man stepped back and cursed under his breath. He leaned over the side of the truck bed, set the butt of the rifle on the ground, and propped it against the truck.

He forced Billy to roll over on his back, looped a chain through the handcuffs, and attached it to an anchor on the cab. He slid a chain through the leg irons and hooked it to the tailgate so that Billy was stretched out on his back. The man picked up a rolled-up tarp that lay in the truck bed, unfurled it, and spread it over Billy. It was coarse and rough against Billy's face and carried the scent of gasoline.

Billy could see nothing with the tarp covering his face, but he felt the truck bed rise slightly and heard the crunch of gravel at the rear of the truck, followed by the creak and clank of the tailgate being lifted and shut. He heard steps moving to each corner of the truck bed, followed by a rustling of the tarp, and he guessed that the man was tying it down. Billy heard the door slam and the engine start and felt the truck move forward. From the shifting of his weight, he thought the truck turned right out of the clearing and climbed the hill to Kirby's General Store, Billy's store. It felt as though it stopped there at the intersection of Whiskey Road and the state road, turned left, and sped up.

Wind surged under the tarp and whipped at Billy's face and he shivered and took his breath in short bursts. Ten minutes into the ride, a corner of the tarp broke free from its tie-down and blew across his chest and he saw steep mountains rising up on both sides of the road and leafless branches arching over the truck like bony fingers clawing at the purple night sky. Much later, he heard the roar of water falling from a great height. A cold mist kissed his brow just before he passed out.

When Billy regained consciousness, dawn had broken. The air was still and cold. The aroma of gasoline was strong, but the truck was parked and the engine wasn't idling. The tarp was gone, but he was still chained on his back in the truck bed. The early morning sun cast shafts of light through trees on a hill to his right, and there was a chorus of birdsong.

Billy knew where the man had taken him. He had felt the truck turn left at the T where Whiskey Road met the state road at Billy's store in Fox Run to head north into Whippoorwill Hollow. Twenty-two miles from the farm town of Fox Run, the state road passed Whippoorwill Hollow Dam and ended at an entrance to Shenandoah National Park, and from there a network of dirt roads maintained by the park for firefighting cut through mountainous wilderness.

Footsteps rustled through a slush of leaves and the ski mask loomed over Billy. The man's dark eyes glistened through the eyeholes.

"I know where we are," Billy said. "I felt the spray off Whippoorwill

Hollow Dam last night. We're in the park. Why did you bring me here?"

The man unlocked the chain anchoring Billy's handcuffs to the cab and moved to the rear of the truck. Billy sat up on his haunches. "Who are you?"

The man dropped the tailgate and dragged Billy out of the truck. He threw him to the ground and kicked him in the ribs, and Billy curled up and gagged. The man went to the cab and returned with his rifle. He motioned with it for Billy to stand, and Billy struggled to his feet. He grabbed Billy by the shoulder and turned him to face a steep hill, poking him in the back with the rifle. Billy staggered forward, but the restraint of the leg irons made him stumble. He stopped to regain his balance; the man prodded him in the back again; and Billy hobbled forward slowly. His bare feet were tender and his ankles were sore from abrasions inflicted by the irons. Each step was torturous, but the man gave Billy no mercy. He punched Billy with the rifle whenever he hesitated, and each blow was more painful than the last.

The climb was steep and arduous. Near the top of the hill, exhaustion overcame Billy and he fell to his knees, gasping for air. The man poked him in the back with the rifle and Billy fell forward on his face. "I can't go on," he said.

The man put the barrel to the back of Billy's head. Billy squeezed his eyes shut, fear choking him. The man held the gun to his head for a few seconds and then pulled it away. Billy rolled over on his back and looked up at the man, who was standing over him and glaring at him, trembling. The man motioned for Billy to stand.

"I can't," Billy said. "I'm spent."

The man cursed, bent down, and grabbed the leg irons. He twisted Billy around and dragged him up the hill, stopping once to catch his breath before he pulled Billy the last few feet to the summit. He dropped the leg irons and leaned against a big oak tree, gasping for air.

Billy rolled over and slowly got up on his hands and knees. His head hung down between his shoulder blades and spittle ran from his mouth to pool on the carpet of leaves beneath him. After a while, he lifted his head and looked around. A deep ravine lay at the bottom of a cliff about twenty feet to his left. He could see the face of the opposite mountainside and a good ways down the hill they had just climbed. There was nothing but wilderness as far as he could see.

The man kicked Billy in the side again and Billy fell and rolled over on his back, clutching his side and gagging. The man picked up a long chain that was coiled at the base of the oak tree and dragged it to Billy. He grabbed Billy's hands and stretched them over his head, looped one end of the chain through Billy's handcuffs, and padlocked the end links together to bind it tight to Billy's cuffs. Then he carried its other end to the oak tree, slipped the chain through a steel ring attached to the end of a metal stake that protruded from its trunk, and padlocked the chain to the ring.

Billy rolled over and got up on his hands and knees. He looked up at the man. "Do you aim to kill me?"

"I do." The man's voice was choked with anger.

"Why?"

The man turned without a word, trudged down the hill, and disappeared in the growth below.

Billy crawled to the oak tree and sat leaning against it. He felt the wound to his head. It was swollen. A crusted scab under his hair was sore to the touch and his ribs ached from the man's kicks. Billy pressed his hand against his side and winced.

A cold wind blew across the top of the hill. He pulled the collar of his nightshirt tightly around his neck and looked up at the stake he was chained to. He grabbed the stake and pulled himself up to stand beside the tree with his legs quivering. He tried to pull the stake out of the tree trunk, but it was pounded deep into the oak.

He slumped to the ground and rubbed his shins and his bare feet to warm them. The sky darkened and the wind blew. Tree branches clattered together like brittle bones. A hawk floated just under the cloud cover, searching for prey. It tilted its wings and banked down behind the opposite mountain.

Billy thought about his assailant. The truck's presence inside the park meant he had a key to the gate. To have a key, he had to be someone who worked for the park, a ranger or a fireman, or someone who owned property on its far side. He had to be someone who knew Billy couldn't cry out, because he hadn't bothered to gag him. He was familiar with Billy's house because he'd come straight to the bedroom. Billy knew the man's stiff legs and shortness of breath all too well as the infirmities of old age. The man had to be old, perhaps as old as Billy. Billy reviewed his acquaintances searching for a match, but he could think of no one who would attack him so violently.

The wind blew harder and the cloud canopy descended upon the summit of the hill like a slate ceiling. Billy gathered his nightshirt more tightly around him and thought about the man's stated desire to kill him. He should embrace the man's homicidal intention, he told himself. His misery was so deep that he had considered death by his own hand. Why not give in to this man's murderous rage?

A gust of wind blew Billy's hair across his face. He brushed it back and stared into the gray miasma, pondering his own death. After a few moments, he stirred from his thoughts, put his hand inside his nightshirt, flattened it over his chest, and felt his heart beat, steady, strong, persistent.

Chapter 2

The Cabin

Earlier that same morning before dawn, Selk County Deputy Sheriff Toby Vess climbed a mountainside. His lean six-foot-three frame was strong, but he was winded and nauseous from the exertion. He laid his rifle on the ground and put his hands on his knees to catch his breath. His stomach rolled and the bitter taste of bile soured his palate.

Toby looked down the mountain at the hunting cabin where he had slept. From his spot near the summit of Buckhorn Mountain, the cabin was a postage stamp in a grove of elm trees in the moonlight.

Toby swiped his hand across his face and sighed. He knew exactly what his problem was. He and his hunting companion, Stogie Morris, had spent the night sitting on the cabin's cinderblock steps drinking white lightning. The powerful brew numbed their aches and pains and lifted their spirits, and for a short while, they didn't feel the stiffness in their joints or the aches of their tired muscles. The hooch made them feel young again.

They talked about all the good times they'd had in that old hunting cabin. They recalled the card games, jokes, tall tales, and big drunks. They remembered the time Billy Kirby got so snookered he fell against the woodstove and knocked the stovepipe loose and covered them all with black soot. They laughed about how they drove out of the park into Fox Run and paraded through Kirby's General Store looking like coal miners coming off a double shift, reveling in the hoots and laughter of their friends.

Way too late in the night, they ran out of old stories to retell; they fell silent; and the positive effects of the hooch wore off. They stared at the stars. Stogie mumbled a few words about the last trophy buck he shot on Pine Top Mountain. Then he fell mute and his eyes misted over. Toby could think of nothing more to say, so they turned in. But by then they had drunk too much shine.

Toby was paying for their foolishness that morning on the steep climb. He breathed deeply, long plumes of vapor streaming into the dark. A dog bayed at the moon somewhere far away. The faint howl floated on a cold wind that swirled up the mountainside from the valley below the cabin. Probably a frightened deer hound lost on a hunt, he thought, searching for the way back home.

He picked up his rifle and resumed his climb. He and his three oldest friends built the one-room shack forty years ago, when they were young men. They bought acreage in the back country on the far side of Shenandoah National Park that they could access only by navigating a four-wheel-drive vehicle in sub-low gear over the park's primitive fire roads.

They built the cabin for next to nothing and did all the work themselves, throwing it together with plywood, two-by-fours, and tar paper. Indoor plumbing wasn't an option in the wilderness, so they built the cabin beside a mountain spring and carried water to it by bucket. They dug a pit for an outhouse on the other side, away from and below the spring. They slept in sleeping bags thrown on bare mattresses in wooden bunks.

The nausea returned and Toby stopped his climb again. He took off his hat and leaned over. He breathed in and out deeply, looking down at the cabin. He and his friends loved that old pile of sticks. For forty years, they had wetted their whistles with moonshine and laughed and told lies at night and hunted white-tail deer, black bear, and wild turkey during the day.

The problem was there weren't many good times ahead. He and his friends had grown old all of a sudden when they weren't looking. Toby was the youngest of the four at sixty-eight. He was still hearty and healthy, but his three buddies hadn't fared so well. Stogie was pushing seventy-five. In his prime, he killed trophy bucks with racks of ten points or more and filled his big game ticket every season. Then old age ambushed him in the form of a mild stroke. He recovered from it quickly, but it left him weaker on his right side and he limped when he walked. He still made every hunting trip and strained to reach the summit of Pine Top Mountain each morning, but lately his breath grew short before he came to the steep part of his climb. His right hand shook with palsy when he aimed his rifle and he hadn't killed any game in years.

Billy Kirby was Toby's closest friend of the three. He was eighty, but he had the strength and vigor of a much younger man. Most of his life he had been a study in contradictions. Spectacularly selfish in many ways, he was known to be a relentless womanizer, a ruthless businessman, and a convincing liar, but when a neighbor was in need, he was the first to offer help and was unfailingly generous with his time, energy, and substantial resources. Late in his life, his selfish side toned down a lot. The incarceration of his son eight years ago and the death of his wife more recently seemed to make him question the way he had lived his life. He had made every hunting trip without fail until this year, when he said he'd been feeling poorly since Mary Jo died and didn't know if he had the spirit to overcome his regrets.

Amos Hukstep, who was seventy-eight, canceled out the Tuesday before Thanksgiving. He wouldn't give Toby a reason, but Amos was a man of few words, and when he made up his mind, there was no changing it. Toby didn't bother to argue. He knew Amos thought he was too old to have fun and that his good times were behind him.

Old age had claimed Stogie Morris' strength, Billy Kirby's spirit, and Amos Hukstep's disposition. Toby was worried about old age, too; not for himself, because he didn't feel that old, but for the other three. He didn't want to lose them.

He swept his hand across his feverish brow, put on his hat, and climbed higher. When he reached the summit, the sight of the doghouse chased his somber thoughts away. The squat wooden structure sat on the park line in a clearing next to an old apple orchard. The hunters called it the doghouse because that's what it looked like. It was just large enough for a man to crawl inside on his belly and peer out its gun holes at approaching game. A rusty barbed-wire fence between the orchard and the doghouse marked the border between the park and the hunters' private property.

Hunting in the park was illegal, and decades of hunting seasons had taught the white-tail deer the game warden's rules. They were smart and skittish. They grazed on the hunters' land at night and hopped over the fence to the old orchard inside the park just after dawn, and they came out of the park's sanctuary into the pasture again at dusk. To have a chance at bagging a white-tail deer, a hunter staked out a position along the park line before dawn or at dusk and waited for one to cross over. Toby had built the doghouse twenty years earlier to give a hunter cover while he waited.

He walked to the doghouse in the dark. The frost on its tar paper roof sparkled in the moonlight as he approached. He crawled inside and stretched out on his belly then checked the chamber of his thirty-thirty rifle, set the scope in place, and peered through the slits he had cut in the plank walls twenty years earlier. With the coming of daylight, he would be able to see down the mountain and in both directions along the park's border on the summit. The sun had begun to brighten the sky, and he guessed that dawn was no more than fifteen minutes away. If a buck was going to cross the park line that morning, he would be coming along soon. Toby leaned his aching head against the wall.

Toby coughed in mid snore and awoke with a start. He rubbed his eyes and gazed out of the gun holes at the clearing. The mountaintop was enveloped in fog, and it was raining. He felt feverish and edgy. Streams of sweat coursed down his face. He unsnapped the buttons on his hunting jacket, glanced at his watch, and blanched. Eight thirty.

Rain pounded on the pasture and steam rose into a thick gray soup. He couldn't see twenty feet from the doghouse. No doubt all the game had hopped the fence and retreated into the park at first light, anyway. "Damned fool," he said to himself. He had wasted the morning. The hunt was done, and he might as well go back down to the cabin.

Toby crawled out of the doghouse, turned up the collar of his jacket, and pulled the brim of his hat low. The rain was unseasonably warm, and it poured down hard. He picked his way down the mountainside hurriedly, jogged to the cabin and burst through the door. Stogie lay flat on his back on the bunk with his mouth open, snoring.

When Toby slapped his hat against his thigh to shake off the rain, Stogie coughed and sat up in bed. His face was the color of rancid milk. His bloodshot eyes widened. He rushed to the door and retched. He leaned against the door and ran his sleeve across his mouth. "Those Vienna sausages must have been bad." He wiped sweat off his bald head and staggered back to the bed. "I've been sick as a dog since I woke up."

"It's not the sausages. We drank too much shine last night."

"We didn't drink no more than we ever did."

"We're longer in the tooth than we used to be. It doesn't take as much to make us sick."

Stogie stretched out on the bunk and groaned. "I guess we'll have to back off a little next time." He closed his eyes and rubbed his temples. "You see any game?"

Toby stripped off his wet jacket and plopped down in a cane chair next to the woodstove, swiping his hand over his gray hair. "I fell asleep in the doghouse like an old fool. Shoulda stayed in bed, for all the good I did. How about you?"

"Hard to see good when you're pukin your guts out."

Stogie wouldn't look Toby in the eye. Toby thought he probably hadn't climbed the mountain to his deer stand that morning but didn't want to admit it. Toby shook his head. They were a sorry duo—old, tired, and hungover. This hunting trip was a failure in all respects. He cursed, looked out the window at the fog and rain and looked at Stogie prone on the bunk, sick and breathing hard. "The hell with it," he said. He stepped over to his bunk and rolled up his sleeping bag.

"What are you doing?" Stogie said.

"Pack up your gear. Two old dogs like us ain't fit to carry on like young wolves on the prowl. This hunt's a bust. Let's call it quits and go home."

Stogie hauled his carcass off the bunk and packed his bag without a word in protest. They padlocked the cabin, loaded their gear into Toby's old blue Ford pickup, and drove down the fire road in the rain. About halfway through the park, Stogie said, "I guess that's it, then."

"What?"

"That's all she wrote. I didn't want to admit it, but it's true. Billy and Amos already gave it up. I thought they were wrong, but I was the one who was wrong. I'm giving it up, too. I'm too old to hunt."

Toby stared at Stogie and then looked back at the road just in time to steer around a deep rut. "We're not giving up. Neither are Billy and Amos. We're taking a break. We're regrouping for the next hunt."

Stogie clenched his fists and then opened them, flexing his gnarled fingers. "I lied to you back there at the cabin."

"About climbing the mountain?"

"No. I didn't lie about that. I climbed Pine Top. I was sick and it was hard on me, but I made it to my stand. I lied when I said I didn't see anything. I saw a two-pointer with a doe. They walked right up the trail to me. I had a clear shot at the buck."

"What happened? Your rifle jam up?"

"I'm the one jammed up. I drew my gun sight down on that young buck but I couldn't pull the trigger. My eyes watered up and I couldn't see to aim."

"That happens sometimes. The cold and the wind get in your eyes."

"It didn't have anything to do with the weather. I put my sight on the buck's front shoulder. While I tried to steady my aim, the doe came up beside him and nuzzled his neck with her snout." Stogie paused. "That was when my eyes watered up. I couldn't see and my hands started shaking." Stogie wiped a tear from his cheek and shook his head back and forth. "I couldn't kill that young buck with that doe standing there and all. I lost my nerve."

They were silent for a while. Then Stogie said, "It's been a good run, Toby. We've had some good times." He rubbed his arthritic knuckles. "This was my last hunt."

As Toby drove over the fire road through the park toward Whippoorwill

Hollow, he thought about the passage of time, good friends, and old age. Thanksgiving had begun as a sad morning after a long hard night, and there was still a lot of the day left to go.

Chapter 3

The Note

Jolene Hukstep didn't wake up until nine on Thanksgiving morning. She lay in bed and stared at the wall, listening to rain patter on her trailer's aluminum roof and thinking about the lonely day ahead of her. For the last ten years or so, her daughters and their families hadn't come home for the holiday or invited her and Amos to their homes. She'd cooked Thanksgiving dinner for Amos and they had eaten it alone at their kitchen table without saying much to each other. This year would be the same.

She sighed and rolled over to reach for Amos, but he wasn't there. He had been an early riser for sixty years, and of late, he slept fitfully, if at all. Then she remembered that he hadn't come to bed that night. He hadn't come to bed for the last three nights. Not that it mattered much. Nothing had happened in their marriage bed in more than a decade.

Jolene sat up and wiped the sleep from her eyes and listened for his sounds in their double-wide, but she heard nothing. Maybe he was outside in the rain, working on the slabs for the two new trailer pads. He never rested, even in bad weather. She wished he wouldn't drive himself so hard. There were already thirty-three trailers in the park, not counting their double-wide. They wouldn't get rich off the rent from the hookups, but they made enough to get along. They didn't need the two new concrete pads. They were in their seventies, for Pete's sake. It was time to slow down and savor what time they had left, but Amos didn't think that way. He worried about money. All the time. All his life.

She crawled out of bed, put on her housecoat and slippers, and went to the window to separate the spindly Venetian blinds and look outside. The sky was dark gray. It was raining hard in Saddleback Cove. Huge puddles gathered in the ruts of the trailer park's gravel road, and the gutter next to Whiskey Road overflowed with runoff. Even Amos wouldn't try to work in that big mess.

He must have gone somewhere again without telling her. He would sometimes go for a week or more without saying a word to her. She gazed at the rain for a while, wondering where he was, then stretched her arms over her head and yawned. She padded listlessly to the bathroom, took a hot shower, toweled off in the humid little room, and wrapped the towel around her body. Cinching it at her breasts, she assembled her makeup on the shelf under the mirror.

The mirror was all steamed up. When she wiped it clear, she saw the image of her grandmother staring back at her, and her hand froze in place. The hair on the old lady in the mirror was thin and gray, like spider webbing ironed over her crown. Her face was crosshatched with dark fissures. Jowls sagged from her jaws. Liver spots stained her forehead and cheeks. The hand pressed against the mirror was bony and withered.

She looked down at the porcelain sink and sighed. Her gaze drifted to her waistline. She was still thin, at least. The change of life had been kinder to her than to most of her friends. She hadn't bloated up with a big potbelly. She hadn't developed beefy shoulders or a bovine neck, but it was small consolation. She shuddered at the sight of her once firm, taut legs that were now wrinkled slabs of loose flesh. They looked like her mother's legs when she lay dying in the nursing home.

Jolene stared in the mirror at the old woman's eyes. They were rimmed with crow's feet and underlined by puffy, purple bags, but her pale blue irises sparkled. They were bright and clear, and if she ignored the face of the old woman around them, her eyes were still beautiful. They proved she was still young Jolene, even though she was trapped inside a used-up decaying cocoon of withering flesh.

Her eyes welled with tears and she wept quietly. Then she dried her eyes angrily with a corner of the towel. There was nothing to cry about. Old age was the way of all living things. It was natural and ordinary. All creatures are born, grow old, and die. Jolene was near the end of the cycle of life, and there was no point in crying about it.

She took a few deep breaths and began to apply her makeup. She brushed her hair, trying to give it some body, and put on her red blouse because it was bright and cheerful and her black slacks to show off her waistline. She slipped on her penny loafers and walked through the living room to the kitchen.

She warmed the frying pan on the burner, cracked two eggs into it, and stared out the kitchen window while they crackled. The rain had stopped, and the sun broke through the clouds. The trailer park had the fresh, clean look to it that came after a hard rain.

The eggs sizzled until Jolene spilled them onto her plate. She put the pan in the sink and sat on the barstool at the kitchen counter. That's when she noticed Amos' note beside the toaster. She held it up to the light with a palpable sense of dread because he never wrote her notes.

Gone to Richmond for building supplies. Be back in a few days.

In a few days! She smoothed the note on the counter and read it again. It made no sense. Amos had ordered all the supplies for the new trailer pads last week from Shenandoah Building Supply. Concrete mix, planks to frame the concrete sets, galvanized pipe for the water connection, sewer pipes, electrical wire. Shenandoah delivered the goods Monday. All of it was piled under a tarp out by the pads.

Certain Amos had not gone to Richmond, Jolene reread the note. It was written in his cramped scrawl, as though it was painful to squeeze the few cryptic words from his closed mind. The note read the way he talked to her, like each word was a thorny thistle that had to be pulled out of his gut through his constricted throat past a swollen tongue. She stared at each word. Two short sentences. Twelve words. Nothing at the end, no "love you" or "XXX" for hugs and kisses. He hadn't even signed it.

She dropped the note on the counter and looked out the window. The note bore Amos' most distinctive character trait: he couldn't tell a lie to save his soul. He was up to something.

She thought about his recent taciturn mood; he'd been sleeping in his easy chair with the television on all night. He was troubled about something, but she had no idea what it was. He had always been a private and inward man and he'd withdrawn even more as he grew older. She grew more uneasy as she stared at the note.

She looked out the window at her old lime-green 1954 Hudson Hornet sitting under the awning of the carport. Amos fired the old heap up every once in a while, but Jolene hadn't driven it since her eyesight deteriorated. When she ran over a row of mailboxes trying to navigate the turn into the trailer park five years ago, she gave up driving for good.

The eye doctor said she was myopic. She could see just fine up close to read and do handiwork, but everything in the distance was fuzzy and blurred. He gave her a pair of thick, ugly glasses and told her she was legally blind for driving without them, but she didn't want to wear them so she gave up driving. Driving wasn't important to her, she told herself. Amos drove her everywhere anyway.

She looked at the Hudson and sighed. The truth was, she had given up driving to preserve the last vestige of her youth. She refused to bury the last remnants of her beauty under the bottoms of pop bottles, and without the glasses she couldn't drive. She'd mourned the freedom she lost when she parked the old car.

Jolene found her glasses in the cupboard, put them on, and looked at herself in the mirror. She looked like a bullfrog. She glared at her reflection. "You're not Jolene," she said. She snatched the glasses from her eyes and put them back in the cupboard and rummaged around in the silverware drawer until she found the keys to the Hudson. She grabbed her purse, gloves, and winter coat, and rushed out to the carport.

Chapter 4

The Passerby

Fog enveloped the summit of the hill where Billy sat chained to the oak tree. He leaned against it, its rough bark pressing against his back through his nightshirt, and thought about dying at the hands of the ski-masked man. He told himself he should be grateful. He had longed for death for months, but he had the strength and health of a much younger man and longevity ran in his genes, so suicide had seemed his only way out. Now this angry man would play the role of the grim reaper. No suicide note required. No one could blame him or think less of him for being this man's victim. It was a good way to die.

The world would be better off without him, he thought. No one would mourn his passing. Some would even celebrate it. His son would be the most cheered by his demise. Billy ran his hand across his brow, stared into the gray haze, and thought about the night Blakey had committed crimes so serious that Billy couldn't pay to make them go away. His friend Toby Vess, deputy sheriff of Selk County, had telephoned him. "Blakey attacked Carter Embry," he'd said. "Beat him near to death. Beat up Raylene Gibson pretty bad, too. We've got him in the holding pen down here. He's asking for you."

Billy drove to the sheriff's office in Jeetersburg and found his son stretched out on his back on a cot in a chain-link pen in a room off the lobby. A partially burned-out fluorescent light cast a dull yellow pall over the room. The air was hot and close and stank of whiskey, sweat, and disinfectant. Blakey lay with his arms crossed over his face. His long black hair was oily and sweaty and grimy stubble darkened his big square jaw.

Billy stood outside the pen and laced his fingers through the chain link. "Blakey," he said in his flinty voice.

Blakey dropped his arms to his sides and looked at Billy. His eyes were tortured, desperate, hopeless. "Get me out of here, old man."

"Howard Raines is on his way. If there's a way to get you out of this mess, he'll find it."

Blakey stared at Billy with a hollowed-out look. "They should put *you* on trial," he said. He looked up at the ceiling, drew in a deep breath, and let it out. "You made me what I am." He rolled over on his side and turned his back to Billy.

Billy stared at Blakey's back for a while and then retreated to the lobby and sat in a metal folding chair near the front door. He leaned forward with his arms on his thighs and clasped his hands together. Blakey was right. He had raised Blakey wrong. But Blakey was to blame, too. Billy might have set him on the wrong path, but he was forty-two years old. No one had forced him to commit crimes.

Howard Raines was one of the best criminal defense attorneys in Virginia, but his best wasn't good enough. The commonwealth's attorney, Nate Abbitt, put Raylene on the stand and led her through a sordid story of long-term physical abuse culminating in Blakey's vicious attack after she ran away with Carter to escape Blakey's beatings.

Howard approached Nate at counsel's table when the court adjourned that day. They talked for a while and then Howard approached Billy. "Nate's willing to recommend ten years if Blakey pleads guilty. It's a generous offer."

Billy blanched. Blakey would be over fifty years old when he got out of jail. Billy, over eighty.

Howard put his hand on Billy's shoulder. "Raylene's testimony sealed his fate. The jury will find him guilty on all counts, and Judge Blackwell is tough on violent crime. He's likely to send him away for twenty years."

Billy gripped the railing and looked down at his whitened knuckles.

"Sorry, Billy," Howard said. "It's the best we can do."

It was hard to accept. Billy watched Nate put his files in his briefcase and start down the aisle to leave the courtroom.

"Thank you," Billy said to him.

Nate stopped and looked at Billy. He nodded and moved on down the aisle. Blakey rejected the plea bargain at first. "He blames everyone but himself," Howard told Billy. "Raylene, Nate, Judge Blackwell, me, and most of all, you." But Howard made Blakey understand he would likely serve twenty years in prison if he didn't accept the deal, and he knuckled under. As the guards led Blakey out of the courtroom at the conclusion of the sentencing hearing, Blakey stopped and looked back at his father, his face twisted with hatred. That was the last time Billy saw his son.

After they transferred Blakey to the state penitentiary, Billy traveled to Richmond twelve times over the course of a year, but each time Blakey refused to come out of his cell. Blakey sent all his letters back unopened and refused to take his calls, and Billy eventually stopped trying. Blakey had been in prison now for almost eight years and Billy had made no attempt to reach out to him in the last five.

As Billy sat chained to the oak tree, he wondered if he would ever speak to his son again. The fog thickened and a light mist began to fall. It became a steady rain and soon quickened to a downpour. The tepid water soaked Billy's head wound; his blood mixed with the rain; and pale red streaks coursed down his face and stained the front of his nightshirt. He got up and crouched under a big branch in an effort to gain shelter, but the rain still found him. He buried his face in his hands and whimpered.

When the temperature climbed higher, the rain slacked off. The fog lifted and the sun broke through the clouds. Billy stretched out on his back and closed his eyes. Wet leaves clung to the back of his head. He brushed them away clumsily with his cuffed hands. He lay still in the warm sun for a long time. His nightshirt dried out somewhat and his head wound scabbed over.

In the distance to the west, Billy heard the groan of an engine. The grinding hum rose and fell as it labored over difficult terrain. He sat up and looked in the direction of the sound. It grew louder and louder, but he couldn't see the vehicle. He heard it skirt the base of the hill below him, but its path was hidden from him by the growth down there. When the sound of the motor was loudest and clearest, he recognized it. That truck had taken him to Saturday night poker games, saloons and dance halls, Stogie's farm, Hukstep's Trailer Park, and the hunting cabin. It was Toby Vess' old Ford pickup with its faded blue paint, the big dent in the driver's door, and the gash in the middle of the front bumper. Billy knew Toby and Stogie had gone to the cabin the previous night. They had planned to hunt through the holiday weekend, but they must have abandoned the hunt for some reason.

A surge of energy ran through Billy. He jumped up and tried to yell to his friends, but his crushed vocal cords could muster only a flinty rasp. He cupped his hands around his mouth and tried to project his cries. "Help. Toby, Stogie. I'm here. Help me."

The engine droned on to the south, its groans growing fainter until Billy could no longer hear them. His energy drained away. He slumped to the ground and fell over on his side. His face sank into the damp, spongy forest floor. The pungent odors of decaying leaves and moist loam filled his nostrils. He drew his knees up to his chest and thought about all the good times in the old cabin. He wished he could go back there and relive the hunting trips. He wished he had more time with his friends. He wished he had a few laughs yet to go.

Despite his many regrets about Mary Jo and Blakey and the cold logic that told him he should welcome his death, a sense of anxiety came over him. It took hold and grew in strength. His chest swelled up with it and it cut off his air. He took several short breaths and then a long one and tried to fight it off, but it gripped his throat like a cold fist. Billy rolled over on his back, put his hands over his eyes, and wept.

When he had cried himself out, he wiped his face and looked at the sky. The clouds had cleared. The gray had given way to blue. The hawk he had seen earlier circled above him. It banked its wings and glided toward the opposite mountainside. Its screech pierced the air as it plunged beneath the trees.

The leaves stirred on the slope below Billy. He sat up. The ski-masked man was climbing the hill toward him. Billy looked at him carefully. He was tall and stout and bowlegged, with a large round head inside the ski mask. When the man reached Billy and looked down at him, Billy stared at the holes in the mask where the man's angry eyes nested like hard little stones and he knew who the man was. A wave of hope washed over Billy. This man was dimwitted, dull, and gullible. He was no match for Billy, never had been, never would be. "You can take off the mask," Billy said. "I know who you are."

The man hesitated and then pulled the ski mask off his head. Amos Hukstep glared at Billy, his face flushed and sweaty, his eyes filled with rage and pain and despair. A vision of an ancient betrayal flashed through Billy's mind, a selfish act, a profound provocation.

Amos raised a tire iron above his head and brought it down on Billy.

Chapter 5

The Store

Toby drove out of the park past Whippoorwill Hollow Dam and traveled south through the hollow. He and Stogie reached Fox Run about ten thirty. Kirby's General Store stood at the head of the T intersection where Whiskey Road met the state road and Billy's house sat on one of the corner lots across from the store. As they passed the store, Toby saw movement inside and the OPEN sign posted in the window. Billy normally sat on a bench in the back next to a potbelly woodstove, spreading gossip and telling jokes. Toby felt blue about the aborted hunting trip and Stogie's sad words. He craved a distraction. Even during Billy's recent jag of moping about his regrets, he still had some of his old spunk and could lift Toby's spirits from time to time. "What say we stop at Billy's store?" he asked Stogie.

"Okay by me. I could use some aspirin tablets."

Toby pulled into the dirt lot beside the store. It was a rectangular frame box with peeling paint. Smoke curled from its stovepipe and the morning rain still dripped from rusty gutters that clung desperately to the roofline by scattered nails. The storefront was a concrete porch with a single gas pump in front of it. Two long wooden benches sat on the porch on each side of the door. Four rotting wooden pillars buckled under the weight of the porch's sagging roof. The old store had already been remodeled and repaired a hundred times, and another facelift was overdue.

The history of the old house and store was common knowledge in the hollow. They were pre-Revolutionary War buildings. In the olden days, travelers who took the stagecoach from Hayesboro across the Blue Ridge Mountains to Jeetersburg would spend the night in Fox Run on the downhill side of Feather Mountain. Billy's great-great-grandfather owned a farm at the foot of the mountain in the 1700s. He boarded the travelers in the upstairs rooms of Kirby's Hall, which was now Billy's old house, and sold provisions and spirits out of Kirby's Tavern, which Billy's grandfather converted into Kirby's General Store. Billy's forefathers made a small fortune investing the profits from the farm and store in local real estate. Billy followed their lead and greatly increased the family wealth, speculating in land and building rental homes in Whippoorwill Hollow and apartment buildings in Jeetersburg while still operating the farm and the store.

Years ago, the crusty, high-toned Virginia Historical Society designated Billy's house and store official historical sites. Toby smiled when he remembered Billy's reaction upon learning that his family's ramshackle buildings had become monuments to the past: he'd quipped that he planned to become a historical artifact, too. He claimed he wrote a clause in his will to instruct his heirs to hollow out his corpse, petrify it in stone, lacquer it, and stand it on the porch of the general store as a public historical exhibit— a genuine fossilized Whippoorwill Hollow redneck. Stepping off the running board of his truck, Toby's smile faded. He thought Billy probably wouldn't find his old joke so humorous now that he had passed his eightieth birthday. He imagined history was less amusing when you were about to become part of it.

Toby and Stogie climbed the steps to the store. "Don't the skinflint ever close this place?" Stogie said. "It's Thanksgiving Day, for Christ's sake."

"He's afraid he'll miss a nickel or two, I reckon."

Billy's grandson stood behind the counter. Porter was in his early twenties, a younger version of Billy: average height, lean, and handsome, with a dark complexion, square jaw, black eyes, and coal-black hair.

Toby had known Porter all the boy's life. His mother died when he was a toddler and Blakey abandoned him when he was nine years old. Billy tried to raise him right, but he was constantly in trouble. He failed several successive grades in school and was eventually expelled for fighting. Soon afterwards, he got his girlfriend pregnant. They married, but after Maureen lost the baby, Porter abandoned her and joined the army. He came home from Vietnam last winter with a drinking problem, more rebellious than when he left. A few weeks later he was arrested for stealing a car and wrecking it on a drunken joyride in Wise County. The commonwealth's attorney would have charged Porter with DUI, reckless driving, and grand larceny auto theft, but Billy stepped in and convinced him to recommend no jail time, a three-year probation, and a six-month suspension of Porter's driver's license in exchange for rehab, a brand-new car, and guilty pleas to unauthorized use of a vehicle and DUI.

When Porter got out of the Roanoke Drug and Alcohol Rehabilitation Center in June, Billy gave him a business interest in the store and started training him to run it, and the boy began to straighten up. Toby knew from Billy that Porter had worked hard to convince Maureen to take him back. She finally agreed about a month ago, and Billy rented them a small home he owned in the hollow, but the reunion was off to a rocky start. Maureen's family and friends didn't believe Porter had reformed and their skepticism fueled her own doubts. Despite the problems in Porter's marriage, as far as Toby knew, he had been sober since he left the rehab center, and under Billy's guidance he seemed to be maturing and stabilizing.

Toby walked back to the potbelly stove at the rear of the store and was disappointed to see that Billy wasn't there. He went to the drink case on the back wall, selected a grape Nehi, returned to the front counter, and gave Porter a nickel. "Where's Billy?"

"Still in bed, I guess. He was supposed to take over at ten, but he hasn't showed up yet. I hope he gets here soon. I need to go home."

Stogie paid for aspirin tablets and a root beer. "Why don't you shut her down? You won't miss any customers. Ain't nobody out and about but lame old dogs with nobody to cook turkey for em."

Porter shook his head. "Grandpa wanted to keep her open. He hasn't got much else to do today."

Stogie looked aggravated. "I guess you and Maureen couldn't trouble yourselves to set a place for him at your Thanksgiving table."

Porter gave Stogie a hard look. "Actually, we invited him, but he turned us down. Maureen's family is comin over and he said he didn't feel like socializing with everyone. He's been kinda down in the mouth lately."

Porter and Stogie stared at each other for a few moments and then Stogie turned away and meandered out the front door. Toby followed him and they sat down on the porch bench.

A green Chevrolet pickup truck climbed the hill on Whiskey Road and Eva Gitlow parked beside the porch. Eva owned Twin Ridge Farm in Saddleback Cove; she was sixty years old and as tall as Toby, gangly and thin with a long plain face. She climbed the steps and walked across the porch toward the front door. Most days she wore a man's work shirt, muddy jeans, and rubber work boots, but that day she wore a red wool winter coat that was open in front to reveal a pleated plaid skirt and a white blouse. Her cheeks were flushed with a gloss of rouge and her lips glistened with blood-red lipstick. She wore eye shadow that drew attention to her green eyes, and her snow white hair was flipped up in a smooth wave at her shoulders, silky and soft.

Toby felt a smile creep across his face. He touched the brim of his hat. "Eva," he said with a tone of wonderment in his voice.

She stopped in front of the bench. "Toby," she said in her deep voice. She looked at Stogie, who was staring at her with his mouth hanging open. "Stogie," she said. Stogie was speechless. "Pretty day, gentlemen."

"Yes, ma'am," Toby said, his smile widening.

She flashed a dimpled grin at them and went inside the store.

As soon as she was out of earshot, Stogie said, "What's Eva done to herself? She looks like a different woman."

Toby peered in the store window at her. "I'd say somebody took her to the beauty parlor."

Stogie looked in the window, too. "Well, they sure as hell painted her up good. She looks downright pretty."

"That she does," Toby said, still smiling. He turned back to face the road, shook his head in awe of her transformation, and took a swig of his grape Nehi.

Stogie popped an aspirin tablet into his mouth, washed it down with root beer, and belched.

Toby gazed at a baby blue car parked across the street in Billy's driveway. It had an ornamental grille and fancy rear tire skirts. "Nice car," he said.

"It ought to be," Stogie said. "Brand new, top-of-the-line Plymouth VIP. Cost about as much as you'd pay for ten acres in the hollow. Title's in Porter's name, but Billy paid for it."

"Mighty generous."

Stogie snorted. "That boy wouldn't have a pot to piss in if it wasn't for Billy's fat wallet. Don't know why the old fool wastes money on him. That boy's a hellion and a drunkard and he always will be."

"He's calmed down a lot since Billy put him in the store."

"He's walkin the straight and narrow now, but it won't last. Mark my words. He'll turn out just like his daddy. It's in his blood."

"You oughta go a little easier on him. Give him a chance to prove he's changed his ways."

"Won't do no good," Stogie grumbled. He took two more aspirin tablets, rubbed his eyes and groaned.

A warm wind swept across the porch. Toby unbuttoned his shirt and rubbed his chest. It was sixty degrees or more, a beautiful Indian summer day, probably the last warm spell before the long cold winter rolled in. Toby picked up a newspaper from the bench and read the first few paragraphs of an article about the progress of the Vietnam War.

"What's the news?" Stogie asked.

"President says we're winnin the war. The protestors who marched on Washington last month say he's a liar." Toby's gaze dropped down to a headline near the bottom of the page. "People say Nixon's gonna run for president."

"Won't make no difference. He's as big a liar as Johnson."

Toby leafed through the paper while Stogie sipped his root beer and rubbed his sore head.

The door opened. Eva came out of the store with a grocery bag in her arms and Porter followed with two more. They put the bags in her truck and then climbed the porch steps to return to the front door. Eva waited there while Porter went inside and came out with another grocery bag, which he handed to her.

They stood on the porch, facing each other.

"Thank you, Porter," Eva said. "You're a good …" Her voice broke. She looked down and cleared her throat. "Thank you so much." She went down the steps, got in her truck, and pulled it into the road.

"What was that all about?" Stogie said.

Porter put his hands in his pockets and watched her truck coast down the hill on Whiskey Road and cross the one-lane bridge. "Nothin much. I helped her pick out a turkey and some fixins so she could make Thanksgiving dinner for her hired hand and his family."

Stogie squinted at Porter. "She looked like she was about to cry."

Porter shrugged. "Wasn't nothin more to it. She's just a nice lady is all."

Toby studied Porter's face. It was common knowledge that Eva was headed toward bankruptcy. Toby guessed that Porter had given her the groceries. He scratched his chin, thinking that Stogie was wrong about the boy.

Porter stood on the porch for a while, staring at the opposite hill until Eva's truck crested it and disappeared on the other side. Then he seemed to stir from his thoughts and looked over at Billy's house. He glanced at his watch and frowned. "It's almost eleven. Wonder where he is?"

Stogie went still for a moment. "Good question. It ain't like him to miss a chance to turn a profit."

A sense of uneasiness came over Toby. He placed his empty Nehi bottle in a wooden crate next to the bench and stood slowly, staring at the house. "Let's go across the road and have a look."

He stepped off the porch and crossed the road, and Stogie and Porter followed. They walked over the brick walkway and climbed the porch steps to the front door. Toby knocked on it. There was no answer. He called out, "Billy! Billy Kirby!" Still no answer.

Stogie cupped his hands around his eyes and peered in the parlor window. "It's dark inside."

"You have a key?" Toby asked Porter.

"I gave it back to him when I moved out, but he hides one under a flower pot on the back porch."

Toby stepped off the front porch and loped around the house, his concern growing. He froze when he saw a red stripe trailing down the back porch steps. The rain had watered it down, but the pale red line looked like blood.

Porter came up behind him. "Jesus."

Stogie limped to Porter's side and emitted a low whistle. "This don't look good."

"Stay where you are," Toby said. "Don't touch anything." He climbed the steps. A red streak ran across the porch from the back door to the top of the steps where Toby stood. He crossed the porch, found the door unlocked, and went inside. "Billy!" Spots of blood trailed through the dining room to the foyer. He followed them up the steps to Billy's bedroom. There was blood splatter on the wall by a closet door, and a handgun lay on the floor nearby. Toby picked it up with his kerchief. He recognized it, a Colt Python .357 Magnum. It was Billy's gun. Toby was with him when he bought it at a gun shop in Jeetersburg about ten years back. He broke it open. It wasn't loaded. He sniffed the chamber. It smelled like it hadn't been fired. The top drawer of a bureau was open. Bullets for the Colt lay in the drawer.

Toby searched the other rooms upstairs, ran down the stairs, and looked in all the rooms on the first floor. There was no sign of Billy. He ran out the back door, crossed the porch, and came down the steps to rejoin Porter and Stogie.

Toby looked at Porter. He looked fearful. "What happened to Grandpa?" Porter asked.

"I don't know, son." Toby looked around at the yard. A separation of fallen leaves on the lawn began under a sweetgum tree and stretched across the yard to a break in the boxwoods bordering the driveway. "Stay here."

He ran across the yard to the driveway. There was a shallow trough in the gravel where something had been dragged across it to the split-rail fence. He went to the fence, climbed over it, and found more signs of something having been dragged down the hill. He followed the trail down to the foot of the hill near the barn and on through a gate to a clearing beside Whiskey Road. There were several sets of tire tracks in the mud in the clearing.

Toby took off his hat and rubbed his head, looking back up at the house as a flock of red-winged blackbirds swooped down the hill and over the barn. He watched them alight in the maple tree by the river. It appeared that someone had attacked Billy in his bedroom, dragged him to a vehicle in the clearing, and hauled him away, but to the best of Toby's knowledge, Billy didn't have an enemy who would go to all this trouble. The situation made no sense.

Chapter 6

The Motive

Billy awoke, sat up, and held his head in his hands. It was throbbing. There was a new lump the size of a duck's egg above his left ear. It stung and oozed blood. He squinted up at the sunlight slicing through the trees. The sun was directly above him. He must have been unconscious for more than an hour.

He looked around at the terrain and realized he was in a different place. His hands and legs were still manacled and he was still chained to a tree, but the tree was not an oak. It was an elm. And he was not at the top of a hill. He sat in a copse of elm trees on a mountainside. He heard a trickling sound behind him and turned to see spring water emerging from rocks above him, running down to a little pool, and spilling into a stream that ran downhill from there. Through the trees below him, he saw a wall of tar paper glistening in the sunlight, and he knew where he was. Amos had moved him to the hunting cabin.

A purl of smoke rose from the cabin's stovepipe into the sky, but it was too warm outside to burn wood for heat. A moment's reflection told him why Amos had moved him: the cabin gave him shelter and a stove to cook food. The cabin gave him the opportunity to drag out Billy's death as long as he wanted.

The fear that had gripped Billy earlier seized him again. He struggled to rein it in. He needed to calm down and gather his wits. He needed to clear his mind of the cobwebs caused by the blows to his head. The pool was within reach of his chain, so he crawled on his hands and knees to it, then stretched out on his belly and submerged his head in it. The cold spring water braced him. He stayed underwater for a time, and then raised his head and drew in big gulps of air. He got up on his knees and drank water from his cupped hands. When he had slaked his thirst, he hobbled on his knees a few feet away from the pool and sat on his haunches.

He looked up at the azure sky and thought about Amos: his personality, his strengths, his weaknesses. Of all the men he knew, Amos was the last man he would have expected to come after him. He was introverted and sullen. An unremarkable man. Billy had spent hundreds of hours with him in the hunting cabin over the last forty years, but he couldn't recall a single joke Amos told or a prank he pulled. He drank, but he never drank much. He listened to their stories, but he never said much. Billy couldn't remember a single time when Amos had laughed out loud. There was only one brief display of silent mirth when Amos flashed a shy grin after Billy knocked the pipe loose from the woodstove during a big drunk, and even then he covered his mouth with his hand as though he was ashamed of losing control.

Billy looked down at the cabin. The main attraction of the hunting trips for Billy was the raucous fun, the foolishness, the drinking and joking and carrying on. The hunting was merely an excuse to run away with the boys and have a good time. But Amos hadn't come for the drinking and joking; he'd never joined in the fun.

He hadn't come along for the hunting, either. He climbed to the summit of Pine Top every morning and afternoon and mounted the same deer stand next to the same game trail, but in all the years, he never shot a deer, bear, wild turkey, or anything else.

Billy pulled his knees up to his chest and wrapped his arms around his legs, remembering the time twenty-five years ago when Amos' attitude toward killing game first became clear to him. Billy climbed a game trail on the western slope of Pine Top, tracking a white-tail buck in the snow. The track was large and fresh and the steps were evenly spaced, indicating that the buck was walking along easily, calm and undisturbed.

Billy had released the safety on his rifle and crept up the slope, squinting into the falling snow. As he crested the ridge and began to descend the other side of the mountain, he heard the rattle of loose shale below him and he saw the big buck trot by Amos' deer stand. Billy had unintentionally played the role of a good deerhound, driving the buck right to Amos, but Amos never lifted his rifle to his shoulder. The big buck ambled past him and hopped the fence into the park.

Billy stomped down the trail to Amos' stand, outraged. "What the hell are you doing, Amos? I drove that buck right to you. Why didn't you fire at him?"

Amos seemed startled to see Billy. "He was a little too far off," he said.

"He was so close you could have brained him with the barrel of your rifle!"

"You must have seen it from an odd angle. That deer was a little too far."

"Too far, my ass."

That night, Billy spouted off to Toby and Stogie about Amos' failure to fire at the buck. Amos sat in the corner and turned beet red while Billy ranted and raved. He went on and on about it until Stogie grabbed a fistful of Billy's hunting jacket and tugged him outside. Standing by the cabin wall in the dark, Stogie dressed Billy down. "Lay off Amos," he said. "You're ridin him too hard."

"Well, hell, he watched a trophy buck walk right by him. That buck was so close he could have pissed on Amos' boot."

"Amos can't kill nothin."

"What?"

"Amos can't kill a living creature. He ain't got it in him. He can't help it, so just leave him be."

"Well, what the hell's he doing up here?"

"He doesn't come on these trips for the huntin. Just leave him be."

Stogie was right, Billy thought, as he sat under the elm tree twenty-five years later. Amos didn't come on the trips for the hunting or the carousing or the drinking.

Billy looked down at the tarpaper wall of the cabin glistening in the sunlight. Amos' reason for coming along was obvious to Billy, and it made him uncomfortable. Amos didn't have many friends. Toby, Stogie, and Billy were his only close relationships. He came on the trips to be with them, with his friends.

Billy hung his head between his knees, spat on the ground, stared at the spot of saliva as it seeped into the dirt, and thought about Amos' friendship. There was no question that Amos was a good friend to Billy. He'd removed any doubt about that in 1938, when Billy played his game with a woman who lived on a farm near Rock Castle Creek. He'd caught her on the rebound from her second divorce, and she found out he was married and confronted him. They had a big fight and he gave up on her. He drove to a saloon in Scottsville to wash away his frustration, and when he walked in, he saw Amos at a table in the corner by himself, nursing a beer.

Billy sat down with him, but they didn't talk much. Billy was in too bad a mood to talk and Amos was too shy to carry the conversation by himself. Billy was pretty well soused when the woman's brother, a big strong farmer, stormed into the saloon and picked a fight with him. The farmer quickly gained the advantage and got his hands around Billy's throat. His grip felt like a blacksmith's vise, choking off Billy's wind and crushing his Adam's apple. Billy scratched and clawed at the man's fists, writhed and kicked, all to no avail. The farmer's contorted face and the saloon faded away and Billy remembered thinking, "So this is how I will die."

When he awoke in Dolly Madison Hospital, Toby Vess was by his bedside. Toby had been a Selk County deputy sheriff for about ten years back then and he was the first officer to respond to the dispatcher's call. "Amos went plumb crazy," Toby told Billy. "He beat that man nearly to death." Toby said Amos had to be pulled off the man and held down. He was still fighting when Toby got there. "It was all we could do to restrain him long enough to put the cuffs on him."

Billy looked up at the sky above the cabin and blew out a long breath. Amos saved his life, but Billy had not been a good friend in return. A warm wind moaned in the trees. Golden dust motes floated in the cones of light sifting through the branches. Billy lay down and rolled over on his belly, his chain dragging across his back, and sipped water from the pool.

"Most men your age wouldn't recover from a hard blow to the head, much less two of em."

Billy rolled over on his back to see Amos standing over him. "Why'd you wear a mask? If you mean to kill me, I wouldn't live to tell anyone you were my murderer."

"I wanted you to feel helpless. At the last minute, I planned to show you my face so you'd know who killed you. What tipped you off it was me?"

Billy sat up and wiped water off his face with the sleeve of his nightshirt. "Your height and weight, your gait, the shape of your head."

Billy stared at Amos, searching his face. Maybe Billy was wrong. He had told no one about his ancient betrayal, and decades had passed. He didn't understand how Amos could have learned of it. Maybe he had some other reason for attacking him. He hoped so. Otherwise, Billy was doomed.

"Why do you want to kill me? What have I done to you?"

"It won't do you no good to pretend you don't know."

"I'm not pretending. I don't know what's made you hate me so. I thought we were friends."

Amos sprang upon Billy, grabbed him by the collar, and jerked him to his feet, holding their faces inches apart. "You're no friend. A friend doesn't steal the only thing you care about in the whole wide world. A friend doesn't cut your heart out." Billy tried to pull back, but Amos tightened his grip. He held Billy's eyes for a few moments and then threw him down to the ground, stepped back, and leveled his rifle on Billy. Amos' hands shook and sweat coursed down his face. Billy held his breath.

Almost a full minute passed before Amos lowered the rifle and swiped a trembling hand over his face. "God knows I want to blow your head clean off. God knows I do."

Billy tried to swallow the lump of fear in his throat. He stared at Amos' watery eyes and shaking hands. "Back there in the house," Billy said, "when I had the drop on you, you didn't know my gun would misfire, but you stood there while I pulled the trigger. I would have killed you if my gun hadn't failed me." Billy paused. "That's what you wanted, isn't it?"

Amos put his hand to his brow and took several deep breaths. When he dropped his hand, his eyes were filled with anger. "You shouldn't be thinking about me. You should be thinking about how you want to die."

"What do you mean?"

"My plan was to gut-shoot you. I figured you'd last a couple hours if I aim my bullet careful." Amos paused and stared at Billy, hatred etched on his face. "You'd die slow. You'd beg me to kill you before it's over."

Billy wrapped his arms around his knees, licked his chapped lips, and looked down at the ground, trembling.

"But I decided to give you a choice. If you confess and tell me the truth, I'll shoot you in the back of your head. Tell me all of it, and you'll die quick. You won't feel a thing."

Billy studied Amos' face, hoping to see some ambivalence in his resolve to kill him, but there was none. There was only rage and determination, and Billy was too frightened to speak.

"I'll give you time to think. I'll come back at nightfall and you can tell me if you want the gut-shot or the bullet to the back of the head." Amos gave Billy a last long menacing look, turned, and walked down the hill.

Billy watched him until he disappeared around the corner of the cabin. Then he hung his head and pressed his hands together to make them stop shaking. Stogie was wrong. Amos could kill a living creature after all. He would kill Billy, and when Billy was dead, he would kill one last creature. He would turn the gun on himself.

Chapter 7

Jolene's Closet

It was almost noon when Jolene Hukstep drove the Hudson to the other end of the trailer park to the new trailer pads, and she did okay, considering that anything more than ten feet ahead of the car was a blur. She drove slowly and guided the old car carefully over the dirt road between the trailers. The trailers were big walls of white and gray on each side of the road, and they weren't hard to steer clear of. The ditch next to the road was the problem. The Hudson kept sliding into it and scraping its underside on a hump between the road and the ditch. She would jerk the steering wheel to the left and pull the car out of the ditch, but each time the car would slide back in the rut again like there was a big magnet drawing it down into the trough.

Despite almost gutting the Hudson, she finally reached the new trailer pads. She didn't see the first one until she drove up on top of it. There was a loud noise, and she slammed on the brakes. She figured she must have beached the car on the pad because her seat leaned back and the hood pointed up in the air. She didn't worry about it, though, because you couldn't do much damage to a trailer pad. It was just a raised slab of concrete.

She got out of the car, looked around for Amos, and called out to him. As she suspected, he wasn't there, so she got back in the Hudson and sat there for a while, thinking about places he might have gone. Her thoughts soon settled upon her mother's house. Her mother died two months ago. She was ninety-four years old, and the doctors said her old heart just stopped pumping. Jolene cried a little that night, but her mother's death wasn't too sad because she'd lived a long, full life. Her death was painless, and she was ready to go. Jolene told herself that over and over again, and it helped a little bit.

Jolene's mother had been admitted to a nursing home a couple years before she died. Amos and Jolene had thought about moving into her old farmhouse back then, but they decided against it. The house was musty and drafty and in severe disrepair. Plus they liked the double-wide, and it was easier for them to manage the trailer park from there. When she died, she left the farmhouse to them in her will, and they decided to fix it up and sell it.

Amos had worked on it off and on for the past several weeks, patching the roof, replacing the rotten porch planks, and repairing the plaster in Jolene's old bedroom. He was more sullen than usual three or four days ago after he returned from there, and as far as Jolene knew he hadn't been there since. Maybe the house had something to do with his recent taciturnity. Maybe he went there that morning to resume his repair work. It was worth a look-see.

Jolene backed the Hudson off the pad, and something hit something else real hard when the front wheels slammed down to the ground, but the engine kept running so she figured it couldn't be all that important. She revved it up and pulled forward. She made it across the dirt road and eased onto Whiskey Road. She could discern the outer edge of the asphalt as the right side of the Hudson's hood swallowed it up, so she kept the hood ornament lined up with the edge of the road and crawled forward. The trip went pretty well for about two miles. Then some blue blur of a car or a truck whipped around a turn and came hurtling toward her. The blue thing's horn blared and it swerved away from her. She didn't see it in her rearview mirror, so she assumed it passed by safely and kept going.

She made it all the way to her mother's house without another incident. When she turned in the driveway, she ran over a row of bushes before she saw them. She got out and looked under the front wheel. She had smashed her mother's azaleas flat. It was too bad, but they were old and their limbs were spindly and brittle and most of them no longer bloomed in the summer. Maybe it was a good thing she finished them off. She and Amos could brighten up the yard this spring with healthy new shrubs.

Jolene climbed the porch steps and unlocked the door. "Amos? Are you here?" She walked through the foyer and down the hallway to the kitchen. Her mind flooded with memories of her mother bustling about the room. Her mother loved to cook, and Thanksgiving was her favorite day of the year. She would create a feast, and the whole family would gather around the dining room table: Jolene and Amos and their three girls, her father before he passed on, her brother and his wife and their two kids before they moved to Blacksburg, her uncle Fred and her aunt Clara and her cousins. The kitchen would be hot as an oven, and her mother would flit around between the stove and the dining room table with her face flushed, shoving food at everybody, never sitting down or taking a bite for herself, in seventh heaven until the last dish was cleared, washed, and put away in the cupboard.

Jolene smiled as she walked into the dining room and pictured everyone sitting around the big table gorging themselves. The musty room was cold and quiet as a tomb, but she remembered it warm and filled with laughter and excited chatter. She could almost hear the clinking china, crystal, and silver, the voices of her family, the high-pitched squeals of her daughters. The sounds of her family were still there in the walls and floors of the old house. They surrounded her and made her feel warm inside.

She crossed the dining room and went down the hall to the foyer. Along a side wall, stairs climbed to the second floor where her and her brother's bedrooms were located. She stood at the foot of the steps and looked upstairs. She saw herself as a child, bounding up the steps two at a time and sliding back down the banister. She stroked it fondly. Its once-shiny sheen had dulled, but that was understandable. It was older than Jolene, after all.

She looked up at the landing and at her bedroom door. She'd dreamed dreams in that room. She had mapped out her entire life, and it had pretty much followed her dream. She planned to marry Amos and have kids by him and raise them with him, and that's exactly what she did.

She frowned as she pondered the one deficiency of her youthful planning: it hadn't gone far enough. It didn't extend to where she found herself at this moment, with almost all of her shine dulled down like the old banister. Her plan ended when the girls married and moved away. Her plans didn't anticipate a time when she and Amos would be alone and old and tired, when he wouldn't come to bed and wouldn't tell her what was wrong, and when he didn't seem to care for her anymore.

She shuddered in the cold gloom, wrapped her arms around her shoulders, and climbed the stairs to the second floor. She pushed open the door to her bedroom and swept away a spider's web that clung to its eave. Maybe her parents hadn't planned for the last part of their lives either, because her room looked the same as it did when she was a girl. The bed resting against the window was covered with dust, but it was neatly made and ready to receive her with the musty old bedspread and throw pillows of sixty years ago. The oval rug that she and her mother made from rags covered the floor. Her crude charcoal drawing of a horse hung over her bed and her awkward painting of a grist mill in autumn still hung over her desk, both the products of school projects. Her little knickknacks and keepsakes still sat on her desk: dolls, porcelain figurines of the king and queen of England, and the little brown teddy bear her father bought for her on a trip to the state fair in Richmond. The room was dank and smelled of mildew, but nothing else about it had changed in sixty years.

A bag of plaster leaned against the wall next to the closet, where water had seeped into the ceiling from the leaking roof. Amos had chipped some of the crumbling plaster away and pried the rotting wood loose from the frame. His hammer and chisel lay next to the bag of plaster. The closet door stood open. Jolene went to it and looked inside. The old crossbar for hanging her clothes was empty. The shelves on the opposite wall were dusty and scarred. Several musty cardboard boxes sat on the shelves, and beside one of the boxes on the middle shelf sat a little yellow basket.

Jolene gasped. She put her hand over her breast as her heart moved into her throat. She stepped into the closet and pressed her hands down on a shelf to keep from falling, staring fearfully at the little yellow basket she'd put on that shelf so many years ago. She remembered everything about it now and it frightened her almost to the point of passing out. She closed her eyes and took deep breaths.

Five or six years after she married Amos, Jolene had returned to her childhood bedroom and placed the basket on that shelf behind the boxes to hide it from everyone in the world. She thought her secret would be safe there, and it had been safe for half a century, so safe that she had forgotten about it.

She gathered her courage, picked up the basket, and went back to the bed. She sat down and passed her shaking hand across her brow. Maybe Amos hadn't looked inside. Please, God, she thought. Make it so he didn't look inside.

She reached in and withdrew one of the notes. The old paper crackled in her hands as she unfolded it. Her heart stopped when she saw Amos' smudged fingerprints, soiled from his work on the plaster. He had seen the note. He had read it. She held the note in her lap and wept feebly for a long time.

She finally pulled herself together and stared down at the note. She couldn't remember what it said. Maybe there was still a chance. Maybe it didn't say enough. She held the note up to the light, but her hand shook so violently she couldn't read it. She grasped it with both hands to quell the trembling and held her breath and read it.

Jolene,
Meet me by the river at noon under that maple tree where we
made love in the moonlight Tuesday night.
Wear that yellow dress.
Billy

She dropped the note on the bed and cried. She rocked back and forth and cried and cried. After a long time, she cried herself out, and forced herself to take the other two notes out of the basket. She laid one on the bed and read the other one. In that one, Billy told her to meet him behind Purcell's Sawmill. She tried to remember. That was the first note he gave her, the first time she stole away to meet him.

Her thoughts returned to that summer. It was around the time of the big war, 1915, as she recalled. She was twenty-two and Billy was five years older. He was handsome, with coal-black hair, dark skin, and fierce black eyes, and he had a winning smile and a wicked throaty laugh. All the girls swooned over him.

She married Amos when she was seventeen. She never dated anybody else and no one ever courted her. Even Amos never courted her. He grew up on the farm behind her father's property. From the time they were children, everybody, including her and Amos, assumed they would get married. He didn't have to chase her or court her or win her over. He grew up standing next to her, and one day he just took her hand and they got married. There was never any question about it or any thrill or suspense or romance.

She never dreamed she would cheat on him, but that summer Billy Kirby began to flirt with her. He stared at her at church, at his store, at the barn dances, at the hay rides. He was always smiling that smile of his that told her exactly what he wanted to do with her. He smiled at her and winked at her and nudged her when he could get close enough, but never when Amos was looking. It made her uncomfortable at first, but after a while, she looked forward to his flirtations despite her best efforts to be good.

When Amos got drunk and passed out at Stogie Morris' barn dance, Billy threw him in the back of his buckboard and drove Jolene and Amos home. He tried to kiss her and rub her legs while she sat next to him on the buggy seat, but she fought him off. He reined the buggy horse to a halt and leaned into her with his broad grin. "You're a beauty, Jolene. You're too pretty to go to waste on Amos Hukstep." He tried to kiss her, but she turned away. Then he said, "I want you, Jolene. I want you bad." She glanced at Amos, lying flat on his back behind them, snoring, dead to the world. Billy looked at him and smirked. "I guarantee you Amos Hukstep don't want you as bad as I do. He don't know what he's got. If he did, he wouldn't drink himself stone drunk and let me get so close to you." Billy gazed into Jolene's eyes. "You have the prettiest eyes in Selk County, Jolene." He said it so confidently, like the mere fact that he said it made it so. He said it every time he saw her after that, and for a few months she believed it. Fifty years after Billy noticed her eyes, she was still trying so very hard to believe she had the prettiest eyes in the county.

Billy handed her the first note at a church picnic while Amos stood under the trees talking to the men. She hid the note in her blouse. When she and Amos got home that night, she locked herself in the bathroom and read it. "Meet me behind the sawmill tomorrow night at eight." Jolene hid it in her underwear drawer where she hoped Amos would be too shy to look. The next night, when he left for his job on the night shift at Murray's Visible Records, she found the bottle of perfume her father had given her for Christmas and rubbed some of it behind her ears and on her chest and legs. She got to Purcell's Sawmill early and hid in the cedar trees, afraid that someone might drive up and ask her what in the world she was doing there in the dark. Her heart pounded when Billy emerged from the pine forest into the moonlight.

She followed him into a shed and she sat on the sawdust floor with him and they talked for more than an hour. She let him kiss her, but nothing more. She wanted to do a lot more, but she knew it was wrong. She had always been a good girl. Maybe that was part of the reason she was so attracted to Billy. She had never done anything against the rules, and he was as far outside the rules as she could get without going to jail.

A week after that first night at the sawmill, she was shopping for staples with Amos at Billy's father's store. She was looking at a can of green beans when Billy passed behind her and dropped the second note in her tote bag. Amos was standing right beside her but he didn't notice because Billy whacked him on the back and started telling him a dirty joke. She slipped the note inside her blouse and almost went crazy waiting for Amos to take her home so she could lock herself in the bathroom and read it.

She did exactly what the note told her to do. She put on a yellow dress and waited for Billy behind Kirby's General Store just after dark while

Amos was at work, and Billy came and grabbed her up in his strong arms and twirled her around and kissed her on the mouth before she had a chance to stop him, and then he took her hand and they ran through the wheat field down to the meadow on the banks of Little Bear River. That kiss broke down what little resistance she could muster. Billy spread a blanket in the moonlight, and she gave in to her desires. She let him do what he wanted to do and she did what she wanted to do, too. It was wonderful and glorious and thrilling beyond belief. She would have stayed there all night if there had been any possible way to get away with it. God knows she wanted to stay with him, but she had to be home by midnight when Amos got off work. It was all she could do to tear herself away from Billy, and when Amos came home she feigned sleep so she wouldn't have to face him because she was afraid she would lash out at him because he stood between her and a lifetime of bliss with Billy.

Jolene trembled all over as she remembered those fiery times. Billy swept her clean off her feet that summer. She put her hand to her mouth and shook her head. She was so stupid. She thought she was in love with Billy, and she thought he loved her, too. She was wrong on both counts.

She picked up the third note. Billy slipped it to her Sunday morning after church. He knew Amos had to work overtime at the plant that afternoon, so the note told her to meet him by the river. It was a beautiful summer afternoon and they spread a blanket in the same meadow under a maple tree. She made love to him in the warm sun, right out there in broad daylight, and she was the happiest girl in the world. Then she told him she loved him.

In that instant, her world turned upside down. Billy said something about how she didn't love him, she just loved the good times, but his words didn't matter to her. It was his eyes that gave him away. She saw the truth in them. He hadn't courted her because he thought she was special, the way he said. That was a fool's lie. He courted her because she would let him do what he wanted to do. He didn't want her love. He wanted what she gave him on her back on the blanket in the meadow. That was all he cared about.

She cried as she lay on the blanket that day, and she cried again as she sat on her bed in her old bedroom fifty years later. All that was left of that time so long ago were the three short notes. She put them back in the basket and stared at it, wondering why she had kept the notes. Why hadn't she burned them? They weren't protestations of love or expressions of tender feelings. They were merely commands from a lustful man. Meet me here. Meet me there. Wear this. Wear that. They contained no kind words of special affection. They weren't precious keepsakes.

She looked out the window down at the front yard, at the lime-green blur of the old Hudson. She knew why she kept the notes. She kept them because Billy wanted her that summer. He could have had any woman in Selk County, but he wanted Jolene. He broke her heart and it took her more than a year to heal the wound, but at least he wanted her for a while. No one else had ever wanted her the way he did. He craved her. He lusted after her.

Amos never wanted her in that way. He took her when they were in their marriage bed, but he was plodding and dull with it. He followed the rules and did what he was supposed to do. He never whispered in her ear or told her she was special or nice or fun to be with. He never said her eyes were pretty. He never even said he loved her. She thought he loved her, but he never said it and he never showed it. It wasn't in his nature. With Amos, she had to tell herself that he loved her and that was all she ever got, self-assurances of his love. He bedded her at night and did his business silently and dutifully, like cleaning the gutters or washing the truck. He spawned babies with her, but that was all there was. No flowers, no sweet talk, no wicked throaty laughter, no fire or sparks or screams or groans of passion or ways to touch you which were against the rules and would drive you wild.

With Billy, Jolene got all of that. He made her feel like he wanted her more than anything in the world. It lasted only a few weeks, but it was the only time in her life when she felt so wanted. That's why she kept those three cryptic notes from her youth. They were dried out, crusty remnants of those few days in the summer fifty years ago when she felt pretty, desirable, and special. Those memories were precious only to her. Now Amos had found them, and he knew Jolene had cheated on him and had covered it up for fifty years. That was why he was so sullen and why he hadn't come to bed the last few nights. He knew about her ancient trysts with Billy, and he was deeply, profoundly hurt.

Jolene lay down on the bed and sighed, breathing in the stale scent of the old bedspread and thinking about how Amos must have felt when he found the yellow basket and read the notes. She imagined a stabbing, searing pain in his chest. She saw his florid face and his shaking hand when he read about what she did with Billy.

She lay on the bed for a long time, thinking about Amos and his awful moment of realization, and then it hit her and she bolted upright. Amos was more than hurt. He was enraged. He was very slow to come to full-throttle anger, but when he finally got there, he was hell-bent to beat someone to death.

When they were in high school, there was gossip that Amos' mother was having an affair with a preacher from Staunton. One boy teased Amos relentlessly for a week, but when he called his mother a whore, Amos charged him like a rabid bull. He broke the boy's arm and two of his ribs and knocked out most of his teeth before the others pulled him off. It took four big strapping farm kids to save that hateful boy from Amos' wrath. Then Amos went to Staunton and beat the preacher within an inch of his life. He spent six months in reform school and was held back a grade that year.

Amos' rage about Jolene's betrayal would be worse than that. Jolene's eyes widened as she realized where he had gone. She jumped up from the bed and rushed out of the bedroom, down the stairs, and out the front door to the Hudson. She fired it up and floored the accelerator, speeding out of the driveway and hurtling over Whiskey Road toward Fox Run.

Chapter 8

Toby's Discovery

That day shortly after noon, Toby called the sheriff's office from Billy's store and told the dispatcher to find Selk County Sheriff Coleman Grundy and Frank Woolsey, the county's crime lab technician, and tell them to come to Billy Kirby's house.

Frank arrived first. He was a short, stout middle-aged man with a wide bald head, a perpetually flushed face, and a white handlebar mustache. Toby told him what he had discovered, left him in charge of the crime scene, and went home to change into his uniform and fetch his service revolver. Toby lived on Whiskey Road in Saddleback Cove about ten miles west of Fox Run. The winding road was narrow and flanked by steep mountains that blocked out the sunlight except for a few hours around high noon each day. The sun was bright and warm that day, and water from the morning's rain glistened in the ditches by the road.

Toby's house was a small red-brick cottage that sat in a grove of cedar trees at the foot of one of the steep mountains. Toby parked in the gravel driveway and got out of the truck. A warm breeze moaned in the cedars as he followed the flagstone walkway to his front stoop, where he stopped cold. His front door had been kicked open. The dead bolt had busted through the doorframe and ripped the plaster away from the adjoining wall. He stepped inside quietly and listened. He walked through the house slowly to make sure the burglar wasn't still there. The house seemed largely undisturbed and all his valuables were in their proper places until he entered the little back room he used as his home office. A pair of handcuffs and a set of leg irons were missing from a desk drawer, and yet the service revolver, which lay in the same drawer, was still there.

Toby propped his hands on his hips and stared at the desk, troubled. Leg manacles and handcuffs were the tools of a kidnapper. Only a few of Toby's close friends knew he kept the restraints in his desk drawer, but none of them had a motive to kidnap Billy. The situation made no sense.

He took his service revolver from the drawer, went to his bedroom, changed into his uniform, and strapped on his holster, all the while thinking about the break-in. He went through the house again, searching for any evidence the intruder might have left behind. He found nothing. He returned to the office and stared at the drawer. He resolved to tell Frank Woolsey to flyspeck his house for evidence after he'd completed his work at Billy's house.

Toby closed the front door from the inside, went out the back door, and headed back toward Fox Run. About halfway there, he came around a sharp turn to find Homer Sprouse's blue Pontiac Bonneville wrapped around a telephone pole. Deputy Will Garrison was already on the scene. He told Toby he had radioed the dispatcher to send an ambulance for Homer and a tow truck for the Pontiac. Homer sat on the bank beside the road, looking forlorn with his head wrapped in Deputy Garrison's bloodstained kerchief. There was a gash on the bridge of his nose and both his eyes were blackened.

Toby went over to him. "What happened, Homer?"

"I come around that turn yonder and ran up on a big old green car, biggest car I've ever seen. Looked like a commercial fishin boat floatin along on my side of the road. I blew the horn, threw my Pontiac in the ditch, and slammed into that damned pole. Smashed my face on my steerin wheel. Totaled my Pontiac. The worst part is I don't have no insurance."

"Did you get a look at the driver?"

"It happened too fast. I'll never forget that car bearin down on me, though. It was a big old lime-green boat. Don't know what make it was. Some kind of off brand I ain't ever seen before."

"I'll keep an eye out for that car," Toby said.

Deputy Garrison seemed to have the situation under control, so Toby moved on to Billy's house and parked his truck in Billy's driveway. Stogie stood at the break in the boxwood bushes by the driveway, gazing at the house.

Toby got out of the truck and walked over to Stogie. "Where's Porter?"

Stogie made a sour face. "Said he had to go home to his wife's family get-together. Claimed he'd be back soon as he could. I'll believe it when I see him."

Toby went inside the house and talked with Frank. He had found a screen, which had been removed from a dining room window and was propped against the side of the house, and some mud on the dining room floor just inside the window, leading him to conclude the window was the point of entry. He'd also taken blood swatches and dusted for fingerprints. Toby told Frank about the break-in at his house and he agreed to head over there when he finished his work at Billy's house. Toby left Frank collecting the mud he'd found under the dining room window and went outside.

When Toby rejoined Stogie in the driveway, Porter pulled up behind Toby's truck in his new Plymouth. He walked over to Toby and Stogie looking hangdog. "I'm sorry I had to leave. Is there any sign of Grandpa?"

"I'm afraid not," Toby said. He noticed a spot of blood beading in the corner of Porter's mouth, and when Porter turned his head to look at Billy's house, Toby saw a purple bruise under his eye just above his cheekbone. "What happened, Porter? You look like you've been in a fight."

Porter glanced at Toby, swiped at his mouth, and looked at the smear of blood on his hand. His face reddened. "It's nothin."

Toby squinted at the bruise. "Someone hit you. Tell me what happened."

Porter put his hands in his pockets and heaved a sigh. "Had a little run-in with Maureen's dad at my house."

Stogie snorted. "I bet you did."

Toby shot Stogie a hard look. Stogie put his hands in his pockets and scowled at the ground.

"How bad a fight was it?" Toby asked.

Porter toed the gravel in the driveway. "Bad enough for Maureen to throw me out."

"Is Zeke hurt?"

Porter shook his head. "I went easy on him. His pride's hurt, I reckon, but I didn't do much damage to him otherwise."

Toby would have asked more, but Sheriff Grundy pulled into the driveway and walked over to them. He was in his late fifties, a head shorter than Toby, and portly. His ample girth strained against the buttons of his uniform. He took off his hat and wiped his bald head with a red kerchief. "What have we got here, Toby?"

"Looks like Billy Kirby's been assaulted and kidnapped." Toby recounted the evidence he and Frank had found.

"Any boot tracks in the yard or the field?" the sheriff asked.

"The rain washed them away. There are tire tracks in the clearing, but the rain washed out the patterns of the tread. Tire tracks wouldn't help us identify the attacker anyway. Lots of people park down there at night. The teenagers use that spot to neck, and farmers sit down there in their trucks, hiding from momma to drink their hooch."

The sheriff turned to Porter. "When's the last time you saw your grandpa, son?"

"Late yesterday evening. He was in the store, jawing with his old pals."

"Was he still there when you went home?"

"I worked late. He went home before I left." Porter paused, frowning. "Let's see. When I left the store about nine, the light was on in his bedroom. I came in to the store this morning before dawn to total yesterday's cash receipts because I wanted to get home by ten, when Grandpa was supposed to take over. There were no lights on in Grandpa's house when I got here. They never did come on and he never showed up at the store."

The sheriff said, "It sounds like someone attacked Billy sometime after nine last night and before dawn this morning."

Stogie said, "From the looks of all the blood, it had to be somebody with a powerful grudge."

"You know anybody with a grudge against Billy?" the sheriff asked

Stogie.

"Not in the last twenty years. When he was young, lots of men hated him, but those days are long gone."

The sheriff scratched his chin. "Who are some of the old dogs who had disagreements with him?"

"Me, for one. I tried to kill him when I caught him in bed with my first wife."

The sheriff nodded. "I heard those old stories about Billy and Bea. I reckon Billy was none too pleased with you when you took up with Mary Jo, either."

"We hated each other back then." Stogie frowned. "I left Bea after that. She was no-account before Billy got ahold of her, and her cheatin on me gave me good cause to throw her out. Mary Jo and Billy got back together after she broke up with me. I don't know why. They never seemed to get along too good. Took Billy and me about ten years to heal our wounds and become friends again. I'll tell you what, though. I wasn't the only man Billy put the horns on. He chased a lot of married women and made goats out of a whole lot of men. You could fill up a good-sized barn with married men who wanted to do him in." Stogie paused. "Still, as far as I know, all those old grudges got settled up some way or other or their holders are long since dead."

There was the roar of an engine on Whiskey Road, followed by a loud thump, a crash, and scraping metal. Toby looked up to see a car careen across Billy's driveway, smash flat the boxwoods that bordered the yard, and stall out on top of them. Steam rose from the hood. Toby recognized the car as Amos Hukstep's Hudson Hornet, and it immediately occurred to him that the big lime-green off-brand model fit Homer Sprouse's description of the monster that chased his Pontiac into a telephone pole.

Toby and the others rushed over to the car. While Porter pulled Jolene Hukstep out of it, Toby saw that a post and a section of the split-rail fence that fronted Billy's property had been knocked down. Porter's Plymouth hadn't fared much better; the driver's door was smashed in and splinters of glass were scattered across the gravel driveway.

Porter was so busy with Jolene he didn't seem to notice the damage to his car. He led her by the arm across the yard toward the porch with the rest of them trailing along behind. "Are you all right, Mrs. Hukstep?"

"I'm fine." She flinched when she saw the sheriff. "Why is the law here?"

The sheriff took Jolene's arm from Porter and guided her to sit down on the porch steps. "Did you lose control of the car?"

Jolene squinted at the Hudson. "I guess so. I was driving too fast. I didn't see the fence and it was too late to stop when I saw the bushes." She squinted at the rest of them. "Stogie? Toby? Is that you?"

Toby stepped closer to her. "Are you sure you're all right? You hit the car in the driveway pretty hard."

"Was there a car in the driveway?"

Porter blanched and ran across the yard.

Jolene frowned at Toby. "Why are you wearing your deputy's uniform on Thanksgiving Day?" She looked at the sheriff. "Why is the law here? Where's Billy Kirby?"

"He's been kidnapped," Toby said. "Or worse."

Jolene sucked in her breath. "Oh my God."

Toby was surprised to see something akin to guilt flash across her face. He knelt beside her. "Do you know something about this, Jolene?"

She put her hand to her mouth and averted her eyes from his probing look.

Toby paused. "Do you know something about Billy's disappearance?"

"I don't know if I should tell you."

Toby took her hand. "That's not a good answer." She pulled her hand away, but he took it back. "Tell us what you know about Billy."

Jolene's eyes brimmed with tears. "I can't tell you."

Toby gave the sheriff a confused look.

The sheriff said, "Where's Amos, Jolene?"

She wiped her tears and shook her head. "I don't know. He was gone when I woke up."

"Jolene?" Toby said. "Does Amos have some reason to be angry with

Billy?"

Jolene withdrew a handkerchief from her coat pocket and blew her nose. "It's a private matter."

Toby shook his head in amazement. "What in the world is going on here?"

Stogie grabbed Toby's arm. "I need to talk to you alone."

"Not now, Stogie."

"It's got to be now—right now." Stogie pulled Toby away from the group to the driveway. He glanced at Porter, who was kneeling beside the Plymouth looking at its caved-in door, and dragged Toby to the split-rail fence that bordered the pasture where they were out of earshot of Porter and the others. "I know something I ain't supposed to know." He put his mouth near Toby's ear and dropped his voice. "Billy put the horns on Amos."

Toby winced. "Billy and Jolene? I don't believe it."

"It's true. Billy told me so a couple weeks after Mary Jo died. We were the last ones sitting around the stove in his store one night. He'd been nipping from a jug of shine all night long. By the time everybody else left, he was crying in his booze and muttering gibberish about the past. He was so drunk I don't think he knew I was there." Stogie glanced at Jolene and lowered his voice. "Billy said it flat out. Him and Jolene did the deed. He said she was the only one he ever really loved in his whole life but he missed his chance cause he made some kinda mistake."

Toby looked at Stogie incredulously. "That's ridiculous. It can't be true."

"Look at her," Stogie said. Jolene sat on the porch steps, weeping uncontrollably. "If I'm wrong, why do you suppose she's so upset?"

Toby stared at Jolene and tried to adjust to the shock of Stogie's revelation. Ludicrous images of Billy and Jolene, both way past seventy years old, locked in a passionate embrace, ran through his mind. Then it dawned on him that Amos was one of the few people who knew where he kept his handcuffs and leg manacles. "I'll be damned."

He and Stogie went back to the porch. Toby knelt beside Jolene and said, "Jolene, we need your help. Tell us the truth. Amos has a powerful reason to be angry at Billy, doesn't he?"

Jolene looked Toby in the eye for an instant and then turned away. "Yes, but I won't tell you the reason. It's too embarrassing."

Porter returned to the group with a grimace on his face.

"Help us, Jolene," Toby said. "Maybe it's not too late. Maybe we can find them. Where is Amos?"

She wiped her eyes and shuddered. "I don't know. Amos and his truck were gone when I woke up."

Porter perked up. "I saw Mr. Hukstep's truck this morning."

Everyone turned to Porter.

"His red Chevy pickup drove past the store before dawn," he said. "I didn't think anything of it at the time. I figured he was making his way to a deer stand before first light. He came up the hill on Whiskey Road and stopped at the sign."

"Which way did he go?" Toby asked.

"He turned left at the T and took the state road into Whippoorwill Hollow."

The sheriff looked north. "Why would Amos take Billy into the hollow?"

"Amos didn't stop in the hollow," Stogie said.

Everyone turned to him, and he shrugged. "I know how Amos thinks. He drove through the hollow and on past the dam. He took Billy into the park. That's where I'd go if I wanted to kill a man. Nobody could see you or hear you in the park, and there's a thousand places to stash a body where no one could find it. That's where Amos took Billy."

"Oh my God!" Jolene cried.

"Why would Amos want to kill Billy?" the sheriff asked.

"He wants revenge." Stogie glanced at Jolene and looked back at the sheriff with a knowing expression on his face.

The sheriff looked at Jolene and raised his eyebrows.

She balled her handkerchief in her fist and hit her knee with it softly. "Good Lord."

The sheriff took off his hat, ran his hand over his bald head, and put it back on. He looked at Jolene again, shook his head, and then looked up the road toward Whippoorwill Hollow. "You're right, Stogie. If I wanted to get away from everyone to do some serious harm to a man, I'd take him into the park." The sheriff looked at his watch. "It's almost five. It'll be dark in less than an hour. Amos has a twelve-hour head start on us. There's a hundred miles of fire roads in there. He could be anywhere and time is not on our side." He turned to Toby. "You head on up now."

"My county truck's in Jeetersburg at headquarters. I've been drivin my Ford pickup over the holiday weekend."

"We could radio for your county truck, but it'll take more than an hour for it to be driven out here." He looked at his patrol car. "My car doesn't have four-wheel drive." He turned back to Toby. "There's no time to waste. Head on up there in your Ford. I'll call the other deputies and send them up there behind you in four-wheel drive vehicles. Leave us some sign on the roads you search so we don't cover the same routes."

Stogie grabbed Toby's arm. "I want to go with you."

Toby hesitated.

"I know Amos better than anybody," Stogie said. "I can help you find him."

"Stogie's right," the sheriff said. "Take him with you."

Toby and Stogie rushed across the yard, climbed into Toby's old Ford pickup, and sped toward the park through Whippoorwill Hollow.

"When did it happen?" Toby said to Stogie as they drove along.

"What?"

"Jolene cheating on Amos with Billy."

"Billy said it was a long time ago. Back around World War I."

Toby braked the truck to a stop. "World War I?"

"That's what Billy said."

"Fifty years ago? Why the hell is Amos taking his revenge on Billy now?"

"I don't know, but I'll tell you this. When a man messes with your wife, it takes a long jag of time to get over it, and you don't ever really forget it. Believe me. I know."

Toby shook his head, shifted his truck into gear, and drove on.

Chapter 9

Billy's Lie

That evening Billy lay in the leaves under the elm tree. The temperature dropped considerably as dusk approached, but it was still much warmer than usual for the time of year and the mild chill didn't bother him. He had other discomforts to distract him. He was hungry and tired. His head hurt and the lacerations on his back were inflamed and sore and he was dizzy, nauseous, and weak, but his primary discomfort was psychological. He pondered his impending death and he was filled with fear.

Billy wasn't afraid of going to hell when he died, like the preacher at Grace Church had warned him would happen. He didn't believe in God or heaven or hell. He knew what would happen to him after he took his last breath: nothing would happen. Nothing at all. When Billy told Amos the truth, he would blow Billy's brains out. His bodily juices would melt into the dirt. The mountain spring would take his decayed cells and spill them into the stream that trickled into Little Bear River. The river would carry them through Whippoorwill Hollow, and they would ride the river on and on, mixing in with everything and moving farther and farther away from each other until they were everywhere and nowhere.

That was Billy's afterlife—dissolution into a ubiquitous nothingness. He would cease to be. There would be no more mistakes or lies or misery … and no more blue sky or Indian summer breeze or fresh cold spring water or jokes and tall tales told beside the woodstove in the store or nights drinking shine in the hunting cabin or soft touches from the gentle hand of a pretty woman. No sunshine. No moonlight. No warm nights under the maple tree. No fire. No cold. Nothing.

Billy sighed heavily. He wasn't afraid of the nonexistent afterlife. He was afraid of losing this life. Amos' attack made him realize he didn't want to die. He wanted to live as long as possible, no matter how many mistakes he'd made that would come back to plague him in his old age.

As darkness approached, Billy's anxiety mounted. He crawled on all fours to the spring, dragging his chain along with him, and sipped the cold water. When he was finished, he sat up and looked at the purple sky. A soft breeze blew across the side of the hill, and he gazed at the opposite navy blue mountainside, the eastern face of Pine Top Mountain. Pleasures in life he had come to ignore meant more to him now that he was faced with his imminent death. The land around the cabin was spectacularly beautiful, he thought, even in winter when the vegetation was dormant.

He wiped the moisture of the spring water from his lips and looked down at the darkening form of the cabin. Smoke curled from the stovepipe. Amos was cooking his supper. Billy rubbed his belly and winced. He was hungry and his sides were bruised and sore from the times Amos had kicked him.

Night fell. Time was growing short. He let out a heavy breath. His mind was addled by pain and hunger and fear, but he tried to gather his wits. There had to be a way to live another day. Amos was dimwitted. Maybe a well-crafted lie could pull Billy back from the abyss of nothingness. Lying was his special talent, his gift. He had told lies all his life to escape responsibility, to get out of trouble, to gain the upper hand in a business deal, to impress a pretty woman. He had convinced a lot of men and a whole passel of women to believe his lies, and all of them were smarter than Amos. With his life on the line, Billy certainly ought to be able to summon the skill to persuade a man as gullible as Amos to believe an artful deception.

Bald-faced, insistent denial had persuaded other cuckolded husbands of his innocence. It might work here. The embryo of a lie of denial took seed in Billy's imagination and came to life and grew into a fleshed-out creature of deceit. He turned it over in his mind and silently rehearsed its delivery.

Amos might believe it. He could sell this lie to Amos if he calmed down and focused his energy.

Billy ran his hand through his hair, the cold metal link binding his cuffs pulling his other hand along with it. Certainly Amos would believe him. Most men in Amos' shoes wanted to believe such a lie. They were predisposed to hope that their wives had been faithful. A good story pulled them across a line into self-deception because they didn't want to resist. Of course, Amos was different from other men. He was so honest he had probably never lied to himself, and he might not allow himself to believe Billy's lie the way a normal man would.

No, don't doubt yourself, Billy thought. The secret to a convincing lie was confidence. Even a wisp of doubt could undermine his credibility.

"What's your decision?"

Billy looked up into the blinding glare of a flashlight. He took a deep breath. "All right," he said. "I'll tell you the truth."

Amos sat down cross-legged in the leaves. His flashlight washed over the barrel of his rifle resting across his lap. "I want to know what you and Jolene did with each other."

Billy gathered his courage. "You've got it all wrong, Amos. We did nothing. Nothing at all."

"What?"

"I wanted her. I tried hard to get her, but she wouldn't give me the time of day."

Amos pointed his rifle at Billy. "Don't lie to me."

Billy looked directly into Amos' light and projected all the sincerity he could muster. "I don't know who told you she went to bed with me, but they got it wrong. I wanted her bad and I chased her hard, but she was faithful to you. She didn't betray you. She turned me down. Over and over again."

Amos looked confused. "That's not true. She ran off with you."

The look of confusion in Amos' eyes encouraged Billy. "You're wrong," he said. "Someone convinced you Jolene cheated on you when it never happened. You want to kill her, but you can't bring yourself to do it because you love her too much. So you decided to do the next best thing.

You decided to kill the man you think made love to her. Well, Jolene didn't betray you. I tried to get her in bed with me. God knows I tried every trick in the book, but nothing worked. She wouldn't do it. She wouldn't cheat on you. You can kill me for trying to bed your wife if you want, but you can't kill me for doing the deed with her because she wouldn't give in to me."

Amos stood up and stared at Billy. He seemed speechless, and Billy was convinced his denial was working. "Unlock these manacles," he said. "Take me home. I ought to have you jailed, but I won't. I understand your blood was up when you thought Jolene slept with me. Jealousy makes men crazy. I'm willing to make allowances for that, but you've beaten me mercilessly and I'm tired and sore and hungry. If you let me go now, I'll forget this ever happened and I won't tell anyone, but if I have to endure one more minute of your torment, I'll turn you in and see to it the law brings its full measure against you."

"You're lying."

Billy shook his head resolutely. "I never touched her."

"I know better. I found the notes."

Billy's blood ran cold. The notes. All the confidence drained out of him with the uncertainty produced by those two words. What notes? He couldn't recall writing any notes to Jolene. God knows he wrote a lot of love notes in his day. The sappy letters worked their charm with a lot of women. He must have written love letters to Jolene, but he had no recollection of them.

Billy tried to convince himself the love letters didn't matter. He couldn't change strategy midcourse anyway. Whatever the contents of the notes, he was already committed to the denial. He had to keep going with it and hope the letters didn't contradict him, but he had lost his greatest strength—confidence in his lie.

"Sure I—" Billy's throat was dry and his voice broke. He gathered himself and started again. "Sure I wrote her notes. That was all part of my scheme to lure her into bed with me, but it failed. I tried to win her over, but she wouldn't take the bait."

"One of the notes says you did it with her under that maple tree in the pasture below your house."

Billy reeled. He had contradicted his own word in some ancient note he couldn't remember. "It was … just a ploy, a lie, you know … I wrote that note to let her see it wouldn't be so bad if we went ahead … I thought maybe she would fall for it if I said it in writing even though we never did it."

Amos leveled the rifle on Billy. "You lying bastard. You steal Jolene from me, and you have the gall to try to tell me it never happened. Well, I know better. I found three notes you wrote to her, and they prove she didn't turn you down."

Billy hung his head.

Amos put the mouth of his rifle barrel against the top of Billy's head, just over the hairline. Billy cringed, waiting for the explosion. Amos held the rifle there for a long time, the mouth of the barrel vibrating against Billy's head with the shaking of Amos' hands. Then Amos pulled the rifle back and brought it down to his side. He stepped back and put his hand over his eyes and wept.

Billy let out his breath and waited, afraid to say anything.

After a long time, Amos wiped his eyes and looked down at Billy. "I'll give you one last chance, you lying son of a bitch. When I come back here at daybreak, if you don't tell me the truth, I'll gut-shoot you and watch you bleed to death. You better think long and hard on that tonight. If you know what's good for you, you've told your last lie." Amos wheeled around and marched down the slope toward the cabin.

"Amos," Billy rasped.

Amos turned. "What?"

"If I tell you the truth, all of it, is there no chance you might let me live?"

"Tell me the truth and I'll shoot you in the back of the head. Tell me another lie and I'll gut-shoot you. Those are your only choices." Amos turned and walked down the hill.

Billy fell back in the leaves. The notes to Jolene he couldn't remember told the truth. No lie would be credible against those notes. The truth was all Billy had left, but the truth was an unfriendly stranger to him. The few times he had been forced to tell the truth when it ran against his interests, it lay in his mouth like ground glass and it cut him up on the way out. He rolled over on his side and drew his knees up to his chest. He lay on his side for a long time, trying to dispel the image of his skull being split by a thirty-aught-six shell.

Chapter 10

Jolene's Dream

Just after dark that night, the sheriff asked Porter to drive Jolene home. She was crying when she followed him to his car. She hadn't been able to stop crying since Toby and Stogie left in Toby's truck because she knew what had happened to Billy and Amos. Amos killed Billy, and then he killed himself. Only *she* killed them both, because she was the one who cheated on Amos. She was the one who pledged the wedding vows to him and then stole away to make love to Billy. She was the one who concealed her infidelity from Amos for half a century. And now he knew what she had done, and he had killed Billy for it and then he had killed himself.

Billy's grandson took Jolene's arm and politely opened the door of his car for her. She climbed in, sat down, and clasped her hands in her lap. She stared out the windshield at the night and waited for him to round the car and get in, but for some reason he couldn't open the door on his side. He called out to the sheriff, who brought a long iron bar over to the car. They wedged the bar in the door and pushed and pulled, grunting and heaving. It made creaky sounds and then sprang open.

Porter climbed in behind the steering wheel and slammed the door, but it wouldn't catch hold. He slammed it three times, but it still didn't catch. Then he slammed the door as hard as he could one big time. The door caught hold, but there was a clanging sound. He looked out the window at the ground. "Door handle," he said under his breath. He looked over at Jolene with a hard expression on his face. She began to cry again, and his expression softened.

He pulled onto the state road, turned left on Whiskey Road, and drove west toward Saddleback Cove and the trailer park. When they reached the park, he stopped just inside the entrance. "Which one is it?"

She pointed at the double-wide. He parked the car under the carport and cut off the engine. He jerked on his door and slammed his body against it, but it didn't open. He sat still for a moment, massaging his temples. Then he turned to Jolene. "You'll have to get out, Mrs. Hukstep. I'll slide across and come out your door and walk you to your trailer."

"Yes, of course," she said. Porter reached across Jolene and opened her door for her, and she saw him up close for the first time and noticed a large bruise under his eye. "You're hurt."

He looked at her and frowned. Then he touched the bruise. "Oh, you mean this? It's nothin, ma'am."

When he touched his face, she took in his entire aspect and was startled. He had coal-black hair and dark skin. His jaw was square. His shoulders and chest were lean and strong. He was Billy fifty years ago. The sight of young Billy took her breath away. She raised her hand to her lips. "Oh," she gasped.

He looked alarmed. "What's wrong, ma'am?"

"Nothing is wrong. It's just that … I can't believe how much … You're the spitting image of your grandpa. Did you know that?"

"No, ma'am."

"Well, you are. You look exactly like he did when he was your age." She reached up to touch his cheek, but she thought better of it. Her hand hung in the air for a moment, and she brought it to her mouth and shuddered. "He was a handsome man," she whispered. "He made me feel so … It was long ago, so many years."

Porter shifted in his seat and looked at her uncomfortably. "We better get you inside, Mrs. Hukstep."

Jolene looked at the blurred gray wall of her double-wide. "I don't want to go in there." She hung her head and whimpered.

Porter put his arm around her. "Well, I don't know what else we can do." He patted her shoulder and looked all around the trailer park. "Is there someone you can stay with? Is there somewhere else you'd like me to take you?"

She looked into his black eyes, Billy's eyes. Billy was there in the car with her. He was inside this young man. "Billy," she whispered. She knew it was wrong, but she touched his cheek with the palm of her hand. She could feel the sharp prickles of his beard stubble, and memories of Billy flooded over her and warmed her. His beard felt good. She hadn't touched a man's cheek in ten years. Jolene missed the soft scratch of a man's beard on her hand, on her cheek.

He looked apprehensive, but he didn't pull away. She slid her hand around behind his head and gently pulled him to her. She pressed her cheek against his cheek. It was warm with youthful vibrancy, and it was smooth and tight and hard and pleasantly rough. For a euphoric instant she was in the meadow on the banks of Little Bear River in the afternoon sun, and Billy wanted her. "Billy," she murmured. She buried her face in the crook of his neck and nuzzled against his warmth and brushed her lips against his throat.

"Mrs. Hukstep," the young man said softly. He gently pushed her away. "I'm not Billy. I'm his grandson. I'm Porter. Porter Kirby."

She put her hand to her mouth, her lips trembling. "I'm sorry." She looked away, mortified. "I'm so ashamed."

"It's all right," he said softly. "I understand. It's confusing, I reckon, me looking like Grandpa and all." He squeezed her shoulder. "You've been through a lot today. We'd best get you inside."

She looked at the double-wide and trembled. She didn't know what to do. For decades, she'd plodded through her life one predictable step after another. She knew what would happen every day when she got up in the morning. All she had to do was get out of bed and sleepwalk through it. But now she didn't know what would happen the next minute, much less tomorrow or the day after that. She was terrified.

"With Amos gone," she said, "I don't know who to turn to. Momma's dead. My brother moved to Blacksburg years ago. His wife died ten years back, and last I heard, he was an invalid in a nursing home. My oldest girl lives in Danville and the other two live in Norfolk. I haven't seen them in more than a year. They haven't called for months."

Porter nodded toward the trailer. "If there's nowhere else to go, ma'am, I think we should go inside."

Jolene looked at him fearfully. "Could you stay with me for a spell? I don't want to be alone. I'm afraid."

She saw Porter look at his watch and wince, but when he looked at Jolene, his face softened. He wasn't like Billy, she thought. He was a kind young man. Maybe if he had been the one to sweep her off her feet fifty years ago, instead of Billy, they would have run away together, somewhere far away, North Carolina or somewhere like that, where the acid tongues of the Selk County gossips couldn't reach them. She stared at Porter longingly for a moment, but then she thought about her daughters. They hadn't called or visited for a long while, but she loved them and missed them. They were Amos' children. They wouldn't have been born if she had run away. Her grandchildren would never have come along, and she loved them so. She placed her hand over her eyes. It was all so confusing.

She lowered her hand and looked at Porter. He couldn't have swept her off her feet in 1915. He hadn't been born, and Billy had to marry Mary Jo to conceive Blakey so Blakey could spawn Porter, or he wouldn't be sitting in the car with her in front of her double-wide, Amos' double-wide. Jolene felt weak. She put her hand to her brow. "I'm so confused. Please sit with me for a spell."

"All right. I'll stay for a few minutes."

Porter reached across her and opened her door and she climbed out of the car and he slid across the seat and got out. He took her arm and guided her to the double-wide. They climbed the steps and opened the door.

Jolene felt a little better when she went inside and turned on the light. It was comforting that everything was in the right place. The foundations of her life had been blown to bits in the past few hours, and she expected the interior of her home to have exploded while she was gone. She expected her anchors of normalcy—the furniture, the kitchen fixtures, the tin walls of the trailer—to have been obliterated or turned upside down or stolen, but they were all there in their proper places. Everything was the same as the day before. The easy chair, the couch, the kitchen counter and stools, the television set. Everything was there except Amos.

Jolene turned on the space heater, took off her winter coat, and sat down on the couch. She folded her hands in her lap and looked around.

"Can I use your telephone, Mrs. Hukstep?" Porter said.

"Yes, of course. It's on the counter in the kitchen."

Porter went to the kitchen counter and talked quietly into the phone for a few minutes. Jolene knew she shouldn't eavesdrop, but she couldn't help hearing his end of the conversation. At one point, he said, "What was I supposed to do? He came at me." Later, he said, "I relapsed. I was wrong to do it, but it's not easy to quit. There's a powerful urge to go back to it." And after a pause, "Well, your dad's wrong. I'll lick it one way or another. I promise." And then in a measured tone of voice, "All right. I understand." He laid the phone in its cradle and stared at it.

"Was that your wife on the phone?"

"Yes, ma'am." He blew out a short, heavy breath. "For the time being, at least."

Jolene felt guilty. "I'm sorry for all the trouble I've caused you."

"You didn't cause my troubles. They started long before I met you." He looked out the kitchen window for a long time. Then he came around the counter and looked at her. "Maybe I should call your daughters and let them know what's happened."

Jolene thought about Amos lying dead in the park. She couldn't tell them about him. She couldn't face the questions they would ask or the thought of giving them truthful answers. "I don't want to call them until we know where Amos is. I don't want to worry them."

"I understand. What do you want to do, then?"

"I'll just stretch out on the couch here and rest a minute."

She laid her head on the arm of the couch. She asked Porter to fetch one of her mother's quilts from her bedroom and told him where it was. He went and got it and spread it over her. Porter was so kind. If only he had been the one instead of Billy. Or Amos. She sighed. If only Amos had been Billy, or

Billy had been Amos, or either of them had been as kind as Porter. She was so tired and confused. She closed her eyes. A little while later, she was in the meadow by the river on a sunny afternoon, and she was young. She sat next to Billy on a blanket. He turned to her and said, "You have the prettiest eyes in Selk County." She smiled at him, and she felt warm all over.

Then she saw that Billy wasn't Billy. He was the young man, Porter. She reached up and touched the bruise under his eye and stroked his cheek. The prickling of his beard felt good on the palm of her hand. She closed her eyes and kissed his throat. When she opened her eyes, he was Billy again, but he looked so sad. One big tear pooled in his eye and slid down his jaw to land in her cupped hand. She stared down at the precious droplet. She was surprised because she had never seen Billy cry. He was always so happy, grinning and laughing, joking and reveling in the fun of the moment, fun that he created. "Grab the good times and ride em hard," he had said.

Jolene stared at the precious tear and then looked up into Billy's face, but it wasn't his face or Porter's face. It was the face of Amos. Another big tear gathered at the corner of Amos' eye and coursed down his cheek to bead at the base of his chin. "Goodbye, Jo."

Jolene clutched her chest, bolted upright on the sofa, and cried out. Porter was asleep in the easy chair. When she screamed, he jumped up. Jolene coughed and gasped for air. Porter rushed to her and put his arms around her. "Mrs. Hukstep, what is it? What happened?"

She buried her face in his chest and wept, and he hugged her and rocked her back and forth. "It'll be all right, Mrs. Hukstep. It'll be all right. You had a bad dream. That's all. You'll be all right now that you're awake."

Porter held her in his arms, and she cried for a long, long time. It seemed to her she cried forever. When she'd cried herself out, she sat in Porter's embrace and stared out the window at a black night where Billy was dead and Amos was dead and she had killed them both.

Chapter 11

The Confession

That morning at three A.M., Billy Kirby lay in the leaves beneath the elm tree in an uncomfortable place between dream and memory. Jolene lay in his arms in the sunlight on the blanket, her silky hair spread across his chest. Tears streamed down her flushed cheeks. He held her close. "Don't cry, now. Don't cry, darlin."

She cried softly for a long while. Then she looked up at him and said, "Take me home, Billy."

They dressed. Billy gathered up the blanket and the picnic basket. She took his arm and they walked from the riverbank across the meadow to the road without speaking to one another. A crow flew across the river and alit in the maple tree behind them, cawing raucously. In the clearing by the road, the chestnut gelding hitched to the buggy switched its tail and flies swarmed and resettled on its back. The gelding looked back at Billy and tossed its head.

Billy helped Jolene climb the step to the buggy seat. He climbed up beside her, took the reins, and gave them a shake. "Git up, now." The buggy lurched forward. Billy pulled the gelding around; they crossed the narrow wooden bridge; and the gelding began a long pull up a steep hill, its hooves clip-clopping on the sun-baked dirt surface of Whiskey Road.

Jolene held onto Billy's arm and rested her head on his shoulder. Maybe there was still a chance, he thought. "It's not love," he said gently, "but we've had fun, haven't we?" She didn't reply. Billy rode along silently for a while and then tried again. "There's not that much fun in this life, you know. I figure it's best to grab all you can get and ride it hard. I live by that rule. That's my creed." She said nothing.

After a long while, Billy gave up. "Well, we had us some good times. At least it was fun while it lasted."

She rode silently beside him with her head on his shoulder, clutching his arm with both her hands, all the way to her house. He pulled back on the reins and the gelding stopped in the road beside a scrawny dry-brown hedge that flanked the front stoop. A cloud of dust from the buggy's trail swirled around them. She didn't move or speak, still holding his arm tightly with both hands.

Billy didn't know what to do, so he just sat there. He looked at the house, a dingy little cinderblock hovel with a rusty tin roof. She and Amos were dirt poor. He imagined her inside that little sweatbox, cooking over a woodstove, mopping the concrete floor, hand-washing his soiled underwear, writhing underneath his heavy body on a hot humid night. Billy looked down at her blonde hair still resting on his shoulder. She deserved better. He pushed a lock of silk back from her forehead. His hand lingered there. "I'm sorry, darlin," he said. He stroked her cheek, gently and slowly, once, twice, three times. His hand moved down her neck and rested on her shoulder. When he grasped the top button of her dress, her hand clasped his wrist and held it firm. She held it for a long time and said nothing. Then she pushed his hand away gently, climbed down from the buggy, and went inside the house without speaking to him or looking back at him.

Billy sat staring at the flimsy screen door Jolene passed through. Then he jiggled the reins and the chestnut gelding trotted forward and pulled the buggy back into the road.

A blood-curdling scream electrified Billy. He jumped up on all fours, his eyes wide. There was another scream, and he recognized the cry as the squall of a bobcat. His muscles relaxed. He let out a long breath and looked around. It was dark. He wasn't riding in the buggy on a pretty summer afternoon. He was in the wilderness chained to the elm tree. He lay down and burrowed into the leaves.

A vision came to him of his cold blue corpse stretched out under the elm tree, rigid with rigor mortis, the top of his head blown off, a large ring of dried blood staining the leaves around his head like a macabre halo. He rubbed his eyes and tried to purge the vision from his thoughts, but fear clutched him by the throat and choked him. His breath came irregularly and in short gusts. He sat up and arched his back to make his breath come easier. After a while, he caught his wind and looked up at the black form of Pine Top Mountain. Trees began to emerge from the darkness on its eastern face in the first faint light of day. Billy squeezed his eyes shut and tried to will the sun to stand still, but when he opened them, the mountainside was a brighter gray. The day was coming on faster than any other morning in his long life.

A warm wind swept through the bower of elms, but Billy trembled. He lay down on his side, wrapped his arms around his waist, and hugged himself, trying to shut down his body's reaction to his fear. He lay like that until he heard Amos' steps below him climbing the hill.

"Get up."

Billy slowly rolled over and sat up. Amos stood ten feet from him beside a big flat rock under the elm tree, a breeze lifting the collar of his jacket.

"I want the truth," Amos said. "Don't try my patience. If you start to tell a lie, I'll shoot you before you can finish a sentence." He sat down on the rock with the butt of his rifle between his feet and wrapped his hands around the barrel. "When did it start?"

Billy looked over at the spring and drew in a deep breath. The wind died down. Birdsong filled the forest and he watched the stream trickle down the hill. The peacefulness of the forest was ironic, he thought, given the imminence of his violent demise. He crawled to the pool and sipped water, stalling, desperate to extend his life, even if only for a few seconds.

"Answer me," Amos said. "When did it start?"

Billy rolled over, sat up, and wiped his mouth with his sleeve.

Amos pointed the rifle at Billy. "When did it start, you son of a bitch?"

"Sometime in the summer. July, I think."

Amos paused and then set the rifle on its butt again. "This past year?"

"1915."

Amos frowned and didn't move for a few seconds. Then he shifted his weight on the rock. "That long ago? Y'all have been carrying on for fifty years?"

"I got with her three times that summer. She broke it off after that."

Amos looked confused. "That was it? Three times fifty years ago?"

"You said you found three notes. I don't remember them, but there must have been one for each time we met."

Amos was quiet for a long time, gazing into the distance. Then he said, "How did it come about?"

"I chased after her when you weren't looking. At church. At the barn dances. In the store. You passed out on moonshine at a square dance at Stogie's farm, and I drove y'all home. I tried to talk her into it that night, but she wouldn't go for it. I kept trying."

Amos pressed his forehead against the barrel of his rifle, anguish written on his face.

Billy felt sorry for him. "For what it's worth, she didn't give in to me easy. I chased her hard for a long time."

"How did you talk her into it?"

"I don't know exactly. I usually found a way to talk women into giving me their favors, but I didn't always understand what did the trick. It was just something I could do. It was a gift, I reckon."

"It don't seem like a gift to me. It seems more like a curse."

Billy wrapped his arms around his knees and looked across the way at Pine Top and remembered the passionate trysts in the summer of his life. He saw his lovers float by in his mind's eye one by one, each one special and unique. They were lovely and gentle. The affection they gave him was tender and sweet, and he wished he had savored their favors more when he was young. He wished he had appreciated their company more and had treated them better.

"It didn't seem like a curse at the time," he said softly. He looked up at the sunrise over Buckhorn. A peach-colored arch glowed over its crest. Layers of orange, pink, and lavender fanned out above it. He remembered that so many of the women he courted seemed so sad and lonely. They craved to hear a kind word, a tidbit of flattery, a simple statement of praise. It took so little. It always seemed to surprise them to hear how special they were. It was so easy to tell them. He didn't even need to lie. He never understood why he was the only one who told them what they so desperately needed to hear, what they deserved to hear. "They all had good qualities," he said. "I never understood why I was the only one who told them so."

"What?" Amos said. "Speak up. I can't hear you."

Billy tried to clear his broken voice box. "I told them they were pretty or smart or shapely. I told them they had silky hair, or skin like velvet, or sweet lips—whatever I liked about them that others seemed to overlook. It was always such a surprise to them, like nobody ever noticed their good parts but me." Billy remembered Jolene's eyes sparkling in the sunlight. "With Jolene, it was her eyes. She had the prettiest eyes, like clear blue pools of ocean water. I told her how pretty they were, and it was a surprise to her." Billy looked at Amos. "Maybe you never told her, Amos."

Amos didn't say anything.

"Maybe you didn't notice her eyes. Or maybe you noticed them, but you didn't think to tell her how pretty they were. I told her she had the prettiest eyes in Selk County, and it was true. Her eyes were the prettiest eyes I'd ever seen. They still are."

A pained expression came across Amos' face. He stared into the distance for a few seconds. Then he stirred. "What did y'all do?"

"What do you mean?"

"What did you do with her? How did y'all touch and all?"

"You don't want to know, Amos."

"I want to know all of it."

"No. You don't. Believe me, there's nothing you can imagine that we didn't do. You don't want to hear it."

Amos wiped his mouth with his sleeve. "Where did you do it?"

"The first time was in the old shed at Purcell's Sawmill. We talked and kissed a little, but she wouldn't do anything more. Later on, she met me one night behind the store. I took her down to the river and spread a blanket in the moonlight. That time she gave in." Billy paused while the ghost of the excitement and exhilaration of that night passed through him. Then he said, "There was one other time in that same meadow beside Little Bear River near the barn below my house. It was a pretty summer afternoon." Billy saw her there again on the blanket beside him and the pain gathered in her eyes and she turned away. Billy's own eyes welled with tears. He fought them back. "That was the last time," he rasped.

"You're sure that was it? There were no other times?"

"Those three times fifty years ago. That's all there was."

Amos paused. "Did she love you?"

Billy closed his eyes. The truth was an uncomfortable guest in the chambers of his mind, ugly and unwelcome, but it was there to stay and it would plunge a knife into Amos' heart. Billy took a deep breath, gathered his nerve, and looked at Amos. "She said she loved me that last time in the meadow."

Amos was silent for another long time. Then he said, "Did you love her?"

"I didn't love her in the summer of 1915."

"What does that mean? Did you love her some other time?"

Billy glanced at Amos and then looked away, ashamed of the worst mistake of his life. "I came to love her later, when I had time to reflect on it."

"How much later?"

"A few months ago."

Amos furrowed his heavy brow. "I thought you said those three times in 1915 were the only ones."

"They were."

"I don't understand. You fell in love with Jolene months ago, but you haven't touched her since 1915?"

"I don't understand it either." Billy wrestled with the truth. "That's not true. I do understand. I understand perfectly." He took a deep breath. "When Mary Jo died, I grieved over the pretty young girl she was when I married her, the girl I cheated on and lied to and drove crazy." Billy ran his hand across his eyes. "I thought about how my life had turned sour because I married the wrong woman and I wondered what would have happened to me if I had picked the right one. I thought about all the women I'd held in my arms, and I imagined living with every one of them and I thought it probably wouldn't have mattered who I married. I thought my life would have followed the same sorry pattern no matter who had been my partner." Billy brushed his lips with his hand. "Then I remembered those few special times with Jolene, and I realized she was the one who could have made all the difference in my life. She was the brightest diamond in the pile of pretty jewels I laid down with, but I didn't understand that in 1915. I didn't figure it out for fifty years. That afternoon in the meadow by the river Jolene told me she loved me, but I let her go. I didn't know what was ahead of me, all the mistakes and the heartache. I could have taken Jolene to my heart that day. I could have run away with her, had babies with her, and made a good happy life for us." Billy looked at Amos solemnly. "I could have lived your life with Jolene, but I made a fatal mistake in 1915. I turned away from her and it's too late to fix my mistake now. You don't get second chances in this life. That's the pity. When you're young you're too stupid to make good decisions. By the time you learn enough to make the right choices, it's too late and you're too old to straighten out the mistakes you've made, and that's why I'm lonely and miserable. I need a thousand second chances to clean up the junk heap I've made of my life, but I won't get a single one." He paused and then said, "The worst ..." His voice ground to a halt. He swallowed and tried again. "The worst mistake I made was turning away from Jolene when she said she loved me. If I could have one second chance in my whole life, that moment when I turned away from her would be the one I'd take."

Amos didn't move or say anything for five long minutes. Billy stared at the ground between his knees, hoping for a merciful miracle he knew would not occur.

Amos finally broke the suspense. He stood and pointed his rifle at Billy. "Roll over on your belly."

Billy looked at the gun. In a few moments, his death would rush down the barrel and all his rational thought about the misery of his life and the virtues of dying fell away like the wall of an iceberg crashing into the sea. Billy did not want to die. He wanted to live on and on and savor every minute of life.

"Roll over," Amos said again.

"It was a long time ago, Amos. Jolene went back home to you and lived with you for fifty years. She wouldn't lay with me again after that time in the summer of 1915. I tried, but she turned me down cold. She's been true to you ever since. Can't you see your way clear to forgive her? And me?"

"Jolene lied to me for fifty years by not telling me. She lied every day, every minute. My whole life has been based on one big lie, and I hate her for it." Amos' barrel chest shook. "And I hate you because you talked her into it." Amos motioned with the rifle. "Roll over. It's time."

Billy could see his death in Amos' tormented visage. There was no point in begging and pleading. He rolled over on his belly and pressed his face into the palms of his hands. Choking, mind-numbing fear swelled up inside him. He tried to quell it by telling himself yet again that he wanted to die, that he wanted to end his misery, and that he should be thankful and joyful, but he knew it was a lie. At the threshold of death, his body and mind betrayed him. His long-dormant senses, dulled by age and misery, came to life. He could smell the leaves and the rich loam of the mountainside. He could feel the warm sunlight on his back.

Billy's past flashed through his mind. Mary Jo and Jolene and all the others burst forth inside him. He touched their soft skin and smelled their hair and kissed their lips and felt their embraces and he loved them all. He saw Blakey and Porter and Maureen and all the faces of his friends and he saw himself, laughing, joking, cursing, weeping, shouting, whispering, loving, hating.

Billy tried to steel himself but he couldn't stop shaking. Amos pressed the cold mouth of the rifle barrel against the back of Billy's head. Standing on the edge of the cliff of death, Billy looked down and there was nothing there, no afterlife, no heaven or hell. This life was all there was, and with all his failings and infirmities, he wanted to live on. He wept for his lost future, no matter what it might have held for him. His muscles tensed. His breath grew short. He squeezed his eyes shut and waited.

The mouth of the barrel vibrated against Billy's head. The vibration became a pounding. The skin on the back of his head broke, and he felt blood trickle down the back of his neck. He cried choking, rasping sobs.

Billy heard Amos sobbing behind him, and then the pressure of the barrel against his head was gone. Billy held his breath, expecting the rifle to fire, but nothing happened. He opened his eyes, twisted around, and looked behind him. Amos wasn't there.

Billy gasped and rolled over on his back. He was covered with sweat and he was spent. He gulped in air and saw and heard nothing for a while. Then he sat up and looked around. Amos was sitting on the flat rock under the elm tree with the butt of his rifle on the ground. The gun was propped upright between his knees. His chin rested on the mouth of the barrel. His hands slid down the barrel.

Behind Amos, Billy saw the end of the chain looped through the anchor in the metal stake Amos had pounded into the tree. The chain trailed down from the anchor to the base of the tree next to the big rock Amos sat on, and laced its way between Amos' feet beside the butt of the rifle. It snaked from there across the ten or twelve feet to Billy's wrists, where it was looped around the handcuffs. Billy's eyes followed the chain backwards from his wrists to the ground at Amos' feet.

Amos' hands slid down the barrel toward the trigger guard. They reached it. His thumb moved inside the guard and rested on the trigger. There were no second chances in life, Billy reminded himself, but strangely, Amos had given him a second chance, one he didn't know he wanted.

Billy jerked the chain as hard as he could. The chain grabbed the butt of the rifle and kicked it to one side. The rifle exploded and the discharge blew off Amos' ball cap. The bullet sheared off a branch of the elm tree, which crashed to the ground beside Amos, raking the side of his face on its way down. Billy planted his feet in the dirt, flexed his legs, and pulled the chain again. It drew taut against Amos' boot and rode up his leg. It flipped Amos backwards off the big rock and he dropped the rifle. It slid down the slope below the rock and came to rest a few feet below the fallen branch. Amos thrashed on the ground behind the rock, his leg entangled in the chain.

Billy crawled on all fours to the rifle. He heard the rustle of leaves beside him just as he grabbed it and pulled it under him. A great weight fell on his back and he collapsed on top of the rifle. Amos grabbed him from behind and lifted him to a standing position. Billy clutched the rifle with his cuffed hands and held it out in front of his body away from Amos' reach. Amos clawed at Billy's outstretched arms, but Billy held on.

Amos squeezed Billy in a powerful bear hug. He jerked Billy's frail body this way and that, Billy's chain lashing through the air and clanking against the big flat rock. Amos' constriction of Billy's chest cut off his air and his grip on the rifle began to loosen. Amos tightened the bear hug even more, digging his chin into Billy's shoulder. Spittle flew from Amos' mouth. His cheek was pressed against Billy's cheek, his head beside Billy's head. The barrel was pointed skyward.

Billy jerked it toward them as hard as he could, and the barrel struck Amos in the face. He jerked it toward them again and it struck Amos again and blood sprayed the fallen elm branch in front of them. Amos' arms loosened a bit and Billy sucked in air and pulled the barrel hard toward them again. Another mist of crimson sprayed the branch at their feet. Amos' grip relaxed more and then completely and his heavy body slid down Billy's back and collapsed on the ground in a heap.

Billy fell to his knees, still clinging to the rifle, gasping and heaving. Multicolored spots danced in front of his eyes. He fell back on his haunches with the rifle across his legs and searched his memory for Amos' rifle's firing mechanism. He remembered it was bolt action and held several shells in its chamber, but he couldn't remember how many. He pulled the bolt back and shoved it forward, reloading. He pointed the rifle into the air and fired. The barrel exploded. The rifle recoiled and the butt struck Billy in the chest. He groaned in pain, but he forced himself to pull the bolt back again. The next bullet slid into place. Billy fired again, holding the rifle tightly against his shoulder to brace against its kick. He pulled the bolt back again and fired. And again. And again. The bright spots before Billy's eyes grew larger. He fired the rifle. He worked the bolt action and tried to fire again but the rifle wouldn't fire. He tried again and heard the hammer click harmlessly against the firing pin and then the bright spots blinded him and he fell over in the leaves and the spots went black.

Chapter 12

Young Billy

Billy's legs ached and his hand shook as he pressed down on a cane to support his weight. He walked from the barn across the meadow to the maple tree beside Little Bear River. A young man sat on a blanket there with his back to Billy. "Where's Jolene?" he asked the young man.

The young man turned to face him. "She left a long time ago."

Billy was surprised. The young man was his grandson, but that wasn't possible. "What are you doing here, Porter? You haven't been born yet. Your daddy hasn't even been born yet."

"I'm not Porter. I'm you when you were young. I'm you in 1915."

Billy scowled. "You're the one who made all the mistakes that got me into so much trouble."

"I've made my share of mistakes, but I didn't know as much as you do about the world. I didn't know how things would turn out."

"You should have been more thoughtful. You've made a mess of my life."

"I was counting on you to straighten out some of my mistakes, but you didn't set things straight. You sure let us down on that score."

"How was I supposed to correct your mistakes? I can't go back in time and fix up what you did wrong."

"Oh, get off it, old man. I've heard your complaints about not getting second chances. That's just an excuse to keep on making mistakes till we die."

"That's easy for you to say. You don't have to deal with the misery you caused. You left me a long time ago."

"I didn't leave you, you old fool. I'm still alive."

"You're not alive. You died long ago."

"I'm not dead. I live inside you. Here. I'll show you." Young Billy stood, grabbed Billy, and embraced him. He pressed his strong hard body against Billy's brittle bones. "You've got to help me," young Billy said. "Hug me." Billy dropped his cane and grabbed the young man, and they grappled with each other. Billy could feel the young flesh and bones melt into his own. The spirit of youth washed across his misery like the waters of a hot spring poured over a block of ice. "It's working," Billy said. He clutched young Billy's sleeve and pulled him toward him. "Help me." Young Billy seemed to resist and tried to pull away. "No," Billy said. "Stay with me."

Young Billy's sleeve broke free from his grasp, and Billy raised his hand to shield his eyes from the sun's glare and saw a face looming over him. He squinted and Toby Vess' features came into focus. His wide-brimmed deputy sheriff's hat was ringed with a fiery gold line of sunlight. Billy put his hand to his brow and looked around. He was under the elm tree where Amos had tried to kill him and failed and then tried to kill himself and failed at that, too. He tried to sit up. "Amos? Where's Amos?"

"He's over there with Stogie. Don't worry. We got him under control." Toby helped Billy sit up, and Billy saw Amos. He sat on the big flat rock. Blood oozed from gashes on his forehead. His nose was swollen and purple. His hands were cuffed in front of him. He was staring at the ground with a blank look. Stogie stood next to him with his rifle pointed indifferently in Amos' general direction.

"Tell me where you're injured," Toby said.

"I'm all right."

"You don't look like you're all right. What did he do to you?"

"Nothing serious. Hit me on the head. My back's scratched up, but I'm all right. God almighty, I'm hungry."

"Here. This is all I've got." Toby withdrew a Baby Ruth candy bar from his shirt pocket and handed it to Billy.

Billy tore the wrapper off, shoved it in his mouth, and swallowed it in one bite.

"Looks like he starved you out," Toby said. He felt Billy's arms and legs and probed his head wounds. "You don't seem to have any broken bones, but your head's swollen up like a rotten tomato and there's dried blood all over your nightshirt. You need medical attention, but I don't have a radio in my pickup. I can't call an ambulance to come in here and haul you out. Our best bet is for me to drive you to Jimmy Baber's house below the dam and call the hospital. The paramedics can come and take you to Dolly Madison from there faster than my old Ford can cover the distance."

"I don't want to go to the hospital." Billy grabbed Toby's arm and tried to pull himself up. "Take me home. I want to go home."

Toby helped Billy to his feet. He almost collapsed, but Toby caught him and draped Billy's arm over his shoulders. "You're headed to the hospital whether you like it or not." Toby turned to Stogie. "Bring Amos along. Watch him close."

Toby walked Billy down the slope. Billy's legs were weak, and his bare feet were torn and tender. He couldn't put one foot in front of the other. Toby tightened his grip around Billy's waist and carried him down the hill.

As they descended, they approached the cabin. A few hours earlier Billy thought he'd never see the inside of it again. Now he was saved. He would live. He would come again to the cabin with his friends. He would tell dirty jokes and tall tales and slap backs and laugh and talk trash about the people in Selk County and drink moonshine and carouse all night. He would come back there every chance he got and he would have fun with his friends, Toby and Stogie and Amos ... No, that was wrong. Amos wouldn't be there. Billy twisted around and looked at Amos. He was walking along beside Stogie with his head down. His face had always been dull and blank, but Billy saw a new vacancy there. Billy dug his feet into the turf and stopped. "Amos," Billy called out.

Amos didn't respond.

"Don't worry about him," Toby said. "He can't hurt you now."

Billy looked at Toby, confused. "What?"

"Come on. Let's get you to the doctor." Toby lugged Billy on down the hill.

Billy looked over his shoulder at Amos and a great apprehension swelled up inside him. "Stop," he said. "I can't breathe." Toby eased Billy down to a sitting position. He put his hand over his chest and gasped.

Toby stretched Billy's arms over his head. "Breathe deep."

Billy sucked fresh cool air into his lungs, and with it sympathy and guilt came alive and took shape inside him. He was uneasy and uncomfortable in their presence. He wanted to usher them to a room in the back of the house, shut the door on them, and ignore them, but they wouldn't retire to a rear chamber. They sat in rocking chairs on the front porch and frowned at him like unwelcome guests who had dropped in for coffee, judged him, and then insisted on bunking down for a long visit.

Billy listed to one side and almost fell. He reached out to catch himself and his hand hit something hard and rough. He looked at it, dazed and confused. It was the cabin wall. He sat at its front corner.

"Billy?" Toby said. "We need to go. You need a doctor."

"He never laughed," Billy said.

"What?"

"He never killed any game."

"What are you talking about?"

"He came to be with friends. Came to be with us. With me."

"You're out of your head." Toby pulled Billy up and walked him down the hill toward the truck.

Billy thought about where they were headed. He would be hailed as a hero, but the law would charge Amos with kidnapping and assault and he would likely spend the rest of his life in jail. "Stop," Billy said feebly. "Set me down. Leave me here."

"Can't do it, Billy. You need a doctor."

"I don't want to go back. I can't face it. Leave me here. I'll be all right."

"You're talking crazy."

Toby pulled Billy along to the truck, propped him against the front fender, opened the door, and began moving things around inside to make room for Billy and Amos. Billy leaned against the cold steel, watching Stogie lead Amos down the hill. He might as well be dead, Billy thought, and I'm the one who killed him. A heavy mantle of guilt cloaked Billy, and the weight of it was too great to bear.

He swiped his hand across his feverish brow, his addled mind racing in search of an escape from the miserable future he could see coming at both of them. At first he could think of no way out. Then he leaned over, propping his hands on his knees, and out of the ether of his confusion a lie took form and became people and places and the people began to talk to Billy and do harm to him. The lie had ragged edges and loose ends dangling from a flimsy structure, but he could see its contours and he could feel its words rising from his heart into his crushed vocal chords. It might work, he thought. People might believe his lie if he could summon the wit to present it skillfully. Certainly he could do that. Lying was his special talent, his great gift.

He took a few deep breaths, gathered his remaining stores of energy, and said in as strong a voice as he could manage, "Why have y'all handcuffed Amos?"

Toby stepped back from the truck cab and looked at Billy. "You're talking out of your head again."

"My head's clear. Why have you cuffed Amos?"

Toby squinted. "He's under arrest, of course."

"Under arrest? For what?"

"You know good and well why I arrested him. For kidnapping you, chaining you to a tree, beating you to a pulp, and trying his best to kill you."

Billy feigned incredulity. "Have y'all lost your minds? If Amos hadn't come along, I'd be a dead man. He saved my life."

Toby searched Billy's face. "Amos tried to kill you. You know that."

"You've got it wrong. A ski-masked man attacked me."

Toby paused. "What ski-masked man?"

"A man wearing a ski mask broke into my house, hit me over the head, hauled me up here, and chained me to a tree."

Billy had known Toby for forty years. He was intelligent and intuitive and he understood Billy. Billy hoped he would grasp the advantages of the lie quickly and become his conspirator in his effort to exonerate Amos. Billy grabbed Toby's sleeve and pulled him closer, willing Toby to read his mind. "The man who kidnapped me said I sparked his wife years ago. I don't remember anything about her, but he said I ruined his woman and blew out his marriage. All day yesterday and all night long, that man kept me prisoner. He kicked me in the ribs, punched me in the face, beat me with a tire iron, and threatened to gut-shoot me. If Amos hadn't come along and chased him away, he would have killed me."

A knowing look came across Toby's face. Billy let out a long breath and let go of Toby's sleeve.

"That's ridiculous!"

Billy looked up to see Stogie scowling at him.

"No one will believe such a cock-and-bull story."

In his exhaustion, Billy had forgotten about Stogie. He wasn't like Toby. He was a plodder with no imagination. It would be a challenge to persuade him of the merits of Billy's lie before the authorities questioned him. Billy wasn't sure he was up to it, but he gathered what little energy he had left. "It's the truth. Amos is a hero. You ought to pin a medal on him."

"Are you crazy? Amos damned near killed you."

Billy shut the door to the truck, sat down on the running board, and blew out a heavy breath. "The man who attacked me wore a black ski mask. He was tall and skinny. He drove a green pickup, a '62 Ford with South Carolina license plates. I was too woozy to get the number. He gunned his truck away from here when Amos shot at him. You and Toby must have heard the gunfire."

"Of course we heard the shots," Stogie said. "That's why we came barrelin up here lickety-split, but Amos didn't fire the shots. You did."

"No," Billy said, so exhausted he had to strain to speak loudly enough to be heard. "Amos fired the shots at the ski-masked man. He saved my life."

Stogie threw a hand in the air dismissively. "What a bunch of malarkey!

If some unknown man attacked you, how come we didn't see his pickup on the fire road? There's only one way out. He didn't pass by us because he don't exist."

Billy put his hand to his eyes and struggled to rein in his temper. When he'd gained control, he said, "The man's truck had four-wheel drive. He must have circled above you off-road on Pine Top and dropped down to the fire road after you came through."

Toby rubbed his jaw. "Maybe there's something to this story, Stogie."

Stogie scoffed. "Bullshit! There's no path off-road on Pine Top. The brush is too thick and the ground's too rough."

"It's not bullshit," Billy said, on the edge but still in control. "The man's truck was high-bodied. It could have cleared the brush easy enough."

"This ski-masked man, what's his name?" Toby asked.

Billy glared at Toby, surprised that he seemed to be turning against Billy. "How the hell do I know? He wore a mask."

"You took his wife to bed," Toby said. "How come you don't know his name?"

"I laid down with a lot of women over the years. It's unreasonable to expect me to remember the names of every last one and their husbands to boot."

"Why did some man from South Carolina bring you to our cabin? How did he know where our cabin was and how did he get through the park's locked gate?"

Billy's temper flared. He started to rebuke Toby, but he saw smile lines around Toby's eyes and he understood why Toby asked the questions. They were questions that required credible answers for Billy's lie to have a chance of saving Amos.

Billy paused and reflected upon the questions. He was a good liar and the answers came to him in a rush of creativity. "The man said he was going to take me someplace to torture me before he killed me. I knew you and Stogie were hunting at the cabin. I figured if I could convince him to take me here, you two might be able to overpower him and save me. I told him about the cabin and how it would be more comfortable for him to sit inside next to the stove in between the beatings. He fell for it, and he drove me up here. My plan would have worked if you two had been here, but you were gone when we got here."

"That's right," Toby said. "We cut our hunting trip short. We left here Thanksgiving Day in the morning."

"The masked man and I didn't get to the cabin until noon that day. When you two weren't here, I lost hope. But Amos changed his mind about joining your hunting trip. If he hadn't showed up this morning, I'd be dead by now."

Billy worried that Amos might contradict his story, but one look at Amos allayed his fears. His jaw was slack. He looked too stunned and bewildered to understand Billy's lie, much less refute it.

But Stogie was relentless. "What the hell are you trying to pull? Me and Toby spent the whole damn night roaming the park looking for your sorry carcass. It ain't been no picnic driving rough roads searching for you, and to make matters worse, we were both hungover something fierce. We save your life and you thank us with this hogwash about Amos shooting it out with some mystery man."

Billy glared at Stogie and pointed at the cabin. "We spent forty years drinking and carrying on in that cabin. Amos was there with us through it all. He's one of us. He's our friend."

"He may be our friend, but he's the one who tried to kill you. No one will believe this tall tale about some masked man with no name driving some truck we didn't see and you laying down with some woman you can't remember. Nobody beds down with a woman and forgets all about her. Your story's a lie from top to bottom. It's ridiculous."

Billy rubbed his temples. He felt faint. "What's ridiculous about it? I'm old. My memory fails me. I chased damn near every woman in Selk County over the years, and I caught a lot of them. You can't expect me to remember all the details."

"The whole pack of lies makes no sense, but the looniest part is that you sparked so many women you can't remember who they are. Nobody will believe it."

Billy snapped. "What the hell's the matter with you? This story makes perfectly good sense! I slept with a lot of women and I made a lot of husbands madder than hornets! Think on it, Stogie. I sparked your wives, didn't I? You tried to kill me, didn't you?"

Stogie staggered backwards as though he had been hit in the face with a hammer. "My wives?" Stogie dropped his rifle and pushed his hat back from his face. He swayed in his tracks. "You and Polly?"

Billy's anger evaporated. His temper had overwhelmed his discretion. "I said that wrong. I meant to say I took up with the one wife, Bea. Just the one."

"You said wives. I heard it clear." He studied Billy's face, his eyes boring in on Billy. Billy looked away. "You got with Polly," Stogie said, choking up. "I can see it in your face." Stogie almost fell, but Toby caught him and eased him down to the ground. Stogie's hat fell off. The sun glinted on his sweaty bald head. He looked up at Billy, his eyes glistening. "I knew about Bea, but I never dreamed Polly turned to anyone else. How could she? I loved her so much."

"Wait a minute," Billy said. "You got it wrong. I never touched Polly. The word wives was just a slip of the tongue. I meant wife. Bea, your first wife. Not Polly. Polly was faithful to you, like you thought."

Stogie wiped the sweat off his bald spot with a trembling hand. "I was married to Polly for twenty years. I loved her more than anything. I never knew."

Billy swallowed hard. "I didn't ... I said it wrong."

Stogie stared at Billy like he didn't know him. The hurt spread across his face and tears welled in his eyes. "I loved her and all this time you and she ..." A sob burst from Stogie's lips, followed by another. He buried his face in his hands and wept.

Billy rubbed the back of his neck. He didn't know what to do. Too much of the truth had slipped out. His frantic lies of denial had only made matters worse. He knelt beside Stogie. "I'm sorry. I'm tired and weak and I lost my temper." Stogie continued to weep, feeble muted sobs. Billy said, "I wouldn't do it today ... with all the time we've spent together, with our friendship and all." He shook his head, searching for an excuse for his

behavior. "I was young and brash. I didn't think about anyone but myself."
He rested his hand on Stogie's shoulder. "I'm sorry, Stogie. So sorry."

Stogie's shoulders shook with each sob. He cried for a long time. When
he finally stopped crying, he looked down at the ground blankly. Then he
flinched as though he had been awakened from sleep and pushed Billy's
hand off his shoulder. He stood, wiped the tears away, limped to the truck,
and climbed in the truck bed. He sat on his haunches with his back leaning
against the cab, crossed his arms over his chest, and stared into the distance.
His message was clear: he wouldn't ride in the cab with Billy.

Throughout Stogie's fit of crying, Amos had stood silently beside them,
staring at nothing. When he saw Stogie climb into the truck bed, he lurched
over to the truck and climbed in beside Stogie.

Toby gave Billy a hard look. He gathered the rifles, put them in the
truck, and helped Billy into the passenger seat. Toby climbed in behind the
wheel and stared at Pine Top for a few moments, his lips pressed together
tightly. Then he started the engine and drove away from the cabin.

At the base of Pine Top, he slowed the truck and eased it over the rutted
fire road into the park. Billy looked through the cab's rear window at his
two old friends, jostling along in the truck bed. Both stared vacantly into
the distance.

Billy turned back to the front and looked out the windshield. It was high
noon. Another Indian summer day of bright sunlight and warm temperatures
was half gone. A little stream trickled through the pine tags down the slope
of Pine Top into the fire road and ran along ahead of the truck in the deepest
rut. Its rivulets looked like silver string in the sunlight.

"Do you think Sheriff Grundy will believe me?" Billy asked Toby.

They drove on in silence for a short spell. Then Toby said, "How did
the man from South Carolina get through the park gate? How did he get into
the cabin?"

"I gave him my keys," Billy said. He pressed his hands together and
looked down at them. "Now that he's run off with em, I'll have to have new
ones made."

Toby drove on for a while. Then he said, "I found a ski mask on the table in the cabin."

Billy nodded. "Makes sense. The man who attacked me took it off yesterday. He said it was too hot to wear it and he figured he didn't have to worry about me identifying him since he planned to kill me any way. He must have left that mask on the table."

"How do you explain the keys to the handcuffs and leg irons? I found them in Amos' pocket."

Billy thought for a moment. "This morning the man said he was going to march me down to his truck and shoot me and haul my body into the park to bury it where no one could find it. He was in the process of unlocking the cuffs so he could take me to his truck when Amos drove up. I called out to Amos, and he came running up the hill. The man dropped the keys and ran into the brush to hide. Amos joined me by the tree, found the keys, and started to unlock the cuffs when we saw the man run across the clearing toward his truck. Amos jammed the keys in his pocket and started firing at the man, but he missed him. The man got to his truck and Amos started down the hill after him, but he tripped and hit his head on a rock and the blow knocked him out. I crawled down to Amos and picked up his rifle, but I was so weak that I passed out without firing a shot."

Toby shook his head. "I don't know, Billy. Sounds far-fetched."

"I don't care how it sounds. That's what happened."

Toby drove on for a while and then said, "Frank Woolsey combed your house for evidence of the intruder. You better hope he didn't find anything."

"Like what?"

"Fingerprints, for one."

"I'm sure Frank will find some signs of Amos in my house. That doesn't prove he broke in. He's been in my house a hundred times. He's bound to have left some signs behind."

Toby smirked. "Well, there's one big problem with your story you can't get around. The cuffs and leg irons are mine. Someone broke into my house and stole them out of my desk drawer while I was at the cabin with Stogie. Amos is one of the few people who knows where I keep my restraints."

Billy thought for a long time. Then he said, "Maybe the thief stole some other things, things you might have lost over the years, things you don't need any more."

Toby shook his head. "Sorry, Billy. I won't lie for you."

"Forget about me. Think about Amos. Think about what they'll do to him. Can't you stretch the truth a bit for his sake?"

Toby looked over at Billy and then back at the road. "I'll tell the sheriff what I found at the cabin when I got there. I'll tell him what you said happened to you and I'll recount your answers to the questions I asked you. I won't dispute your story, but I won't lie to the sheriff for Amos or anyone else."

Billy sighed. "Is the fact that Amos knows where you keep your manacles enough for the law to put him away?"

"I don't know. The commonwealth's attorney will decide that."

"I'm the victim, damn it. Don't that count for something? I'll refuse to press charges. The county can't jail Amos if I don't want it."

"That's not the how the law works. His crimes run against the commonwealth, not just you. If there's enough evidence against him, they'll prosecute him whether or not you agree to it."

Billy scowled. "Well, they'll have a hell of a time makin a case. I'm the only one who knows what happened, and I'll tell everybody that Amos is innocent. I'll shout it from the rooftops!"

"You can tell any story you want," Toby said, "but I won't back you up by telling lies."

They rode on in silence for a while. Billy looked back at Amos and Stogie again. He turned back to the front, pressed his hands together more tightly, and looked down at them. "All right, Toby, I understand you won't lie. I'll carry that load alone, but maybe there's a favor you can do that won't require you to break your rules."

"What's that?"

"I know I'm the last person with any right to ask you, but if I can convince the county to let Amos go, I'd appreciate it if you'd take him home with you and watch over him. Don't let him go near Jolene and keep him away from his gun until he has time to heal up and come to his senses."

Toby was quiet for a while. Then he nodded. "I can do that." Toby fell silent for another spell and then said, "I'll take Stogie home with me, too. Just for a while. Until he calms down a bit."

"Thank you, Toby. You're a good friend to all of us." He looked down at his hands, rubbed the sore places where the cuffs had chafed his wrists, and sighed.

They reached Jimmy Baber's house at the foot of Whippoorwill Hollow Dam an hour later and parked in his driveway. Toby and Billy got out of the cab, and Toby helped Stogie climb out of the truck bed. Stogie seemed weak and listless, but he was able to stand on his own.

Billy said, "It'll help Amos if you don't tell the sheriff you think my story about the kidnapping is a lie."

Stogie glared at Billy. "You can tell all the lies you want. For Amos' sake I won't argue with you, but when this is over, you'll stay out of my sight if you know what's good for you."

Toby looked at Stogie and then at Billy. "I don't feel comfortable leaving you two together," he said. "You'd better come with me." He led Stogie to Jimmy's house.

Amos sat in the truck bed and Billy stood beside the truck. He gazed at Whippoorwill Hollow Dam looming above them, about fifty yards upriver from Jimmy's house. A rush of water slid over the lip of the concrete dam and plunged a hundred feet down to the pool at its base. A rainbow arched up through beads of mist from the pool to the top of a hill beside the dam. Billy stared at the rainbow's crescent and then looked at Amos.

"Amos," he said.

Amos' eyelids fluttered. He glanced at Billy and then looked away.

"I'm sorry for what I did to you," Billy said. "I'm trying to make up for it. I saved your life back there at the cabin. You would have killed yourself if I hadn't grabbed the gun."

Amos' eyes were flat, his expression blank.

"Now I'm trying to save your life a second time. I lied to Toby and Stogie. I told them you chased my attacker away and saved my life. I'm going to tell that lie to the sheriff and everyone else. The law would put you away for ten years if I told the truth. Ten years is about all you've got left."

Amos didn't look at Billy or say anything.

"They're going to ask you what happened," Billy said. "Don't talk to them. You're not a good liar. You'll just get in trouble if you talk."

Amos looked off into the distance, apparently oblivious to Billy's presence.

"You're lucky I'm the one you tried to kill," Billy said. "No other man in the county would have a chance in hell of telling such a big lie and getting you off with it." Billy put his hand on Amos' shoulder.

Amos slowly turned, looked down at Billy's hand, pushed it away, and looked off into the distance again, his face blank.

Billy stared at him for a few seconds. Then he climbed back into the truck and thought about the questions he would be asked and the answers he would give.

Chapter 13

The Separation

Back at the double-wide, Jolene fell asleep on the couch just after dawn and slept fitfully through the morning. Midafternoon, Porter woke her with a smile on his face. "They found them. They're safe and sound."

Jolene sat up and rubbed her eyes. "Amos is alive?"

"Yes, and Grandpa, too. Mr. Vess called. He said Grandpa told him a man from South Carolina kidnapped him and tried to kill him. Mr. Hukstep saved Grandpa's life, but the kidnapper got away."

"Amos is all right? You're sure?"

"Mr. Vess said Mr. Hukstep fell and busted his head and Grandpa is beat up pretty bad, but Mr. Vess took them to Dolly Madison and the doctors think they'll be okay."

It took Jolene a few moments to digest the turn of events. Then she buried her face in her hands and cried. Porter hugged her. "They're going to be all right, Mrs. Hukstep. There's no need to cry. They're going to be all right."

She sat up straight and wiped her tears away. "I want to see Amos. I have to explain. I have to tell him …" She hesitated. What would she tell Amos? What could she say? She would tell him the truth, she supposed. She had always told him the truth. Except about this one little sliver of her life, which she hadn't really lied about. She had kept quiet and said nothing. Of course, Amos would consider her silence a lie.

Well, no matter. It was time to confess and to ask him to forgive her.

She hesitated again. Surely he would forgive her. She failed him only once for a few brief moments more than fifty years ago. Surely he would understand how a young woman could make a mistake with a gay young blade like Billy.

A chill of anxiety came over her. Amos very well might not forgive her. Forgiveness wasn't in his nature. After he beat that hateful boy in high school, and after he beat the preacher within an inch of his life, he never spoke to his mother again. After he married Jolene, he refused to set foot in his childhood home, and when his mother died, Jolene and the girls went to her funeral without him. He had not spoken her name in the fifteen years since her death.

Jolene put her hand to her lips. "Oh my God," she said under her breath. She turned to Porter. "I hate to impose on you again, but could you please take me to the hospital?"

They went out to the Plymouth and got in the car. Porter had taped a big piece of cardboard over the broken driver-side window. Jolene watched him slip baling twine under the cardboard and tie the door to the doorframe to hold the door in place before he cranked up the Plymouth. As they drove through Saddleback Cove over Whiskey Road to Fox Run, turned right at the T and went south on the state road thirty miles to Dolly Madison Hospital in Jeetersburg, Jolene turned over in her mind what Toby told Porter. It didn't make sense. Amos had to be enraged. Saving Billy's life was the last thing he would do.

When Porter pulled into the parking lot at five o'clock, the sun was a gold disc setting on the mountain range on the western horizon. It bathed the four-story hospital and the coal-black asphalt in a buttery glow. Porter followed the muddy streaks made by other vehicles to a spot near the center of the horseshoe-shaped building. Jolene's skepticism increased. Six county sheriff's office trucks and Toby Vess' old Ford pickup were parked there. "Why are so many policemen here? Why aren't they out looking for the man who tried to kill Billy?"

"I don't know," Porter said. "Maybe they need to get all the details from Grandpa and Mr. Hukstep before they search for the criminal."

Jolene didn't believe it. She was sure Amos was in trouble with the law. She got out of the car and walked toward the main entrance at a brisk pace with her heart in her throat. Porter had to jog to catch up. She pushed through the glass double doors and headed toward a reception desk on the wall to the left, but Porter took her arm. "There's Mr. Vess," he said, pointing to the other end of the lobby.

Toby and Sheriff Grundy stood in front of an elevator. The elevator doors opened. Jolene rushed toward them. "Wait!" Toby looked back at Jolene and then said something to the sheriff. The sheriff nodded, stepped into the elevator alone, and its doors closed as Jolene rushed to Toby's side. "Where is Amos? What have you done with him? Is he under arrest?"

"Let's talk over here." Toby tried to guide her to a waiting area to the right of the elevator. She resisted, but he took her arm and pulled her toward a row of chairs. "Sit down."

"I don't want to sit down. I want to see Amos."

"Sit down," he said firmly.

Toby had never spoken to her so sharply. She sat down.

Toby turned to Porter. "I need a few minutes alone with Jolene, son."

Porter looked at Toby curiously and then nodded. "I'll go out in the parking lot and get some air." He walked across the lobby and exited through the double doors.

Toby sat down beside Jolene. "You can't see Amos right now."

She felt like she was going to cry, but she fought it off. "Why can't I see him? Why is the sheriff here?" She put her hand to her breast. "Amos attacked Billy, didn't he?"

"Amos is a suspect for kidnapping and attempted murder, but Billy claims someone else attacked him. The sheriff and the commonwealth's attorney are questioning Billy now. They're pressing him pretty hard."

Jolene's fear made it hard to speak. In a small voice, she said, "Why can't I see Amos?"

"This is not the right time."

"Why?"

Toby looked around to make sure no one was listening, then in a low tone of voice, he said, "Billy claims Amos saved his life by chasing his attacker away. More than a few people are skeptical about that. There's some circumstantial evidence against Amos, but Billy's story makes it hard to prove a case against him. Billy and Amos are the only ones who know what happened. Billy says Amos didn't do it. Right now, Amos isn't talking, but he's unstable. Your sudden appearance might cause him to say something that would cut against Billy's story."

"But I need to make things straight between Amos and me."

"I'm sure you and Amos will work this whole thing out in due course, but now is not the time to talk to him about it. His future hangs in the balance." Toby patted her shoulder. "You go home. I'll call you when I know what they're going to do with him."

"I'd rather wait here so I can take him home if they turn him loose."

"That isn't a good idea."

"Why?"

"It'll be a good while before they make a decision."

"I'll stay here as long as it takes."

Toby looked down, sighed, and then looked up at her. "If they decide to let Amos go, I plan to take him home with me."

Jolene was startled. "Why does he need to go to your house?"

"He'll need some time to adjust. You will, too."

She shuddered.

Toby took her arm and gently lifted her out of the chair. "If they let him go, I'll do my best to get him back home to you as quick as I can. Believe me, I don't want that big old bear in my house any longer than necessary."

He guided her out of the emergency room. Porter was standing just outside the door. Toby led her across the parking lot to the Plymouth and Porter followed them. Toby helped her into the passenger seat and shut the door.

"Take her home," he said to Porter.

Porter nodded, got into the car, and began tying twine to the doorframe.

Toby leaned in the passenger window. "I'll call you tonight and tell you how things are going."

"Tell Amos I came to see him," Jolene said. "Tell him I love him."

"I'll tell him."

Night fell as they drove from the hospital back to Saddleback Cove. Jolene stared out the window at the darkness and said nothing to Porter along the way. Porter must have guessed she didn't want to talk, because he stayed silent too. He parked the Plymouth under the carport and helped her inside the trailer. Jolene sat on the sofa and cried.

Porter went into the kitchen and made a phone call. He spoke so quietly Jolene couldn't hear what he said until near the end of the call when he said, "All right, if that's what you want." He paused. "I'll come pick up my things when I can." He hung up the phone and looked out the kitchen window for a while. Then he came around the counter and sat in Amos' easy chair. "Is it all right if I stay with you tonight, Mrs. Hukstep?"

"Yes, of course. I want you to stay." It registered with Jolene that Porter's wife had told him not to come home. She knew she should ask him about his troubles, but she couldn't bring herself to do it.

They sat silently for a few minutes, both lost in their own thoughts, and then Porter turned on the television set. She sat on the couch the rest of the night, staring at the television blankly while she worried about Amos and waited for the phone to ring.

Toby called just before midnight. The sheriff had not placed Amos under arrest, but the investigation was ongoing. He said it would take weeks to complete it, but his guess was that Amos would not be charged unless they found more evidence against him. He told her the doctors were going to keep Amos in the hospital for a few days to treat his injuries and then Toby would take him home if he hadn't been charged by then.

"Did you tell him I want to see him?" she asked.

Toby didn't answer.

"Toby?"

"There's no gentle way to say this, Jolene. Amos said to keep you away from him or he couldn't be responsible for what he might do."

Jolene fell silent.

"Amos' wounds are fresh. Give him a little time to heal."

She hung up the phone, went back to the living room, and sat on the couch, feeling lost.

Porter turned off the television. "What did Mr. Hukstep say?"

"He doesn't want to see me."

"I'm sorry." Porter looked at her pensively. "I realize it's none of my business, Mrs. Hukstep. You don't have to answer if you don't want to, but exactly what's the trouble between you and Mr. Hukstep?"

She blushed. "Your grandfather is the problem." She looked down at her hands. "Your grandfather and me."

Porter stared at her, perplexed. Then the light dawned in his face. "You mean you and Grandpa are romantic?"

"We were at one time."

"Oh … well, that explains why Mr. Hukstep won't talk to you, I suppose." Porter knitted his brow. "Grandpa just turned eighty and you're … I mean, it's not that you can't … it's just that—"

"It was fifty years ago."

Porter looked confused. "Fifty years is a long time back. Why is Mr. Hukstep so mad about it now, all of a sudden-like?"

"He just found out."

Porter paused. "But if it was fifty years ago, I mean, you and Mr. Hukstep were married for all those years since then, right?"

"Yes."

"It seems like all the years y'all spent together ought to count for more."

"Apparently, Amos doesn't think so." Jolene was on the verge of breaking down. "Excuse me." She got up and rushed back to the bedroom. She closed the door, threw herself on the bed, and tried to muffle her sobs in the bed covers.

After a long time, she cried herself out and rolled over on her back and stared at the ceiling. Her eyes wandered to the light fixture directly above her. The light was on and a dead fly's carcass rested at the bottom of its opaque pink bowl. She rested her forearm over her eyes to block her view of the little gray lump. She took several deep breaths, trying to calm down, but she could not suppress the thought that Amos might never forgive her.

Jolene rolled on her side and drew her knees up to her chest. She was so tired she could barely hold her eyes open. Her last thought before she fell asleep was that she had plunged a knife through Amos' hard-shell exterior to pierce his heart, and the wound was so deep it might never heal.

She awoke the next morning with the sun in her eyes, dazed and confused. She sat up on the edge of the bed and rubbed her face, and was surprised to find that she was still dressed. She got off the bed and went to the Venetian blinds and pulled them shut, but there was still light in the room. She squinted at the overhead light and realized she hadn't turned it off the night before.

She ran her hand across her brow. It felt warm and damp. She must be catching something, she thought. She drifted into the living room, still in a daze. She saw a blanket ruffled up on the couch and Porter standing in the kitchen at the coffee pot with his back turned to her, and the nightmare of the past two days came back to her in a rush and sickened her stomach.

She took deep breaths and fought off nausea and dizziness. Porter said good morning. She replied in a voice that sounded thin and reedy to her ear. She put her hand on the arm of the couch to steady herself and glanced at the telephone on the kitchen counter. Toby said Amos didn't want to talk to her, but maybe he had changed his mind after spending the night away from her. He was in the hospital all alone. He'd had time to think by now. Maybe he missed her as much as she missed him.

She bit her lip, went to the counter, and snatched up the phone. The hospital switchboard operator rang Amos' room. She listened to the phone continue to ring while Porter placed a cup of coffee on the counter in front of her and sat in Amos' chair. The phone rang more than ten times before a woman's voice finally answered. "Mr. Hukstep's room."

"Who is this?"

"Nola Fisher, day-shift nurse for the 300 hall."

"This is Jolene Hukstep. I want to speak with my husband."

"Hold on just a minute."

There was a short silence and the nurse came back on the line. "I'm sorry," she said, sounding uncomfortable. "Mr. Hukstep says he doesn't want to talk to you." The nurse hung up.

Jolene held the phone to her ear and listened to dead air. She placed the receiver in the cradle and left her hand resting on it. The telephone was smooth plastic and cool to the touch. It was fire engine red. She'd chosen that color because she thought it looked cheerful and helped brighten the room. Her vision blurred with tears. She wiped them away, went into the living room, and sat on the sofa.

"He still won't talk to you?" Porter asked.

She shook her head.

"I'm sorry. Are you going to be all right?"

She was afraid a sob would burst forth if she spoke. For sixty years, she'd walked through life with Amos by her side. Now he might never come back. It was like losing an arm or a leg.

After a long silence, Porter leaned forward, set his cup on the coffee table, and clasped his hands together. "Well, Mrs. Hukstep, I'll be moving along now."

Jolene looked up at Porter. A thin line of steam drifted from the coffee cup up to his face and the choking fear of being left alone welled up inside her. "You're going home?" she asked in a small voice.

He shook his head. "No, ma'am. Maureen don't want me around. I'm going to ask Grandpa if I can move back in with him."

"The trouble between you and your wife is my fault. She's angry because you left her on Thanksgiving to stay with me."

"No, ma'am. That's not the reason. It's got nothing to do with you."

"I don't believe you. You're trying to ease my guilt."

"No, Mrs. Hukstep. Our problems are my fault. I hurt Maureen bad. She doesn't trust me."

"That doesn't make sense. You're a kind young man. It's not in your nature to hurt anyone. I want to talk to your wife and explain what happened."

"That wouldn't help," he said. He stood, turned his back to her, looked out the window, and fiddled with the string to the Venetian blinds.

Jolene was unconvinced. "I'm sure I can make her understand why you stayed with me. I want to talk to her. I insist."

He was silent for a long time. Then he turned and looked at her. "It's like this, Mrs. Hukstep." He jammed his hands in his pockets and bowed his head. "I got Maureen pregnant when we were seventeen. I married her, but I wasn't much of a husband." He looked off to one side, his face flushed. His voice dropped so low Jolene had to lean forward to hear him. "One night I came home real late from tom-cattin around with another girl, and Maureen's dad was waiting for me. Maureen had lost the baby while I was cheating on her, and he was mighty hot with me. I was drunk and I got hot, too. I said I was glad she lost the baby." His voice fell even lower. "I didn't see her standing in the hallway until she busted out cryin."

A chill ran through Jolene as she stared at him, trying to reconcile the young man who had been so good to her with the one he had just told her about. She could not.

Sunlight poured in the window behind him. A bright gold line limned his head and shoulders. "I'll get out of your way now," he said. His coat was draped over Amos' chair. He put it on and headed toward the door.

The instances of kindness and sensitivity he had shown her over the last few days flashed before her. "Wait," she said.

He looked back at her.

"What you did back then was selfish and cruel, but you're not like that now. You helped me through a terrible time and I know you. You couldn't do something like that today. That's not who you are. You've changed."

He shook his head. "You barely know me, ma'am. We've only spent a couple days together."

"When you go through a trying ordeal with someone, you see their true nature. Our time together has been short, but I know you."

Porter bowed his head. "There's a lot you don't know, I'm afraid. I've made some big mistakes lately, and Maureen has good cause to doubt I've really changed my ways."

"What sort of mistakes?"

He hesitated and then looked out the window. "Couple weeks ago I ran into one of my old drinkin buddies." He swiped his hand across his mouth. "I was drunk for two days. When I sobered up, I promised Maureen I wouldn't do it again, but she didn't believe me. We were still trying to get over my relapse when Thanksgiving came along. Her family came over. Grandpa disappeared that morning and I was late coming home. She got worried that I had run off to get drunk again and she told her dad about my relapse. When I finally showed up at the house, he came at me and we mixed it up a little bit." He shook his head. "Maureen's not the only one who doubts me. The truth is, I've got my own doubts."

He stared at Jolene for a few moments. "Goodbye, Mrs. Hukstep." He reached for the doorknob.

She stood. "Wait."

He stopped and looked back at her.

"You were wrong to do all those things, but I still believe in you. You're a good person, trying to do what's right."

He put his hand to his eyes and then dropped it to his side. "Thank you, Mrs. Hukstep. I hope you're right." He opened the door.

She stepped over to the door and grasped his arm. "I don't want you to go."

He turned to face her. "I don't think—"

"Please stay." She gently pushed the door closed. "It would be a great favor to me."

"Mrs. Hukstep—"

She pulled his hand away from the doorknob and cradled it in her hands. "I need your help. I'm all alone. Please stay with me."

He stared at her upturned face and touched her cheek with the palm of his hand. She pulled him to her and hugged him and held him for a long time. Then he stepped back and turned away from her so she couldn't see his face. He stood with his back to her and she put her hand on his shoulder.

"I've got to go home and get my things," he said softly. "I'll be back in a couple hours."

He opened the door and went outside. She stood in the doorway and watched him drive out to Whiskey Road. On the horizon, dark clouds gathered over Hawk's Nest Mountain and a chill wind blew into her face. She shut the door, sat on the couch, and waited for his return.

PART II

CHRISTMAS

Chapter 14

The Second Chance

Billy sat in the sanctuary of Grace Church in the third pew back from the altar. Whiskey-colored globe lamps hung from the ceiling, shining amber light on the maroon carpet and dark-stained oak pews, railings, and altar. Three floor-to-ceiling stained glass windows stood on each side of the sanctuary. Billy sat beside the one depicting Jesus praying in the garden the night before the mob crucified Him. The morning sun beamed through the stained glass, casting red, blue, and green stripes across his hands and the black fedora he held in his lap.

Billy hadn't come to church to worship. He was a nonbeliever. He had come there to find refuge from his loneliness. He had lost his wife and alienated his son and his best friends. The cold silence and emptiness of his old house had frozen his heart so he had come to the one place where there would be a crowd of people who could not turn him away.

He looked around the sanctuary. To Billy's right was Hugh Gibson, a dairy farmer who was built like a bull, his shiny brown Sunday suit giving off the faint scent of sour milk. Next to Hugh sat his wife, Franny, a lumpier female version of Hugh, and down from her sat a string of four fat children, a boy and three girls. In the pew behind Billy sat George Frazier and his wife and five children. He was a diesel mechanic, tall and skinny with a florid face, jug ears, and tobacco-stained buck teeth. His wife was a short, frail woman with stringy hair. Their children sat in order of descending height, all hopelessly ugly and unkempt with mouths full of crooked teeth.

A girl of about ten in the middle of the pack stared at Billy with her buck-toothed mouth hanging open.

Billy sighed heavily. The sanctuary was chock full of the people he lied to and cheated when he was younger. He had no peer among them. Gazing across the sea of faces, he saw no one who would care the least bit if he keeled over and died right before their eyes. In the midst of the crowd of worshippers, he was still alone. He looked down at his hands. They quivered and tears beaded in his eyes.

Billy was close to breaking down when the door to the sanctuary swung open behind him, and he turned to see Jolene Hukstep walk down the aisle. She turned into the second row of pews and sat down directly in front of Billy. He leaned toward her. "Where's Amos," he whispered.

"He left me."

"I'm sorry," he said, although he wasn't sorry at all. He was cheered by the news, and hopeful.

Jolene turned and smiled at him. She was young and beautiful, her hair silky and blonde, her blue eyes shining and bright. "I love you, Billy."

His breath grew short. He clutched his chest.

"You all right, Mr. Kirby?" Hugh Gibson grabbed Billy's arm. "You don't look well."

"I don't understand."

"Don't understand what, Mr. Kirby?"

"Look at her. Don't you see? She's young again."

Jolene's ocean blue eyes were filled with passion. "I love you, Billy."

Billy's heart beat so hard he felt it might burst. Young strong blood coursed through his veins and the skin on his hands cleared and tightened and he felt a surge of energy and power. The sanctuary faded away and he found himself beside the river on the blanket with the scent of honeysuckle in the air and sunlight breaking through a canopy of maple leaves. Jolene was beneath him, her lips parted, her cheeks flushed, her breath coming in short gusts, her warm legs wrapped around him, pumping.

He was living it again! He was being given a second chance!

Hugh Gibson appeared beside him on the blanket and tugged his arm.

"Mr. Kirby."

"Get away from me!" Billy said. "Let me go. You'll ruin it."

"Mr. Kirby!"

"No! Leave me be."

"Mr. Kirby! It's time for your pain pill."

Jolene's smell and touch and feel slid away and her face and body receded into darkness. "Don't go," Billy said. "Stay with me. I love you, too! I love you!"

But she didn't hear him and she was gone and some other woman was there with him, a frumpy middle-aged woman with a concerned look on her face. The sight of her restored his presence of mind and he remembered where he was and how he got there. He let out a long breath. "Oh, God," he moaned. "I was so close."

"It's time for your pill," the woman said.

Billy remembered her. She was the day-shift nurse, the one who was nice to him, Nola or Norah or something. "Why did you bring me back? I was so close this time, so close."

"It was a bad dream, Mr. Kirby. The medication causes dreams sometimes."

"You don't understand. It was so real." Billy put his hand to his eyes and felt a sharp pain in his arm. He looked down, confused. A tube was taped to his flesh below a purple bruise. It ran to a bag of fluid on a metal pole beside his bed. Billy tried to pull the tube out of his arm, but the nurse stopped him.

"Don't, Mr. Kirby. We don't want to put you in restraints again. Leave the IV alone. Let it do its work."

Billy dropped his hand feebly to his side. The nurse raised the head of the bed so he was tilted upright. He wept.

She stroked his brow. "There, there, Mr. Kirby. What's got you down? All the tests came back negative. You've come through your ordeal amazingly well. In fact, the doctors say you're remarkably fit. Doctor Munger says you have the body of a sixty-year-old. You're the envy of the senior ward. You should be pleased."

Billy choked back his sadness and wiped away his tears. "How long have I been here?"

"Six days. Healing takes time, but you're doing quite well for your age."

"What time is it?"

"Nine o'clock. You slept well last night, all the way through." She handed him a pain pill and a cup of water.

Billy put the pill in his mouth, took a sip of water, and pretended to swallow. When the nurse turned her back to make an entry on his chart, he spat the pill into his hand and slipped it under the pillow. She finished with the chart, tucked in the sheets at his feet, and pulled the blanket up to his chest.

"There you go. Doctor Munger will be in to see you soon."

"Is Amos Hukstep still here?"

"Mr. Hukstep is down the hall. He's doing fine, too. He's going home this morning."

"What room is he in?"

"Room 312. If you want to call him, dial seven and the room number."

"I want to go see him."

"That's not possible. You have to stay in bed, but I'll tell Mr. Hukstep you'd like him to drop by on his way out." She smiled and left the room.

No chance of that, Billy thought.

He took a piece of tissue from a box on the bedside table, buried the pill in it, and dropped it in the trash can by the bed with the rest of the pills.

He needed to escape. He didn't trust doctors, and he had no use for hospitals. They were full of diseases and rife with infection. Too many of his friends had died in such dreary places. He had to get out before the place killed him, but it would not be easy. The doctors were determined to keep him bedridden. He had tried to flee on the first night. The hospital lackeys had hidden his filthy nightshirt so he had been reduced to making a break for it in the flimsy hospital gown. He made it to the elevator before a big burly colored man in a white uniform caught him and restrained him.

The hospital staff tied him to the bed, robbing him of his independence and free will in furtherance of the supposedly laudable goal of "taking care of him." He knew where their care and attention would take him. They would eventually condemn him to a nursing home, strap him into a wheelchair, hook him up to an oxygen tank, and stab him with tubes attached to bags of fluid. With each "helpful" treatment, they would make his world smaller and smaller until it was the size of a pine box.

Billy had other plans. He wanted to live out the last years of his life with vitality and gusto, savoring every moment of joy he could generate. He wanted to hunt and fish and drink and cuss and tell jokes and slap backs and laugh and carouse. And most of all, he wanted to love someone. He wanted to love Jolene. He wanted to correct the worst mistake of his life. He wanted to tell Jolene he loved her and ask her to spend the rest of her life with him.

But his vision of a joyous exultant life of love with Jolene was impossible because of Amos. The first few days Billy was in the hospital, the sheriff and the commonwealth's attorney made several hard runs at him trying to get him to recant his story about the ski-masked kidnapper from South Carolina, but Billy stood firm and they finally gave up. Since then, Billy had spent every waking moment thinking about his betrayal of Amos' friendship. Again and again, he replayed in his mind's eye the look of abject misery on Amos' face as he sat on the big flat rock under the elm tree with the mouth of his rifle under his chin and his hand sliding down the barrel toward the trigger. Billy's affair with Jolene of fifty years ago had ruined Amos' life and driven him to the brink of suicide. A second modern-day love affair between her and Billy would surely shove Amos into another deep hole. Billy couldn't have Jolene, he told himself. It would be immoral and base and selfish for him to take her away from Amos. He would stay away from her. He would sacrifice his greatest wish for Amos' sake.

That was what Billy told himself when he was awake, but when he slept, his dreams were about Jolene and his time with her under the maple tree. He saw her pale blue eyes, moist and limpid, her smooth white shoulders, her silky blonde hair. He kissed her and caressed her and stroked her. He heard her voice, husky with emotion: "I love you, Billy." He yearned to go back there to the meadow. He wanted a second chance to tell her he loved her, too.

Each time he awoke from his dreams he was in tears because he wanted Jolene and he needed her and he loved her. That morning, he had emerged from his dream of Jolene in tears yet again, and after the nurse left his room, his thoughts turned to Amos as always, but this time his resolve to stay away from Jolene weakened. He had lived most of his life figuring out ways to get what he wanted, and that morning his powers of rationalization slowly nudged his newfound morals aside.

Maybe Amos didn't really want Jolene any longer, he reasoned. When Amos spoke about her during the kidnapping, he seemed to hate her as much as he hated Billy. After all, he said she had lied to him for fifty years; he said his life had been ruined because it was based on her lies; and he said he hated her for it. Amos was a brooding, sullen man. He nursed grudges for decades and he was unforgiving. Maybe he hated Jolene so much he wouldn't care if Billy courted her. Billy's reasoning gave life to a seed of hope in his heart. If Amos truly hated Jolene, maybe Billy could have her without breaking his heart yet again.

There was only one way to find out. Billy pulled the tube out of his arm, crept to the door in his hospital gown, and leaned into the hallway. Room numbers were displayed on placards beside each door. The progression of the numbers indicated that room 312 was down the hall on the same side as Billy's room. He looked around for hospital personnel. There was a counter at the end of the hall. Two nurses stood behind it and a third was seated at it with a telephone to her ear. He watched and waited. When the two standing nurses turned their backs and the nurse on the phone began to pore over a medical file, he darted down the hall to room 312, slipped inside, and shut the door.

Amos sat in a chair beside a window dressed in bib overalls, a denim shirt, and work boots. He held a jacket and a red ball cap in his lap. There was a gauze bandage wrapped around his head. His gray hair stood up straight inside the rim of the bandage, his eyes were blackened, and his nose was brownish-purple and bulbous, giving him the appearance of a circus clown. He scowled at Billy. "What are you doing here?"

Billy crossed the room and sat in a chair facing Amos. "I came to ask you a question."

"I won't talk with you. Get the hell out."

Billy could think of no subtle introduction to his topic. "I want to know where you stand with Jolene."

"What do you mean?"

"Do you plan to make up with her?"

Amos' face reddened. "It's none of your business what I do."

"In a way it is."

"I don't see how."

Billy leaned forward in the chair. "I told you when you were fixing to kill me that I'm in love with Jolene. I want to spend the rest of my life with her, but I won't court her if you still want her."

Amos clenched his fists, and his voice rattled up from deep in his chest. "You expect me to give you permission to run off with Jolene?"

"I don't expect you to give me your blessing. I just want to know what you intend to do. If you don't plan to make up with her, I'll ask her to spend the rest of her life with me. But if you still want her, I'll try to leave her alone."

Amos sat perfectly still for a while.

Billy waited it out, sweating and losing hope.

"She's a liar," Amos said, "just like you. You deserve each other. I hope you both rot in hell." His eyes were flat and menacing, like the eyes of a copperhead. "Get out of my sight."

Billy was ecstatic. He had gotten the answer he wanted. He could live the rest of his life with Jolene and feel no guilt about it. He stood and started to leave, but he glanced at Amos on his way out and stopped cold. Amos stared out the window. His face twitched and a solitary tear slid down his cheek. Billy's joy faded and the sense of guilt he had hoped to avoid returned to him. He tried to think of something that would comfort Amos. "Amos, I'm sorry how this—"

"You're not the least bit sorry for anything." Amos glared at Billy and then looked out the window again. "Just get the hell out and leave me alone."

Billy stared at Amos pensively. He could think of nothing he could say that would ease Amos' pain. Billy went to the door and looked back. "Are you sure, Amos?"

"Do what you want," he said without looking at Billy. "I don't care anymore." He waved his hand at Billy angrily. "Go on. Get out. Leave me alone."

Billy went out in the hall and walked back to his room. When he came through the door, the nurse stood at the foot of his empty bed, staring at it. She turned when she heard him behind her. "Mr. Kirby, what do you think you're doing?"

Billy ignored her and crawled into the bed.

"You're a sick man," she said. "You'll harm yourself if you don't do as we say." She jammed the IV into his arm more roughly than he thought necessary, pulled the covers up to his chest, and tucked them in as tight as a straitjacket. "I'll have to report this to Doctor Munger. He will not be pleased." She shook her finger at him. "I'm going to alert the nurses and orderlies to watch you every minute from here on." She went to the door, turned back, and cast a severe look at him like a school teacher glaring at a misbehaving child. "No more funny business. If you won't behave yourself, we'll place you under restraints again." She shook her head disgustedly and walked out.

Billy looked out the window and tried to distance himself from Amos' misery. He replayed the scene in Amos' room. Amos had been angry at first. His hatred for both Jolene and Billy had been etched on his face. "You deserve each other," he had said. "I hope you both rot in hell." He spat the words out like venom from a timber rattler. But then there was the tear.

Billy stared at a mulberry tree in the courtyard. Maybe Amos had shed that tear in anger, he told himself. Great rage moistened the eyes sometimes. Billy had shed tears in anger once or twice. He hoped so, but even if Amos' tear was shed in sorrow for his loss of Jolene, Billy shouldn't be blamed for that, should he? Amos was only losing Jolene because he wouldn't forgive her. His refusal to forgive her was a choice, not a requirement. If he chose to turn his back on Jolene, he should bear the guilt for his broken heart, not

Billy. After all, Billy had promised to stay away from her if Amos wanted her. He had done all he could do. He had saved Amos' life under the elm tree at the cabin. It appeared the county wasn't going to jail Amos for kidnapping Billy, so Billy had saved his life a second time, but Billy couldn't be responsible for making him live it. He had done his best for Amos. He owed him nothing more.

Billy watched a light breeze stir the branches of the mulberry tree and frowned, not sure he was right about Amos. Or anything else, for that matter. A pearl gray dove flew across the hospital courtyard and alit on a branch of the tree. The dove ducked its head once and then again and cooed, and his thoughts about Amos gave way to visions of a happy life with Jolene by his side. Billy smiled wistfully.

Chapter 15

The Sled Run

In mid December, a snowstorm blanketed Saddleback Cove and Whippoorwill Hollow. Twelve inches fell overnight, and the blizzard continued into the morning. Jolene parted the spindly blinds of her bedroom window and gazed at the snow swirling in the wind. There hadn't been such a furious storm in the cove since she and Amos were kids. She could barely see the hazy outline of Hawk's Nest Mountain in the distance.

Jolene remembered that snowstorm of sixty years ago. Amos had appeared at her front door decked out in a billowy wool jacket, black high-topped boots, and a brown leather aviation cap. The cap wrapped Amos' big head in a tight ball, circled his beet-red face, and snapped under his meaty chin. His winter garb was caked with frozen snow from head to foot, as though he had wallowed in the deep white powder drifts like a hog in mud. He looked ridiculous. She covered her mouth and giggled when she saw him, and he flashed an embarrassed grin at her. "Thought you might want to go sleddin," he said. He shifted from one foot to the other, uncomfortable and shy. He lifted his chubby arm and pointed at Hawk's Nest Mountain. "I packed down a sled run up there."

Jolene grinned at Amos impishly. He looked down at the porch planks, his already crimson face turning redder every second. "Might be somethin to do," he said. "Ain't nothin else to do. Roads are all closed."

"Wait here," she shouted. She darted back inside, leaving him standing on the porch as she ran up to her room and put on her heaviest winter clothes.

She ran down the stairs and flew out the front door, startling him. She grabbed his hand and pulled him off the porch. They stumbled through the knee-deep snow to the foot of Hawk's Nest Mountain. There was a hard-packed snow trail three feet wide from the top of a steep hill down to the bottom of the mountain. "I made this sled run this mornin," Amos said.

Jolene poked at his snow-covered jacket and laughed. "What did you do, Amos? Roll around in the snow like a big barrel?"

Amos blushed, grinned, and shrugged. "Packed it hard. It oughta be fast."

They climbed to the top, breathing hard from the exertion of scaling the steep slope in such deep powder. He had left his sled at the peak of the hill, waiting for them. He positioned it carefully at the head of the run. "You lay down on your belly. I'll give you a shove, and you can ride her down."

Jolene grinned at him. "I'm afraid," she lied. "I don't know how to steer it. I'll get on, but you have to climb on top and steer it for me."

Amos stared at her, paralyzed.

She giggled and lay down on the sled on her stomach. She looked up at him. He stood there, motionless and completely befuddled. "Get on, Amos." She wiggled her butt at him and laughed. His face looked like an overripe tomato.

He knelt down awkwardly and spread his heavy body over her as gently as he could, trying not to touch any sensitive parts, which was, of course, impossible. He was sweating in the freezing cold. "I'm not sure we oughta do—"

Jolene put her hands in the snow and pushed the sled forward. The sled tipped over the peak of the run and sped down the hill. The cold air whipped her face raw and the spitting snow stung her cheeks. Amos' barrel chest pressed against her back and his pelvis bounced against her butt as they hit each rut in the run. Amos grunted with embarrassment as he tried to restrain his body from reacting naturally, but he couldn't do it. He was simultaneously aroused and mortified. She laughed.

The sled hit a rock near the bottom of the run and they lost control. They fell off and slid the rest of the way head first on their backs, holding onto each other for dear life. Jolene screamed as they smashed into a snow bank at the bottom of the hill. She landed with her head on Amos' chest, laughing hysterically as he groaned and wiped a cake of wet snow off his face.

"I didn't see that rock till we were—"

Jolene grabbed his jacket collar, pulled herself up to his face, and wrapped her arms around his thick neck. Amos recoiled, but her mouth found his lips and she kissed him long and hard. It was their first kiss. Amos' muscles tensed, all of them. His big body was a solid rock and he didn't move at first, but he eventually put his arms around her and hugged her and his embrace grew tighter and they lay there in the snow and kissed for so long that their mouths almost froze together.

She put her hand to her lips and stared out the window remembering that first kiss. It was so long ago, but she could still feel Amos' cold lips on hers and she could still see his red face in her mind's eye. Through this new snowstorm she could barely see the old mountain where they groped each other when they were kids. The snowflakes swirled in the air the same as that day so long ago, but she and Amos were not the same. They hadn't laughed together or hugged one another in more than a decade. And when they released Amos from the hospital, he moved in with Toby Vess instead of coming home to be with her. A few days ago, Toby said the county had closed its investigation of Billy's kidnapping without finding sufficient evidence to file charges against Amos, but he still didn't come home. She'd called Toby every day since Amos was released from the hospital, but he refused to talk to her each time.

Jolene's eyes filled with tears. He wouldn't even talk to her. She clenched her fists and struck the top of the bureau. He was wrong to freeze her out of his life. She'd made up for her solitary transgression with a half century of loyalty and love. She had been a good wife to him, and it wasn't fair that he wouldn't speak to her. She pounded the top of the bureau again and wiped the tears from her cheeks angrily. She had endured enough of this nonsense, dang it!

Jolene put on her boots, grabbed her heavy coat, and marched into the living room. Porter sat in the easy chair reading a magazine. "Take me to

Toby Vess' house," she said.

Porter looked up at her wide-eyed. "The snow's blocked the roads. I can't even get the Plymouth out of the trailer park."

"There's a snow shovel in the shed and chains for your tires in the trunk of the Hudson."

"But the snow's three feet deep out there."

"I don't care. I'm going. If you won't drive me, I'll walk."

"Walk? It's four miles to Mr. Vess' house. You'll catch your death in this blizzard."

"I'm going to see Amos. Now."

Porter's face softened. "All right, but it may take me a while to dig out the car. I'm not sure we can get there, even with chains." He looked at Jolene and waited. She stared at him resolutely. "All right," he said. "I'll do the best I can." He put on his boots and heavy clothes. "I hope we don't get stranded and freeze to death." He looked at her again.

"I need to see Amos."

Porter plodded through the snow to the shed. Jolene found her glasses in the cupboard and watched from the window. He dug out the Plymouth's wheels and struggled with the chains, slipping and falling twice. He stepped away from the car to the shelter of the shed to take off his gloves and blow on his fingers and warm his hands inside his jacket. Then he attacked the Plymouth again. The snow came down so thick and fast that he had to dig the tires out of the drifts a second time after he finished putting on the chains.

He returned to the double-wide huffing and puffing. He stomped the snow off his boots and knelt before the space heater, holding his red chapped hands up to it, rubbing them together and shivering. "It's mighty cold out there."

She took off her glasses and left them on the kitchen counter, then put on her heavy gloves and one of Amos' hunting caps that had ear flaps. She snapped the flaps under her chin and turned to Porter. "Let's go."

The Plymouth plowed a path through the deep snow in the trailer park road without much difficulty, but Whiskey Road was another story. The road had been plowed, but even with the chains, the car fishtailed all over the place. "State snow plow came through here last night and packed the snow down," Porter said. "Turned the road into slick glass. We'd be better off if they didn't plow it at all."

The car slid completely off the road into the ditch about a hundred feet from Toby's driveway, and Porter got out and tried to shovel the snow away from the back wheel. He had thrown some planks in the trunk in anticipation of getting stuck in a rut. He placed them under the wheel to give it traction and kept digging.

While Porter was struggling with the ditch and the planks, the red blur of Amos' Chevy pickup truck skated past the Plymouth and slid into the ditch just ahead of them. Jolene squinted at the truck cab window. She could barely see an outline of the back of his big round head. A lump rose into her throat.

She heard Amos rev the engine; the truck's rear wheels whined as they spun furiously. The wheels stopped and the pickup sat still, listing heavily to one side, its right rear wheel mired in the icy ditch. The truck door creaked open and she saw Amos' stout form step down from the running board.

Jolene caught her breath when he turned to face the Plymouth. For a fleeting moment, she thought he might come to her window and talk to her, but her hopes were dashed when he went to the rear of the truck. He dropped the tailgate and lifted two melon-sized objects from the truck bed. She squinted at them, but couldn't make out what they were. He cradled them in his arms and trod carefully over the slick road. His figure grew smaller. He was headed toward Toby's driveway, away from the Plymouth and Jolene.

"No," she said. "No!" She opened the door, stumbled out of the car, and charged off into the blizzard toward her husband.

"Mrs. Hukstep!" Porter called out, but she ignored him. She slipped and slid and staggered on toward Amos.

"Amos!" Jolene yelled. "Amos!"

Amos walked on without looking back. She scurried over the slippery road, leaning into the wind and moving as fast as she could. Her feet slipped out from under her and she fell. She struggled to her hands and knees and then carefully stood upright. She stumbled forward again and increased her pace. She was gaining on him. "Amos! Wait! Wait for me!"

She caught up to him at the mouth of Toby's driveway, grabbed him by the shoulder, and wheeled him around to face her.

"Amos," she said softly, shocked by his appearance. He had big scars on his forehead and a bruised bent nose, but it was his eyes that stunned her. They were hollow, dull, and glassed over. There was no warmth in them, no feeling, no life.

Jolene stepped back and put her hand to her breast. Amos' tall stout body swayed in the wind while bits of snow and sleet swirled around him. Her eyes fell on the objects he clutched to his sides. He held a gallon mason jar full of clear liquid in each arm, cradling them like they were precious twin babies.

He coughed and cleared his throat. "I don't want to talk to you." The stench of alcohol knocked Jolene back. She placed her hand over her nose and frowned at him. Anger flared inside her. She had been stewing in the double-wide, worried to death about him, and he was drunk. She was on the verge of bawling him out, of telling him that he was a stubborn old fool for throwing their lives away over an ancient mistake, but his lifeless eyes disarmed her and her words stuck in her throat.

She looked him up and down. He had fallen apart, and it was her fault. She fought back tears. "I came to apologize."

He didn't respond.

"What I did was wrong. I cheated. I … I slept with Billy." She swallowed hard. "I lied to you and covered it up. I was cruel and selfish."

No emotion registered in his eyes.

She took a deep breath. "There's no excuse for what I did. I hurt you, and I'm sorry."

He didn't react for a long time. Then he said, "Is that it?"

Jolene's eyes brimmed with tears. She looked down at the ground and clenched her fists because she didn't want to cry. She held her breath and made the tears go back down inside. Then she looked up at Amos. "Please forgive me, Amos." Her voice broke despite her efforts to be strong. She covered her mouth with a shaking hand and gathered her strength. "I made a terrible mistake and I hurt you badly, but I love you and I want to be with you. Please come home with me."

"I can't do that," he said in a dry, flat tone of voice.

Jolene saw her life with him slipping away. It was like the two of them stood on a chunk of ice in the Arctic Ocean. A fissure cracked down the middle between them, and his slab was drifting away from hers into a frigid fog. She felt as though she were reaching out to Amos across a great cold divide, but he wasn't reaching out to her in return.

"Please, Amos. I stayed with you afterwards. I was faithful after that one mistake. That proves I love you."

His face didn't change.

"We had babies," she said desperately. "We raised them together. Doesn't that count for something?"

Amos furrowed his brow and his eyes hardened. "You lied to me for fifty years. You lied every time you opened your mouth and didn't tell me, every time you looked at me, every time you touched me."

She shuddered. "It wasn't a lie when we touched. My love was true."

The hard look in Amos' eyes died out. He looked down at the ground and shook his head slowly. When he looked up at her, the sullen lifeless expression had returned.

She pushed all her feelings into her voice and made one last try. "I've loved you through all the years we've been together. I still love you."

"I don't believe you." He turned his back, walked toward Toby's house, and faded into the miasma.

Jolene stared at the curling white lines of swirling sleet and snow, and she was suddenly very cold. She wrapped her arms around her waist to still the trembling. She swallowed hard and staunched the flow of her tears. She turned and looked for Porter and the Plymouth, but she couldn't see them. She couldn't see anything. The wind howled. She leaned into it and walked in the direction she thought the Plymouth might be. The wind chafed her face and stung her cheeks. She shielded her eyes with her hand and plodded on, but the car didn't appear before her. She turned and squinted into the gray behind her. Maybe she had walked in the opposite direction of the car. The snow whipped around her, so thick she couldn't see ten feet ahead. She was lost. She dropped her hands to her sides feebly and wept. "What difference does it make? I might as well lie down here and finish up."

Then Porter's voice came to her in the wind. "Over here, Mrs. Hukstep." She looked all around, but she couldn't see him. His call seemed to come from all directions and it sounded miles away. She pushed back the bill of Amos' sheepskin cap and peered into the storm, but her myopia and the water in her eyes blinded her.

Then a hand grasped her elbow and Porter's voice was at her ear, although she couldn't see him. "You turned the wrong way. The car's over here." He led her through the gray wall of weather to the car and helped her inside. He rounded it, got in behind the steering wheel, pulled off his gloves, and blew on his hands. "Are you all right?"

"We can go home now."

"Are you sure you don't want to go in and sit by the fire to warm up?"

"There's no point to it. Take me home, please."

Porter revved the engine and rocked the Plymouth back and forth on the planks and it spurted out of the icy ruts. He got out and threw the planks into the trunk. He got back in, turned the car around, and headed back to the trailer court.

"I saw you talking to Mr. Hukstep." He drove on for a while. "How did your talk with Mr. Hukstep go?"

She couldn't speak. She couldn't compose thoughts to send them to her mouth and she couldn't command her tongue to shape the words. She stared straight ahead and didn't say anything and Porter must have given up because he didn't ask her any more questions.

The Plymouth plowed a return path through the deep snow in the trailer park to the double-wide. Porter helped Jolene inside. She shed her snow-covered heavy coat and boots and gloves and sat down on the couch and stared out the window at the blizzard. Her eyes were dry. Her nerves were still and calm. She was surprised that she felt nothing. Her sixty-year relationship with Amos was dead, but she felt nothing.

Porter sat down next to her and put his arm around her. "What did Mr. Hukstep say?"

"He said he doesn't believe me."

"I'm sorry."

Jolene put her head on his shoulder and closed her eyes. "At least I know the truth. Amos doesn't love me. I don't think he ever loved me."

Chapter 16

The Escape

After almost three weeks in Dolly Madison, Billy still couldn't convince the sons of bitches who ran the place to turn him loose, so he took matters into his own hands. He called Porter and told him the doctors had released him. "Come get me. And bring me a suit of clothes."

When Porter showed up, Billy ripped the tubes out of his arm and got out of bed. He dressed hurriedly, put on his overcoat and hat, and thrust his hand at Porter. "Give me the car keys, son."

Porter looked confused. "Don't we need to talk to the doctors before we take off? Don't you need prescriptions and discharge papers and such?"

"The hell with the doctors. I'll never get out of this hellhole if I wait for them to turn me loose."

Porter looked nonplussed. "I thought they cleared you to go home."

"I might have exaggerated a bit when I told you that." Billy snapped his fingers. "The keys, son."

Porter hesitated.

"If you don't give me the keys, boy, I'll make a run for it on my own. I'll hitchhike home if I have to."

Porter made a wry face and handed the keys to Billy. Billy went to the door and leaned into the hallway. No nurses tended the counter. He darted down the hall to the fire stairwell, rushed down the steps, and scurried to the parking lot with Porter trailing along, casting furtive looks behind them.

In the parking lot, Billy ran over to the Plymouth and stopped cold beside it, surveying the caved-in door and the cardboard in the window. "What the hell happened?"

"It's a long story."

Billy scowled at the baling twine tying the driver's door shut. "How am I supposed to get in?"

"You untie her and then tie her back up after you get in, or you can go around to the other side and slide across."

Billy muttered a curse and proceeded to the other side of the car. When he slid behind the steering wheel and wrapped his fingers around it, he smiled. It felt good to regain some control over his life. Doctors had probed him, poked him, shoved pills down his throat, and jammed needles in him for three weeks. They decided when he would eat, sleep, empty his bladder, and void his bowels. They recorded each bodily function on little charts, pored over the putrid samples of his waste, and discussed his body parts among themselves in his presence as though he wasn't there. Billy treated his livestock with more sensitivity than they accorded him. He wished them all a fond farewell and hoped he'd never see them again.

Billy revved the engine, spun out of the parking lot, and sped north from Jeetersburg toward Fox Run. Snow still covered the fields from the blizzard of a week ago. Most of the snow and ice had been cleared off the road by plows and the spreading of salt, but the shady spots were still slick. Billy hit one and the Plymouth fishtailed toward a road sign, but he managed to straighten out the car at the last second.

Porter buckled his seat belt. "Hey! Slow down! Where's the fire?"

"I've got things to do, and I'm eager to get started."

"You won't get to do anything if you kill us both."

It took all Billy's self-control to rein in his enthusiasm and hold the Plymouth down to a safe speed. The fifty-minute drive to Fox Run seemed to take all day, but he finally braked to a stop in the store's snowy dirt lot and Porter gave him the key to the front door. He climbed the steps, unlocked the door, and burst through it. He stood beside the cash register and drew in a deep breath of the familiar aromas—cheese, cinnamon, and burnt pinewood, all mixed together.

Porter came in behind Billy. Billy beamed at him. "God almighty, I missed this old store." He went to the back of the store, sat on the bench, and gazed fondly at the cast-iron wood-burning potbelly stove with its glazed window across its bulging front-side and its big round black stovepipe stretching up from its back-side through the rafters to the roof. He looked around at the front counter, the rows of shelves stacked with staples and supplies, and the drink case standing against the back wall and smiled. "She looks just the same. Set a fire in the stove and open her up for business."

There was a little locked room behind the stove at the back of the store that housed a safe for cash and valuables, cleaning products, and a box of firewood. Porter went to the back room, gathered an armload of kindling and pine logs, and lit the fire. It crackled and popped and soon warmed up the place. Billy took off his coat while Porter put the OPEN sign in the window.

Shorty Clatterbuck was the first to saunter through the front door. He saw Billy by the stove and flashed a smile. "Can't keep a good man down, I reckon."

"Don't know about a good man," Billy said, "but they can't keep Billy Kirby down."

Shorty grinned and sat beside Billy. "I heard tell some fellow tried to kill you for stealin his wife."

Billy nodded. "A man from South Carolina. I ruined his marriage back in thirty-five. He said he couldn't measure up after his wife slept with me. I don't remember her that well. Big brunette with juicy lips is about all I can recall. That man was hellacious riled up about what I did with his wife, though. The sheriff's men chased him all over the park, but he got away. I tell you one thing. It sure as hell pays to have good friends. That crazy man would've killed me if it hadn't been for Amos Hukstep." Then Jake Shifflett traipsed in, and Billy told his big lie all over again, warming to the task and adding a few details.

Word soon seeped out of the store into Whippoorwill Hollow and Saddleback Cove that Billy Kirby was out of the hospital and holding court in front of the potbelly stove. Half the farmers in the county showed up to hear his version of the recent events. A broad outline of his harrowing ordeal had already made its way through the rumor mill and some had expressed skepticism about it, but Billy's enthusiastic telling of the tale was convincing and his version was even more exciting than the rumors. His personal embellishments gained a life of their own as the day waxed on, and his story was a powerful draw on customers. The store did almost as much business that day as it did the first day of trout fishing season.

Along about nine o'clock, the last straggler left the store and the lateness of the hour made it unlikely more customers would drop by that night, so Billy told Porter to close up. Billy put on his coat and joined Porter at the cash register. "It was good to see everybody again," he said as Porter placed the CLOSED sign in the window. "I almost went crazy in the hospital. Thanks for helping me break out, son."

"I'm not sure I should've done it. I hope your health holds up."

Billy laughed. "I've never felt better."

Porter shoved his hands deep in his pockets, hunched his shoulders, and looked at the floor. "I need a favor, Grandpa."

The somber tone of Porter's voice caught Billy's attention. He gave Porter a concerned look. "Is something wrong?"

Porter hesitated and then said, "I need a place to stay. Maureen threw me out."

Billy was disappointed. He knew Porter cared a great deal for Maureen and was trying hard to save their marriage. He put his hand on Porter's shoulder. "What happened?"

Porter told Billy about his relapse and his fight with Maureen's dad. "Maureen lost confidence in me after my big drunk, but I thought we had a chance of gettin past it until my dust-up with her dad. That was the last straw for her."

Billy withdrew his hand from Porter's shoulder and stared out the window at the moonlit night.

Porter shifted from one foot to the other. "I'm sorry I let you down, Grandpa."

"Don't apologize to me. Maureen is the one you let down. Maureen and yourself." Billy continued to stare out at the night, worrying about Porter's strength of character. The headlights of a truck coasted down the opposite hill on Whiskey Road to the one-lane bridge, climbed the hill to the intersection, and stopped at the T. Its headlights flashed directly in the store window. The truck turned left and rolled south toward Jeetersburg. Billy stared at its red taillights, winking in the dark. "You know you can't drink, son," he said. "What in hell were you thinking?"

Porter swallowed hard. "I wasn't thinking. That was the problem. Cletis, my sponsor at the rehab center, said you can go sober a long time and almost forget you're a drunk, and that's when you fall back. You think you can take a drink and the world won't come to an end, but that first sip puts you back on the path to hell. Cletis says I can't ever let my guard down."

Billy stared at Porter for a long time. Porter slouched with his hands in his pockets, his eyes down, beads of sweat popping out on his forehead. He'll have no chance of success, Billy thought, if no one believes in him. He returned his hand to Porter's shoulder. "All right," he said. "You slipped and fell. Let's move on from it, but make sure you don't do it again."

Porter put his hand over his eyes. "I'll try my best," he said. He took a while to pull himself together. Then he wiped his eyes and cleared his throat. "I was hoping I could move back into the big house with you."

"Where are you staying now?"

"Mrs. Hukstep took me in."

A tingle ran up Billy's spine. "I didn't know you were staying with Jolene."

"I moved in with her when you and Mr. Hukstep disappeared so she wouldn't be alone, but I feel like I've worn out my welcome."

Billy stared at Porter, thinking. Amos had said he didn't plan to make up with Jolene, but he could have changed his mind. "Is Amos there, too?"

"No, sir. He's staying with Mr. Vess."

"Why didn't he go home?"

"Mrs. Hukstep asked him to come home, but he turned her down. It looks like he doesn't want to be married to her any more. She said she thinks he never really loved her. She's torn up about it. It's a sad situation."

Billy thought about Jolene being left all alone for the first time in her life and he remembered how he felt the first time Mary Jo walked out on him. "I don't think now is the time for you to leave Jolene, son. She needs your company."

"That's what she says, but she cooks for me and cleans up after me. It's bound to be a bother to her."

"I don't think so. She's never lived alone. It's not easy to abide the silence of an empty home if you're not used to it. I think you should stay with her until she rights herself. Then you can move in with me if you want to."

Porter nodded. "I see your point. She's awful lonely without Mr. Hukstep around. I reckon I can stay with her a little while longer."

Billy looked out the window and thought about the last time he saw Amos in the hospital. Billy put his hand to his eyes and heaved a deep sigh. When he dropped his hand to his side, his eyes wandered to the spot down the hill from his house. In the moonlight he could make out the silhouette of the barn and the maple tree beside Little Bear River and in his mind's eye he saw Jolene there on a summer afternoon. He stared at the barn and the tree for a long time. Then he stirred from his reverie and said to Porter, "I want you to take a note to Jolene for me."

Porter hesitated. "Grandpa, I don't know what you have in mind, but I don't want to see Mrs. Hukstep get hurt. She's been through a lot. She can't bear any more heartache."

"I don't intend to hurt her, son." Billy went to the counter and found a note pad and a pencil. He wrote a note, shoved it into an envelope, and handed it to Porter. "Make sure you give this to her tonight."

Porter agreed to deliver the note and went outside to his car. Billy locked up the store and crossed the road to his house. He stopped in the side yard and looked down the hill at the river again. Snow blanketed the pasture and the trees beside the river were iced over, but Billy saw the meadow in the full bloom of summer.

Chapter 17

Jolene's Quest

Jolene rode along in the Plymouth on Whiskey Road. It was a sunny day and the sky was cloudless, but it was bitter cold and high winds whipped through the trees. She adjusted her thick glasses on her nose. She wasn't used to them and they were uncomfortable, but she was determined to wear them. She had done a lot of thinking about her life and how she would live out her last years. To have any chance of finding some level of contentment in her uncertain future, she decided she must face the hard truths of her new reality. Amos was unlikely to come home; she was seventy-five years old; and she would never be young again. She resolved to see the world the way it was, not the way she wished it to be. So she got the ugly old glasses out of the kitchen cupboard and put them on, but that afternoon in the Plymouth, looking at the snow-covered pastureland sliding by outside, she wasn't so sure she had made the right decision. "Everything's so sharp," she said.

"What's that?" Porter said as he steered the car through a bend in the road.

"Everything's got sharp points. The ends of branches, the corners of barns and houses, the edges of road signs. It's all pointy and razor-sharp. Everything was rounded off smooth when I didn't wear my spectacles. The world looked soft and easy. Now it's all prickly. Everything looks so, I don't know, hazardous is the right word, I guess."

The Plymouth crested the last hill on the way to Fox Run, coasted down its steep slope, rolled across the one-lane bridge over Little Bear River, and came to rest in the clearing by the gate to Billy's lower pasture. Porter cut off the engine and pointed at the barn. "That's the spot, right?"

With her spectacles, Jolene could see downriver past the barn to the old maple tree where she'd made love with Billy in 1915. "Yes, that's the spot."

Porter scanned the area. "I don't see him. It's mighty cold today and the wind's blowing awful hard. The mercury didn't break above fifteen at high noon, and it's colder now. Seems crazy for Grandpa to ask you to meet him by the river. Y'all could freeze to death. You sure you want to go over there?"

"I'm sure." Jolene looked at the ice on the hill that rose up to Billy's house and the wind blowing through the big trees up there. She had no choice but to brave the weather. One of the hard truths that she wanted to face was something only Billy knew. She had to talk to him to get the information. There was no other way, so she had to meet him no matter how cold it was. She looked over at Porter. He gripped the steering wheel and clenched his jaw. "What's the matter?"

Porter rubbed his face and looked over at her. "With the history between you two, are you sure it's a good idea to talk to him like this? He's my grandpa and he's been good to me and to a lot of other folks around these parts, but he's a might selfish and he can hurt people sometimes. You've been hurt pretty bad already. I'd hate to see you suffer any more."

Jolene smiled. "If your grandpa wasn't such a stubborn mule, he could learn a lot from you." She pried his hand off the steering wheel and held it in her hands. "Don't worry. Billy hurt me once, but that old wound healed with hard tough scars that are wide and deep. I was young and foolish back then. I know who Billy is now, and I know who I am. He can't hurt me anymore." She patted Porter's hand reassuringly. Then she opened the door and climbed out.

"Mrs. Hukstep?"

"Yes?"

"I'll have the engine running and the heater on. You come back if it's too cold, and you call out if you need help. I'll come running and carry you back here if need be. It's no trouble at all."

"Thank you, but I'll be fine. You won't have to wait long. I'll only be a few minutes."

Chapter 18

The Proposal

Billy stood beside the barn, seeking shelter from the frigid wind, leaning on a cane, shivering. He cursed under his breath. He didn't know why he hadn't anticipated the entirely predictable logistical difficulties of a meeting with Jolene at the river in cold weather. He'd planned this reunion to rekindle the flames of passion of fifty years ago, but his enthusiasm about his memories had blinded him to immutable facts of life: it was December; it was the dead of winter; and it was icy cold.

The morning had started out well, before he realized how cold it was. He had combed his hair carefully to sweep the front wisps across his forehead in the hope of making himself look younger. He peered in his bathroom mirror at the reflection of the prickly mustache he had grown in the hospital. It was an unfortunate shade of dirty gray and he needed more growth to fill in the bare spaces. In its current state, it resembled a smear of axle grease. He considered shaving it off but ultimately decided to keep it as a symbol to Jolene of the fact that he was a changed man.

He dressed in a black three-piece suit and a crisp starched white shirt. He cinched a black string tie tightly to his neck. He spit-shined his high-top black boots and placed his wide-brimmed black hat carefully on his head so that his hair would stay in place when he took it off. He looked at himself critically in the bedroom's full-length mirror. He didn't look half bad for a man who had been kidnapped, starved, and beaten only a month ago.

The black cane was the finishing touch. He found it leaning against the wall in the foyer. He hadn't intended to use it, but he thought it added an air of class and dignity to his outfit. Besides, his legs were still a bit shaky from the beating he had taken.

He donned his long black winter coat and fetched a blanket to spread under the maple tree. It was when he picked his way carefully down the slope from his house to the river that reality slapped him in the face and brought him out of his memories of the summer of 1915. The side of the hill was frozen solid. Snow and ice left over from the blizzard lined the slope. The high winds screamed in his ears and he had to press his hat down on his crown to keep it from blowing away. The cane became more than a dapper addition to his wardrobe. He used it as an anchor and a pick to hold his position and to steady his balance against the gale winds.

It took Billy more than a half hour to descend the treacherous hill to the bottomlands and to stagger to the barn. The trek was a taxing ordeal. He was out of breath and chilled to the bone. He leaned against the barn, using it as a windbreaker, clutching his chest and breathing deeply.

When he regained his breath, he looked around and realized the situation was hopeless. The spot under the maple tree downriver from the barn was hard cold ground covered with solid ice. Billy pulled the collar of his coat tightly around his throat. His teeth chattered.

He was considering climbing the hill back to the house, telephoning Jolene, and relocating their rendezvous when he heard the groan of the Plymouth's engine on the hill. He leaned around the corner of the barn and looked at Whiskey Road. Vapor swirled from the Plymouth's tailpipe as it coasted down the hill and came to rest in the clearing. The car sat there for a few minutes with the engine running. Then Jolene disembarked and walked to the gate. She came through it, closed it, and slipped and almost fell when she started across the icy pasture. Her arms jutted out wide and she caught her balance. She stood still for a moment, looking down at the ground uncertainly, straining against the force of the wind. She finally took a tentative step farther along and then another step.

Billy ducked behind the barn. It was too late to call off their meeting. He would have to make do as best he could. He shook his head in disgust.

He should have arranged to meet her in the store by the potbelly stove or in his house by the fireplace. He flattened his back against the barn and closed his eyes, his mind racing in search of a way to save the day.

"Who died?"

Billy turned to the sound of Jolene's voice. She stood at the rear corner of the barn with her arms wrapped around her waist, shivering. "What?" he said.

"Who died? You look like an undertaker."

He stared at her. Her eyes looked strange. She wore glasses with lenses as thick as the headlights on Porter's Plymouth. They protruded from her scarfed head like the antennae of a giant insect. When she blinked, her lids looked like shutters falling over windows and then retracting back up. Billy took a tentative step toward her, disarmed by her bugged-out eyes. "What did you say?"

Jolene tiptoed carefully across the ice alongside the barn until she reached him. She looked him up and down with her binocular-sized glasses. "You look like you're going to a funeral."

Billy stared at her, dumbfounded.

She grabbed the sleeve of his coat and shoved it roughly toward his face. "You're dressed in black from head to toe. Who died?"

He looked down at his clothing. "Oh. You're right. It's all black. I didn't think, you know, about the way it looks. All the black, I mean."

He had thought about this moment for three weeks. He envisioned sweeping Jolene off her feet. It seemed so smooth and easy in his daydreams. Now the moment was upon him, and he felt as though his mind was clogged with viscous mud. "I just wore my best," he said. "Nobody died. I guess." He looked down at his clothes again. He looked at Jolene and swallowed. He couldn't verbalize a complete thought. During the most important moment of his life, his brain seemed to have unhooked itself from his mouth.

A strong gust of wind whipped alongside the barn and almost blew them down. Jolene pulled her collar tightly around her throat. "We'll catch our death out here." She stepped around Billy and slipped and slid toward the front of the barn. Billy tripped along behind her like a stray dog. They rounded the corner and entered the barn.

Billy's hay barn was tall and open on the front end so the cattle could come in out of the wind. Ten or twelve cattle standing under the hayloft at the back of the barn turned their heads slowly toward Jolene and Billy when they stepped inside. A big Angus bull stretched his neck toward them and bawled.

Jolene stopped in her tracks. Billy stepped on her heels and bumped up against her. "Oops … I—"

Jolene turned to him and grabbed his arm. "The bull. Is he dangerous?"

Billy stared at her, confused. "What?"

"The bull," she said again, pointing.

Billy looked at the bull. "You mean Maximus?"

"I mean that big bull that looks like he's about to charge at us. Is he dangerous?"

"Oh, no," he said. "He won't harm us. He's just trying to stay out of the weather."

She scowled. "Well, that proves he's got more sense than you do." Jolene walked along the wall to the rear of the barn. Billy followed her and felt the ground give way under his foot. He heard a sucking sound as he pulled his newly spit-shined boot out of a cow pie. He looked around the barn. Cow pies were everywhere, mostly frozen solid, but he'd managed to step squarely in the only fresh one within twenty yards.

An Angus cow standing next to Maximus chose that moment to lift her tail, scrunch her body into a massive black ball, and piss a steaming stream of urine into the barn muck. Billy looked sheepishly at Jolene, who was staring at the cow with revulsion. She put her hand over her nose and made a face. "It stinks in here."

He glanced down at his beshitted boot and tried to scuff some hay over it. "Yes, well, cattle do their business in here."

"I noticed that."

Nothing about their rendezvous was proceeding as he had planned. He needed to get it back on track or all would be lost. He tried to forget the weather, the cattle, and the stench. He gathered his wits, positioned himself directly in front of Jolene, and squared his shoulders. "I'm sorry about all this, Jolene. It isn't what I had in mind."

She smirked. "What did you have in mind?"

"I wanted to go back in time, back to that summer when we sat on the blanket out there by the river, back to that last time we were together."

Jolene grimaced. "We can't go back. We're fifty years older. Besides, even if we could be kids again, it's the dead of winter. We'd freeze to death out there."

"I know. In my excitement about seeing you again, I forgot how cold it is. I should have asked you to meet me in a warm place. There's so much I want to say, words I should have said fifty years ago when we were on that blanket." Billy stepped closer to her. "Jolene, I made a mistake back then when you said you loved me—"

"I don't want to talk about that." Her insect eyes blinked stubbornly.

"But I want to tell you—"

"I know what you want to tell me, Billy Kirby. You want to tell me you love me. You want to tell me you always loved me. You want to tell me a pack of lies."

Billy was taken aback. "No. Absolutely not. I wouldn't lie to you, Jolene. I wouldn't."

She waved her hand in the air like she was batting at a pestering horsefly. "Oh, please, Billy. I'm not the silly, lovesick girl you fooled out there by the river way back when. Give me some credit for learning a few tricks in my seventy-five years."

"You don't understand. It's the truth. I do love you. It's the God's honest truth."

Jolene's bulbous eyes blazed. "You wouldn't know the God's honest truth if you heard it from Jesus Christ's own lips. Your romantic malarkey is not what I came here to talk about. I don't want to hear it. What I want to know is what happened between you and Amos in the park. I want to know all of it. What happened up there in the mountains?"

"Wait a minute. There's something important I want to ask you."

Jolene scowled. "No! I won't stand for it. I want an answer to my question. What happened in the park? Amos tried to kill you, didn't he?"

Billy stepped back. "It wasn't Amos. It was a man from South—"

"You just said you would never lie to me, Billy Kirby. I guess that was a lie, too."

Billy coughed. "Well, I—"

"Tell me the truth! What happened between you and Amos in the mountains?"

Billy hunched his shoulders and looked at the ground. In his long life, he had never encountered such a frustrating day. Virtually everything had gone wrong. There seemed to be no way to avoid disaster. He wanted to impress Jolene with the idea that he was a changed man, a man she could trust, and everything in nature was working against him—the cold, the wind, the cattle. Now the events of the past few weeks had turned against him as well.

There was no point in resisting. Jolene was intractable. "Amos hit me over the head with his rifle."

"Then what?"

"He hauled me up to the cabin."

"I know that much. I figured that out on my own. What did you tell him about us?"

"I told him about the three times we met."

"What did you say about those meetings? Did you … did you tell him what we did?"

"I told him we made love."

Jolene's big eyes misted over. "That was a lie," she said in a small voice. "We didn't make love. We had sex."

"You're wrong, Jolene. What we did was more than that—"

"Why didn't Amos kill you? What happened to stop him?"

Billy puffed out his cheeks and looked up at the loft. He might as well tell her and get it over with. "Amos couldn't do it. He put the gun to my head, but he couldn't pull the trigger."

"What happened then?"

Billy looked away.

"Amos tried to kill himself, didn't he?"

Billy looked down at the ground and nodded.

"I knew it." Her eyes brimmed with tears. "Why didn't he go through with it? Why didn't he kill himself?" Billy started to turn away from her, but she grabbed his sleeve. "Tell me!"

She was staring at him fearfully. He didn't want her to know that their ancient affair robbed her husband of his will to live. "He lost his nerve, I guess. He couldn't do it."

She gritted her teeth. "You're lying. I can see it in your eyes. You owe me this much after all the trouble you've caused. Tell me the truth!"

Billy let out a long breath. "He would have killed himself, but I got the gun away from him. Then Toby and Stogie came along."

Jolene put her hand to her lips and cried. While she wept, Billy tried to think of a way to get her to focus on him instead of Amos. He took her hand and cradled it in his own hands. Her old hand was rough, bony, and mottled, the spindly claw of an old woman. He stared at it fondly. He could have held that precious hand as it grew old if he hadn't been such a fool.

She pulled her hand away. Her lined and creased face sagged. "Did Amos say anything about me?"

"Let's not talk about him, Jolene," Billy pleaded.

"Tell me! What did he say about me?"

Billy hesitated, and then said, "He said I stole from him the only thing he ever cared about. I stole you."

She shook her head feebly. "He said that?"

"He said I cut out his heart."

"I thought he didn't love me," she whispered.

Billy let out a deep breath slowly. "He loved you. He still does. That's why he's sick to death, I suppose." He turned away from her and hit the plank wall softly with an open hand. Jolene cried. He looked at her and shook his head. Nothing had gone according to his plans. He had envisioned a joyful coupling with her. Instead, his answers to her dogged questions had made her miserable. His dream of a happy life with her was fading away.

He had to do something to save it.

He faced her, took the ugly glasses from her eyes, and put them in his coat pocket. She looked up at him through her tears. "Give me back my glasses," she said.

Billy didn't respond. He was mesmerized by her blue eyes, pooled with tears. They were still beautiful. He was more convinced than ever that the Jolene of 1915, the Jolene he longed for, was still inside her. "I guess you don't want to hear it from me, Jolene, but you still have the prettiest eyes in Selk County."

"More lies," she said, but her voice had softened.

Billy brushed the tears from her upturned cheeks with his withered fingertips. "That's no lie. That's the truth, the God's honest truth. It's the truth that Amos still loves you, and it's the truth that I love you, too." He tried to kiss her, but she pulled back.

"Don't," she said.

Billy put his hands on her shoulders. "I love you, and I invited you here so I could ask you to marry me."

"What?"

Billy stretched his arms out wide and looked around the barn. "It didn't work out the way I'd hoped, what with the freezing cold and the cattle and the barnyard aromas, but none of these setbacks change what I want. I want you to marry me. I want to live the rest of my life with you."

"But I'm married to Amos."

"Leave him, and marry me." Billy took her chin in his hand and kissed her full on the mouth. She let him kiss her this time. He knew she only allowed him to do it because she was shocked and stunned, but the kiss was a wondrous joy for him anyway. Her lips were thin and drawn with age and a little rough, but they revived his memories of her sweet kisses in the summer of their youth. He closed his eyes and he saw her in the meadow on the blanket in the warm sun.

She pulled back and looked up at him with a dazed expression on her face. In his mind's eye her creases and wrinkles were gone, and he saw the vibrant, flushed face of young Jolene.

"Your eyes are even prettier when you're happy," he said. He put his arms around her and pulled her to him. "You haven't been happy enough all these years. You haven't been as happy as you deserved to be. Let me make it up to you." He kissed her again and hugged her and she went limp in his arms. He kissed her long and deep and he didn't feel the brittle-boned old woman in his embrace. He felt the ripe, taut curves of a young girl. He nuzzled his cheek against hers and ran his hands up her back. He kissed her neck under her ear. "Marry me," he whispered. "I'll make you laugh every day. I'll make you happy the way you were with me fifty years ago."

Jolene seemed to melt in his arms for a short while. Then her back stiffened in his embrace. She put her hands on his chest and leaned back, looking up at him. She looked skeptical.

"I love you, Jolene," he said insistently. "I love you with all my heart."

A solemn expression settled into the corners of her mouth, and she pushed him back gently but firmly until she freed herself from his clutches. "You don't love me, Billy. You love the good times."

Billy felt a sharp pain in his chest, like an ice pick piercing the core of his heart, and it took his breath away.

Her face softened. "Those words hurt, don't they, Billy?"

He couldn't catch his breath.

"They were true when you said them back then, and they're true again today."

"No. You don't understand."

"I thought I loved you," she said gently, "but I didn't love you. You were right. I loved the good times you brought me, the excitement and the fun. I lusted for you, but I didn't love you and you don't love me now. You think you love me, but you don't. You love the young girl I was that summer, and you love your own youth. That's what you love." She put her hand on his cheek. "God knows I longed for you to say you loved me back then, and it might be fun to go back there and live it all over again a different way. It might even last, if you have some of your grandson in you. But we can't go back. We've lived long lives, you with Mary Jo and me with Amos. We can't undo all we've done over the years. We can't take away the lives we've led. We wouldn't want to even if we could."

Billy put his hand over her hand as it rested on his cheek, and he pressed his lips against her palm and kissed it. "Why not, Jolene? Those two young people are still inside our hearts. They still want each other." He cupped her hand in his like a delicate flower. "Let me bring those two young people back to life."

She stared at him for a few moments and he thought he saw affection in her beautiful eyes, but then she pulled her hand away and took a step back and frowned at him. "Give me my glasses," she said. The tone of her voice was firm and cold and it chilled him. He withdrew the glasses from his pocket and handed them to her.

She walked around him to the front of the barn, stopped at the corner, and looked back at him. Her eyes caught the sunlight and sparkled like sapphire. Billy's breath caught in his throat.

She frowned at him. "Grow up, Billy. Our youth is gone and you can't bring it back. You're eighty years old. Face up to it and make the most of it." She put on her glasses and her frown deepened. "And shave off that silly mustache. It takes away from your good looks."

She stepped around the wall out of sight and left him standing in the barn with his knees trembling. He looked at the cattle and then down at the cow dung on his boot. He shuddered in the cold. He pulled the collar of his coat tightly around his throat and looked at the corner of the barn where she had stood with her blue eyes shining. He had told her the truth. She had the prettiest eyes in Selk County. Then she had covered them up with ugly glasses and stood there scolding him. Billy knitted his brow and sighed.

He went to the front of the barn and looked over at the clearing by Whiskey Road. Jolene had reached the gate. He watched her go through and close it behind her. She walked toward the Plymouth like an old lady, stiff-legged, hunched over. He clenched his fists.

All was not lost. He couldn't have conceived of a more disastrous plan for resurrecting their passion for one another, and yet it had almost worked. He had revived young Jolene for a few moments in an open-air barn in the dead of winter, standing in the midst of stinking cattle with fresh cow shit on his boot. Under the right conditions, he had no doubt he could persuade her to accept his proposal.

Billy smiled, pulled his hat low over his eyes, and caned across the pasture to the foot of the hill, pondering the appropriate time and place for their next encounter.

Chapter 19

Jolene's Choice

Jolene opened the car door and plopped down on the seat of the Plymouth, shivering and out of breath. Porter reached across her and pulled the door shut. "I hope you didn't catch your death. It was cold as an icehouse in here even with the heater going full blast. Are you all right?"

Jolene's teeth chattered. "I'm fine."

"What happened down there with Grandpa?"

She pulled her coat more tightly around her. "He asked me to marry him."

Porter's jaw dropped. "What?"

"He asked me to marry him," she said. "He says he loves me." She looked over at Porter. The stunned look on his face coupled with the sheer audacity of Billy's outrageous proposal made her burst out laughing. She laughed raucously, rocking back and forth, and Porter began to laugh, too, and they couldn't stop laughing for a long time.

When they had finally laughed themselves out, Jolene gazed out the window. With her glasses on, she could see Billy clearly as he climbed the hill. He moved quickly and didn't seem afraid of falling. "Look at the old boy. Dressed to the nines all in black. Something's come over him. He's recovered his old spunk."

"Grandpa says life served up a second chance, and he means to make the most of it."

Jolene watched Billy reach the top of the hill and climb effortlessly over the split-rail fence bordering his backyard. "He's off to a good start. There's a lot of fun left in that old rogue."

"Are you going to do it, ma'am?"

Jolene turned to Porter. "Going to do what?"

"Will you marry Grandpa?" he asked, looking much less amused.

"Of course not," she said. "There's too much heartache that comes along with his brand of fun." She turned to look at Billy, but he had gone inside. She stared at the big old two-story farmhouse at the top of the hill and thought about Billy Kirby. He had surprised her. It was understandable, she supposed, that he swept her off her feet again for a few moments, but it didn't last. She was too old and wise to fall for his tricks. He might be more stable, but he was still a bucking bronco. An older horse, but still wild. She wanted the work horse, the strong horse that plowed straight ahead. She wanted Amos.

She knitted her brow and thought about Amos. The way he acted in the blizzard made her believe he had never loved her, but he told Billy she was the most important thing in his life. She thought about Amos' introverted nature. He kept his feelings so well concealed that he was hard to read. Maybe he really still loved her, as Billy had said.

She turned to Porter. "Take me to Toby's house."

"Are you sure that's a good idea? It made you awful sad last time."

"I want to tell Amos that Billy asked me to marry him."

Porter looked askance at her. "I don't know, ma'am. Mr. Hukstep was mighty riled when he found out you and Grandpa got together fifty years ago. No telling what he'll do if you tell him Grandpa is after you again."

"No matter what he does, he can't make things worse than they are now."

Porter stared out the window for a moment. "I guess you're right," he said. He started the car, turned it around, and drove west over the one-lane bridge into Saddleback Cove. Cold shadows fell across the road and ice-blue snow covered the slopes and clung to trees. Ten miles into the cove, a clearing emerged on the right-hand side of the road where Toby's house stood in a grove of cedar trees.

Porter pulled into the driveway and parked behind two pickup trucks: Amos' red Chevy and a blue Dodge. Snow was banked up on the hoods and windshields of both of them. Jolene told Porter to wait in the car.

When she got out, a gust of wind blew snow mist from the cedars into her face. She wiped it away and picked her way carefully over an icy flagstone walkway to Toby's front stoop. She stepped up on the stoop and rapped on the door. No one came. She beat the door hard with her fist, but still no one answered. She knew Amos was in there because his truck was in the driveway, so she kept pounding until the door finally swung open. Stogie Morris stood before her with his slick bald head all sweaty and his face covered with gray stubble. One red suspender was draped over the shoulder of a filthy, tobacco-juice-stained undershirt. The other dangled at his knees. The strong scents of sweat and liquor poured out of the house. Jolene put her hand to her nose and looked Stogie up and down. She had never seen him look so slovenly.

"What are you doing here, Stogie?" she said.

"It's none of your business."

She paused, surprised by his animosity, and then said, "Is Amos here?"

"That ain't none of your business either."

Her surprise gave way to irritation. "I want to see Amos," she said firmly.

"Well, he don't want to see you."

"Tell him I'm here!"

Stogie arched his back. "You can't boss me around. Me and Amos are done with women like you. We're holed up here by ourselves, having us a high old time despite what you and your kind did to us. You ain't welcome here. You ain't fit to keep our company."

"I'm the same person I was before y'all found out what I did with Billy."

"That's where you're wrong. You lied to Amos all those years. You lied to everyone. You ain't the person you claimed to be."

"That's not true!"

"It is true! And I don't blame Amos for hating you for it. I know how it feels, by damn! It hurts bad to find out the woman you trusted lied to you and pretended to love you and never told you the truth. Then, when you find out the truth, she's long since dead and gone and you can't talk to her to try to understand it and there ain't a damn thing you can do to fix it. I know how it feels! It hurts so bad you can't think about nothin else!"

Jolene was more confused than before. "I'm not dead and gone." Then it dawned on her. She could see it in his bleary eyes and in the twitching creases of his face. He was very badly hurt and Polly was gone.

"Oh, Stogie. I'm so sorry."

He stared at her wildly for a few moments. Then he seemed to realize where he was and who she was and he hung his head. "Of course, what went on between you and Billy ain't none of my business." He blew out a long breath. "I'm sorry for my harsh words. I'll fetch Amos." He disappeared into the shadows.

Jolene turned around and looked at the road and the forest on the other side. Billy's charm masked a cruel selfishness. He had lived his life with no one else in mind, chasing thrills and taking what he wanted. Now his friends were paying the price in misery and heartache for his recklessness.

"What do you want?"

Jolene turned to face Amos. He stood in the doorway dressed in filthy long johns, gripping one of his mason jars. His face was grimy and pasty. His oily gray hair was flecked with bits of grit and it stuck out wildly in different directions. He looked even worse than he had the day of the blizzard. It took her a few moments to adjust to the shock of his deterioration. Then she said, "Billy Kirby asked me to leave you and marry him. He says he loves me."

Amos' shoulders slumped. He lifted the jar to his lips, swilled the painkiller, and dropped his arm to his side listlessly. A line of saliva dribbled from the corner of his mouth. He dragged his sleeve across his lips and cleared his throat. "What's it got to do with me?"

She hesitated, wounded by the question. Then she gathered her resolve and said, "What do you want me to do?"

He said nothing for a long time, swaying in the doorway, his eyes flat and empty. "I don't care what you do." His voice sounded like dry cornstalks rustling in the wind.

Anger welled up inside her. She wondered why she had entertained any hope that Billy's proposal would change Amos' mind. She had forgotten who he was. He was a bullheaded, taciturn old grump who was determined to throw away their sixty years together. "You won't forgive me no matter what I do, will you?" she said in a sharp tone.

"You lied to me."

"Yes, I lied to you! I slept with Billy Kirby! I gave in to temptation. I was wrong to do it. I'm not perfect, but neither are you."

Amos straightened his back. "I never even looked at another woman. I was too busy working myself to the bone to put food on the table for you and the girls. I gave you everything I had in me, and what did I get for it? Lies. Sixty years of lies."

Jolene put her finger in Amos' face. "You stopped talking to me. You shut me out. You haven't touched me in so long I don't remember the last time, but I never complained. I never said a cross word to you about it. I forgave you because I thought you loved me, even though you never said it and you didn't show it, but I was wrong. You don't love me. You don't love anyone. You're a cold, stubborn man who's determined to be miserable." She stepped back from him and clenched her fists. "I'm through calling you on the phone and lying awake nights worrying about you and chasing you around and begging you to take me back. Go ahead and throw away our lives. I don't care. I'm done with you." She turned and started up the walkway.

Behind her she heard Amos' strained, gravelly voice. "You hurt me, Jo."

She turned and looked back at him.

His chin quivered. "I wish I could forget what you did with Billy, but I can't. I can't stop thinking about it." He swiped his hand across his eyes. "It hurts too much." He lifted the mason jar to his gut and cradled it in front of him with both hands. He looked down into it for a few seconds. Then he looked up at her. "I'm sorry." He turned and receded into the shadows of

Toby's house.

Jolene stared at the empty doorframe. She was right, she thought. He was foolish and stubborn. But he was right, too. He couldn't change who he was. He held grudges. He brooded. He couldn't stop thinking about her betrayal. The spirit of those few fiery summer moments with Billy so long ago had lived on, hovering over the banks of Little Bear River. In the winter of her life, those moments had descended on Amos like a poisonous cloud and they had smothered him. He would never be able to forget, and he would never be able to forgive her.

She walked the flagstone path back to the Plymouth, opened the door, and got in. She looked straight ahead at the snow-covered pickup trucks in the driveway. She felt Porter's eyes on her, waiting to hear what happened. "Amos wants no part of me."

"I'm sorry, Mrs. Hukstep."

"I'm sorry, too." She looked over at Toby's house. "I'm sorry I'm in love with a stubborn old fool who doesn't love me back."

They were quiet for a while. Then Porter started the car, backed out into Whiskey Road, and drove west toward the trailer park.

Chapter 20

Billy's Second Try

A few days later, Billy gave Porter another message to deliver to Jolene. This one asked her to forgive him for the frigid debacle in the barn. He wanted to start over and make his case to her in a more comfortable, appropriate setting. He proposed that she come to his house on Christmas Day for a catered dinner, followed by a long visit sitting by the fire in his parlor.

When Billy entered the store on the morning of Christmas Eve, Porter handed him an envelope from Jolene. Billy carried it to his bench by the stove and ripped it open eagerly. He held the note up to the light and read it.

Dear Billy,
I can't marry you. I don't love you. I like you fine, but I love Amos even though he doesn't love me anymore. Please don't send me notes or come to see me or ask me to marry you again. It's too hurtful. Maybe there will come a day when I can be in the same room with you without feeling sad, but not now.
Please respect my wishes and leave me be.
Sincerely,
Jolene

Billy was stunned and shaken. He sat by the stove for the remainder of the day reading and rereading the note, searching for loopholes. He lay awake in his cold bed on Christmas Eve, thinking about the meadow and the speckled sunlight and the blonde curl at the nape of Jolene's neck and her bare shoulders shuddering with quiet sobs when he wouldn't say he loved her. He didn't sleep at all.

At dawn on Christmas Day, he arose and read Jolene's note yet again. Amos couldn't be the reason she'd turned him down. She was alone and miserable. So was Billy. Together they could be happy. Her rejection wasn't logical. She had made the wrong choice. He had to find a way to make her understand that.

He went into the bathroom and shaved off his mustache. He dressed in his black suit and winter coat, donned his wide-brimmed black hat, and went out to his truck. On the drive through Saddleback Cove to the trailer park, the sun peeked over the mountains, streaking the sky with pink and lavender. He pulled up to Jolene's double-wide and parked his truck beside Porter's Plymouth. The crisp air chilled his face and the cold tin of Jolene's front door stung his knuckles when he rapped on it.

When the door opened, he was taken aback. Billy had thought about young Jolene all night long, but the Jolene in the doorway was an old lady. Her thick glasses enlarged her tired, red-rimmed eyes and she wore a long, wrinkled, loose-fitting black wool dress with support hose and high-topped leather boots. She put her hand to her breast and frowned.

"I asked you not to come here. Please go away."

It took Billy a few moments to recuperate from the shock. He reminded himself that he had revived young Jolene when he embraced her in the barn. He could revive her again if he was determined and persuasive. He took a breath and summoned his memory of their time in the meadow together. "I'll honor your request to leave you alone if you still feel the same way after you hear me out. Can I come inside and talk to you?"

She gave him a sour look. "That would only lead to more pain for both of us. I want you to leave here now. Don't ever come back."

Billy plodded doggedly forward, telling himself she didn't have to be as old as she looked at that moment. He took off his hat. "Jolene, I've got ten good years left in me. I want to spend them with you. If you'll let me, I'll show you fun times for the rest of our lives. My father and his father made a fortune and I've doubled it. I couldn't spend it all if I tried. We can do anything you want. If you want to go to Florida and lay on the beach, we'll do it. You want to travel the world and see the sights, we'll be on our way in the morning. You want a mink coat, a diamond ring, a string of pearls, a fancy new car, a brand-new house, just say the word. I'll give you anything you want."

"I'm sorry, Billy. What I want you can't give me."

"That's not true, Jolene. There's nothing I won't do for you. Just tell me what you want. Tell me."

"I want Amos to realize he's made a terrible mistake and come home."

Billy's breath caught in his throat.

She shut the door.

Billy stared at the tin door, desperate to save his dream of a life with Jolene. He considered breaking down the barricade, but he could think of nothing he could say once he forced his way inside. She was right. What she wanted he couldn't give her, and even if he could talk Amos into going home to her, Amos' return would extinguish any chance that she would ever embrace Billy. He hung his head.

"Do you want me to drive you home, Grandpa?"

Billy turned to see Porter standing behind him, looking concerned.

"I was in the shed," he said. "I saw you talking to Mrs. Hukstep. You want me to drive you home?"

"No, thank you, son."

"Are you sure you should drive? You look mighty rattled."

Billy stared at Porter. He put on his hat and placed his hand on his grandson's shoulder. "For a long time I thought you'd turn out like your daddy. I was wrong. I don't know where you got it from, but you've turned into a good young man." Billy felt his eyes welling with tears. He bowed his head. "Thank you for your offer, boy, but I need to be alone for a bit." He went to his truck, opened the door, and climbed up on the running board and looked over the top of the cab at the trailer. Jolene was at the window.

He saw the sun flash on the thick lenses of her ugly spectacles.

"Merry Christmas, Grandpa."

Billy swallowed and nodded to him. "Same to you, boy."

Chapter 21

A Widow's Christmas

Christmas Day at ten in the morning, Eva Gitlow stood in the Grace Church cemetery beside her deceased husband's cousin, facing her husband's headstone. Harvey Gitlow was a tall, stout, bald-headed man in his early sixties, with wide-set black eyes and a full black beard. He put his hand on Eva's shoulder and said, "God, I miss him."

The cemetery sat behind Grace Church on a flat expanse of land at the foot of Feather Mountain. The Gitlow plot was off to the left of the front gate, four rows in. The graves of Nelson's mother and father lay at the head of the plot. His sister, Rachel, who died in infancy, lay to their left, marked by a small, crumbling stone topped by a weather-worn marble carving of a lamb. Nelson was buried to the right of his parents.

As Harvey knelt and placed a plastic vase of red roses at the head of his cousin's grave, tears beaded in his eyes. He and Nelson had been close. Harvey was a long-haul truck driver based in Jeetersburg, and when Nelson was killed, he'd been in California on a run and couldn't make it back in time for the funeral. He insisted that Eva meet him at the cemetery every year on Nelson's birthday, the date of his death, and Christmas Day; the boys' families had spent every Christmas together when they were young.

Eva wasn't keen on these memorials, but she liked Harvey and didn't want to hurt his feelings so she met him at Nelson's grave on each of his designated days. That morning, she had made a wreath of evergreens clipped from a fir tree near her barn. She laid it on the grave beside Harvey's roses.

She and Harvey stood side by side staring at the polished granite headstone. It was pale gray, slick, smooth. *Nelson Taylor Gitlow/ b. June 20, 1904/ d. April 6, 1965.* Harvey clutched a grease-stained gray Goodyear ball cap to his chest, bowed his head, and closed his eyes.

Eva bowed her head. Out of the corners of her eyes, she watched Harvey's lips move as he worked his way through his typical interminable silent prayer for Nelson's nonexistent soul. The temperature hadn't risen out of the teens the last few days and it was bitter cold that morning. A low gunmetal-gray cloud cover masked the top half of Feather Mountain and cast a blue-gray haze over the barren, skeletal trees on its lower slope. A chill wind blew Eva's white hair across her face, and she swept it out of her eyes. She was wearing a wool coat over a hooded blue sweatshirt, but the cold seemed to cut right through it and she was shivering uncontrollably.

Time passed and Harvey prayed on. A cow lowed somewhere off to the east. She heard a car pass on the road in front of the church heading toward Fox Run. Eva's teeth began to chatter. She was on the verge of telling Harvey she'd had quite enough when he finally said amen and opened his eyes, which were wet with tears.

The wind died down. They stood together without saying anything for a while. Then Harvey took a deep breath. "Are you all right?"

"Yes," she said.

"Musta been mighty hard on you, the way he went out and all."

"It's been more than two years. I've adjusted."

Harvey looked at her curiously and then looked back at the gravestone. "Well, if there's ever anything I can do ..." His voice trailed off.

She didn't bother to reply. They both knew there was nothing he could do. If a rich relative had survived Nelson, there would have been quite a lot he could do. He could pay her feed bill or her delinquent property taxes or her defaulted mortgage payments, but Harvey was Nelson's only living relative and he didn't make enough to pay his own bills.

Harvey turned to Eva and hugged her tightly, cheek to cheek, her breasts flattening against his chest. His scraggly beard scratched the side of her face, and the rabbit's fur collar of his jacket smelled of stale cigarette smoke. He finally let go and stepped back. "See you next time," he said, apparently too choked up to say more. He kissed her on the forehead and walked away quickly, his hands shoved into his jacket pockets, his head down.

Eva sighed. She would prefer to put her dead husband behind her, but almost three years after his death, Harvey showed no signs of allowing Nelson's memory to fade away.

Harvey cranked up his tractor-trailer and she watched him pull out of the church parking lot and onto the state road. She looked back at Nelson's grave and Harvey's roses one last time, wrapped her arms around her waist, and walked back to her truck.

She drove to Fox Run, turned on to Whiskey Road, and headed into Saddleback Cove toward her farm. A couple miles into the cove, she came up behind a red Chevy pickup sitting on the side of the road at an odd angle with its right front wheel lodged in the ditch. She slowed as she passed by and looked in its window. Amos Hukstep was slumped behind the steering wheel, his head leaning back against the back wall of the cab as though he was unconscious.

Alarmed, she pulled off the road, ran back to the truck, and opened the driver's door. A dense cloud of alcohol vapor billowed out of the cab. She stepped back, covering her nose with her hand, and frowned at Amos. His eyes were closed; his mouth was open; and he was snoring. His hair was oily and mussed up, and several days' growth of beard stubble darkened his jowls.

She grasped his elbow and shook it. "Mr. Hukstep. Are you all right?"

His eyelids fluttered. He stirred and looked around groggily. His gaze settled on Eva. A wan smile came to his face. He raised his arm and waved to her as though he was passing her as she stood on the side of the road. Then he looked forward and gripped the steering wheel with both hands. His head fell back; he closed his eyes; and he resumed snoring.

"My word," Eva said. She glanced back at the truck bed. A cardboard box with six one-gallon mason jars filled with clear liquid sat behind the cab. Grain alcohol. Bootleg, no doubt. She was surprised. Amos Hukstep was known for being sober and somewhat sullen. This was wildly out of character. She stared at the jars curiously. Maybe this was a holiday celebration run amok.

She wasn't sure what she should do, but it was clear she couldn't leave him there. If he didn't wake up, he might freeze to death. If he woke up, he might kill himself or someone else trying to drive home. Lugging him to her truck and driving him to his trailer wasn't a viable option. She couldn't carry him, and he was in no shape to walk, even with her help.

She grimaced. She had to drive him home in his truck and then find someone to drive her back to her truck. It amounted to a large pain in the ass, especially on a day when she'd overslept and left without feeding the livestock. In another hour, the cattle would be gathering around the barn, bawling their protest at her failure to spread hay in the field.

She looked at her truck and then back at Amos, trying to think of another course of action, but there was no other way. The cattle would have to wait. She had no choice but to take him home.

She stepped up on the running board and pushed Amos across the bench to the passenger side. He fell over against the door and cracked his head against the window. He gasped and grabbed the side of his head. Eva climbed in behind the wheel, started the engine, and pulled into the road.

Amos grabbed the dashboard and looked around, wild-eyed. "What's going on?" He gawked out the window and then jerked around to see Eva behind the wheel. "What the hell are you doing?" he shouted.

"I'm taking you home."

"What? You have no right. Who the hell do you think you are, hijacking my truck and all?" He grabbed the wheel and tried to wrestle control away from her. The truck veered toward the ditch. Eva hit him on the bridge of his nose with her fist. He let go of the wheel and fell back against the passenger door and she pulled the truck back into the road.

He sat back in the seat, holding his nose. "You hit me."

"I had no choice. You almost killed us."

His eyes filled with tears. "I think you broke my nose. Am I bleedin?"

"Of course not. Don't be such a baby. I didn't hit you that hard."

He wiped his eyes, sat up straight, and scowled at her. "Stop the truck and let me drive."

"You're too drunk to drive."

He gave her a sour look, but he didn't argue the point. "Where are you taking me?"

"I'm driving you home."

He seemed to chew on that for a moment, and then said in a low voice, "I can't go home. I don't live there anymore."

Eva glanced at him and then looked back at the road. "Where do you live?"

"I'm staying with Toby Vess. Take me to his house."

Eva saw the slump in his shoulders and the downturned corners of his mouth. Maybe his drunkenness wasn't the result of a festive celebration after all.

"All right," she said. "Toby's house it is."

Amos crossed his arms over his chest and rode along silently with a taciturn scowl on his face the rest of the way to Toby's house. Eva pulled into Toby's driveway and followed Amos as he staggered over the walkway to the front door. He stopped on the stoop and grabbed one of its posts to steady himself. Then he opened the door and went into a little sitting room where Stogie Morris was stretched out on a sofa clad in nothing but his long johns. He lay snoring on his back, his arm dangling down to the floor where his hand rested on the mouth of a half-empty mason jar. The room stank of alcohol and stale sweat.

Amos teetered past the sofa and through a doorway behind it. A moment later, Toby came through the doorway. He flinched when he saw Eva. "Eva, what are you doing here?"

"I found Mr. Hukstep passed out drunk in his truck on Whiskey Road. He wasn't fit to drive. I set out to drive him home, but he told me to bring him here." She gestured at Stogie. "I take it you're running an alcohol rehabilitation center out of your home."

Toby shook his head. "No, ma'am. There's absolutely no rehabilitation going on here."

She gave him a wry look. "A flophouse for aged drunks, perhaps?"

"That's about the size of it, I'm afraid."

Toby volunteered nothing more. He was averse to spreading gossip, and Eva was against gathering it.

"I need a ride to my truck," she said.

Toby drove her back to her truck. When he pulled up behind it and stopped, she got out and started to shut the door.

"Merry Christmas, Eva."

She paused and stared at him blankly. "Merry Christmas to you," she said with no conviction.

She shut the door and Toby waved as he drove past her. His truck swept around a turn and disappeared. A light snow had begun to fall. She looked up at the pewter cloud cover. From the looks of the sky and the smell and feel of the air, she guessed it would be a deep snow. Christmas wouldn't be merry, but at least it would be white.

PART III

THE NEW YEAR

Chapter 22

The Fix

A few days after the turn of the year, on a sunny, cold day at noon, Billy sat in his truck with the engine idling and the heater running full blast. He was parked under a big sycamore tree facing a little white clapboard church on the other side of a dirt lot. Ivy Ridge Baptist Church was founded by a small group of slaves in the early 1800s; a few colored families worshipped there now and did their best to maintain it, but the building was in sad shape.

Billy had driven by the church countless times recently without noticing how much it had deteriorated. It had always been a plain little box with no stained glass and no steeple, but now it was close to falling down. The wooden arch over its front stoop was rotten and buckling, and its wrought iron railing was loose and leaning to one side at a forty-five-degree angle. The dirt-streaked windows flanking the front door were cracked, and the door, once bright red, had faded to a dull pink. The felt roof tiles were worn and curled with patches of tar paper peeking through.

Billy stared at patches of snow from the Christmas storm that still lay in shady spots in the lot and at layers of white-capped mountains that stretched out on the horizon and remembered Ollie Shanks, the preacher at Ivy Ridge when Billy was a boy. Six days a week he worked as the lead farmhand on the Kirby farm, and on the seventh day he preached. Billy's father worked Ollie hard, paid him little, and blamed him for everything that went wrong, but Ollie was unfailingly kind to Billy. One of Billy's earliest memories was sitting in Ollie's lap and steering a mule-drawn wagon with

Ollie's calloused hands covering his on the reins.

Billy gazed at the church pensively, puzzling over why he had stopped there. He had driven deep into Whippoorwill Hollow to Cecil Garrison's house and bought a gallon of moonshine. On the way back out to Fox Run when he came around a bend in the road, the sun glanced off the church windows into his eyes and he spontaneously pulled into the dirt parking lot and stopped under the sycamore.

He looked down at the gallon jar of shine that sat beside him on the truck seat. The demise of Billy's dream of a life with Jolene had set him adrift. His newfound lust for life, borne out of the threat of death at Amos' hands, had faded away and he had broken down again. Amos and Stogie turned to whiskey to ease their pain; that morning he had thought he would do the same, but it didn't seem like such a good idea now. He lifted the jar and moved it away from him, setting it on the floorboard under the glove compartment.

He was staring at the church thinking about Amos, Jolene, and Stogie when Toby's county patrol truck pulled into the lot. Toby got out and climbed into Billy's Dodge, and when he swung his legs into the cab, his foot bumped against the jar. He raised his eyebrows and nudged it aside with his boot. "Looks like you're fixin to pull a big drunk."

Billy didn't reply.

"It won't help," Toby said. "When the shine wears off, you'll be more miserable than you are now."

"I don't need advice about hooch. I'm old enough to know what to do with it."

Toby nodded. "I reckon you are." He took off his gloves and held his hands up to the heater's vent. "I've been looking for you. Blakey's getting out of jail."

Billy looked at Toby, surprised. "When?"

"Two weeks from tomorrow."

"I thought he had two years to go."

"They decided to put him on parole. They've assigned him to a parole officer in Richmond."

"Why Richmond? Why not here?"

"He says he's not coming home. Says he wants no part of his past." Toby paused and then said, "He claims he wants no part of you."

Billy looked out the window. A flock of starlings streaked across a field beside the church. They alit on the top line of a barbed-wire fence, twelve or fifteen of them side by side between two weathered posts. Their black feathers glistened in the sun.

Toby said, "Sheriff Grundy is worried about it. So am I."

Billy turned back to Toby. "Why?"

"The sheriff called the warden at the state pen and asked about Blakey's state of mind. Apparently, he's been on his best behavior the last few years. He told the parole board he wouldn't come back here if he was released because he wants to start a new life away from all his past troubles. The parole board believes him. The warden agrees with them. They think he's reformed." Toby opened and closed his hands. He blew on them and held them out to the heater again. "Sheriff Grundy and I ain't so sure. He nursed some mighty big grudges against you and others when we had him locked in the county jail during his trial. Maybe he's put all that behind him, but there's no way to know for certain. We plan to keep a wary eye out for him when he gets out. We think you should do the same."

Billy stared at the starlings and thought about Blakey. A cold wind blew and the birds leaned into it, fluttering their wings to hold their position on the barbed wire. Billy recalled the last words Blakey had said to him: "You made me what I am." He remembered the look of hatred on Blakey's face at the end of his sentencing hearing.

"When Blakey gets out," Toby said, "it might be a good idea to carry that .357 Magnum with you."

Billy contemplated the prospect of firing a gun at his son. He didn't think he could do it, even in self-defense. His chin quivered.

Toby put his hand on Billy's arm. "Maybe the parole board is right. Maybe prison changed him for the better. Let's hope so." Toby gave Billy's arm a gentle pat, got out of the truck, and drove away.

Billy stared at the old church balefully. The wind whistled through the truck window. The cab vibrated rhythmically with the idle of the engine, and the heater emitted a steady whine. Billy's thoughts drifted back thirty years to the only time he had ever set foot inside the sanctuary of Ivy Ridge.

It was a scorching hot day in July. Billy had stood in the dirt lot, staring at the church's broken windows and at the dark red paint that had been splashed on its walls. He crossed the lot, opened the door, and stepped inside. A threadbare maroon carpet ran down a center aisle. It had been shredded into tatters. Ten rows of dark-stained pinewood pews had been overturned and chopped to pieces. A half-circle altar at the front of the sanctuary had been reduced to a pile of kindling. A lectern that stood in the pulpit lay on its side, battered and broken. Hanging on the wall behind the pulpit was a large painting. As best Billy could determine from the slashed strips still clinging to its frame, it had depicted Jesus in a white robe on his knees, praying. The same dark red paint that streaked the walls outside had been poured on the floor and thrown on the interior walls and on most of the wreckage. Several empty buckets lay beside the broken pews to Billy's left and one lay on the ruined carpet at his feet. He picked it up and read the label. *Dunn-Edwards Paints, Semi-Gloss Exterior,* and below that, *Arabian Red.*

The door opened behind Billy. He turned to see Ollie Shanks and his son, Patrick. Ollie was in his late eighties by then, still tall and strong, but cataracts had blinded him. He clutched Patrick's elbow with both hands and stared into space. "The devil did this, Mr. Billy," he said. "We don't have the money to rebuild." His milky eyes watered up and tears slid down his withered cheeks. "I called on you cause I didn't know who else to turn to."

Billy looked at Patrick. Patrick had succeeded his father as the preacher at Ivy Ridge. He was tall and strong like his father, but he wasn't blind and his eyes weren't tearful. They were angry and fierce, and they bored into Billy.

Billy turned away from Patrick to conceal his shame. He dropped the empty paint can to the shredded carpet at his feet and swept his eyes over the ruined sanctuary once more. "I'll hire Tom Wilcox to rebuild the place," he said softly. "We'll start work in the morning. I'll pay for a complete

restoration and any improvements you wish to make. You have my word."
He walked around Patrick and Ollie, avoiding Patrick's glare, and went
outside.

He was making his way unsteadily toward his truck feeling nauseated
and dizzy when Ollie called out to him.

"Mr. Billy."

Billy stopped, but couldn't bring himself to face them. He wanted to
flee in the worst way, but he couldn't run from Ollie. Patrick led his father
across the lot and placed him directly in front of Billy.

"You don't understand, Mr. Billy," the old man said. "We don't want a
handout. We want a loan. It'll take us a while to raise the money, but we'll
pay you back."

"Mr. Kirby don't want us to pay," Patrick said, glaring at Billy.

Billy dropped his eyes to the ground. He took off his straw hat and
wiped sweat from the headband with his handkerchief. Rivulets of sweat
ran down his back and sides inside his shirt.

"Now hold on, Patrick," Ollie said. "It ain't right to put it on Mr. Billy
just because he's rich. We can pay our own way once we got the time to
raise the money. We don't need no charity."

"It ain't charity," Patrick said. "It's justice."

Billy took a deep breath and looked Patrick in the eye. "I'll pay for
everything," he said. He walked around them, got in his truck, and drove
out of the lot toward Fox Run.

When Billy turned right onto Whiskey Road, he coasted down the hill
and stopped in the clearing by his barn. He rolled down the window and
took several deep breaths. The air near Little Bear River was fresher and
cleaner than other places, and the rapids below the one-lane bridge made a
soothing sound. Proximity to the river had always calmed him.

When he recovered some peace of mind, he allowed himself to look at
his freshly painted barn. Billy had bought the paint at the Fruit Growers Co-
op, a dark red shade: Dunn-Edwards, Arabian Red. Buck Abel painted the
barn for him and left the excess in the tool shed so Billy could return it to
the co-op for a refund.

Billy gave up on Blakey that day. The boy was twenty-three that summer, and Billy could no longer tell himself his son would grow out of his cruel ways. From then on, he didn't try to reason with him or discipline him or control him. He merely tried to clean up after him. He apologized to Blakey's victims, plied them with money, and begged them not to press charges. His efforts served to postpone Blakey's demise until he went too far and committed crimes that couldn't be papered over.

Sitting in his truck in the dirt lot thirty years later, Billy heaved a deep sigh and surveyed the old church building again. No doubt it hadn't been renovated since he repaired it thirty years ago. He resolved to talk to Leo, Ollie's grandson, who had succeeded Patrick as the preacher, about a donation.

The starlings sprang up from the fence and streaked a black line over the church. Billy watched them in the distance until they were only a small dark speck on the horizon. He gave the church a last look, shifted the truck into gear, and headed back to Fox Run.

The following week, Billy was sitting by the stove when Toby strolled into the store at noon and grabbed his usual grape Nehi from the drink case. He walked over to the stove and greeted Billy. Billy was mired in depression and didn't want to socialize with Toby or anyone else. He wanted to be left alone to plumb the depths of his misery about Blakey and Jolene and his myriad mistakes.

"I'm feelin poorly," he said to Toby. "I'd appreciate it if you'd move on and leave me be."

A half smile creased Toby's face. "What happened to the friendly cuss that used to sit here by the stove tellin tall tales and crackin jokes with his buddies?"

"Just leave me be," Billy mumbled.

Toby's smile went away. He took off his hat, ran his hand over his close-cropped gray hair, and seemed to be thinking something over. Whatever was on Toby's mind, Billy wanted none of it. "I asked you politely to leave me be," he said gruffly.

"Stogie tells me you asked Jolene to marry you," Toby said.

"I don't want to talk about it."

Toby sipped his Nehi. "What did she say?"

Billy heaved a disgusted sigh. Maybe if he answered Toby's question, he would leave him in peace. "She turned me down."

Toby shook his head. "I'm sure to God relieved to hear that."

Billy scowled. "Why do you say that?"

"If Jolene accepted your proposal, Amos would kill himself. Jolene would kill herself over Amos. You'd kill yourself over Jolene. Stogie would kill himself just to keep pace with the rest of you."

Billy grimaced and rubbed his temples. "I'm in no mood for humor."

"I'm not joking. At least about Amos and Jolene."

"I said I don't want to talk about it."

Toby was quiet for a long while. He finished off his Nehi and sat down beside Billy. "Amos and Stogie are still living with me," he said. "They're a couple of sad sacks. They drink till they drop, sleep it off, and start in again as soon as they wake up. You're sober, but you don't seem much better off than they are."

Billy scowled. "I'm miserable, but it's none of your concern. Go away and leave me alone."

"There's only one way you'll ever be happy again. Amos has to go back to Jolene and you have to move on and leave them alone. Jolene knows that, but you and Amos can't seem to figure it out."

Billy slapped his hand on the bench. "Damn it, Toby. I don't want to talk about this."

Toby waved his hand in the air. "All right, all right. I'll leave you alone." He stood and went to put his empty bottle in a wooden crate by the drink case. He hesitated there for a moment and then returned to the stove. "You're the only one who can fix this big mess, you know."

Billy glowered at Toby. "How the hell can I fix it?"

"I don't know. I'm not smart enough to figure it out. All I know is Jolene can't fix it because Amos won't listen to her. Amos can't fix it because he's drunk all the time and he's dull-brained even when he's sober. That leaves you. You've spent your life fixing problems so they come out in your favor. If you'd set your mind to it, maybe this one time you could figure a way to make things come out in favor of someone else." Toby headed toward the door.

Billy said, "Next time you come in here, I'll thank you to keep your advice to yourself."

Toby stopped and looked back at Billy. "Whenever people around here need a helping hand, you give it to them even when they're not your close friends and you didn't cause their problems. Amos is your lifelong friend. He's broken down because of deeds you did a long time ago. All I'm asking is for you to take a break from feeling sorry for yourself and try to figure out how to help him get his life back."

Billy glared at Toby. Toby stared back at him evenly. Then he turned and left the store.

The following week, Billy sat in the store just after dark reading an article in the *Jeetersburg Daily Progress*. Doctors in South Africa had performed the first human-to-human heart transplant in December when Billy was in the hospital. They placed the heart of a twenty-five-year-old woman in a fifty-four-year-old man's chest. The man lived eighteen days and drew his last breath three days before Christmas. Then at the turn of the year, three doctors at Stanford University in California performed the first adult heart transplant in the United States. That patient died fifteen days later. The article explained that the patients' immune systems considered the new hearts a threat and attacked them and killed them. The heart was a delicate organ, the doctors said. When diseased, it was difficult to mend, and when it ceased to function, it had thus far been impossible to replace. Billy stared at the newspaper, pondering this.

"Blakey's out."

Billy looked up from the paper to see Toby Vess standing beside the stove.

"His parole officer says he rented a flat in Richmond," Toby said. "He's looking for a job down there. Shows no interest in coming home so far. The Richmond police and his parole officer are keeping a close eye on him, but they can't watch him full time. You should be careful the next few weeks."

Billy stared at the shadows cast by the outer aisle of shelves on the far wall. He wasn't worried about what Blakey might do to him. Billy's life wasn't worth living anyway, given his choices thus far. His thoughts rolled down a well-worn path through his foolish mistakes and their manifestations in his present miserable circumstances, from his broken marriage to Mary Jo through his ruptured relationship with Blakey to his ruination of Amos' life. Most of the heartache he had caused couldn't be fixed.

He sighed despondently and looked down at the newspaper in his lap. Toby's words about Amos came to his mind yet again: "You're the only one who can fix this big mess." Difficult to mend; impossible to replace, the doctors said. Billy folded the paper and laid it on the bench beside him. "I've been trying to think of a way to convince Amos to go home to Jolene."

Toby perked up. "You come up with any ideas?"

"There's no quick and easy way, but I might be able to reason with him if you help me."

"What do you want me to do?"

"Sober him up and give me some time alone with him."

"I can't sober him up. He lives with a jar of shine glued to his right hand. He sleeps with it so he can get drunk quick if he happens to wake up sober during the night."

"I can't reason with him when he's drunk. Take him to a place where he can't get to his jar. Take him to the hunting cabin."

"He won't go. He only leaves the house to buy a new batch of shine. I can't even get him to ride the piddling three miles to Lacey Bibb's pool hall to drink beer."

"Tell him he has to go with you or you'll throw him out of your house. He's got nowhere else to live. He'll have to do what you say."

Toby stroked his chin. "That might work, but I'd have to bring Stogie along. Amos won't go anywhere without him."

"Bring him along, then. Take them to the cabin Friday night. I'll be waiting for you, but don't tell them I'll be there or they'll refuse to come. When you get there, I'll deal with Amos."

"What about Stogie? You need to set things straight with him, too."

"I can't solve both problems in one sitting. I'll fix things up with Stogie later. It shouldn't be that hard. He's told lies and cheated and such. He understands the ways of the world. Amos is the hard case. He walked the straight and narrow all his life. He doesn't understand the weaknesses of others. When we're up there, you'll have to keep Stogie occupied while I try to convince Amos to forgive Jolene."

"I don't think you can do it," Toby said. "Amos' hurt runs deep. I'm not sure he could forgive her if he wanted to. What's more, he won't listen to you. He hates you. A meeting between the two of you could lead to disaster."

"We can take a risk, or we can leave things where they are."

Toby nodded his head slowly. "I'll give it a try, but whatever you do up there, be careful." He put on his hat and stood. "While we're fixing problems, there's another needy soul I'd like you to take care of. Homer Sprouse. He rammed his Pontiac Bonneville into a telephone pole. He's got no insurance and he can't pay to fix it. I want you to foot the bill for the repairs."

Billy frowned. "What the hell's it got to do with me?"

"Jolene's Hudson ... It's complicated. Just take my word for it that the accident wasn't his fault. He works hard and he's a good man with a family to feed. He can't work without his car and he can't afford the repair bill."

Billy knew Homer. He was no saint, but he wasn't a bad sort. If he was facing certain ruination, shelling out a small sum of money that was of no consequence to Billy was an easy fix. "Tell Homer to bring his repair estimate by the store in the morning."

Toby touched the rim of his hat. "You're a good man, Billy Kirby." He smiled. "Sometimes." Toby turned and walked out of the store.

Chapter 23

Estrangements

The next morning, Jolene stood in the double-wide's second bedroom, the girls' old room, wearing a red-and-white-checked shirt and jeans, one of her work-around-the-house outfits. She stripped the single bed and put clean sheets and a navy blue bedspread on it. She and Amos used the girls' room for storage after they moved out. When Porter agreed to stay with her, it was cluttered with old furniture, holiday decorations, Jolene's sewing machine, Amos' back issues of *Popular Mechanics*, and old clothes they hadn't yet given to Goodwill. It had taken her and Porter most of a day to move the items worth keeping out to the tool shed and to dispose of the junk in the burn barrel. When they finished cleaning the room, only the furniture remained: a single bed, a bunk bed, a bureau, and a chifforobe.

That morning just after dawn with all the clutter removed, the room seemed larger and more cheerful. She stood, holding the soiled bedding in her arms, and looked around at the bedroom and smiled as she recalled how happy she'd been when she and Amos first moved in. When they married, her father let them live rent-free in a cinderblock house on his farm that had three dingy little rooms, each about the size of a jail cell. They hated the little house, but they couldn't afford to live anywhere else. The only work Amos could find was a low-paying job in the maintenance department at Murray's Visible Records in Jeetersburg. Jolene had cleaned houses and washed and ironed clothes for some of the well-off farmers to make ends meet. When Amos worked his way up to print press operator, they were able to set aside Jolene's income each month, but the meager savings accumulated slowly. To make the money required to buy a place of their own, Amos hatched the idea of owning and managing a trailer park.

Jolene sat on the single bed, set the bedding down beside her, and ran her hand over the clean bedspread. Navy blue was her oldest daughter's favorite color. When Amos thought they'd saved enough to try his trailer park gambit, Julie was a toddler, Clara was an infant, and Jolene was pregnant with Linda. Amos bought the land with their savings and a big bank loan, but the property had drainage problems that prevented it from absorbing sewage waste. They'd had to install an elaborate system of French ditches that cost them so much they couldn't start up the trailer park for another five years. For Jolene, that was the most trying time of their marriage. The girls almost drove her crazy, bouncing off the walls of the cinderblock house like bugs trapped inside a jar.

When she and Amos finally loaded their belongings and the girls into their truck, drove to the double-wide, and opened the door, she was stunned by the new carpeting and gleaming kitchen fixtures and furniture, but it was the expanse of space that took her breath away. The trailer seemed as big as a palace, 28 feet wide by 48 feet long, 1300 square feet in all, with a kitchen-dining-sitting area that the manufacturer called "the great room," a master bedroom with its own bathroom, a little washroom, and a second bedroom and bathroom. The girls charged inside and ran from one end of the train of rooms to the other, shrieking and laughing. Jolene threw her arms around Amos and kissed him and he lifted her off her feet and twirled her around.

Jolene smiled again, remembering Amos' hearty laughter rumbling through the trailer, but her smile faded when she pondered how long it had been since she'd heard him laugh. Twenty years, she guessed. She gazed at the top bunk. Linda, the youngest, had slept there. She searched her memory for an instance of Amos' laughter since Linda moved out. Only once, she thought. About 1950 Julie left her two kids with them for a weekend, and Amos had laughed when he wrestled with Tommy on the bedroom floor. She wondered if he'd ever laugh again, and if he did, she wondered if she'd be beside him to hear it.

She picked up the bedding and cradled it in her lap. When she confronted Amos at Toby's house, she'd told him she was through begging him to come home, but her resolve had weakened. She missed Amos and wanted him back, but she could think of nothing she could do to convince him to forgive her. So she pined for him and drifted and hoped for a miracle.

She sighed heavily, stood, and went into the living room. Porter was in the kitchen on the phone with his back turned to her, talking quietly. As she entered the room, she heard him say, "I'll do what you want, but I miss you." There was a pause. Then he said, "All right, if that's the way it has to be." He hung up the phone, leaned against the counter, folded his arms over his chest, and bowed his head.

Jolene took the bedding into the washroom and returned to the kitchen, where Porter had set out plates of food and cups of coffee. He insisted on cooking breakfast every morning "to earn his keep." He sat on a stool at the counter and Jolene took a seat beside him. She picked up her knife and fork and sliced a piece of Canadian bacon. "Was that your wife on the phone?"

Porter nodded.

"Are things any better between you?"

He ran his finger around the edge of his plate and shook his head.

Jolene set the knife and fork down and swiveled her stool toward him. Her knee touched his thigh. She put her hand on his forearm. "Go to her. Tell her how much you love her. Tell her how sorry you are for the times you hurt her."

The morning sun coming through the kitchen window glinted in his black eyes. "I can't. She's staying with her folks. Her dad won't let me see her."

"Talk to him. Tell him how much you love her."

"He won't believe me," Porter said. He leaned on his forearms on the counter and looked down at his plate. "It's not hard to see how he looks at it. I hurt Maureen really bad and I ran off. For years I was a drunk and a bully. He's got good cause to hate me."

Jolene stared out the window. The sun cast a pale gray hue on the western face of Hawk's Nest Mountain. She thought about how she would feel if one of the girls' husbands had been cruel and selfish and then claimed to have reformed. She wouldn't take his word for it, especially after a big relapse of drunkenness. She looked at Porter pensively for a few moments. Then she took his hand and held it on her knee. "Tell me what made you change."

He looked down at their clasped hands. "I hit bottom."

"What do you mean?"

Porter was quiet for a while. "Last winter I got drunk with an army buddy down in Wise County. We were looking for a thrill. I stole a Cadillac in Big Stone Gap for a joyride." He made a wry face. "I didn't get much enjoyment out of it. I ran her through a fence and rolled her over. Totaled the car and almost killed my buddy, but I came through without a scratch." He closed his eyes and blew out a heavy breath. "I was facing five to ten years in the state pen."

Jolene tightened her grip on his hand. "How did you get out of trouble?"

"Grandpa made it all go away. He paid for all the damages and worked out a plea deal with the prosecutor. He came and got me out of jail and drove me straight to the rehab center in Roanoke. On the way, he told me stories about my daddy and all the people he hurt. He said I was headed in the same direction, to a place where everyone hates you, including the people who started out loving you."

Porter withdrew his hand, stood, and looked out the window. "When I was growing up, Daddy would get drunk and beat my mom. She died of consumption when I was a little boy and he turned on me." Porter gripped the edge of the counter and looked down at his hands. "Sometimes I hated him so much I wanted to kill him."

After a few moments, he let go of the counter and put his hands in his pockets. "Grandpa told me a hundred times before I stole that Cadillac that I needed to straighten up, but he'd never compared me to Daddy. When I dried out in the clinic, I thought about all I had done and I knew he was right." He shook his head back and forth slowly. "That was the bottom for me. I knew how much Daddy hurt me, and I realized I hurt Maureen that same way. I couldn't live with it." He looked at Jolene, determination in his eyes. "That's why I can't slide back again. I won't be like him. I won't."

She rubbed his back with the palm of her hand and put her head on his shoulder. "You're not like your father."

He put his arm around her waist and they stood there for a while. Then he said, "I'd better get going to the store." He went in the bedroom and came back out with his coat. "Thanks for talking to me. I'll see you tonight." He put on his coat and went outside.

Jolene went to the window and watched the Plymouth pull out of the trailer park and head up Whiskey Road. She stood staring after it for a long time.

Chapter 24

The Confrontation

As Toby predicted, Amos didn't want to go to the cabin. Neither did Stogie, but Toby did what Billy suggested. He threatened to throw them out of his house if they didn't go. Amos agreed on the condition they take a case of moonshine with them. Stogie agreed because he didn't want to be left alone.

Friday night when Toby carried a box of groceries out to his Ford pickup, he found Amos' crate of mason jars sitting in the truck bed. While Amos and Stogie were inside the house fetching their rifles and rolling up sleeping bags, Toby removed the crate from the truck and stashed it in his garage. Then he herded the two old codgers into the truck, started her up, and began the long drive from Saddleback Cove to the cabin.

It was a cold, clear night. A yellow half-moon cast streaks of gray mist through the trees. Amos sat between Toby and Stogie. Just after Toby passed the dam, unlocked the gate to the park, and drove through it, Amos withdrew a jar of moonshine from the big side-pocket of his hunting jacket and took a swig. Toby cursed under his breath. Amos cradled the jar in his lap and sipped from it as they rode along. He made no conversation.

Stogie sat by the passenger door, staring into the night, trancelike. He had kept pace with Amos drink for drink since the kidnapping until two days ago, when he appeared to have quit cold turkey. His somber sobriety and uncharacteristically quiet demeanor made Toby uneasy.

"What are you thinking about?" he asked Stogie.

"The day after Thanksgiving, 1934."

"What brought that to mind?"

"I almost shot Billy up on Pine Top that day. I know it was 1934 because Polly died in '44, and it happened ten years before she died. I tend to count time based on when she died."

Toby's uneasiness grew. "What do you mean you almost shot him?"

"I was on my deer stand when a buck with a trophy rack hopped out of the brush in front of that big rock up there that's shaped like a goose egg."

"I know the spot."

"I squeezed off a quick shot. My bullet whizzed past the buck and ricocheted off the rock. The buck jumped into the brush and ran off, and then I saw Billy. He had been tracking the buck and he was standing behind him when I fired. My bullet made a mark on the rock just above his head."

The truck plunged into a deep rut and stalled out. Toby restarted the engine, accelerated out of the hole, and wrestled the truck back onto the road.

Stogie gripped the dashboard and grimaced. "If I'd aimed a few inches lower that day, I'd have killed Billy."

"I don't see how that matters now if—"

"It might have mattered a great deal, or it might not have mattered at all."

"What do you mean?"

"I don't know when Billy worked his way into Polly's bed. If he didn't get to her until after Thanksgiving of '34, a fatal stray bullet that day would have kept him away from Polly. But if he'd already slept with her by then, it wouldn't have made any difference."

Toby rubbed his jaw. "I don't think that mishap is a healthy subject to dwell on. You ought to let it go."

"I'd let it go if I could, but I can't stop thinking about it. It won't let go of me."

Toby steered the pickup around the last bend in the fire road, pulled up to the cabin, and parked beside a black Dodge D-100 half-ton pickup truck, Billy's truck. Billy was visible in the cabin window, sitting at the table beside a lit kerosene lamp.

Stogie glared at the truck and then at Billy. "You didn't tell us Billy would be here."

"He asked me to bring Amos up here to talk things out. You insisted on coming along."

"Talking won't help." Stogie got out of the truck, grabbed his hunting rifle from the rack over the back window, and headed toward the cabin.

Toby jumped out of the truck and ran after him. "Stogie. Don't!"

Stogie kicked open the cabin door, stepped inside, and leveled his rifle on Billy.

Billy put his hands in the air.

Toby came up behind Stogie. "I unloaded your rifle before we left the house."

Stogie lowered the rifle and glared at Billy. Toby took it from him and propped it against the wall.

Billy dropped his hands and blew out a long breath.

Stogie fell into a cane chair by the table.

Billy said, "I'm sorry I hurt you so bad, Stogie."

"You're a liar. You're not the least bit sorry."

There was the sound of grinding outside, and they all looked out the window at Toby's truck. Its engine kicked over and revved up. It lurched toward the cabin, turned left, and pitched into the creek below the spring, sinking up to its hubs in mud and plowing its bumper into the opposite bank. It stalled out and its horn blared.

"Damn it," Toby said. He ran out to the truck while Billy and Stogie watched from the cabin door. He opened the truck door and pulled Amos off the steering wheel. He was unconscious, but Toby found no wounds or blood on him. He dragged Amos out of the truck, lugged him into the cabin, and stretched him out on one of the bunks while Billy hustled outside to douse a towel in spring water. He sat on the bunk beside Amos and swabbed his brow. Amos' eyelids fluttered and he groaned.

"You all right, Amos?" Billy said.

Amos' eyes came into focus. His face twisted into a sour pile of wrinkles and he swatted Billy's hand away. He lifted himself up on his elbow and glared at Toby. "You should have told me he would be here." He jerked free from Billy, got up, and staggered toward the door, but he lost his balance and fell into Toby's arms.

Toby dragged him back to the bed and stretched him out on it again. "You need to stay down for a spell," Toby said. "Your balance is gone. You must have taken a blow to the head."

"The crash didn't make him dizzy," Stogie said. "It's the shine."

Amos moaned. His face was the color of mildewed plaster. He closed his eyes and began to snore.

Toby checked his pulse and felt his forehead. "Stogie's right. It's the liquor. He smuggled a jar of hooch into the truck and drank all of it on the way up here. It's a miracle he didn't pass out before we got here."

"I never knew Amos to drink so much," Billy said.

"He didn't drink at all before he found out what you did with Jolene," Stogie said. "Now he's drunk all the time."

Billy wiped Amos' face down with the cold towel. "If I could go back in time and change what I did, I would."

Stogie snorted. "You wouldn't do any different. You took what you wanted every chance you got, and you never cared a whit about anybody else. You still don't."

Billy fell silent. He sat on the bed with Amos for a while. Then he folded the towel and placed it on Amos' forehead. He put on his coat, went outside, and sat on the front stoop in the cold.

After a while, Toby went outside to take a look at his truck and Billy joined him. They tried to dig the truck out of the creek while Stogie watched over Amos. The old Ford was too mired in mud to back out under its own power, and they couldn't use Billy's Dodge to pull it out because they didn't have a chain or a rope to hitch to the tow bar. They finally gave up and went back inside the cabin. Stogie had crawled inside his sleeping bag and had fallen asleep on his bunk. Amos snored loudly on another bunk.

Billy sat down at the table and turned the kerosene lamp down low. Toby tossed a couple of logs in the stove, stoked the fire, and sat across the table from Billy. The fire warmed the room. They took off their hats and coats. Toby took off his muddy boots, stripped off wet socks, and draped them over the back of a chair to dry out. He propped his bare feet on a chair beside the stove, swiped his hand over his crown, and looked at Billy. "What do you plan to do with Amos?"

"He'll sober up by morning. I'll talk to him then."

"Be careful what you say to him. He's obviously in a bad way and he's unpredictable."

Billy nodded toward Amos' inert carcass. "Nothing I can say will make him more miserable than he is now."

Toby looked at Amos and sighed. He was tired and frustrated. "If we come through this, I suggest you consider mending your ways. Two of your three best friends have tried to murder you for betraying their trust."

"I guess I'm lucky you never married, or you'd make it a clean sweep."

Toby paused, irritated. "It's not a laughing matter. You broke down two good men. Maybe next time you could consider how your actions hurt your friends before you do whatever the hell makes you feel good."

Billy folded his hands on the table, stared at them, and said nothing.

Toby stripped to his long johns and crawled into his sleeping bag on his bunk. He watched Billy blow out the kerosene lamp, move to the bunk on the opposite wall, and lie down. The branch of an elm tree split the moonlight pouring in the window into two shafts. One fell across the kitchen table. The other fell across Billy's chest and face. He was still staring at the ceiling when Toby fell asleep.

Chapter 25

The Advocate

Billy arose well before dawn, started a fire in the woodstove, and cooked breakfast. Toby arose early, too, and Billy served him pancakes at the table. Stogie crawled from bed pale and listless. He refused breakfast. Amos stirred in his sleeping bag and groaned a few times, but he didn't wake up.

When they finished eating, Toby asked Billy, "What can I do to help you?"

"Go hunting. Take Stogie with you. I'll stay here with Amos."

"All right. We'll get out of your way."

"I'm not going anywhere," Stogie said.

"Get your rifle." The tone of Toby's voice closed off debate about the matter. Stogie got his rifle and he and Toby went outside.

Billy watched them cross the creek to the foot of Buckhorn Mountain in the moonlight. He sat at the table and nursed a cup of coffee, waiting for Amos to wake up. It was well after sunrise when Amos finally sat up and looked around groggily. Billy was still at the table, drinking coffee. Amos scowled at him.

"Where are the others?"

"They're hunting."

Amos climbed out of bed, grabbed his jacket, and stomped to the door.

"Where are you going?" Billy said.

Amos went to the creek, climbed up on Toby's truck, and rummaged around in the truck bed. Then he came back inside the cabin and looked around the room. He went to the aluminum cabinet they kept canned goods in and rifled through it.

"What are you looking for?" Billy asked.

Amos slammed the cabinet door and punched it with his fist. He got down on his hands and knees and peered under the bunks. He stood and scowled at Billy with his hands on his hips. "Where's my hooch?"

"I don't know."

Amos ran his hand down his face. His hand shook and he was sweating. "You're a liar!"

"I'm not lying. I don't know where your shine is."

Amos glared at Billy for a few moments and then yelled, "You son of a bitch!" He lunged at Billy and lifted him out of his chair by his collar. "You and Toby got no right to hide my hooch! Where is it?"

Billy clawed at Amos' wrists. "I told you I don't know."

Amos shoved Billy backwards. His head hit the wall and stars burst before his eyes.

"Don't trifle with me, you bastard! I want my shine!"

Amos' breath reeked. "I don't know anything about your shine," Billy rasped. "Let me go."

Amos wrapped his fists around Billy's throat and choked him. "I want my shine now!"

Billy pulled at Amos' hands but his grip was too tight. He stuck out his tongue and tried to suck in air to no avail. His vision began to fade and he feared he would expire. When he felt he couldn't last any longer, he lifted his leg hard and fast and kneed Amos in the groin. Amos gasped, let go of Billy, and grabbed his crotch. Billy staggered away from him, grabbed the back of a chair to steady himself, and heaved in air.

Amos backed up to a bunk and fell over on his side into it, his hands between his legs.

"I didn't want to hurt you," Billy said. "You gave me no choice."

"You hid my hooch," Amos said through clenched teeth.

"I don't know what happened to your hooch. Maybe Toby did

something with it. I asked him to sober you up so I could talk to you."

Amos lay on his side for a while and then sat up on the edge of the bed and held his head in his hands. "Talk to me about what?"

"Jolene."

Amos dropped his hands and looked at Billy. His eyes were red and bloodshot. "I'd rather be dead than talk to you about Jolene." He stood, grabbed his rifle, and headed out the door.

"Where are you going?" Billy went to the window and watched Amos cross the creek and begin the climb up Pine Top Mountain. Billy cursed, picked up his rifle, and started the climb.

The sun was a yellow ball over Buckhorn Mountain. Shafts of gold speared through gaps in the trees and cast yellow stripes across the trail. The air was crisp and cold and a chill wind moaned in the pines. The path was icy and slick in shaded spots from the last snowstorm and Billy's legs were stiff and weak from his Thanksgiving ordeal, but he picked his way along until he reached the summit.

He circled around behind Amos' deer stand, a plank platform wedged in the fork of a big oak. Amos sat on the platform with his feet dangling from its planks, hanging his head listlessly. Sunlight glinted off the barrel of his rifle propped beside him on the stand.

"You figure Toby hid your hooch on this deer stand?" Billy said.

Amos flinched and turned. He scowled at Billy. "Leave me alone."

Billy climbed the ladder to the platform and sat next to him.

Amos stared sullenly into the woods. Neither of them said anything for a long time. Then Billy said, "Remember the time I ran that buck by this stand and you sat here like a statue of Humpty Dumpty and didn't shoot at him?"

"You shouldn't rile me. No telling what I might do if I lose my temper."

"I don't mean to rile you. I'm trying to make a point."

"What point?"

"Jolene was like that big buck."

"What the hell does that old buck have to do with Jolene?"

"Fifty years ago you drove Jolene into my arms the way I drove that buck past this deer stand, but I didn't let her walk on by. I reached out and grabbed her."

Amos squinted at Billy. "What do you mean I drove her to you?"

A gust of wind whipped across the stand and Billy pulled his collar tight around his neck. "I chased her hard and she fought me off for a long time. In the end, she gave in to me because you took her for granted. You ignored her. You didn't show her that you loved her."

Amos looked at the sun in the sky over Buckhorn Mountain and rubbed his eyes. "I didn't drive her to you. You chased her and caught her."

"I caught her because I told her she was beautiful. I told her she had the prettiest eyes in Selk County. I told her she was a jewel. All of which is true, but it was a shock to her because you never said a kind word to her. You acted like she was some washerwoman or a housemaid. She loved you, Amos. All you had to do was tell her you loved her back and she never would have given me the time of day. You can blame me for stealing her favors if it makes you feel better, but the truth is you squandered her love with your cold ways."

Amos turned to Billy and poked him in the chest. "You can't twist it all around. It's plain whose fault it is. You and Jolene are liars. You were never my friend and she never loved me or she wouldn't have laid down with you."

"You starved her for affection. I gave it to her and for a few weeks she thought she loved me, but that passed quickly. She came home to you and stayed with you. She had children by you. She loved you, not me, and she still loves you."

"If she loves me so much, she wouldn't agree to marry you."

Billy paused to digest the fact that Amos didn't know Jolene had turned him down. He had brought her note with him, hoping it would be a trump card in his discussion with Amos. Now he thought it might be powerful enough to win the game entirely. He withdrew the note from his pocket and handed it to Amos.

He took the note and looked at it. "What is this?"

"Read it."

Amos read the note. He handed it back to Billy and swiped his sleeve across his mouth. His face reddened and sweat popped out on his brow despite the cold. He pushed his hands down on the plank platform and hunched his shoulders.

"She loves you," Billy said. "She doesn't want me. She wants you."

"I don't believe it." Amos' voice was hoarse and strained.

Billy held the note up to the light and read from it. "I love Amos even though he doesn't love me anymore." Billy stared at Amos. "She had no reason to lie to me in this note. She loves you, and she thinks you don't love her. Is she right about that?"

Amos wiped the sweat from his brow. He took a deep breath and stared into the woods.

"Come on, Amos. Face it. You still love her. The fact is you can't live without her. That's why you would have blown your brains out if I hadn't stopped you. That's why you're trying to drink yourself to death. You're miserable because you love Jolene but your stubborn pride won't allow you to forgive her and go home to her."

"It's not about pride." Amos' breathing was heavy and irregular. He clutched his chest.

"What's eating at you, then?"

Amos shook his head back and forth slowly. "I can see her under that maple tree with you. Naked, brazen. Doing terrible, nasty things. I can't get past it." Amos' face was contorted.

"You've got to get past it, or it will kill you." Billy looked across the horizon at the summit of Buckhorn. A shaft of sunlight fought through an auburn cloud to bathe the crown of the mountain in an amber glow. "You don't understand the ways of the world, Amos. People deceive one another all the time. I've made a good living at it. Jolene's not like me, though. She's more like you, honest, genuine, straightforward, but I gave her something she needed. I was a man who wanted her for her charms. The only way she could have me was to cheat on you and lie about it, so she gave in to me, but it was out of character for her to deceive you. She made a mistake and lied about it by not telling you, but that's not who she is. She's a good woman you can trust, and she loves you. Let it go and forgive her."

Amos took a deep breath and spewed a stream of vapor into the air. "You don't understand how it feels when the person you love cuts your heart out." Amos turned to Billy. His eyes were hard. His voice was strained. "And you don't know what it's like when someone who pretended to be your friend is the one to cause her to do it."

Billy took a deep breath of his own. "I've made some hellacious big mistakes. Polly Morris was one of them. I ruined Stogie's life when I bedded her down. Jolene was another. I messed you up bad, too, but you have an advantage over Stogie." Billy thrust the note at Amos. He looked at it, but didn't take it. Billy took his hand, pressed the note into it, and forced his fingers to close around it. "Polly died before Stogie found out what she did with me. He doesn't know she still loved him when she and I were done. She told me so, but he won't believe anything I say and she's not here to tell him. Jolene's alive. You know how she feels about you. She wrote it down in that note. She wants you to come home and talk it out with her. That's what people who love each other are supposed to do. That's what you should do."

Amos shook his head. "I don't trust her."

Billy gazed at Buckhorn Mountain morosely. A spot halfway to the top caught his eye. The white bark poles of a stand of birch trees glittered in the sunlight. An old crumbling rock wall rimmed the base of the trees. Dirty snow lay on the ground on its lower side, a remnant of the last winter storm refusing to melt away in the cold shadow cast by the wall. Billy stared at the wall and the snow for a long time. Then he climbed down from the deer stand, stood on the ground, and looked up at Amos. "Go home, Amos. Your life won't be worth living without Jolene. You might as well be dead without her. Go home and forgive her."

Amos swiped his hand under his nose and looked down at Billy. "I can't." There was a strange look on Amos' face, an emotion Billy had never seen in his plain, unaffected aspect. In someone else's face Billy would have interpreted the expression as contrivance or guile, but Amos was too dull and straightforward to harbor such feelings. Amos turned away and cut short

Billy's study of his demeanor.

"I'm sorry," Billy said.

"Not sorry enough," Amos said without looking at Billy.

Billy turned away and walked down the trail. When he knew he had gone far enough to be out of Amos' sight, he stopped and took off his hat and rubbed his face. He couldn't win over Jolene and he couldn't convince Amos to go back to her. She was right. Billy couldn't give her the one thing in the world she wanted. He had done all he could do and he had failed.

He heaved a sigh and resumed picking his way down Pine Top. He had reached a tall white pine that marked the halfway point down the mountain when an explosion from the summit sounded and then echoed off the face of Buckhorn Mountain. The report reverberated through the range of mountains behind Buckhorn and then there was dead silence. Billy dropped his rifle. All the wind went out of his lungs. He grabbed his chest and gasped for air and stood frozen in place. That look Billy had seen on Amos' face just before he left him alone, the look in his eye Billy couldn't read, came clear to Billy: it was the look of someone plotting to kill himself. Billy propped his hands on his knees and breathed in and out deeply to fight off a sudden dizziness. It took him several minutes to regain enough wind and strength to begin the climb to Amos' deer stand.

Chapter 26

The Payback

Toby and Stogie reached the doghouse at the top of Buckhorn Mountain before dawn. Stogie crawled in and grunted as he hunched up against the side of the doghouse to make room for Toby. "This box is mighty cramped for two grown men."

"I built it for me alone. I didn't plan to babysit a second man."

"Then don't babysit me. Give me my bullets. I'll climb the tree next to the old apple orchard and sit on that stand. You can have this cramped box all to yourself."

"You're staying here with me."

Stogie leaned his head against the plywood wall and sighed. After a long silence, he said, "It was all for show, you know. I saw you take the shells out of my rifle before we left the house. I figured you did it because Billy was at the cabin. I planned out what I'd do before we got there. It was all a bluff. I wouldn't shoot Billy. I'm not that far gone."

"Your show was pretty convincing."

"Play-acting is all it was."

"For what purpose?"

"For sympathy, I guess. Trying to show all of you how bad it hurts so you'll feel sorry for me. Trying to show Billy most of all."

Toby looked out at the field through one of the slits in the wall. Dawn had come, and he could see the trees in the old apple orchard and the rusty barbed-wire fence that marked the park border.

"It pulls on your heartstrings awful hard," Stogie said, "to find out your wife chose to lay with another man. Especially if you loved her something fierce. And if that man pretended to be your friend."

"Maybe you ought to tell Billy how you feel and talk it through with him. He's not the same hard case who courted Polly behind your back. I think he'd take back what he did to you if he could."

"Maybe, but he shouldn't have done it in the first place."

Toby saw a big buck saunter over the crest of the summit on Stogie's side of the doghouse and amble toward the park fence and the apple orchard. The buck stopped twenty feet from the fence and dropped his head to nibble the leaves of a laurel bush. His rack was four feet wide and sported more than ten points. His sinewy chest rippled in the early morning sun. He was big and powerful, but he was an old buck, too. His muzzle was grizzled, his back swayed just a bit, and his neck and flanks bore scars from jousting with other bucks over many rutting seasons. He raised his head and gazed suspiciously at the doghouse, presenting his forequarter for a perfect shot. Toby withdrew Stogie's bullets from his pocket and offered them to him.

Stogie looked at the old buck for a few seconds. Then he turned to Toby and their eyes met. Toby knew what he would say before he said it.

"Let's let him pass," Stogie whispered.

Toby nodded and pocketed the ammunition. The buck lowered his head and resumed grazing. When he had finished, he strolled to the fence, sprang over it effortlessly, and trotted into the orchard, dappled sunlight sliding over his back.

"His rack would have looked mighty handsome on your trophy wall," Toby said, watching the proud buck prance through the orchard with his head held high.

"It takes years to grow a big rack like that. That buck's survived a lot of hunts, and this season will probably be his last." He swiped at his eyes. "I would have shot him when I was a young man, but I would have been wrong to do it. He's earned the right to go down in a fight with some young buck over a pretty doe in the next rut. He's earned what time he's got left."

As they stared wistfully at the old buck, a rifle report echoed over the valley between Pine Top and Buckhorn Mountains.

Stogie peered across the way and frowned. "That sounded like it came from Amos' stand. I thought they stayed in the cabin."

Toby withdrew his compact binoculars from his jacket pocket and scanned the summit of Pine Top. "No one's on Amos' stand." He returned the binoculars to his pocket. "We'd better go have a look-see."

They crawled out of the doghouse and began the long trek down Buckhorn Mountain. Toby was moving fast and Stogie couldn't keep up. "You go on ahead," Stogie said. "I'll come along as quick as I can. Meet you at Amos' stand."

Toby sprinted up Pine Top to the stand. Billy was already there, circling it.

"Who fired that shot?" Toby said.

Billy's face was bright red and his eyes were watery. He looked terrified and desperate. "It had to be Amos, but there's no sign of him."

Toby paused. "I locked all his ammunition in my glove compartment."

"Amos had to be the shooter. He and I were the only ones up here."

Toby took off his hat and slapped it against his thigh. "He must have brought ammo with him. I should have searched him." He put on his hat and looked at Billy. "What did you say to him?"

Billy swallowed hard. "I told him his life wouldn't be worth living without Jolene."

Toby was stunned. "You told Amos ..."

"If he shot himself, it's my fault." Billy's eyes welled with tears. He hunched his shoulders and made a choking sound.

Toby pushed his frustration aside and told himself his priority was to find Amos, not cast blame. He scanned around the deer stand for signs. A carpet of winter leaves pocked with patches of snow stretched out as far as he could see in every direction. Billy had tromped around the stand and obscured any trail Amos might have left near the oak.

"Where were you when you heard the shot?" Toby asked.

"Halfway down the mountain."

"Are you sure the shot came from here?"

"I think so, but the echo off Buckhorn could have fooled me." Billy looked around. "It could have come from a little way down the western slope." He pointed. "Down there somewhere."

Toby saw a trail of disturbed leaves on the crown of the mountain heading off to the west. He hurried a short ways down the slope on the other side, following the leaves. A hundred feet from the stand, he found a patch of dense brush with a pathway through it marked with a broken twig here and a displaced branch there. On the other side of the brush, Toby followed signs of a trail through a grove of white pines that ended at the edge of a steep cliff. The cliff dropped two hundred feet to the banks of a creek that Toby knew was a tributary to Little Bear River. On the lip of the cliff, he discovered two boot prints that had to belong to Amos. The placement of the tracks revealed that he had stood with his back facing the ravine. There was a narrow five-inch-long depression in the dirt between the two boot tracks. Toby stared at it until he realized what it represented. Amos had placed the butt of his rifle on the ground between his feet.

Toby looked out across the ravine. Amos had tried to kill himself with his rifle once before. The tracks said he had finished the job this time. He had turned his back to the ravine and placed the butt of the rifle on the ground and its barrel to his chin. The force of the blast must have thrown his body off the cliff and the rifle must have plunged into the ravine with him. Toby looked around for blood. There was none, but Amos' blood could have sprayed into the air behind him and fallen to the ground with his carcass.

The canopy of the white pines below the cliff blocked Toby's view of the ground. The wall of the cliff was steep and jagged in both directions as far as he could see. There was no way to climb down to the creek. He peered across the creek at the valley on its other side. He knew the terrain. Although he couldn't see it through the growth, he knew there was a fire road about a hundred yards from the creek. He surmised that the fire road was the quickest way to access the land at the foot of the cliff. He sprinted back to the deer stand.

"Did you find him?" Billy asked.

"No, but I found where he was, and I think I know where he is."

"Is he … ?" Billy's raspy voice caught in his throat.

"I think so."

Billy turned his back to Toby and put his hand over his eyes.

Stogie limped up the trail, huffing and puffing. "Where's Amos?"

"I don't know for sure," Toby said, "but I'm guessing he's at the bottom of a cliff. There's an outside chance he survived the gunshot and the fall somehow. We've got to climb down the trail to the trucks and ride the fire road to that cliff. There's no time to lose. Maybe you boys should stay here, and I'll come back and get you after I find Amos."

"No," Stogie said. "I can keep up."

"I'm coming with you," Billy said.

Toby knew that Billy was as fit as he was and that Stogie would slow them down, but he took one look at Stogie's drawn face and he didn't have the heart to leave him behind. "All right, but we'll have to hurry."

Toby pulled Stogie along and Billy fell in behind them. They struggled down the steep trail more rapidly than Toby would have believed possible. When they reached the cabin, he glanced at his truck still mired in the mud and turned to Billy. "We'll need to take your Dodge."

Billy fished the keys out of his pocket and handed them to Toby. "You drive. I'm in no shape to manage it."

Toby helped Stogie into the truck and Billy climbed in beside him.

The road to the creek bed was one of the least-maintained fire roads in the park. Toby tried his best to make good time, but it was a washboard of icy ruts and the truck slid into ditches and got mired countless times. They had to dig out the back wheels repeatedly and then drive on. Through it all, Billy didn't say a word. He looked hopeless, red-faced, and teary-eyed, lost in his own private chamber of guilt.

It was well after noon when they finally rounded a bend in the road that Toby guessed would be nearest the spot where he thought Amos had fallen. In the distance Toby saw an object he thought might be a man sitting on a big rock. He gassed the truck. As they closed the distance, a red ball cap, a khaki jacket, and the familiar stout body and round head came into focus.

Toby stopped the truck a few feet from the rock. Amos was perched on it with his rifle propped between his knees, staring at the truck with the bored expression of a dumb animal.

Stogie smiled and said, "Well, I'll be damned."

Toby was relieved at first, but his relief was soon overcome by anger. He got out of the truck and walked over to Amos. Billy and Stogie got out and stood behind him. "You scared the hell out of us," Toby said, his voice shaking.

Amos didn't return Toby's glare. His eyes were locked on Billy.

"Where did you get the ammunition?" Toby asked angrily.

Amos climbed down off the rock, reached into the side pocket of his hunting jacket, and handed Toby two bullets and an empty shell casing. Then he walked around Toby to stand in front of Billy.

"I played you for a fool," Amos said.

"What?"

"Years ago, I found the mouth of a cave down the hill from my stand. It goes through the mountain and opens at the bottom of the cliff. I fired my rifle and ran down here through the cave so you'd think I killed myself." Amos stepped closer to Billy so that they were toe to toe. "How does it feel?"

"I ... I don't ..."

"It's a shock, ain't it? It's a shock when someone does something you never would have believed they would do. It's a shock when that person deceives you and doesn't care how much it hurts you. It takes your breath away, don't it?"

Billy didn't say anything.

"It hurts that I made you think I killed myself, don't it? Think how it would feel if you loved the person who tricked you. It's happened to me twice. It almost killed me both times."

Amos stared at Billy hatefully. Billy didn't say a word.

"What you and Jolene did hurt me a thousand times more than you hurt now."

Amos walked around Billy, climbed into the truck bed, and sat with his back against the cab.

Stogie cast a disgusted look at Billy and climbed in beside Amos.

Billy stood silently, staring off into the distance.

Toby took him by the arm and guided him into the cab. Then he climbed in and started the truck. He drove back to the cabin, packed up their belongings, and headed out of the park. Billy didn't say a word throughout the long ride. It was almost dark when they passed Whippoorwill Hollow Dam. Toby said, "Amos said he'd been hurt two times so bad it almost killed him. One was Jolene and you. I wonder what the other time was."

Billy didn't even look at Toby. His uncharacteristic silence and the look on his face worried Toby more as they passed through Whippoorwill Hollow. In Fox Run, Toby stopped at the T and stared at Billy.

"If it's all right with you," he said. "I'll take my tow chain up to the cabin tomorrow in your truck and pull my truck out of the mire. I'll get Porter to go with me and he can drive your truck back home."

Billy stared into the distance and didn't answer.

"Is that okay with you, Billy?"

Billy nodded.

Toby's gut told him Billy needed help to get past the events of the day, so he turned right on Whiskey Road and took Amos and Stogie to his house in the cove, then drove Billy back to Fox Run.

He pulled the truck into Billy's driveway and killed the engine. They sat together quietly for a while. Billy made no move to get out of the truck. Toby looked out the window. It was about eight o'clock. The night sky was clear. A half-moon cast a pale gray hue on Billy's yard and the pasture beyond it. A huge sweetgum tree stood in front of the split-rail fence that divided the yard from the pasture. On the other side of the fence at the top of the hill that fell away down to Little Bear River, there was a grove of locust trees. Their spindly branches were light yellow in the moonlight. About a dozen Hereford and Angus cattle stood under the trees, their red and black hides grayed down in the soft cast of light. Billy's place looked strangely peaceful after such a hellish day.

"Pretty night," Toby said, trying to prime Billy's pump. "Looks nice in the moonlight."

"I love this old place," Billy said.

Toby was mildly surprised to hear Billy express a sentimental thought.

There was another long wait. Then Billy said, "I love those two old boys, too." His voice was more raspy than usual. "Although I didn't realize it till Amos kidnapped me."

Toby laid his hat on the seat beside him, ran his hand down his face, and sighed. He wanted to be careful not to push Billy further down into the pit of depression, but after all he'd been through with his friends, he needed an answer. "Why did you treat them so poorly? Why did you chase after Jolene and Polly?"

Billy rubbed his hands together and looked down at them and didn't say anything for a long, long time. When he finally spoke, his voice was quiet and low and Toby had to lean toward him to hear him.

"My first time was with Jenny Upton," Billy said. "I was fourteen. She was eighteen. She snuck out her bedroom window on a moonlit night in the summertime and met me in her daddy's barn." He touched his lips and stared into the distance. "She sure to God knew what to do." He shook his head. "We lay together till dawn." Billy went still.

Toby sensed that more was coming but that Billy was struggling to get it out so he kept still and waited. One of the steers stepped away from the locust trees and came over to the fence to look at the truck.

"I was afraid at first," Billy said. "I figured her daddy would beat me to death if he caught us, but ten minutes into it, I forgot all about her daddy. Ten minutes into it, I forgot everything I ever knew, and there was nothing but Jenny and me." He stroked the side of his face. "In all the world, there's nothing like a woman's touch." Billy licked his lips and looked out the truck window at a car climbing the hill on Whiskey Road. Toby saw the light from its headlamps flash in Billy's black eyes and a tear slide down his cheek. "Each woman fetched me in a different way. The curve of her hip or the swell of her breasts. Jolene's ocean blue eyes, looking up at me, wide and bright when we made love. The smooth soft place on the inside of Polly's thighs. The scent of Mary Jo's hair and the warm flesh on her throat where

I could feel the beat of her pulse against my tongue when I kissed her there. They all had charms that took my breath away. Sweet full lips, soft white shoulders, the turn of a calf, a sexy lisp. They were wondrous and special." Toby saw sweat on Billy's brow even though the night was cold. Billy swept his hand across his face and wiped the moisture on the thigh of his jeans. He took a deep breath and let it out slowly. "I could never turn away when I had a chance, no matter who it hurt or how dangerous it was. I wanted to hold them and touch them and feel their touch in return." Billy fell silent and looked down at his hands. "Polly, Jolene, and all the others. When I wanted them, Amos, Stogie, Mary Jo, Blakey, no one and nothing else mattered to me. I couldn't stop." He looked at Toby. There was weakness in his eyes. "Can you understand that, Toby?"

Toby pondered whether he should tell his old friend the truth. Then he said, "No, Billy. I can't understand it."

Billy bowed his head. "I guess I don't understand it either. All I know is I couldn't help myself."

They sat for a while longer and then Toby said, "Are you gonna be all right?"

Billy looked up at Toby. The weakness Toby had seen in his eyes had settled in. "I don't know," he said. He got out of the truck and went inside his house.

Toby sat in the driveway, thinking about all Billy had said. His thoughts soon turned to Jenny Upton. She was about fifteen years older than Toby. His first recollection of her was sometime after her marriage to a Baptist preacher, when she was Jenny Tomkins. And he remembered her now as she had appeared late in her life, a scrawny gray-haired woman. When she died, she and the preacher had eight children, a passel of grandchildren, and a few great-grandchildren. Toby had gone to the funeral at Grace Church. Jenny's husband had to be almost ninety now. The last Toby heard, he was living in a nursing home in Jeetersburg. The union between Billy and Jenny seemed an incongruous event in the context of her long life as a preacher's wife.

Toby took a deep breath, put on his hat, and looked at the herd standing under the locust trees. The steer that stood by the split-rail fence strolled slowly back to the herd, stood beside a cow, and nuzzled her neck. She ignored him. A light came on in Billy's bedroom window. Toby looked up at it. It stayed lit for a short while and went out. Toby started the truck and backed out of the driveway.

Chapter 27

The Blame

On a cold, bright morning a few days later, Billy got out of bed, dressed, and went to the store. Porter was manning the register, sorting money into slots in the cash drawer. He greeted Billy. Billy replied with no enthusiasm, went back to the stove, and sat on the bench.

Porter finished with the cash and began straightening products on the shelves. When he reached the end of an aisle near the stove, Billy said, "Are you still boarding with Jolene?"

"Yes. She doesn't want me to move out."

"I suppose Amos is still living with Toby?"

"No, sir. Mr. Hukstep moved into an empty trailer the day after y'all got back from that hunting trip. I saw him this morning working on a hookup for a new trailer pad."

"Is he still soused on shine?"

"I think so. He was sipping from a jar when I saw him."

Billy rubbed his hands together to warm them. Maybe Amos' return to the trailer park was some sort of progress, Billy thought, but his continued devotion to moonshine was discouraging. In any event, there was nothing more Billy could do to persuade him to go home. "What about Stogie? Is he still living with Toby?"

"No, sir. He went home, too. They say he's cut way back on the shine, but I don't know for sure. He hasn't dropped by the store in a month of Sundays."

"He won't drop by ever again," Billy muttered.

"What's that, Grandpa?"

"Nothing. Just talking to myself."

Billy spent the day and most of that night thinking about Stogie and Polly. The next morning he called Stogie to arrange a meeting. When Stogie refused to meet with him, Billy was not surprised. "Polly's not here to speak for herself," he said. "She told me how she felt about you. She told no one else. I'm the only one left who can tell you what she said."

"You'll tell me lies."

"You'll know I'm telling the truth when you hear what I have to say."

There was a long pause. Then Stogie said, "Be here at ten o'clock sharp. I'll give you fifteen minutes. At ten sixteen, if you're still here, I'll draw my rifle down on you and fire away."

Billy drove to Stogie's farm. The sky was gray and the temperature was below freezing. Patches of snow lined the road into Whippoorwill Hollow and filled the low places and shady depressions on the mountainsides. Billy turned off the state road and drove down a long driveway lined with cedars to the clearing where Stogie's house and barn stood. The house was made of stacked river rock and had a tin roof; the barn behind it was painted white and was three times the size of the house. It had been the site of countless parties, square dances, and wild times over the years.

Stogie was standing at the front door waiting for Billy. Billy walked up the cobblestone walkway to the porch and said, "Good morning." Stogie didn't offer a greeting. He led Billy into the parlor. Two easy chairs sat opposite one another before a fireplace. Cordwood was stacked on the hearth and flames licked high in the chimney. Stogie sat in one of the chairs. Billy hung his coat and hat on a rack beside the front door and sat in the chair opposite Stogie.

"Say your piece," Stogie said.

Billy sat up on the edge of the chair and mustered his courage. Words of guilt and confession lay uncomfortably on his tongue, but he was determined to say them. "It happened after one of the wild barn dances you and Polly used to throw. In the wee hours of the morning, everybody had gone home or passed out. You passed out by a water trough next to the corral. Polly and me were the last ones standing. She was so drunk she didn't know where she was." He glanced at Stogie quickly. "I carried her into the house. To your bed." Billy rubbed his hands together and stared down at them. "When she woke up in the middle of the night and found me next to her, she went plum hysterical." Perspiration gathered on Billy's brow. He puffed his cheeks and looked at Stogie sheepishly. "Polly was drunk past knowing anything, and I took advantage."

Stogie searched Billy's face. "You're lying. You cooked up this story to make me feel better."

Billy looked Stogie dead in the eye. "She was so drunk she was barely conscious when I took her. She didn't know who I was."

"I don't believe you," Stogie said.

"It's true. She was senseless. Talking gibberish. She kept repeating a word or name I couldn't understand, Laramie or Larry Lee or something."

Stogie grew still, his eyes shining. "Larravie," he said in a whisper.

Billy nodded. "Larravie. That might have been it. Larravie. You know what it means?"

Stogie put his hand over his eyes. His chest and shoulders shook and then he broke down and wept uncontrollably. Billy sat watching him, clenching and unclenching his fists.

It took Stogie a long time to regain his composure. When he finally wiped the tears away and stared into the fire, Billy said softly, "She made me swear never to tell you I took her to bed because she said it would break your heart. She said she loved you too much to hurt you. She told me she loved you with all her heart."

Stogie said, "There was only that one time?"

"Polly hated me after that. She wouldn't speak to me or look me in the eye after that night. Maybe you noticed how she cut me off."

"I remember the way she stayed clear of you. These last few weeks, though, I suspected she gave you the cold shoulder in my presence to keep me from finding out what y'all were doing behind my back."

"It was no act. Polly hated me. For good reason."

Stogie put his hand over his mouth and looked out the window. It was midmorning, but the sky was so overcast that most of the light in the room came from the fireplace. The flames flickered in his gray eyes.

"That's the way it went down, Stogie. I swear to God." Billy went to the door and retrieved his coat and hat. "Polly hated me, and you hate me now, too. I don't blame you. I have it coming. I did a lot of bad deeds in my day. Taking advantage of Polly when she was drunk was one of the worst. I don't know why I didn't control myself that night." Billy placed his hat on his crown and pulled it low over his eyes and started to turn to the door, but he hesitated. "I reckon that's not true. I know why I didn't control myself. Polly was a fine-looking woman, kind and gentle and smooth as velvet. I was jealous of you for winning the love of such a beauty, and I wanted her bad." He looked down and shook his head. "In those days, I took what I wanted however I could get it. I had no concern for anybody except me."

Stogie stood and joined Billy at the door. Billy faced him. "I know it probably doesn't mean much to you, but I'm mighty sorry."

"When did it happen?"

"What?"

"What year did you take Polly to bed?"

Billy stopped to think, trying to make sure he didn't make a mistake. "It was the summer of 1931, as near as I can recall."

Stogie shrugged. "Then it wouldn't have mattered if I'd shot you on Pine Top in '34."

"What?"

"Nothing. It doesn't matter now." He sighed heavily. "Bea and I were just kids when we got married, and we didn't belong together. We would have broke up no matter what happened. It didn't hurt so much when she cheated on me with you, but my Polly …" Stogie wiped his nose with his sleeve. "I loved her dearly and it pained me to think she turned to someone else to find tenderness I'd failed to give her."

"You didn't fail her. She loved you. That's why she hated me so much for what I did to her. I was wrong to do it. I wish I could take back what I did, but I can't. I hope you can forgive me some day."

Stogie's eyes locked on Billy's and his face turned hard. "If I'd known back then, I would have killed you. I reckon I'm too old to kill you now, but I'll never forgive you."

Billy hung his head, opened the door, and walked out to his truck. He climbed in and looked back at the house. Stogie stood on the porch. His face was filled with hatred, but he no longer looked broken down and defeated. Billy started the truck and drove away from the house.

He braked to a stop where the driveway met the state road, and he looked back at the house. From that spot, a line of cedars blocked Stogie's view of Billy's truck, so he cut the engine and slumped in the seat for a few minutes. He rubbed his eyes and sighed. Taking the blame was much harder than he imagined, but he had rescued Stogie from an old age tormented by jealousy.

Billy looked at the valley stretched out before him across the road. The floodplain of Little Bear River ran along a flat shelf of land to the foot of Crow Mountain. Stogie owned the land on both sides of the road and the mountain. His cattle stood in the pasture and grazed on hay that had been spread that morning. The nearest heifer raised her head and stared at Billy's truck, chewing methodically, a strand of hay hanging from her jaw. Behind the herd, oaks, sycamores, and maples lined the banks of the river. A murder of crows streaked down the mountainside and alit in the biggest sycamore by the river. They cawed at one another, their feathers ruffling in the wind.

It was cold in the truck, but Billy withdrew a kerchief from his coat pocket and wiped sweat from his face. He had worked hard to restore Stogie's peace of mind, harder than he had anticipated. Billy had never told a lie to shoulder the blame for a heinous wrong before. Stogie's grandmother had called him Larravie when he was little because she said he looked like her grandfather, Larravie Wingfield. The only other person who ever called Stogie Larravie was Polly, and even then, only in bed. No one else knew about it, either, until she told Billy one moonlit night when they lay together on a blanket in a grassy clearing beside Whippoorwill Hollow Dam.

Billy blew out a long breath, stared at the crows in the sycamore, and thought about sweet Polly. What a beauty she was. Lustrous chestnut hair, thick sensuous lips that tasted like wine, soft hands that could drive Billy wild, and long lithe legs that wrapped around his waist and locked behind his back. Their nine-year affair came to an end when Polly got cancer. She'd made him promise to keep their tryst a secret; she lusted after Billy, but loved only Stogie.

Billy rubbed the steering wheel with his gloved hands. He missed Polly and Mary Jo and Jenny Upton and all the rest of them. When he courted them, he thought he loved no one but himself. He gave them his body, but not his heart, and that was one of his biggest mistakes. He realized now that he had loved them all in different ways.

The echo of a far-off hunter's gunshot rolled down the face of Crow Mountain and across the valley to Billy's truck. The crows flew out of the sycamore and streaked over the road toward Stogie's house, and Billy drew in a deep breath and headed back to Fox Run.

PART IV

EASTER

Chapter 28

Billy's Surprise

On a cold, cloudy morning in February, Billy crossed the road from his house and opened up the store. He went to the cash register, broke open rolls of coins, and sorted them into the register's slots. Out the window he saw Toby Vess pull up to the gas pump in his county truck, get out, and flip the lid on his gas tank. Blowing streams of vapor into the cold air, he stood beside his truck and filled the tank. When he was done, he climbed the steps and came inside.

"Fourteen gallons," he said to Billy and handed him a five-dollar bill. "Four seventy-six."

Billy handed Toby a quarter in change. "Keep the penny," he mumbled.

"The sheriff called Blakey's parole officer yesterday," Toby said as he pocketed the coin.

Billy looked up at Toby.

"He's doing well," Toby said. "He got a job at a cigarette factory. Goes to work every day on time. No big drunks. He checks in with his parole officer regularly at his assigned times. You probably should be careful for a while longer, but it's beginning to look like he may have changed for the better."

Billy leaned against the register, relieved but morose. "Looks like my son is better off with me out of his life."

Toby looked disappointed. "I thought the good news might cheer you up."

"I'm glad for him," Billy said with no conviction in his voice.

Toby went to the door. He stopped and looked back at Billy. "Not too long ago, I would go out of my way to stop in here, hoping you'd be sitting by the stove, because you could always lift my spirits. Your good mood was infectious. You made your own fun and spread it around." Toby paused, looked down at the floor, and then back up at Billy. "I hope that man hasn't left us for good. I miss him something powerful."

Billy looked down at the cash drawer, avoiding Toby's gaze.

Toby went out the door and down the steps. Billy watched him get in his truck and drive away.

He stood by the register for a long time. Toby doesn't understand, he thought. He doesn't know what it's like to have nothing to look forward to. An iron-colored cloud cover thickened, and bits of ice began to fall, bouncing on the concrete porch steps and the asphalt road. It intensified into streaks of sleet that whitened the fields.

Porter pulled into the dirt lot in his Plymouth, ran across it to the porch, and burst through the door. He brushed sleet off his jacket sleeves. "Another storm's rolled in."

"Hardest winter in my memory," Billy muttered. He conceded the register to Porter and went back to his bench by the stove to mope.

Late that morning, Porter began to take inventory, moving down the aisles slowly. The bell over the door pinged, and Billy looked up the aisle at the front of the store. A tall woman wearing a blue hooded sweatshirt over a shapeless gray dress rushed into the store. She pulled the hood down, shook out a mane of bushy white hair, and stomped ice off her galoshes. Billy didn't recognize her in the dim light until she said, "God Almighty, it's cold in the hollow this winter." Eva Gitlow's deep voice was unmistakable. Billy knew her to be a plain, worn-out farmer's wife in her sixties, with leathery brown windblown skin and a thin frame worked to a frazzle. He turned back to the fire.

A little later, Eva rounded an aisle near the stove carrying a tote bag. "Mr. Kirby."

Billy looked up.

"You look chipper today," she said.

He started to say something scornful but thought better of it when his eyes fell on her face. She looked different than the last time he saw her. She wore red gloss on her lips that seemed to accentuate her straight white teeth and the dimples on her cheeks, and her face was either flushed from the cold or smeared with rouge. Her crimson cheeks contrasted with the dark freckles sprinkled over her nose and under her eyes. She wore a heavy application of mascara that drew attention to sparkling green eyes he'd never noticed before, and her bushy white hair was flipped up in a sweeping wave at her shoulders.

He backed off from the sour rebuke he intended to give her. "Thank you kindly, ma'am." He paused and said half-heartedly, "You look mighty pretty today."

"Really?" she said skeptically. "I guess it's my outfit. Baggy sweatshirt draped over shapeless muddy dress, set off by dainty ice-laden galoshes." She gripped the pleat of her mud-caked dress and held it out to her side in a mock modeling pose. "The latest winter fashion in Whippoorwill Hollow," she said drily.

He was surprised to feel the corners of his mouth turn upward. "It's not the outfit that caught my eye. It's the pretty lady wearing it." He meant it a little more this time, but not by much.

She smirked. "Thank you, Mr. Kirby," and she moved up the aisle away from him.

Billy was mildly perplexed that she had lifted his mood. He watched her approach the register and present her groceries to Porter, who greeted her with a tight smile and complimented her on her hair and makeup.

"Gertie Wilson did it for me. Second time I've been to the beauty parlor since Nelson was killed. First time was Thanksgiving and it lifted my spirits, so I went back yesterday."

Billy stared at her and recalled her husband, Nelson Gitlow. More than two years ago, his tractor slid off a muddy ledge after a big rain, rolled over on him, and crushed him to death. Billy hadn't known him well, but his dealings with him had been satisfactory. He had run an efficient, profitable farm; he paid his bill at the store the first of each month; and he had a kind word for Billy on the few occasions they met. Billy had attended his funeral out of respect for a good customer. A small crowd came to the church service and most of them followed the hearse to the graveside service; Billy recalled that no one stood beside Eva at the casket. Rumor had it her son was serving time in Georgia for armed robbery.

Billy pondered Eva's plight while she stood at the register. She was all alone on a big farm in Saddleback Cove. Most farmers in Selk County lived from hand to mouth; Nelson Gitlow had been more successful than the others, but farms were expensive to operate and they rarely turned a big profit. Billy doubted he could have set aside enough money to sustain Eva for long.

Porter slid a slip of paper across the counter to her. They looked at each other in a strange way, and Billy detected a mysterious tension floating in the air between them. She signed the paper and handed it to Porter. "Thank you so much," she said. Porter nodded and smiled at her. Billy was surprised to see her squeeze Porter's hand. She looked back at Billy. She seemed on the verge of tears. "Thank you, Mr. Kirby." She gathered her groceries and bolted out the door.

Curious, Billy walked to the front window and watched her climb into her pickup truck. Her dress rode up to the knee of her trailing leg when she got in, and her calf looked surprisingly strong for a skinny woman. Her knee was smooth, round, and milk-white. He was surprised to feel a familiar hollow place open up in the pit of his stomach. He had always considered her a plain, undesirable woman, and yet he stood at the window admiring her flushed face and flowing white hair as she passed the store in her truck and turned onto Whiskey Road to head into Saddleback Cove.

"It's too bad what happened to her husband," Porter said. "I hope you don't mind giving her credit."

Billy turned. "What credit?"

Porter looked embarrassed. "I figured you saw it in the books. I've been taking IOUs from her. You don't mind, do you, Grandpa?"

Lately, Billy hadn't been interested in the store's books, or in much of anything else for that matter. "How much is she into us for?"

"A few hundred dollars."

"How many is a few?"

Porter cleared his throat. "She owes us eight hundred thirty-eight dollars."

Billy emitted a low whistle.

"I shouldn't have let her run up such a big bill, I suppose," Porter said. "But I feel sorry for her, what with the bank coming after her and all."

"What's the bank's interest in her?"

"The bank sent her a notice of foreclosure on her farm last month. The county assessor is breathing down her neck about last year's property taxes, too. She doesn't have the money. She's only a step away from the poorhouse." Porter looked abashed. "I should have brought her bill to your attention. I guess there ain't much chance she'll ever pay, but I can't bring myself to turn her away when she comes in here for groceries."

Billy looked out the window as Eva's truck crossed the one-lane bridge over Little Bear River, climbed the opposite hill, and dropped out of sight on the other side.

"I'm sorry, Grandpa," Porter said. "I know it's bad business to give credit to a widow with no prospects of paying us back. I'll cut her off if you say so."

Billy looked out the window at the crest of the hill Eva had crossed. "Groceries on credit won't save her from the bank."

Porter nodded. "Bankers are a cold lot. They'll take her farm unless she pays up."

"They don't have a choice. They have to answer to their shareholders when a loan goes bad."

"You want me to cut her off?"

Billy stroked his jaw. "Not yet. She's in a bind and we don't need the money. Maybe she'll find a way to pay us back."

"I doubt it, but I hope you're right."

Billy meandered back to the stove, sat down, and turned Eva's problem over in his mind. The wolf was at her door and he could think of no way she could save herself. He pondered her predicament for a while before he returned to moping.

Over the next few weeks, Eva made several visits to the store, making a point each time of talking to Billy; courteous remarks designed to keep her credit flowing, he presumed. Meaningless palaver about the weather, the outbreak of pinkeye among the local cattle last summer, the deteriorating condition of Whiskey Road, the outrageous rise in the price of heating oil.

Then she dropped in on a rainy afternoon and lingered at the front window, seeming reluctant to leave the shelter of the store to brave the weather. She walked back to the bench and sat beside Billy to warm up by the stove, and they talked easily for more than an hour. The next visit resulted in the same lengthy interaction. He learned she grew up in Williamsburg, the daughter of a doctor and a nurse. She graduated from Sweetbriar College. She met Nelson on a blind date when he was at VPI studying agricultural science. They married right out of school, bought Twin Ridge Farm, and had their son soon afterwards. She was reticent to talk about Franklin, but from bits and pieces of their conversation Billy gleaned that the boy turned bad in his teen years, that drugs were involved, that he served time in reform school, and that she'd had no contact with him since he left home twenty years ago. She didn't talk about Nelson at all. Billy assumed the wound of his death was still fresh.

After that second long talk, Porter asked Billy again if he wanted to demand payment from her. Her bill was well over a thousand dollars by then, and Billy considered doing so. Her purchases were extravagant. She always bought more than she could possibly consume, and he was generally reluctant to extend credit to customers with little prospect of paying up. The prudent decision would be to cut her off, but he told Porter not to press her.

The reason for his generosity was clear to him by then: he looked forward to his encounters with her, and he didn't have much else to look forward to. What puzzled him was why he was interested in her at all. She wasn't his type of woman. She was plain, tall, and gawky. Her clothes were unflattering. And yet he found her interesting and strangely attractive.

On the first Tuesday in March, she arrived at the store at ten in the morning without a tote bag. Unlike her previous visits, she didn't wander through the aisles. She walked directly down the center aisle, stopped at the stove, and looked at Billy.

As always, she was dressed like a farmer. She wore dirty bib overalls, muddy work boots, a ragged winter coat, and a watch cap. Her eyes were red and misted over, and her lips trembled. She took off a pair of soiled work gloves and held her hands out to the stove to warm them. Her hands were big and chapped and calloused. She stared at the stove and didn't say anything.

Billy broke the silence. "Are you all right, Eva?"

She didn't answer at first. Then she said, "I can't pay your bill."

Billy didn't know what to say, so he kept quiet.

She sat down next to him. The side of her thigh touched his, and his inexplicable physical attraction to her stirred to life.

"You and Porter know I can't pay. Why do you give me credit?"

"Our customers sometimes go through hard times. We usually get paid in due course."

"You and I both know my hard times won't end well. I took advantage of your kindness. I'm ashamed." Her eyes filled with tears.

"You'll come through this somehow."

"You're kind to say so, Mr. Kirby." She put her hand on Billy's knee. "But you know better."

He struggled to conceal the irregular breathing caused by her touch.

"I'm told my truck is worth nine hundred dollars," she said. "It's not enough to cover my bill, but it's all I can offer you at the moment. I'd like you to take it in payment of my debt."

"You won't have any way of getting around."

"That's not the point. I don't have the cash to pay you."

The idea of a lease came to Billy's mind. He had entered into such arrangements with other farmers in the past, setting terms to ensure things would work out to his advantage in the end. "I'll take the title to your truck and lease it back to you," he said. "I'll own it, but you'll have possession of it."

"I can't pay to lease it. I have no income."

It suddenly occurred to Billy that a lease could be the answer to all her financial problems. He was surprised he hadn't thought of it before. "There's a way you could earn enough money to pay your living expenses. Lease your farm to me. I'll operate it. My lease payments should be enough to cover the payments on your mortgage, with money to spare."

Eva frowned. "Why would you want to lease my farm?"

"To make a return on my investment. Your husband made good money off that place. I ought to be able to turn a nice profit on it, too."

She looked at him askance. "I won't stand for being anyone's charity case, Mr. Kirby."

"I don't invest in business enterprises for charitable reasons. I intend to make a handsome profit off your farm."

She looked at him suspiciously.

Porter had been standing at the end of one of the aisles. "Grandpa's telling the truth," he said. "He uses his money to make more money. That's why he's richer than God."

Billy winced. "God's balance sheet is a little stronger than mine, but what Porter said is true. I'm interested in a business deal, not a charity case."

Eva was still skeptical. "What about the bank? They'll take the farm unless I make all the overdue payments on the mortgage in a lump sum now. Monthly lease payments won't be enough to pay off that obligation."

Billy nodded thoughtfully. "You may be right. That could spoil a lease deal. Depends on how much debt you're carrying. I would need to review your financial situation to know if we can work out something that makes business sense for both of us."

Eva refused at first. It took Billy more fast-talking and further assurances from Porter to convince her that his leasehold idea was a legitimate business proposition and not a handout. Given the urgency of the bank's demands, she agreed to allow Billy to look over her books that day.

She drove over Whiskey Road into Saddleback Cove in her Chevy pickup and Billy followed in his Dodge. It was late morning. The temperature had risen into the fifties, and the last vestiges of snow and ice from the storms had turned to slush in the ditches and trickled off the steep slopes into the valley. Pools of water glistened in the low spots.

Twenty miles from Fox Run, at the very end of Whiskey Road, Eva's Chevy slowed and turned onto a gravel driveway. Billy followed her and drove across the bottomlands of Twin Ridge Farm. The driveway ran along the eastern edge of a wide, flat valley flanked by two parallel forested ridges, their faces pale blue in the morning sun. Rabbit's Foot Creek meandered down the center of the valley and on through Saddleback Cove to spill its waters into Little Bear River near Fox Run. The creek found its source in springs in a range of foothills that ran between the far ends of the twin ridges. Mulberry trees lined the creek at the entry to the property and oaks, gums, elms, and hickories took hold along its banks farther along. A dozen Hereford cattle, the sun gleaming on their red backs, grazed beside the creek on hay that had been spread in the pasture.

Billy followed Eva's Chevy to a two-story white house that sat on a knoll overlooking the valley. The house was surrounded by a variety of shade trees. Eva parked under a hickory tree, and Billy pulled his truck up beside her.

He got out of the truck, walked to the crown of the knoll, and looked over the valley. With the snow melt-off, Rabbit's Foot Creek spilled over its banks in wide places spaced almost evenly apart. The string of silver pools shone in the sun like a diamond bracelet.

Eva came to Billy's side and looked across the valley with him. "Nice day," she said. "Warm for this time of year."

"Your farm is beautiful."

"Thank you."

"How did you manage to maintain it after Nelson died?"

"I liquidated the herd to generate money to pay the bills." Billy had heard that Nelson Gitlow ran more than two hundred head of cattle on the property, but only an old bull and a dozen cows were grazing on hay that morning. "I hated to sell them," Eva said, "but I had no choice. I couldn't make enough money off the farm to stay ahead of the mortgage payments and my other bills. I'm at the end of my rope now, though. As you can see, there aren't enough cattle left to make a difference."

Despite the depletion of the herd, the farm appeared to have been well maintained otherwise. A white plank fence encircled the entire valley. It showed no evidence of rot and had been painted recently. The fields were well groomed. Brush and thistles had been bush-hogged away. Eva couldn't have done all the work alone.

"Who helps you?" Billy asked.

She pointed at a small cottage at the foot of the hill. "Farley Grimmett, his wife and three boys."

"I know him. He's a good hand."

"His wife, Bonnie, is as good a hand as he is. The boys, too. Even the eight-year-old works dawn to dusk when school's not in."

Billy looked at the clumps of hay that had been spread that morning. "How much hay and feed do you have left?"

"We cut two stands from the upper fields last season. We've got enough in the barn to finish out the winter. I sold the cattle a few at a time over the course of the year and spent most of the proceeds on grain, supplement, and vaccinations for the ones I kept. I could have stretched out the money longer if I'd sold the bulk of them all at once. The way I did it, I ended up wasting feed and medicine on cattle I eventually had to sell. That's the advantage of hindsight, I guess." She hesitated and then said, "I don't have the heart to sell the last ones. I'll just let the bank take them, I suppose."

Billy stared at the cottage, thinking about Farley and his family. "How are you paying Farley's wages?"

She bowed her head and swallowed. "I haven't paid him since December."

Billy wondered why Farley stayed on. Then he remembered the large supply of groceries she'd bought on credit each time she visited the store. "The groceries were for the Grimmetts," he said.

She didn't say anything.

"You kept next to nothing for yourself, I bet."

She shrugged. "I'm on a diet."

They were silent for a while. Then she said, "It hasn't been that bad." She looked at Billy and made a wry face. "I lied when I told you I wouldn't accept charity. You and Porter gave me credit when I knew I'd never be able to pay you. Gertie Wilson offered me a gift to improve my mood, so I got my hair and makeup done for free."

"She did a good job. You look beautiful."

"You're lying, but thank you just the same."

"I'm not lying."

She smirked. "I know my limitations, Mr. Kirby."

They both stood looking at the valley. Without thinking it through, Billy reached over and took her hand. She flinched and tried to pull back, but Billy held on and her hand relaxed in his grasp. She let him hold her hand for a while and then looked at him with a confused expression. "What are you doing?" she asked.

Billy was confused, too. "I don't know." He let go of her hand. "I apologize."

She stared at him for a few seconds, her brow furrowed. Then she said, "Let's go in the house. I'll gather the papers for you." She headed toward the house.

Billy stared at the valley and Rabbit's Foot Creek and scolded himself. Taking Eva's hand was brash and rude and he didn't understand why he had done it.

"Are you coming, Mr. Kirby?"

He turned. Eva stood waiting for him, her eyebrows raised. She headed toward the house, and he followed her.

Chapter 29

The Tire Swing

Eva's farmhouse was white with burgundy shutters, a tin roof, and a wraparound porch. Several rocking chairs sat on the porch and a burgundy swing hung from the ceiling. She led Billy through the front door into a sparsely furnished parlor. A sofa and two wing chairs with faded and worn material sat around a stone fireplace. The cream-colored paint on the walls had dimmed to a dusty brown. A trail of muddy tracks ran from the front door to the sofa and several coffee mugs were strewn across a coffee table. Old newspapers were tossed on the floor.

"Pardon the mess in here. I lost interest in housekeeping after Nelson died."

"Looks better than my place," Billy said. As soon as the words were out of his mouth, he realized he had lied to curry favor with her, and he again did not understand his own actions.

"Where do you want to work on the books?" she asked.

"I'll need a table or a desk where I can spread out the papers and take notes."

"The dining room's the best I can do." She led him through the parlor to a large dining room with a knotty pine table and eight chairs under a chandelier made of deer antlers. Billy sat at the head of the table, and Eva left the room through a swinging door.

He looked out a row of windows at a side yard. A large oak tree sat in the center of the yard and an old tire swing hung from it, left over from the days when the Gitlow boy was a toddler, he guessed.

He stared at the swing and rubbed his jaw, confused and uneasy about his interest in Eva. She didn't fit the mold of the women he had chased. In a beauty contest, she would have finished dead last. The most attractive among his lovers—Mary Jo, Jolene, Polly—were stunning lookers in their day, but Eva was gangly, with big hands and big feet and a long thin horse face. And she was too tall for him. He guessed she was six feet two or three inches in height. Billy was barely six feet tall when he forced himself to stand ramrod straight. A woman who had to look down on him to make eye contact usually made him uncomfortable, and yet he felt at ease with Eva.

"Here are the records," Eva said.

She'd reentered the room while he was mired in confusion and was standing beside him clutching a big pile of papers to her chest. She plopped them in front of him, leaned over the table, and began to paw through them. The side of her hip brushed against his arm. It was surprisingly soft. A shock of her white hair fell over her eyes and she pulled it back behind her ear. Her hair was snow white, fulsome, and silky. He looked at her face carefully. It was true that it was long and thin, but she had pretty, high cheekbones, dark freckles over her nose and under her eyes, cheeks that dimpled when she smiled, and a wide mouth with full lips that gave her face a sensuous look.

"Here's the deed," she said. "We bought the place from Archie Leake in 1939." She smiled, crow's-feet splitting the flesh around her eyes. "He was a sweet old man." Her smile faded. "Archie had Parkinson's disease and he couldn't work the place. Poor old codger died two months after we bought it."

She set the deed aside and placed another document before Billy. "Here's the deed of trust to the bank that set up the mortgage." She pointed to a stack of documents beside the deed of trust. "Nelson refinanced the original mortgage several times over the years. These papers set up those loans. They're complex and difficult to parse, and I don't fully understand them." She put her hand on a thick black binder. "Nelson made entries of all the expenses and income from the farm in here. It goes back ten years."

She pointed to several blue booklets. "Those are the bank account books. They won't tell you much except that I'm overdrawn." She placed her hand on a pile of manila folders. "These are tax returns for the past five years. If you need to go back further than that, we'll have to search the attic for the files." She turned to Billy. "Is there anything else you'll need?"

Billy stared at her eyes. He hadn't noticed how stunning they were, a startling shade of green, like smooth, clear pieces of jade. He put his hand to his chin and thought about Jolene's pale blue eyes. Eva's eyes were different but they were every bit as beautiful. If Billy had been the judge of a contest to determine which of them had the prettiest eyes, he would have ruled it a tie.

"Mr. Kirby, are you with me? You seem distracted."

"Oh … yes. I was just thinking about the type of lease we might use."

"Do you think you'll need any other documents?"

"No. I don't think so."

"Good. While you're looking at the files, I'll make us some coffee."

Eva left the dining room through the swinging door and Billy heard the clinking of china in the kitchen. He pinched his lip. He was pursuing a fool's folly, he thought. Eva was widowed not that long ago by a man she loved. Billy was too old to court a sixty-year-old woman who had no interest in him. He puzzled over his illogical affinity for her.

He was still lost in thought when Eva pushed the swinging door open by backing into it, a cup of coffee in each hand. She set one cup in front of Billy, held the other, and frowned at him again.

"You don't seem to be digging into the books," she said.

He looked down at the papers. "Yes … the books." He picked up the cup and sipped the coffee, stalling to gain composure. "I'll need a pen or a pencil. And a note pad, if you have one."

She exited through the swinging door. Billy put his hand over his heart. It was racing. "You're an old fool," he said under his breath.

She returned and handed him a pen and a note pad. Billy picked up the deed and began to read it over, stopping occasionally to take notes. She sat in the chair nearest him, facing the windows and sipping coffee. He forced himself to concentrate on the documents, which was no small feat with her sitting so close by.

She came and went twice, and he took short breaks while she was gone to repeat to himself that it was ridiculous to contemplate courting her. Three hours passed. It was midafternoon when he pushed back from the table and rubbed his face. He stood up and stretched. He went to the dining room windows, pulled aside the sheer curtains, and looked outside. He noticed that the oak tree in the side yard with the tire swing was dying. Branches as big around as a twenty-gallon barrel were rotting, their bark flaking off, their ends gnarled and cracked. Several dead branches lay under the tree where they had fallen, probably broken down under the weight of the last ice storm.

"So what do you think?" Eva asked.

He turned and looked at her. She sat at the dining room table with her back arched, her hands folded in front of her, her face tense and drawn.

"The old oak out there is dying," he said, the sadness in his voice surprising him.

She paused. "It's a very old tree."

Billy turned back to the tree. The tire swing's chain had worn a deep ring in the limb from which it hung. The wood in the deepest part of the groove was freshly exposed and unweathered. Someone had played on the tire swing recently and its chain had cut a newer trench in the older deep groove. Eva's only son had long since grown up and moved away. She had no grandchildren. He wondered what child could have visited Eva's swing. "Do Farley's boys play on the tire swing?"

"No. They're all work and no play. When they're not at school, they're in the fields."

Billy puzzled over the freshly worn scar.

"Mr. Kirby?" Eva said in a sharp tone. "Can we turn our attention to the business at hand? What do you think about the farm?"

He turned back to her. She was too smart to deceive, he thought. She would see through a lie, no matter how artfully composed and delivered. "A lease agreement won't work."

She winced and clenched her fists, her knuckles whitening.

"I'm sorry," he said. "The refinancing documents, the ones you said you don't fully understand, they spoil the deal. Nelson refinanced the mortgage three times, taking on larger loans each time. The farm is carrying a mountain of debt, two hundred eighty thousand dollars in total. That's why you've been losing money since he died. You've managed the farm well, but the payments on the debt far outstrip any revenue anyone could possibly make operating this place. No lease agreement can produce enough cash for you to service the debt and stave off foreclosure."

"I see. Thank you for trying." She leaned back in her chair, covered her face with her hands, and wept.

Billy sat down in a chair across from her and watched her. After a long time, she stopped crying and folded her arms over her chest and looked down at the floor. "That's it, then," she said.

Billy knew the answer but he asked anyway, on the outside chance Eva had overlooked the possibility. "I take it Nelson didn't own a life insurance policy."

She smirked. "You obviously didn't know him well, Mr. Kirby."

"I barely knew him at all."

"Life insurance was of no interest to Nelson. He never gave a thought to the future. He poured all the money we made back into the farm, never setting aside anything for a rainy day. When Franklin was born, I told him I thought we should buy life insurance. He said you have to be stupid to bet with a banker that you'll die young and then hope to God you win the bet." She gazed at Billy with a sour look on her face.

Billy had assumed that Nelson and Eva had a good relationship, but the frustration in her voice brought that into question. "He shouldn't have taken on so much debt," Billy said, "but the books show he managed the place well day to day. He seemed to be a good farmer."

"Oh, he was a good farmer. He loved the land. It's a pity he didn't love much else."

Her remark was laden with profound bitterness, and it cheered Billy, which made him wonder what was wrong with his sensibilities. He stared at her for a long time, pondering the impertinence of the question on his mind. He decided he had nothing to lose by asking it. "Did you love him?"

Eva looked at Billy coldly. He expected her to tell him to go to hell, but she surprised him. "I loved him once. Many years ago."

Billy's heart pounded. She had given him a look into her heart. It was a great gift. He swiped his hand over his mouth and turned to look out the window. The old oak was almost done, its branches rotting, its bark falling away. It made him uneasy. Before he thought it through, he heard himself speak. "My wife, Mary Jo, died of cancer in September. She fought the disease for more than a year."

"I know. I went to her funeral. I'm sorry for your loss. It must be difficult for you."

Billy rubbed his hands together and looked at them. "I loved Mary Jo when we married, but it faded away over the years." He hesitated. "That's not true." He sighed heavily. "The truth is I stopped loving her because she stopped loving me. We split up and got back together many times. She left me for good before she died." He sighed again. "All of it was my fault. My actions drove her away."

Eva frowned. "You cried at her funeral. You seemed devastated."

"I cried for me, for my mistakes. And for my loneliness." He took a deep breath. "You're right, though. I cried for Mary Jo, too." He looked out the window at the oak. "I cried for the young Mary Jo. I loved her once." A gentle breeze passed through the yard. The oak's tire swing swayed slowly in the wind.

"It appears we have a lot in common," Eva said. "I didn't love Nelson when he died, but I cried for him because I loved him once. But like you, I cried mostly for myself, for my loneliness and for my bleak chances of surviving without him." She swiped a tear from her cheek. "Apparently, I was right about my chances."

They sat quietly for a full ten minutes. Billy thought about Mary Jo and Jolene and the others. Eva seemed lost in thought, too. He pondered her loneliness and her financial peril. Was she desperate enough to give herself to an old man, he wondered. Could he make her happy if she did so? He shook his head to clear his thoughts of such nonsense, but the thoughts had rooted in his mind and they wouldn't go away.

She stirred and said, "I'd offer you something to eat, Mr. Kirby, but as you know, the cupboard is bare."

"Just as well. I've lost my appetite." He pawed through the documents on the table until he found the deed to the property. He scanned it again. "Have you tried to sell the farm to pay off the bank?"

"I listed it with Caldwell Realty a year ago. A Caldwell agent came out here and appraised the place. A fat, sweaty man who oiled the hair on the side of his head and combed it over his bald spot."

"Burt Rea."

"Yes, Mr. Rea. I don't like him."

"His own mother doesn't like him. He's honest, though, as far as I know."

"He may be honest, but he's utterly ineffective. He said the real estate market had fallen in value over the last several years and the farm wasn't worth the balance owed to the bank, but he went ahead and set a price slightly above that amount, hoping an unsophisticated buyer would come along. There was no interest until this fall. Just after Halloween, a retired dentist from New York made an offer much lower than the asking price and lower than the amount owed to the bank. I countered, but the dentist refused to improve his offer, so I asked the bankers if they would waive the shortfall if I took his offer and gave them all the proceeds. They refused, so I turned the offer down. No one has expressed an interest since then."

Billy looked out the window at the tire swing. He stared again at the place on the limb where the chain had recently carved a newer groove. A strong wind blew across the yard, bending the branches of the oak. The tire swing turned and swayed. The answer to the mystery of the tire swing suddenly came to him out of nowhere in a spectacular vision. He saw her there, standing in the tire in her galoshes and heavy coat, clutching the chain in her gloved hands, pumping the swing back and forth, a sixty-year-old widow alone in winter, laughing like a schoolgirl. "It was you," he said in his raspy voice.

"What was that, Mr. Kirby? I couldn't hear you."

He couldn't speak. He could barely breathe. He put his hand to his eyes and leaned back in his chair.

She stood, alarmed. "Are you all right, Mr. Kirby?"

"Could you fetch me a glass of water, please?"

"Yes, of course." She rushed out of the room.

He stared at the tire swing and tried to regain his balance. The image of her playing on it wiped away any remaining doubt. She was young at heart, intelligent, and beautiful in an unconventional way. Every word she said was meaningful and intriguing. Every move of her tall gangly body captivated him. God help him, he was hopelessly smitten with this fascinating woman who was too smart, too young, and too good for him.

"Mr. Kirby?"

She stood over him with a glass of water. He took it and drank from it.

"Are you all right?"

"I came through a harrowing ordeal recently. It weakened me."

She sat down in the chair next to him, a look of grave concern on her face. "I heard that a man from South Carolina kidnapped you and tried to kill you."

"So they say." He took another sip of water. He stared at her strangely attractive face, at her piercing green eyes. He couldn't allow the bank to sweep her away from him. He needed a ruse to keep her close, and as always in times of need, the necessary lie came to him quickly. "I want to buy your farm."

Eva sat back in her chair and knitted her brow. "I appreciate your kindness, Mr. Kirby, but I can't allow you to do that."

"Kindness has nothing to do with it. I'll hire a competent professional to appraise the property, not someone like Burt Rea. I'll hire an honest but effective broker. I'll make an offer based on what he says the place is worth. Not a penny more."

She paused and searched his face. "You have your own farm, and from what I understand, you own real estate all through Whippoorwill Hollow and rental homes and apartment buildings in Jeetersburg. You don't need more investment property. You want to buy my farm because you feel sorry for me."

Billy spoke in a measured tone. "You're right. I feel sorry for you. You're an innocent victim of a tragic accident, but I've made a fortune speculating in real estate. Those parcels in the hollow and the rental properties you mentioned are gold mines. This is a beautiful piece of property, a fertile farm, well maintained and profitable. I want to buy it. You need to sell it. If you turn me away, you'll pitch your farm into foreclosure for no good reason."

Their eyes locked. It was all he could do not to lose himself inside her limpid pools of jade. He desperately wanted her to agree to his proposal, but she was right. He didn't need or want another farm. He wanted an excuse to converse with this extraordinary woman. He wanted a foundation upon which to build a relationship. He needed time to win her over. He needed a way to persuade her to sell him the farm so he could keep her near him, and the winning point came to him spontaneously, based on the sacrifices she'd made thus far. "You might consider Farley Grimmett and his family. Where will they go if the bank takes your farm?"

After a long silence, Eva said, "Hire the appraiser. We'll see what he says."

Billy rapped his knuckles on the table, picked up his hat, and stood. Eva stood and walked him through the parlor to the front door. She opened it and held it for him.

"I'll be back tomorrow with my appraiser."

"So soon?"

"The bank will grab this farm as quickly as the law allows. There's no time to waste. I'll come by at noon. Will you be here?"

"If I need to be."

"I'll see you at noon." He put on his hat, walked to his truck, and got in. She stood on the porch staring at him. She looked apprehensive.

He started the engine and pulled away. "You're an old fool," he said again.

Chapter 30

Jolene's Drift

By March, the fading embers of Jolene's hopes that Amos would ever come home had gone cold. Amos had moved back to the trailer court in January, but he didn't return to their double-wide. When she heard the familiar groan of his old Chevy truck that day, her heart leapt into her throat and she ran to the window. She watched his pickup roll by and dodge the ruts in the road down to the third trailer on the other side, Elmer Gibson's trailer. She watched Amos get out of his truck and stand in the road, swaying. Then he unlocked the door to Elmer's trailer and went inside.

Elmer's trailer was a little old rusted-out silver Airstream. It had been empty since Elmer died of lung cancer the previous winter. He had no family, and no one ever showed up to claim his trailer. Jolene and Amos took possession of it in July, filled out a passel of complicated forms, wrote numerous letters, and made countless phone calls until the state bureaucrats finally transferred the title to them in October.

Amos was determined to eke out extra rental income from it, but it hardly seemed worth the trouble to Jolene. The Airstream was too small and dingy to deliver more than a pittance in rent. It was designed to be a camper, not permanent living quarters. It was a cramped little sausage-shaped one-room box with a bed that was merely a hard-board cot that dropped down from the wall on hooks and chains. Elmer had been a chain smoker, and cigarette smoke had seeped into the pores of the walls, furniture, and carpet. Jolene scrubbed down the whole place three times to remove the stench, only to be overpowered by the odor of Lysol. She couldn't imagine anyone wanting to rent the place except a miserable old bachelor like Elmer, and as it turned out, she was right: Amos was that miserable old bachelor.

The day he moved into the Airstream, Jolene put on her glasses and watched him from her window. He carried a crate of mason jars inside and closed the door. She watched the trailer for hours after that, but he didn't come outside again that day. She figured he was doing what he had done when he lived with Toby Vess: he was slumped in Elmer's moth-eaten chair, watching Elmer's little rabbit-eared black-and-white television, and drinking himself into a stupor. It was maddening. He was less than a hundred yards away, but he and Jolene were a million miles apart.

Time passed. The weekdays were long while Porter tended to the store and left Jolene alone. She went to the window a hundred times a day, hoping and praying Amos would set the jar down and walk down to her door. She didn't even care if he was drunk. She'd resolved that she would welcome him with open arms no matter what shape he was in. She even tried to visualize his approach, hoping she could will him to her door. She closed her eyes and imagined him approaching the double-wide. She saw him hesitate on her stoop and lift his hand and rap politely on the door. "Jo? You in there?"

But he didn't come to the door, and he didn't call out. He rarely left Elmer's trailer at all, and when he did, he left in his truck and returned with more moonshine. He was drinking himself to death, and there was nothing Jolene could do about it.

And that's where things stood until Tuesday morning the first week of March. By then she had wrested control of breakfast from Porter. She cooked ham and eggs that morning and they sat at the counter. She caught Porter staring at her a couple times before he finally said, "Are you all right, Mrs. Hukstep?"

"I'm middling fair, I guess. Why do you ask?"

"You're not eating your breakfast."

"I'm not hungry."

"You haven't eaten much the past couple weeks. You're uncommon pale and you're losing weight."

Jolene looked down at her plate. "I've had no appetite lately."

"Maybe we should ask Doctor Davis to take a look at you."

Jolene felt tears welling in her eyes. "Excuse me," she said, covering her face. She ran back into the bedroom and closed the door. She took off her glasses, threw herself on the bed, and buried her face in a pillow to muffle her sobs.

When the trailer shook with the force of the slamming front door a few minutes later, she was terrified that Porter might have finally lost patience with her and would move out. His friendship was her only comfort, and now she feared that she had broken down in front of him one too many times.

She jumped up off the bed and looked out the window, expecting to see him throwing his suitcase in the back of the Plymouth and driving away, but she saw the blurred form of the Plymouth parked under the carport and he wasn't anywhere around it. She snatched up her glasses from the bed and ran to the living room window. Porter was striding down the trailer park road without his coat or gloves. He could catch his death.

Jolene ran into the kitchen and grabbed her coat, but when she threw open the door and saw Porter rapping on the door of Elmer Gibson's Airstream, she put her hand to her chest and went still.

The door of the Airstream opened and Amos stood in the doorway. Porter's gestures were animated and angry. He shook his finger in Amos' face. Amos shut the door. Porter banged on it again with his fist, but the door remained closed. Then Porter stepped back and kicked the door open and rushed inside the trailer. The little silver cylinder rocked and shook.

Jolene was on the verge of running down there when Amos staggered out of the trailer and fell on his face. Porter came out and stood over him, breathing hard. He stared down at Amos for a few moments and then reached down and took his arm to help him up. Amos jerked his arm away, climbed to his feet on his own, staggered back inside, and slammed the door. Porter stared at the door for a while and then walked slowly back up the road to his Plymouth.

"Porter!" Jolene called out.

He didn't even look her way. He got in the Plymouth and drove away.

Jolene looked at the Airstream. She considered going down there to make sure Amos was all right, but that would probably only lead to more heartache. Besides, Amos got up and went inside under his own power. He was probably okay.

She was more worried about Porter. She was afraid he would get drunk instead of going to work at the store, but she couldn't chase after him. The Hudson wouldn't start after the tow truck dropped it beside the carport last December, and it wouldn't have been able to catch up with Porter's fancy Plymouth anyway. She went back in the living room and sat on the couch and fretted about him.

She was so upset she'd almost lost her mind an hour later when Porter's Plymouth pulled under the carport. She opened the door and watched him walk to the trailer. His upper lip was busted and swollen. He swiped at it with his hand and she saw scrapes on his knuckles. He climbed the steps, gently pushed Jolene aside, and went into the kitchen to get a carton of milk from the refrigerator. He poured himself a glass and stood at the counter drinking it down.

His eyes were clear and there was no liquor on his breath. She thanked God he hadn't relapsed. She would never have been able to forgive herself. Jolene shut the door and went to his side. "I appreciate what you did, but I wish you hadn't done it."

"You deserve better than a drunk jackass, Mrs. Hukstep. I don't know what you see in him."

"It's not his fault. He can't forgive me. He can't change who he is."

"I'm sorry, ma'am, but that's a load a bullshit. He's like any other man or woman. He can change if he wants to. I know. I did it. He can sober up, bend his stubborn pride a bit, and come home to you. He won't do it because he thinks he's better than everyone else. He thinks he never made a mistake, so he's too good for anybody who did."

She patted Porter's arm. "I appreciate your concern, but you don't understand him."

"I understand him just fine. You're the one who's got him wrong. He's a selfish, coldhearted drunk. He ain't worth all the heartache. Cut him loose and find someone else to love, somebody worthy of your favors." Porter's black eyes were sincere.

Jolene saw motion outside the kitchen window and looked outside. Amos' pickup passed the double-wide meandering from one side of the dirt road to the other. He pulled onto the state road without slowing down to look for oncoming traffic and sped out of sight.

Chapter 31

Billy's Scam

After he convinced Eva to allow him to have her farm appraised, Billy drove back to the store. Porter was in the back room putting cash in the safe. Billy grabbed the phone by the cash register and dialed Ray Woodson, a real estate appraiser who had worked for Billy on several shady transactions more than ten years earlier when Billy's selfishness still dominated his business deals.

Ray answered on the first ring. "Long time, no see."

"I want you to appraise a farm for me."

"Last time we talked, you told me you were cleaning up your act," Ray said coldly. "You said you were done with me and my type."

"I need you for one last job."

Ray was quiet for a few moments, but Billy wasn't worried that he might turn him away. Ray was a mercenary. His sensibilities were irrelevant; Billy's money was all he cared about.

"What's your game this time?"

"There's no game. I need you to appraise Twin Ridge Farm in Saddleback Cove. I'll meet you there tomorrow at noon."

"Short notice. I'll have to move some things around."

"Move em."

"I'll have to charge a premium for all the trouble."

"I don't care."

"Must be a sweet deal. What sale price do you want me to give you this time?"

"You can't come in lower than three hundred thousand."

"Who's the mark?"

"There is no mark."

There was a long pause. "Who's the buyer?"

"I am."

Another long pause. "You want me to come in above three hundred thousand dollars and you're the buyer?"

"You heard me right. Don't screw this up or I'll have your ass."

Ray snorted. "You already have my ass. In the old days, you bought and paid for it many times over."

"Just be there at noon and try to act like a professional."

The fair weather held up through the next morning. The sun was bright and the temperature was mild, but the weather did not lift Billy's mood. He was anxious and worried when he parked his truck in front of Eva's house at noon. Ray Woodson was the best man you could hire to prepare and present a rigged appraisal, but the farm was worth far less than three hundred thousand dollars. Ray would have to put on quite a show.

Ray's ice-blue Buick was beside Eva's truck when Billy arrived. She and Ray stood on the porch together. Ray was short and stout with thick red hair and beady black eyes. He was dressed in a black three-piece suit, a white shirt, and a maroon tie. Billy got out of his truck and Ray waddled down the steps to greet him.

Billy met Ray at the foot of the steps and they shook hands. "I assume you are Mr. Kirby," Ray said.

"Yes, sir."

"I'm Raymond A. Woodson." He withdrew a business card from his pocket and presented it to Billy. "My regional director called me last night and assigned me to this project. He said it was top priority and of the greatest urgency."

"Yes, sir. We need to close the transaction by next week to avoid foreclosure."

"I'll work as quickly as I can, Mr. Kirby, but I'm sure you understand I can't compromise my conclusion simply because you're in a hurry."

"How much time will you need?"

"That depends on how much assistance you and Mrs. Gitlow can provide me. I need a plot map from a recent survey of the property. I'll need to walk the boundaries and perform extensive inspections of the livestock, farm machinery, outbuildings, the cottage, and the main house. To have any chance of completing an appraisal this week, I'll need the assistance of a knowledgeable guide."

Eva cleared her throat. They both looked up at her, standing at the top of the porch steps. "I have a survey that was performed four years ago when the property was refinanced."

"That should be adequate for my needs," Ray said.

"My foreman can show you around. When do you want to start?"

"Immediately."

She went inside the house.

Ray frowned at Billy. "Am I laying it on too thick?"

Billy grimaced. "That suit's a bit much. You look like a fat penguin with the vest and all."

Ray ran his fingers down the lapels and straightened his tie. "Haven't worn it since my daughter got married in '62. I must have put on some weight since then. The pants are cutting me in two."

"Just make sure you do a good job. This woman's no fool."

"I can tell that by talking with her. What I can't figure out is what scam you're running on her. If I jack up the price, you're the one who loses money. So what's your game?"

"Just come in above three hundred, like I told you."

"All right, but this one's going to cost you. Of course, you knew that when you called me on such short notice. I don't know what your scam is, but it must be a sweet deal."

Eva came out the front door, walked down the steps, and handed Ray a rolled-up document. "Here's the survey."

Ray unfurled it and looked it over. "This will do fine."

"My foreman will meet you at his cottage. Take the driveway down the hill and turn right at the bottom. That road will take you straight there."

"Thank you, Mrs. Gitlow." Ray rolled up the map, extended his hand to Billy, and Billy shook it. "I'll do my best." He strode to his Buick and drove down the hill.

Eva and Billy stood together watching him drive away. "How long do you think this will take?" she asked.

"He should be able to finish by tomorrow night."

She looked at Billy, pursed her lips, and said, "I'll be interested to read his report." She turned without another word, climbed the steps, and went inside the house.

Billy got in his truck and stared at the house. She knows, he thought. He could hear it in her voice and see it on her face. His best hope was that she'd pretend to be deceived to get out of the hole she was in. That's what anyone else would do. Of course, she wasn't like anyone else.

The next day, dark clouds gathered over Feather Mountain. A thunderstorm rolled through the hollow at noon and drenched Fox Run in a cold rain that tailed off around four. The temperature dropped into the twenties and ice congealed on the trees, shrubs, and grass. Standing water froze over.

Late that night, there was a knock at Billy's door. He went to the foyer, turned on the porch light, and opened the door to find Ray Woodson on the porch clad in a heavy overcoat, a black fedora, and gloves. His face was flushed with the cold and he blew vapor into the air with every breath. Billy brought him into the foyer but didn't invite him to have a seat.

Ray set his briefcase on a table by the coat rack and opened it. "It's been a hell of a day," he said as he rifled through his case. "I almost froze to death in the rain and sleet tramping all over that big old farm. Then I damn near killed myself trying to get here tonight. My Buick ain't built to drive on an ice slick." Ray held up a manila envelope. "I got your appraisal done well inside your deadline."

Billy snatched the envelope out of Ray's hand and ripped it open. He scanned the first page of a sheaf of papers—a bill for services in the amount of three thousand dollars. He looked up at Ray and raised his eyebrows.

Ray shrugged. "I told you there'd be a premium."

Billy flipped through twenty-two pages to the last one and found the conclusion. "Three hundred twenty-five thousand dollars," he read aloud.

"A little more than you asked for, you know, to make it look good."

"Wait here." Billy went through the parlor to his office, found his checkbook, wrote out a check for the full amount of the bill, went back to the foyer, and handed it to Ray. Ray took the check, put it in his breast pocket, and smiled at Billy.

"I've missed working with you, Billy," Ray said.

Billy took Ray by the arm, guided him out the front door, and turned out the porch light without replying.

The next morning the sky cleared and the sun came out, but no warmth came with it. High winds during the night cracked off some of the tree branches that were weighed down by ice. On the drive to Twin Ridge Farm, Billy stopped twice to get out and drag limbs off Whiskey Road so he could pass.

Eva was getting out of her truck when Billy pulled up in front of the house. She wore dirty yellow rubber bib overalls, galoshes, and a heavy blue sweatshirt with a hood.

"I'm surprised you were able to get here," she said. "With all the wind, I thought Whiskey Road would be closed by downed trees."

"I had to clear some debris, but nothing too big to handle."

"I apologize for my appearance. A tree fell on one of the sheds. Farley and I spent the morning clearing it and repairing the roof."

"Nothing to apologize for. You look fine to me." After he said it, he was surprised to realize she did look fine to him, although he couldn't have explained it to anyone.

She smiled. "You have strange taste, Mr. Kirby."

"Maybe I do, but I stand by my opinion." He held up the manila envelope. "The appraisal came in last night."

She stared at it for a moment and then said, "Let's go inside." He followed her into the house. In the entry hall, she took off her sweatshirt. She wore a man's red and black checkered shirt underneath, too big for her, one of Nelson's old shirts, he guessed. When she shook her hair free, it swirled like snow in a high wind. He stared at her, entranced. Flushed cheeks, dark freckles, crimson lips, framed by a snowstorm of silky hair. She looked back at him curiously, and he looked away, hoping to conceal what was in his heart.

She said, "Perhaps you could make a fire, Mr. Kirby, while I look at the report."

They walked into the parlor. She sat on the sofa. He found paper and kindling in a box by the hearth, placed it under a pile of pine logs, set fire to it, and stoked the fire with a poker. Flames soon licked high in the chimney. The wood popped and cracked. The place warmed up and the scent of burning pine filled the room.

Billy sat in a wing chair near the sofa and watched her read. She paged through the report slowly with no expression on her face. He waited, hoping she would believe Ray's pompous explanation of the current real estate market factors, his lengthy recitation of comparable farm sales going back thirty years, his exaggerated estimate of water rights attaching to Rabbit's Foot Creek, and his phony analysis of the market value of the main house, the cottage, the outbuildings, and the forest timber. Ray's essay was a thorough, well-reasoned effort to mislead the reader. It was good enough to convince most people who knew little or nothing about real estate, but Billy wasn't sure about Eva.

She turned to the final page. Her eyes rested upon a single line and lingered there for quite a while. Billy assumed she was staring at Ray's bogus conclusion of three hundred twenty-five thousand dollars. She set the report on the sofa beside her, leaned back in the cushions, propped her galoshes on the scarred, mud-stained coffee table, crossed her arms over her chest, and stared into the fire. "Convenient," she said. "Enough to pay off the bank and leave me with a goodly sum of money with which to survive."

The heavy sarcasm in her voice told Billy he didn't have much of a chance, but he tried anyway. "You'll have enough left over after you pay off the bank to rent this house from me for a year or two if that's your pleasure."

She smirked at him, picked up the report again, and flipped through it. "This is an impressive document, Mr. Kirby, a lengthy, thorough analysis, replete with charts and diagrams and discussions of supposedly comparative sales. This Mr. Woodson has worked very hard to convince me that my farm is worth a hundred thousand dollars more than the sole offer I received since I put it on the market almost a year ago." She looked at Billy, shook her head, and tossed the report onto the coffee table in front of him. "I'm not an expert in real estate, Mr. Kirby, but I'm not a fool. If my farm was worth as much as Mr. Woodson claims, it would have sold long ago. This report is an obvious fraud."

Billy sat on the end of the chair with his forearms propped on his knees. He looked down at the report and winced.

"How much did you pay this Mr. Woodson?" she said derisively.

"Three thousand dollars."

"You bribed him."

"I paid a premium for the rapid turnaround."

"You bribed him."

Billy could feel her eyes on him. He looked down at the report to avoid them.

"How long have you known this man? How many fraudulent appraisals has he done for you?"

Billy picked up the report, stood, and stepped over to the fireplace. He threw the report in the fire, picked up the poker, and prodded the sheaf of papers until every page had burned away. He propped the poker against the hearth, placed a hand on the fireplace mantle, and leaned into it. The mantle was made of flagstone. It was dusty and barren. No framed family pictures, no vase of flowers, no knickknacks. Eva hadn't bothered to decorate the place or furnish it nicely or clean it. She was a no-frills, no-nonsense woman. It was no wonder he'd failed. He should have known better than to try.

He turned and looked at her. The truth had never been his ally, but she had found him out and he had no other option. "You're right. Twin Ridge Farm is a good farm, fertile land, picturesque and serene, but it's not worth three hundred twenty-five thousand dollars in today's real estate market. The truth is it wouldn't bring much more than two hundred fifty thousand, and that would require a desperate buyer. I apologize for trying to fool you."

She glared at Billy. "I told you I won't accept charity. I may lose everything else, but I will retain my self-respect. I refuse to be pitied."

"Pity has nothing to do with it."

"Then why are you trying so hard to save me from financial ruin, Mr. Kirby?"

Billy looked down at the floor and gathered his courage. When he looked up at her, the light of the fire was dancing in her green eyes. "The other day you said I don't need another farm. You're right about that. I don't need this place. I don't even want it." He took a deep breath. "The truth is I want you."

She looked at him incredulously. Then the lines in her face tightened. "So you decided to buy me, like a prostitute."

He shook his head. "I proposed to buy your farm so I would have an excuse to keep your company. I want to see you, talk to you, be near you."

Her eyes followed him as he went to the sofa and sat down beside her. "When I first saw you in the store several weeks ago, your short visit was pleasurable to me. I've looked forward to every visit you've made since then and treasured every minute of the time you've spent there. At first, I just found you pleasant to talk to. I didn't expect much to come from it, but I was wrong. For reasons I don't understand, I seem to have fallen in love with you."

She frowned and looked at him incredulously.

"I know I'm too old for you," he said. "Hell, at this age, I'm too old for anybody, I guess, but I can't help my feelings for you. You're smarter than any woman I've ever known. You're interesting. We have a lot in common, what with losing our spouses and our sons' problems and all. And you're beautiful."

She raised her eyebrows.

"You're beautiful," he said insistently. "Your eyes take my breath away." He hesitated for a moment, but he figured he'd already made a fool of himself, so there was no point in holding back. "You have the prettiest eyes in Selk County."

A pained expression came across her face. "How many women did you convince to take off their skirts with that hokey line?"

He looked at the fire to avoid her penetrating stare and grimaced. "One," he said softly. "I meant it that time, too." He pressed his hands together and stared at them.

A long silence passed while Billy kept his eyes on the floor because he didn't have the courage to look at her. Then Eva said, "I'm flattered, Mr. Kirby."

When he finally forced himself to look at her, the blank look on her face and the flat tone of her voice didn't give him much hope. He fought back tears.

"Rumor has it," she said, "that you've bedded down almost every pretty woman of your generation in southwestern Virginia. I assume the rumors are exaggerated." She paused. "Slightly." She paused again. "Given my plain looks, I didn't expect to be a candidate for conquest."

Billy shook his head. "Conquest is not my goal."

"What is your goal?"

He thought about the question. "A partnership. Companionship. Affection." He swallowed hard. "My goal is to convince you to marry me."

She laughed. Her gaiety fell away when she seemed to notice his somber expression. "You're serious," she said, knitting her brow.

"I've never been more serious about anything in my life."

A look of confusion came across her face. "You said you only began paying attention to me a few weeks ago. This is rather sudden, don't you think?"

"At my age, it doesn't pay to delay gratification."

She looked like she might burst out laughing again. Then she erased the mirth from her face, turned to the fire, and stared into it for a long time, her face blank and unreadable. He had little chance of an acceptance, he thought, but at least she hadn't thrown him out of the house.

"I want to be alone for a while," she finally said.

His heart sank. "I understand. I'm sorry if I offended you."

"I'm not offended. At least I don't think I am." She frowned at him. "I'm perplexed, I suppose." She shrugged. "Or maybe I'm merely surprised. I don't know. I need to give this a good deal of reflection to know how I feel about it." She stood and walked toward the door.

Billy pulled himself together and followed her out. A cold wind hit him when he stepped out on the porch. He walked past her to the top of the steps and pulled his coat tightly around him.

"Mr. Kirby."

He stopped and looked over his shoulder.

"You keep referring to your age. How old are you?"

He turned and faced her. "I'm eighty years old."

"Isn't that amazing? You don't look a day over seventy-nine."

He flinched.

The corners of her mouth turned upward and then dropped. She stepped closer to him, put her arms around his neck, pulled him tightly to her, and kissed him full on the mouth, her tongue probing. Soft full lips moved over his and her body pressed against his. Before he could adjust to the shock of her advance and react, she abruptly pulled away, stepped back, and studied him. She raised her hand to his mouth and wiped his lower lip. Billy caught her hand and held it. She pulled it away.

"I've never kissed an eighty-year-old man before," she said. "I thought I should see what it's like." She shrugged. "Not much different than kissing a sixty-year-old, but you're not the average eighty-year-old man, I suppose." She tapped him on the chest with a closed fist. "Let's make an appointment, Mr. Kirby. Come back in three days. Be here Monday at noon." She turned and went inside before he had a chance to respond.

Billy staggered out to his truck on unsteady legs. He sat behind the wheel, staring at the house. He touched his lips and thought about the kiss. She was so tall she'd had to bend down to find his mouth. The rubber material of her yellow overalls squeaked when she pressed her groin against his. He looked down at his lap. Tom Johnson stood at attention. He looked at the house and shook his head in wonder at his state of mind. At his age it normally took more than a kiss to arouse him, and certainly more than the mere memory of a kiss. This eccentric, strangely beautiful, unpredictable, smart-as-hell woman had grabbed him by the throat. He let out a long tired breath. The supreme irony of his plight humbled him. All his life he had walked away from women who cared for him. Now in his eightieth year, he had found the love of his life, and the great likelihood was that she would reject him.

Chapter 32

Lot's Wife

Sunday afternoon, Jolene stood on the double-wide's front stoop. It was a cold, clear day. A brilliant gold line rimmed the navy blue clouds that hung over Hawk's Nest Mountain to the west. The Hudson sat in the yard, a stream of vapor floating up from its tailpipe. Porter got out of it, leaving the motor running. He lifted the hood and ducked under it. The engine revved and died down and revved again. He leaned over the cylinder head and wiped oil off the block with a rag.

Jolene walked over to him. "How's it running?"

He stepped back, put his hands on his hips, and stared at the car. "Not too bad. Grover replaced the radiator. A big splinter from that fence you hit punched a hole in it. I thought the axle might be busted, but Grover says it's sound. The front bumper's ruined, though, so he took it off. He tuned up the points and plugs, but she's still missing a bit. Not enough to worry about. She won't quit on you in the middle of a run."

Jolene stared at the Hudson's grille. The chrome design had looked like a big smile before the wreck. Now it was caved in, like someone had punched the car in the mouth and made it cry. "Can he straighten out the front of it?"

"His estimate to repair the grille and replace the bumper is twelve hundred dollars."

"My goodness."

"It ain't worth the money. What he's done so far cost three fifty. I'd forget about fixing the grille if I was you. It ain't pretty, but she'll run fine. And you don't need a new bumper. You won't be pushing anybody out of a ditch with this old crate."

"I guess you're right. Will I be able to drive it tonight?"

"Like I said, she'll run just fine, but I wish you'd let me drive you over there. It's no trouble at all."

"No, thank you. I've got to do this on my own. I can't depend on you for everything."

"I take your point, ma'am, but it might be safer if I drove you. It'll be dark and the weather might turn on you while you're there."

"Thank you for your concern, but I'll be fine."

"All right, then. She needs gas. I'll drive her over to the store and fill her up for you." Porter got in the Hudson and drove out to Whiskey Road.

Jolene stood in the yard watching him drive away. There was honking in the air above her. She looked up. A couple dozen Canadian geese flew across the sky in a V formation. They were a beautiful sight, sleek and graceful, sliding across the sky with ease. She watched them until they melted into the bruised cloud bank over the mountain. Without her glasses, she thought, they would have appeared as indistinct brown lines against the blue backdrop of the sky. She didn't always like the way the world looked with her glasses on, but her myopia had prevented her from seeing much of its beauty, too.

She was headed back to the double-wide when a car turned off the state road into the trailer park. She recognized the gray Dodge Lancer as Reverend Chatham's car. He drove past the double-wide, parked in front of Elmer Gibson's Airstream, and got out of the car. He went to the door and rapped on it. The door opened and the preacher went inside.

Jolene wondered why the preacher was calling on Amos. Amos was not a member of Grace Church and he hadn't spent a single Sunday in the sanctuary with Jolene since their youngest daughter left home. Of course, it was none of Jolene's concern. She was through with him.

She was moving on with her life, and part of moving on involved the church. She had decided to attend the women's Bible study that night, and seeing the preacher reminded her that she hadn't read the assigned passage. She went inside and took off her coat. She went in the bedroom and rooted around in the closet, end tables, and bureau in search of her Bible before finding it at the bottom of Amos' sock and underwear drawer. She went back to the living room and sat on the sofa, wiping the dust off the cover, and cracked it open.

The women's Bible study group had met in the social hall at Grace Church every Sunday night for as long as Jolene could remember. Ten or twelve women sat in folding chairs arranged in a circle and the preacher's wife led them in discussion. Jolene wasn't religious and wasn't a member of the group, but she knew a few of the women and she had to start somewhere if she wanted to make a life for herself. She had called Gertie Wilson the day before for the assigned verses and to catch up on the gossip. As she set her glasses on the table and opened the Bible, she wondered if Gertie might have called the preacher and encouraged him to visit Amos.

She turned to Genesis 19 and read the story of God's destruction of Sodom and Gomorrah. When God sent two angels to warn Lot, his wife, and their two daughters to flee into the mountains because God planned to obliterate the cities, for some unstated reason he told them not to look back when they were running away. Lot's wife disobeyed God's directive and looked back, and God killed her on the spot by turning her into a pillar of salt.

Jolene closed the Bible and held it in her lap and sighed. The story made her sad but she wasn't sure why. It was something about Lot's wife, she thought. The Bible said almost nothing about her. There was no discussion of her history or the type of person she was. There was no explanation of why she looked back, but Jolene felt as though she understood her.

Jolene rubbed the Bible's worn cover. Lot's wife had probably lived her whole life in Sodom and married there and raised her daughters there. Two angels show up out of the blue and command her to abandon all that she cherished to begin a new unknown life of uncertain prospects. She must have been paralyzed with fear and grief.

Jolene traced the faded golden letters of *Holy Bible* on the cover, and below that, *The Word of God*. She saw Lot's wife running along the lip of a precipice in the mountains. Explosions erupted behind her and fire lit up the night sky and she stopped. All the precious experiences of her life were burning behind her. Heartbroken, she took one last look back at her past, and God struck her down for it. Tears came to Jolene's eyes. It seemed so unfair. How could God be so cruel?

She was still crying when someone knocked at her door. She wiped her eyes, pulled herself together, and went to answer it. The preacher stood on the steps. He was a big bear of a man with an unruly mane of black hair, a full beard, piercing violet eyes, and a deep voice. He wore a gray winter coat over a blue suit and a black felt hat. He took off his hat and smiled. "How are you, Mrs. Hukstep?"

"I'm fine, Preacher. Come in out of the cold."

The preacher stepped into the double-wide. Jolene took his coat and hat and draped them over a kitchen stool. She sat on the sofa and motioned for him to sit in Amos' chair.

"Irene tells me you're coming to the meeting tonight," he said.

"Yes, sir."

"I'm glad. I understand you've had a rough winter."

She crossed her legs and folded her hands in her lap. "Who told you that?"

"I just spoke with Amos. He told me he moved out on Thanksgiving Day."

She fingered the pleated edging of a sofa pillow. "Did he tell you why?" She couldn't smooth out the tremor in her voice.

"He wouldn't say. I was hoping maybe you would enlighten me."

Jolene kept fiddling with the pillow. She was afraid she might cry.

"He says he has a drinking problem. I thought maybe that was the reason you separated."

"He didn't drink before he left me."

The preacher sat up on the edge of his chair and clasped his hands together. "If you'll share the cause of your problems with me, maybe I can be of some help in resolving the differences between you."

Jolene folded her hands to still the shaking she didn't want the preacher to see. "Our disagreement is a private matter." She paused to summon firmness in her voice. "I appreciate your concern, but I won't share the details of our differences with you or anyone else."

The preacher looked down at his boots and shook his head. "You and Amos have a lot in common. He turned down my offer in almost those exact words." There was an uncomfortable silence. Then the preacher said, "When were you two married?"

"April twenty-second, 1908."

"Coming up on your sixtieth anniversary. Long time together. How old were you?"

"I was seventeen. He was nineteen."

"You grew up together."

Jolene said nothing more and the preacher fell silent. The sound of a car's engine rolled by the double-wide and on down the road. A dog barked from the far end of the trailer park. The weight of the silence was heavy on Jolene, but she couldn't speak, because her heart was in her throat.

"Well, I guess I'd better be going," the preacher said. He stood.

Jolene stood, got his coat and hat, and handed them to him. "Thank you for caring about us, Preacher," she said without looking at him, struggling to hold it together.

The preacher put on his coat and hat. "If you decide to open up, just let me know. Irene and I want to help in any way we can."

Jolene said nothing.

The preacher went to the door and Jolene opened it for him. He stood beside her, tall and burly with sunlight playing on sandy highlights in his black beard. "Amos is trying to stop, you know," he said. "He doesn't know if he can do it. I'll help him as best I can." The preacher put his arm around Jolene and pulled her to him. She buried her face in the chest of his coat. It smelled sweet, like ginger tea. She let go of her emotions and wept. He held her for a long time, rocking her gently.

When she stepped back her eyes were full. She waved her hand in front of her face. "I'm not crying about Amos," she choked out. "It's the Bible story, Lot's wife." She put her hand over her breast and swallowed. "It's so sad."

"I don't understand," the preacher said.

She waved her hand again. "It's nothing. Thank you again for coming." She took his arm and gently guided him out the door and shut it behind him. She pressed her face against the cool metal door and closed her eyes, trying to purge the image of Lot's wife from her mind.

Chapter 33

The Answer

On Monday morning Billy dressed in his best black suit, boots, winter coat, and hat. He drove the twenty-five miles south to Jeetersburg to a flower shop, bought a bouquet of daisies, and headed back to Fox Run and then on toward Saddleback Cove. The sun pierced through dark gray storm clouds as he turned onto the driveway of Twin Ridge Farm. A shaft of light fell across the far end of the valley and bathed the house in a golden glow.

Billy parked the truck in front of the house under the hickory and got out. The front door opened and Eva walked out on the porch in soiled jeans, a man's black work shirt, a denim jacket, and work boots. Her hair hung down lifelessly and she wore no makeup. Billy's heart sank. Her appearance was not what you'd expect from a woman who intended to accept a marriage proposal.

He gathered his courage, climbed the steps, and handed her the bouquet of daisies. "Flowers for a pretty lady," he said with no confidence whatsoever.

She frowned. "You paid too much for these, Mr. Kirby. They're out of season."

"I thought they might lift your spirits."

"Well, they are beautiful." She turned and went inside. He stood on the porch, confused. The flowers seemed to have angered her, and she hadn't invited him in. He turned and looked at his truck, crestfallen. Maybe he should give it up and go home.

"Mr. Kirby?"

He turned. She stood behind him in the doorway holding a vase with the daisies.

"Aren't you going to come in?"

"Yes, of course."

He followed her into the parlor. She hadn't cleaned up since he was there Friday. In fact, it looked worse. More muddy tracks on the floor and more old newspapers strewn around the room. The cold hearth was filled with charred logs and ashes. She set the vase on the coffee table in the midst of a jumble of half-filled coffee mugs and dirty dishes.

He hung his coat and hat on a rack by the door and went about setting a fire with kindling and cordwood.

She sat down on the sofa. "I apologize, Mr. Kirby. I appreciate the thought, but I'm against cut flowers."

He looked over his shoulder at her. "Against them?"

"I think it's wrong to cut flowers for a parlor table. It's a frivolous, selfish act."

Billy stoked the fire with a poker and closed the mesh screen across the face of the hearth. He turned and cast a dour look at the flowers. "I'm sorry. I didn't know."

"There is a lot about me you don't know, Mr. Kirby."

Billy sat in one of the wing chairs. He took a deep breath and soldiered on in the face of certain defeat. "There is a lot about you I do know. I'm not a fickle teenager, Eva. I've lived long enough to know what I want and why I want it."

A hint of a smile at the corners of Eva's mouth was quickly suppressed. It fired a small spark of hope in his heart. He cleared his throat. "So, what will we do, Eva, about the fact that I'm in love with you and want to marry you?"

She stared into the fire, frowning. "Yes, well, I suppose we have to deal with that in some way or other, don't we?"

"So what is your answer? Will you marry me?"

She glanced at him and looked back at the fire. She took a deep breath.

"I haven't decided."

He did his best to conceal his excitement. Her tone of voice told him he had a chance.

"I've thought a great deal about you and your proposal since you left here," she said. "I've thought about nothing else, but I haven't been able to come to a decision. The advantages and disadvantages seem equally balanced."

He leaned forward. "What do you consider to be the advantages?"

She swept a lock of hair out her eyes. "On the positive side is your wealth. With all my talk about pride, I confess I'm attracted by the security you offer me. I seem to have no other way to survive."

On the drive to her house, he had thought he would be overjoyed if she accepted his proposal no matter what her reason, but now it troubled him that she might marry him solely for his money. "Is there nothing in my favor other than my wealth?"

"Yes, of course. Your best trait is your generosity. Your kind nature and good works have won my respect and the respect of the community."

Billy was surprised. Money had never meant much to him except as a way to keep score in his dealings with other men, as a way to compete. He was obsessed with winning, and he almost always won; the money he gave away meant nothing to him.

"You understand how much the community appreciates your good deeds, don't you, Mr. Kirby?" Eva said.

He started to protest, almost certain she was wrong, but held back, not wanting to undermine his argument.

She raised her eyebrows. "You don't believe me, do you?" She smiled. "Mr. Kirby, you loaned money to almost every farmer in the hollow after the war when no one else would help them. Those farmers will never forget what you did. You were their salvation."

Billy was unconvinced that writing a few checks had trumped a lifetime of lying, cheating, and philandering, but Eva's smile widened and she scooted up on the edge of the sofa. "Your good works are legion. Grayson Sipe says he would have amounted to nothing if you hadn't paid his way through Jefferson State University. Lilah Clayton, Jason Ames, Morris Jones, Hilda Coleman all give you credit for their college degrees. And the Shanks family—when Little Bear River swamped their land, you let a house to them for free while Tom Wilcox rebuilt their home. You paid for the repairs."

Billy blurted out an explanation before he realized it was against his interest. "Ollie Shanks and his family worked for my father for thirty years. He paid them way less than they were worth, and I always felt bad about it. The flood gave me an excuse to square things up."

"Perhaps, but they weren't the only colored family you helped."

No one else had stepped up, so he'd opened his checkbook. Billy fell silent.

"And there's Porter," she said.

Billy looked up at her.

Eva leaned forward and put her hand on his knee. "Porter told me what you did for him. He said Vietnam almost ruined him. He came home with a drinking problem. He got in trouble with the law. You took him in hand and helped him quit."

Billy stared at her large rough hand. He wanted to take it in his, but he was afraid she would be offended.

"You saved that boy's life," she said. "You taught him right from wrong and changed his ways and everyone admires you for it."

"But there's Blakey," he said softly.

The smile fell from her face and she withdrew her hand from his knee. "He's a mean one, so I've heard. Like my son, Franklin. Believe me, I understand how you feel about him, but if you take the blame for him, you have to take the credit for Porter."

Billy rubbed his face. "What about affection, Eva? Do you care for me?"

Eva paused, looking pensive. "I like you. I find you interesting."

"But you don't love me?"

"Love doesn't come easy for me, Mr. Kirby. Nelson hurt me badly. Franklin, too."

"I won't hurt you."

She arose, went to the hearth, and stood with her back to him. "I'm not so sure." She turned. "I don't know if I can trust you."

"You can trust me," Billy said anxiously. "What do you want me to do to prove it? I'll do anything. Just say the word."

She looked around the room, her face tight and hard. Then she looked at Billy. "You have a reputation, Mr. Kirby, for engaging in certain behavior that would hurt me deeply."

Billy's optimism flagged. "I've made some mistakes, Eva. I won't make them again."

She stared at him intensely, her jade eyes shining. "If I'm to consider your proposal, you must agree in advance to certain rules of conduct."

"What rules?" he asked, feeling queasy.

"No whoring around. No consorting with any other woman."

"I can live with that rule."

"Why should I believe you? You were not faithful to your wife."

Billy nodded slowly. "I was not."

"The rumors are that you were spectacularly unfaithful."

"Yes, ma'am." He felt the blood rising into his face. "The rumors are true. I was a fool. I ruined my marriage."

"Why should I think you would be faithful to me?"

"I've learned some hard lessons the last few months. My mistakes caused me and my friends a lot of pain."

"They weren't mistakes, Mr. Kirby. They were intentional choices."

He grimaced and looked down. "I promise you, I'll live by your rule. I'll be faithful. I won't cheat."

Eva stared at him for a long time. "I'm not sure I believe you."

He looked up at her and tried to show her what was in his heart. "You have good reason to doubt me. I can't erase my past. All I can do is tell you I've never met anyone like you. I've never felt as strongly about anyone as I feel about you. Since I met you I can't imagine being with anyone else."

She stared at him for another long spell. Then she went back to the sofa and sat down. She folded her hands in her lap and looked him in the eye.

"The word is you often drink to excess. I'm not against taking a drink now and then, but I will tolerate no big drunks. No binges."

Billy nodded again. "No drunks. No binges. You have my word on it."

She looked down at her hands and pressed them tightly together. "One last rule. No lying."

Billy's stomach turned over. He could make the promise, but he wasn't sure he could keep it no matter how hard he tried. "Spinning a good story," he said uncomfortably, "is kind of second nature to me."

"So I've heard. Some say you are an inveterate liar. I didn't believe them until you and Mr. Woodson presented me with a twenty-two-page appraisal, every word of which was a lie."

"That report was a mistake. I'm sorry for it."

"It wasn't a mistake. It was a conscious lie."

"All right, it was a lie." He blew out a long breath. "Sometimes a lie can soften a hard truth. I've told a lie or two to ease the burden on a friend." He gave her a pained look. "Is there no room for an exception for that type of thing?"

She seemed to search his face. Then she said, "You can deal with your friends however you like, but I want nothing but the truth from you. There will be no lying to me. No soft lies. No hard lies. No lies of any kind. If you can't live with that, we're done here."

Billy moved to the sofa and sat beside her. He took her hand and looked her in the eye, thinking he had cleared the last obstacle. "I won't lie to you."

Eva took in a deep breath and squeezed his hand. "There's one last subject that troubles me. It's rather awkward to discuss."

His anxiety returned. "What is it?"

"You look younger than your years and you seem vigorous, but you are eighty years old and that causes me some concern."

"What do you want me to do? Get a certificate of good health? I could hire a team of doctors."

"That's not what I had in mind."

Billy searched her face. The crimson in her cheeks, the glint in her eyes, and the way she leaned against him suddenly came together. He dropped her hand and edged away from her.

She arose and looked down at him, her lips pressed together into a tight line. "I'm going upstairs to my bedroom." She looked at her watch. "In thirty minutes, at one o'clock sharp and not a minute sooner, you will join me. It's the first door on the left." She marched out of the room and he heard her boots climb the stairs.

Sweat popped out all over him. He wiped it from his face and the back of his neck. His hands trembled. He stood and looked around desperately for a liquor cabinet. There was nothing in the parlor. He rushed into the dining room, where a china cabinet across from the windows had a half-empty bottle of brandy on a bottom shelf. He poured a crystal glass full and downed it in one swallow. He grabbed the corner of the cabinet and gagged. His legs shook. He held onto the cabinet, breathing hard while the brandy's warm glow went through him. He looked at the bottle longingly, but put it back and went into the kitchen to drink water from the tap to cleanse his breath. He wandered back into the dining room, nervous and on edge. He untied his string tie, tossed it on the dining room table, and unhooked the collar button of his shirt. He breathed in and out deeply. Certainly he could pass this last test. He'd been addicted to comely women for sixty-five years and he'd never failed to perform.

He rounded the dining room table and opened a window. The cool air refreshed him. He took deep breaths and looked outside. The tire swing caught his eye. He saw Eva again, standing in the tire, clutching the rope, pulling it hard to make the swing go back and forth, her dimpled cheeks flushed, her white hair fanning out behind her on the upswing, flowing across her face on the downswing. He could hear her throaty laughter. The tightness in his body relaxed. His nerves stabilized. His heartbeat slowed.

At one o'clock sharp, he climbed the stairs. At the top, a hallway stretched out to a window. Sunlight fell on the faded wallpaper of yellow lilies and green leaves. The air in the hallway was cold, and it smelled like overripe apples. The first door to his left was knotty pine. He stepped forward and gripped its brass handle. It was cold to the touch and the cold went through him. He let go of it, wiped his sweaty hands on his pants, and conjured the image of Eva on the tire swing. He took a couple deep breaths, turned the door handle, and stepped inside.

A rush of hot air greeted him. The room was dark except for the light coming from a fire burning in a stone fireplace on the far wall and a lit candle that sat in a saucer on top of a bureau next to the door. There was a sweet aroma in the air, some sort of incense. When his eyes adjusted to the darkness, he saw that all the curtains had been drawn, blotting out the sunlight. A massive bed with a high headboard of burled mahogany was directly in front of him. Eva sat on the edge of the bed dressed in a blood-red terrycloth bathrobe with her legs crossed. She had fixed up for him. Eye shadow, red lip gloss, rouge, silky white hair brushed out and flipped up at her shoulders. Her jade eyes stared at him. She stood, untied the sash of her robe, slipped it off her shoulders, and let it drop to her feet. She trembled. "Close the door, Mr. Kirby."

Billy turned and closed the door.

Chapter 34

The Homecoming

Billy and Eva lay side by side, covered with a sheen of sweat, on the bed in the dark room. They had kicked off the sheets.

"Did I pass the test?"

Eva brushed a lock of damp hair back from her face, rolled on her side, and draped one of her long legs over his thighs. "A plus. You're much younger than your years, but your enthusiasm is impressive for a man of any age."

Enthusiasm had been a necessity, he thought. He might not have survived without it. She had been a challenge, taller than Billy, stronger and more athletic, limber, with legs and arms all over the place grabbing, twisting, pulling, and pumping. "I wish I'd found you fifty years ago."

"You'd have been jailed for child molestation. I was twelve years old."

"Forty years ago, then. You're the most fascinating woman I've ever known." He kissed her on the lips.

She responded and then pulled back and smiled at him. "You want to go again?"

"I'm not that much younger than my years."

She laughed. "We'll wait a while, then, Mr. Kirby."

Billy wiped sweat from his forehead. "Don't you think we know each other well enough now that you can call me by my given name?"

She made a sour face. "Billy is a child's name. You're a man of substance and maturity. I don't want to marry Billy. I want to marry Mr.

Kirby."

"Suit yourself. I don't care if you call me Adolph Hitler. When do you want to get married?"

"I don't care. Whenever you want is fine with me."

"April fourteenth."

She looked at him curiously. "That's Easter Sunday."

"I know."

"I thought you weren't a believer."

"I'm not."

"Why Easter then?"

"I like what it stands for."

Eva frowned thoughtfully. Then she broke into a smile. "The resurrection? You've risen from the dead?"

"I've been through a lot of turmoil the last few months. It almost killed me."

She made a wry face. "You can't arise from the dead unless you die first. You'll need to be murdered by crucifixion on Good Friday. Should I hire someone to take care of that or handle it myself?"

"On second thought, maybe April first would be more appropriate."

She threw back her head and laughed. "Fool's day. Fits like a body stocking." She put her head on his shoulder and pulled him closer to her. The fire died down; the room cooled; and they fell asleep.

The preacher at Grace Church initially refused to marry Billy and Eva on Easter Sunday, but he warmed to the idea when Billy made a big donation to the church fund for the needy. They set the wedding for two P.M. with a reception to follow at Billy's house. They published an announcement in the *Jeetersburg Daily Progress* and sent out invitations to their friends and neighbors. Their marriage quickly became the talk of the county.

Three weeks before the wedding, a late-season blizzard befell Whippoorwill Hollow and Saddleback Cove, dumping more than a foot of snow on the mountains and valleys. High winds blew down trees, telephone poles, and power lines. Porter called Billy from Toby Vess' house to say he couldn't make it to the store. Jolene's telephone and power were out and Porter didn't want to leave her alone until VEPCO sent a truck to turn on the heat. The same power and telephone lines ran to Twin Ridge Farm, so Billy asked Porter to check on Eva.

Midmorning, Billy walked across the icy road from his house to the store. He swept snow off the steps and fired up the stove. From the porch he could see the trunk of a downed hickory stretched across the state road to the north; no one would be able to reach the store from Whippoorwill Hollow until it was cleared away. Most of the farmers would be checking their livestock, mending fences, and clearing snow anyway.

By dusk, no one had come by, but Billy stayed open, sitting beside the stove, basking in its warm glow and thinking about Eva. The light died early under the overcast sky. It was dark at five when the bell above the door pinged. Billy looked up hopefully, searching the shadows for the face of an old friend.

A hulking figure slouched down the center aisle. Even in the store's dim light, Billy recognized the broad, slumped shoulders and the belligerent swagger of his son. An irrational hope of reconciliation flared in Billy's mind until he saw that Blakey was clutching a whiskey bottle in his right hand and a rifle in his left. Blakey sat down in a laddered chair by the bench and set the rifle on the floor beside it. It was Billy's hunting rifle, which had been locked in the gun case in his parlor.

Billy looked warily at Blakey. He had aged in prison. Dark crevices rimmed his sunken eyes; jowls sagged from his jawline; and a scar traced a jagged half-moon path below his left eye through grimy stubble to his chin. Oily strands of coal-black hair flecked with gray stuck out from a dirty blue Philip Morris ball cap. His jacket was torn at the shoulder and his jeans were filthy and tattered.

Blakey propped his muddy boots on the bench beside Billy, unscrewed the cap of the whiskey bottle, and tossed it away. It skittered across the plank floor and bounced off the wall by the drink case. He took a long pull from the bottle and thrust it at Billy. "Care for a taste?"

Billy shook his head.

"What's the matter? You too good to drink with an ex-convict?"

"I don't care for a drink."

"Suit yourself." Blakey took another big swig and cradled the bottle in his lap. "You don't look happy to see your only son."

A line of sweat trickled down Billy's back and he pressed his hands together in his lap. "You don't look like you're here to make me happy."

A wry smile crossed Blakey's lips. "You're afraid of me, aren't you?"

Billy looked down at the floor and said nothing.

"You should be afraid, old man," Blakey said. He turned the bottle up, took a long pull, held it in his lap, and gazed at it for a long time. "I would have dropped by earlier, but my parole officer told me I'd best stay away from you. Eight years in the pen makes you think twice before you break their rules." He rubbed the mouth of the bottle. "God knows I tried this time. I got me a job in Richmond runnin a tobacco shredder. Punched the goddamn time clock every morning and evening and did what they told me in between." He frowned at Billy. "Why do you suppose the boss man had to be an asshole?" He paused as though he expected an answer. "Seems like that's always the way. You do the best you can and some asshole comes along and tells you it's not good enough." He drank from the bottle, swiped his sleeve across his mouth, and winced.

"You shouldn't drink, son," Billy said quietly. "It always leads to trouble."

"I don't recall you turnin down any drinks, and you sure as hell caused more than your fair share of trouble. It's been a long time since I tied one on."

Billy eyed the rifle. "Jim Beam and firearms don't mix. What do you plan to do with my rifle?"

Blakey looked down at the gun. "I thought about going after Raylene when I finish here, but she's already cost me eight years." He knitted his brow. "She lied at the trial, you know? She told em about the times I hit her, but she didn't tell em why. She didn't tell em how she flirted with other men." He shook his head slowly. A tear slid into the crevice of his scar.

"She lived with me for three years. Longest I ever stayed with a woman." He wiped his eyes with his sleeve and looked at Billy. "Did you know she told me she loved me?"

Billy shook his head.

"She did. She said she loved me, said it over and over again." He pressed his lips together and swallowed. "It was a lie. She'd say she loved me one night and the next night we'd be out somewhere and she'd give every man in the room the come-on and I'd have to slap her around. We'd make up and she'd say she loved me again." He pulled the ball cap down low over his eyes and cleared his throat. "Then she up and ran off with Carter Embry, like I didn't mean nothin to her at all." He took another swig from the bottle. "They're lucky I didn't kill em both."

"It's best not to dwell on Raylene," Billy said. "Let her go, son. She's not worth the heartache."

Blakey looked at Billy contemptuously. "You're an expert in heartache, I reckon."

Billy looked at the stove and said nothing.

"You and Raylene have a lot in common, you know?" Blakey said. "She didn't love me, and you never cared a lick about me either. Y'all both treated me like a stray dog you took in for a while and then left on the side of the road."

"That's not true, son. I care about you. I've always cared about you."

"You're lying. You never cared about me."

Billy ran his hand across his mouth and dropped his eyes to the floor.

"I spent a lot of time in the pen thinking about all the hell you put me through, old man. I thought about all the years I lived in that old house across the road, about all the times when I was a little boy and I was so scared I was sick to my stomach and couldn't sleep. I remembered all the times you came home drunk, smellin of whiskey and some cheap whore."

Billy felt Blakey's hard stare on him while the wind blew outside and moaned in the cracks in the old store's walls. He kept his eyes down.

"I remembered all the times you and Mary Jo screamed and yelled at each other, and I thought about that night she brought home a drunk farmer just to spite you and I sat in the corner cryin and screamin while you and him beat each other half to death."

Billy looked up at Blakey with tears in his eyes. "Me and Mary Jo had our troubles," he said, his voice full with emotion. "I know you suffered for it, and I'm sorry for that, sorrier than you can know."

"You're sorry. Well, I guess that makes it all right then. That makes it all go away."

"Nothing can make it go away. If I could make it all go away, I would, but I can't. All I can do is tell you how sorry I am for all of it."

"Bullshit. You're not sorry about anything. You took what you wanted and you ruined my life." Blakey took a long pull on the bottle, dropped it to his lap, and glared at Billy. Then he brought his feet down to the floor and leaned toward Billy. "Here's what I don't understand. They threw Leroy Sipe in the pen last summer for tryin to kill his wife up in the hollow. Him and me pulled a lotta yard time together, and he told me what you did for Porter. Said it was the talk of the county. Bailed him outta jail, put him in a drunk tank to dry out, gave him an interest in the store and a house to live in." A vulnerable look came across Blakey's face, a look Billy hadn't seen before, something he had picked up in prison, Billy guessed. "You treat Porter like he's your son," Blakey said. He paused for a long time and then said in a soft voice, "Why him and not me?"

Billy shifted on the bench, trying hard to bear up under Blakey's tortured stare. "I was a bad father to you." He paused to maintain his composure. "By the time I figured that out and tried to do better, you were too angry to listen. I couldn't make you change and I gave up on you." Billy ran his hand through his hair and sighed. "When Porter got in so much trouble, I knew better what to do. I didn't want to see him go down the same sorry road, so I tried to help him. I tried to do for him what I failed to do for you."

Blakey's eyes brimmed with tears. "Well, ain't that nice? You ruined my life, and to make up for it, you decided to steal my son from me."

"I didn't steal Porter, Blakey. You were in jail. I was here with him and you weren't, so I raised him."

Blakey leaned back in the chair and shook his head. "I was in jail because of you, God damn you."

A cold draft fell from the rafters and chased the warmth of the stove into the shadows. Billy stared at his son and thought about all the years of heartache they had caused each other. Billy's grief about the immense tragedy of Blakey's life pushed aside his fear of him. A great longing to break through Blakey's self-pity welled up inside him, and words he wished he'd said years ago spilled out with as much force as his broken vocal chords could muster. "I treated you wrong when you were a boy, Blakey, but I didn't put you in jail. No one forced you to kidnap Raylene or beat up Carter Embry or tear up Ivy Ridge Church or cause scores of people heartache and misery over the course of your life. You made those decisions on your own and you're responsible for them. You're fifty years old. It's high time to stop crying about your past. You've served your time and you've earned your freedom. Don't fall back into your old ways and blame everyone else for your problems. Take charge of your life and make a good future for yourself."

A look of disgust came across Blakey's face. "Nice speech. Mostly bullshit, of course, to make you feel good and grind me into the dirt, like everything you've ever said to me, but at least you got part of it right. Takin charge of my life is exactly why I'm here." He set the bottle on the bench, picked up the rifle, and pointed it at Billy. "Stand up."

"Blakey, please listen to me. Please—"

"Shut up, you old bastard!" Blakey stood and put the end of the barrel inches from Billy's face. "Stand up or I'll blow your head off, you miserable son of a bitch!"

Billy stood slowly.

"Give me the key to the back room."

"What do you want with the key?"

"Give me the key, God damn it!"

Billy withdrew the key from his pocket and gave it to Blakey.

Blakey motioned with the rifle toward the back room. He unlocked the door and pocketed the key.

"Head on in there," Blakey said.

Billy pulled the door open. Cold air rushed into his face and braced him.

"Open the safe."

Billy flicked the light switch, knelt before the safe on the floor on the back wall, and ran the combination.

"Give me the cash, all of it."

Billy gathered the packets of cash, arose, and handed them to Blakey, who shoved them in his jacket pockets. "How much is it?"

"Three thousand. Maybe a little more."

"That ought to be enough."

"What are you going to do?"

"I'm takin charge of my life, old man. No more job at the goddamn Philip Morris plant. No more meetings with the jackass PO. No more bullshit from you. Me and the boy are leaving here for good tonight."

Billy blanched. "You and Porter?"

"That's right, me and Porter are leaving you and this shit swamp behind. He's my son, not yours. He belongs with me."

"He won't go with you."

"He'll go. He may not want to, but he'll go one way or the other, and when we get down the road a piece, he'll be damned glad to get away from you and all the sons of bitches in Selk County."

"Leave him be, Blakey. He has a chance to build a good life here. Don't ruin it for him."

"He won't have a chance in hell with you. You don't care about him. You don't care about anybody but yourself. You'll turn on him sooner or later and break him the way you broke me."

"Please, Blakey, I'm sorry I did wrong by you. Take it out on me, but leave Porter alone."

Blakey gritted his teeth. "Turn around and face the wall."

"Blakey—"

"Shut up!" Blakey jabbed Billy's chest hard with the rifle. "Do as I say! Turn around!"

Billy turned. A blow to his head stunned him; his knees buckled; and he went down.

Some time later, grit pressed into the flesh of Billy's cheek. He was dazed and didn't know where he was. He passed in and out of consciousness twice more without realizing his circumstances. The third time he came to, he rolled over on his back and his mind cleared a bit. It was cold. A naked light bulb hung from rafters above him. He rolled his head to the side and saw the firewood box and he remembered where he was and how he had gotten there. He sat up and pressed his palm against a throbbing lump on the back of his head. He rose to his hands and knees and stayed in that position until the room stopped spinning. He looked around to get his bearings. He grabbed the safe, pulled himself up, and sat on top of it, holding his head in his hands for a while before he stood slowly, walked unsteadily to the door, and twisted the knob. It was locked from the outside.

He threw his shoulder against it. It didn't give. He gathered his strength, stepped back, and kicked it. Once, twice, three times. It still didn't give way. He leaned against the door, out of breath. The doorframe was old oak, solid and hard, but with leverage he ought to be able to split it at the latch.

He looked around for a tool. Against the back wall lay a stack of metal bars he used for shelf supports. He sorted through them and found several that were long with flat ends. He chose the strongest one and jammed its flat end into the crevice between the door and the frame at the latch. He pulled the bar back toward him, forcing it to bear his full weight. Once. Twice. On the third pull, the frame busted away from the latch and the door sprang open.

Billy tossed the bar aside and staggered out of the back room. The fire had died out in the stove and the store was cold. His legs shook so badly that he had to sit down on the bench to recuperate. He couldn't waste time, he told himself. He didn't know how long he had been unconscious. He arose and forced himself to walk to the front of the store, holding onto shelves along the way. When he leaned on the counter to gather his strength, he saw that the cash register drawer stood open and empty and the telephone wire had been pulled out of the wall.

He went to the window and looked outside. There were no vehicles in sight. The floodlight on the corner of the store cast light across the road at his house. Its front door stood open.

Billy staggered across the road and over the walkway to his front porch. The doorframe was splintered at the padlock and the top hinge had been torn loose. In the foyer, the glass front of his gun case was shattered and the rack was empty. He went into the parlor. The liquor cabinet stood open and the telephone lay on the floor with its wire pulled out of the wall.

He went back to the foyer, climbed the stairs, and limped down the hall to the telephone in Porter's old bedroom. He lifted the receiver and breathed a deep sigh of relief when he heard a dial tone. He dialed Jolene's number. Then he remembered the storm had knocked out her line. There was only dead air.

He dialed Toby Vess and Toby answered. "Blakey was here," Billy rasped. "He's got my rifle. He's drunk and he's looking for Porter."

"What's Blakey want with Porter?"

"He's running away and he wants to take Porter with him. I don't know what Blakey will do when Porter turns him down. I don't think he knows he's staying with Jolene, so we may have some time before he finds him. Go over to Jolene's and get them out of there."

"I'm on my way."

"Toby?"

"Yes?"

Billy hesitated.

"What is it, Billy?"

"Try not to hurt him."

"I'll do my best." Toby hung up the phone.

Billy stared at the phone for a few moments. Then he went to his bedroom for his pistol and headed out to his truck. He spun out of the driveway and sped over Whiskey Road toward Saddleback Cove.

Chapter 35

The Attack

The day had been bittersweet for Jolene. Porter stayed home with her to wait for the linemen from VEPCO and the telephone company. The telephone men never arrived, but VEPCO got there at dusk and restored power to the trailer park. Porter got Jolene's heater working and made the rounds to the other trailers to make sure everyone else had heat, too.

Jolene had enjoyed Porter's company that day, but she knew their days together were numbered. That night, Jolene sat on the couch trying to read next Sunday's Bible passage, but she couldn't concentrate on the text. She put on her glasses and looked at Porter. He sat in Amos' chair flipping through a *Reader's Digest*.

"I overheard you yesterday when you were on the telephone," she said.

Porter looked up at her.

"I shouldn't have eavesdropped, but I couldn't help myself. You and Maureen seem to be getting along much better."

Porter closed the magazine and put it aside. "We've had some good talks, but I don't think we'll be getting back together anytime soon."

"You don't need to stay with me, you know. I'll be all right when you go back home. I can manage on my own."

"That's not the problem." Porter leaned forward, propped his forearms on his knees, and clasped his hands together. "She doesn't want me back yet. Her dad is dead set against it."

"Is he still refusing to talk with you?"

Porter nodded. "He says it wouldn't do any good. Says a polecat can't wipe the stripe off his back. I'm my daddy's son and I'm just like him." Porter sighed. "There's truth to that. I've tried to change, but they can't forget what I did and she listens to them."

Jolene looked down at the Bible and thought about Amos. "Forgiveness doesn't come easy, but there comes a point when a harsh judgment only begets loneliness." She set the book aside. "I want to talk to Maureen's father."

"It won't help. His mind is made up."

"I want to give it a try."

Headlights flashed in the window and a truck pulled up near the carport. The engine died and the truck's door slammed. "Maybe the telephone company finally got somebody out here," Porter said, heading to the window.

The front door swung open and a man stepped into the trailer with a rifle in his hands. The sour scents of alcohol, filth, and sweat rushed into the room with the night's cold air.

"What are you doing here?" Porter said.

The man raised his eyebrows. "You would think a man's only son would be pleased to see his dear old daddy after all these years."

Blakey Kirby had aged so much and looked so slovenly and disheveled that Jolene only recognized him because he said he was Porter's daddy.

"What do you want?" Porter said.

Blakey looked at Jolene and smiled at Porter. "It's a long drop from Maureen Poway to old Mrs. Hukstep. You must be mighty hard up to spend the cold, stormy night with a dried-up old prune."

"Don't speak about her that way."

Blakey's smile fell. "I was just jokin. No offense intended." Blakey closed the door. "I had a helluva time trackin you down, boy," he said in a jovial tone. "Your house was dark, so I headed over to the Poway farm to see if you were there and I got lucky. Nobody was home except Maureen's stupid brother, and he told me where you were stayin. He said Maureen threw you out for bein a drunk. I'm sorry to hear about your bust-up, but it might be a good thing in the long run, especially when you hear what I have to say."

"Get out," Porter said coldly.

Blakey paused, frowning. "There's no reason to be disrespectful, son."

"There's every reason. Get out. Now."

"But I have something important to talk to you about. A chance at a new life."

"You and I have nothing to talk about. Get out and leave us alone."

Blakey looked hurt at first then he seemed to shrug it off. His face brightened and he pulled a whiskey bottle out of his jacket pocket and extended it to Porter.

Porter trained his cold glare on his father. "I told you to get out."

Blakey grimaced. He stared at Porter for a couple of beats and then pointed the rifle at him, holding it with one hand, the bottle in the other. "Have a seat. You and I are going to have a father-son chat, whether you want to or not."

"Who'll be the father? You don't qualify."

Blakey glowered. "That's enough lip for one night. You'd best watch your mouth from here on out." Blakey motioned to Amos' chair with the rifle. "Have a seat."

Porter didn't move.

Blakey put the mouth of the rifle within inches of Porter's face. "Sit down."

Porter still didn't move.

"Sit down, Porter," Jolene said. "Please."

Blakey said, "Do what Grandma says, son."

Porter glared at Blakey for a few moments. Then he slowly sat down in the chair.

Blakey sat on the couch next to Jolene. His face softened and he lowered the rifle. "I didn't come here to threaten you, boy." He leaned across the coffee table and thrust the whiskey bottle at Porter again. "Come on, son. Have a taste."

"I don't drink."

Blakey thrust the bottle closer. "You sure? She's smooth as silk."

Porter stared at the bottle and Jolene saw weakness in his eyes. "Don't do it, Porter," she said.

Blakey shot Jolene a dark look. "Shut your mouth, old woman! I wasn't talkin to you!"

"I told you not to speak to her that way," Porter said angrily.

Blakey turned back to Porter and his expression softened again. "All right. All right. I just thought we could have a drink together is all. I didn't mean to cause trouble between us." Blakey set the bottle on the table in front of Porter. "I'll just leave this here where you can reach it if you change your mind."

Porter looked at the bottle, but made no move toward it.

Blakey settled back into the cushions of the couch, draping the rifle across his lap. "I've been lookin forward to havin a good talk with you, son."

"You and I have nothing to talk about."

"Sure we do. I want to talk about you and me."

"There is no you and me."

The lines of Blakey's face tensed. "It's the old man, ain't it? He's poisoned you against me."

"You poisoned me against you."

Blakey shook his head. "It's the old man. I'm sure of it. I heard all about it when I was in the pen. He's been good to you, set you up in the store, taught you how to run it, right?"

Porter said nothing, his cold stare unwavering.

Blakey said, "Got you out of trouble with the law, kept you outta jail, bought you a new car, gave you and Maureen a house to live in." Blakey sat up on the edge of the sofa. "You know it won't last, don't you? You know there'll come a day when he'll want something, and you'll be in the way and his true nature will take over. You don't mean anything more to him than I do. He'll throw you away like a piece a trash for a pretty smile, a quick thrill, a wild party, a fast buck, anything that catches his fancy. He doesn't care about you. He cares about himself and what he wants and nothing else."

Porter said nothing.

Blakey leaned forward, a pleading look on his face. "Listen to me, boy. You can't trust him. Don't fall for his lies. He'll break your spirit sooner or later. I know. I'm an expert on him." Blakey seemed to search Porter's face for signs of assent. "You've got to believe me," Blakey said desperately. "He ruined me and he'll ruin you. That's why I came looking for you, boy, to get you away from him before he breaks you down. I've found us a way out of his death grip."

"What are you talking about?"

"I'm talking about a fresh start, a new life, away from all the old man's craziness and misery." The pace of Blakey's speech quickened. "An old boy I met in the pen owns a big piece of land in West Virginia. Before they turned him loose, he told me I could join him out there when I got out. We'll run moonshine and make a ton of money, him and his boy and me." An almost childlike look came across Blakey's face. "And you, boy. I want you to come with me."

"What?" Porter looked incredulous.

"He can't leave here," Jolene said anxiously. "He has a wife and—"

"Shut the hell up, you old bitch!" Blakey yelled. "This don't involve you! It's between me and the boy!"

Porter jumped up and took a step toward Blakey. He raised the rifle and thumped the end of the barrel against Porter's chest.

"Don't, Porter!" Jolene shouted.

Porter froze, glaring at Blakey.

"Please don't hurt him," Jolene said.

"I told you to shut up," Blakey said to her without taking his eyes off Porter.

She put her hand over her mouth to stifle a sob.

Porter looked at her and then down at the barrel pressing against his chest. He backed off and sat down slowly.

Blakey took several deep breaths, wiped sweat from his brow, and unclasped the top button of his shirt. "Last thing I want is to fight with you, boy," he said, sounding tired and worn down. "I want us to get along, be good to each other, take care of each other."

"There's no chance of that," Porter said.

Blakey looked down for a moment and seemed to be trying to summon his patience. Then he looked up at Porter and said, "Just listen to me, will you? This place is perfect for us if you'll just give it a chance." His face brightened again. "This old boy's farmland is in McDowell County, way up on the side of a steep mountain, rugged, wild country with mountain springs and cold streams, pure water, perfect for brewin shine. It's so far out in the sticks the state police, the parole board, the sheriff's boys—no one will be able to find us. We'll be miles away from Whippoorwill Hollow and the old man and all the people here who drag us down. No one will know where we came from or what we've done. We'll start all over again with a clean record." He scooted farther up on the edge of the couch. "Come with me, boy," he said eagerly. "We can leave tonight, drive straight through, and be there in the morning."

"I'm not going anywhere with you."

Blakey closed his eyes, swallowed, and then looked at Porter with desperation written on his face. "Please come with me, boy. We'd be together out there with no one to set us against each other. We'd be like family, like father and son."

Porter squinted at Blakey. "When I was little you were too busy whoring and drinking to be a father. The few times you were with me, you beat me. You spent my teen years rotting away in a jail cell. You've never been a father to me, and I don't want to be your son. I don't want any part of you, and I sure as hell won't go anywhere with you."

Blakey sat back on the couch. He looked devastated, as though his closest friend had just died. Jolene would have felt sorry for him if she didn't know better. He sat for a long time. Then his profound disappointment seemed to dissipate and a determined menace gradually took its place and settled into his aspect. He sat up straight and pointed the gun at Porter. "Here's how it is, boy. I'm your father, whether you like it or not. You'll learn to love me or you won't, but you're coming with me. You'll come along of your own free will or hogtied in the back of my truck."

"I'm not going with you," Porter said.

Jolene put her hand on Blakey's arm. "He's a good young man, Blakey. Please don't make him—"

"Shut up!" Blakey yelled. "I told you this is between me and the boy! Stay out of it!"

"But he can't—"

Blakey's fist came at her so swiftly she didn't have time to react, a straight hard left jab, smooth and lightning fast, a forceful, efficient blow perfectly on target, the product of years of practice on his wife, Raylene, and others. His iron-hard knuckles caught her beside her right eye, breaking her glasses. Broken remnants streaked over the coffee table as Jolene flew across the arm of the couch and hit her head on the table. Blood sprayed the table and the reading lamp and she screamed.

Porter jumped to his feet and Blakey raised the rifle to point it at Porter's chest, yelling, "Stay back!" Porter grabbed the end of the rifle and tried to jerk it aside. There was a deafening explosion. A shower of blood splashed over Amos' chair and splattered the wall and the Venetian blinds behind it. Porter fell backwards, kicking the bottle of whiskey off the coffee table, and Jolene screamed again.

She put a shaking hand over her mouth and sat up and peered over the coffee table at Porter's body. Her vision was fuzzy, but he was close enough that she could see that his arm was twisted under him in an impossible way. Blood stained the gray carpet beneath his shoulder in an ever-widening dark circle.

Blakey stood motionless beside her in front of the couch, holding the rifle in both hands, staring down at Porter, his shoulders hunched, his eyes wide, his mouth open, his breath gusting in bursts. She swiped at the blood on the side of her face and tried to get off the couch and go to Porter's side and help him, but her legs were numb and she couldn't stand. "Help him," she said weakly to Blakey. "Do something to help him."

Blakey looked down at her. He seemed dazed. "All I wanted was for him to go with me." His voice was hoarse and it quavered.

"Help him!" she screamed.

Blakey stared at her as though he didn't understand her. He looked at Porter. "I killed him," he said softly. "I killed my boy."

The overpowering odors of blood and whiskey filled Jolene's lungs. She fought back nausea. She sat up and looked at Porter's body. He was dying, if not dead already. She grabbed Blakey's arm and tried to pull herself up. His arm was hard, like stone, and he stood as stiff and still as a statue. He looked down at her, a blank look on his face, not seeming to understand what she was doing.

"We have to help him," she said.

He put his arm around her and grabbed her under her armpit and lifted her up. Her legs quivered and her knees began to buckle, but she leaned into his chest and he tightened his grip and held her up.

The trailer door swung open and a rush of cold air swirled inside. "Let her go," a gravelly voice said. Jolene turned to the sound and saw Amos standing in the open doorway with his rifle pointed at Blakey.

Blakey looked at Amos vacantly. "What?"

"Let her go."

Jolene's face was pressed to Blakey's shoulder, looking up at him. She was so close she could see the jagged edges of the scar that cut through his cheek, a piece of grit lodged in the beard stubble at the base of his chin, and a spot of saliva in the corner of his mouth.

He frowned at her, looking confused and disoriented.

"You let her go now," Amos said.

Blakey looked at Amos again and turned back to Jolene and his look of confusion gave way to a wounded, vulnerable expression.

"Let her go," Amos said again.

Blakey looked at the mouth of Amos' rifle and the wounded look went away. She felt the tension in his body go soft and she saw the lines in his face relax. He turned to Jolene, and in his face she saw resignation, acceptance, peace, and she knew what he would do. He looked at Amos and raised the rifle slowly with his free hand to point it at her head.

The explosion concussed her eardrums. Blakey's feet left the ground and he soared backwards over the couch and crashed against the wall and slid down to the floor. Jolene was thrown back onto the couch. She lay there stunned and motionless for a time. Then she held up her hands to look at them and saw that they were spattered with blood. Behind them she saw the blurred form of Amos, standing in the doorway, staring at Blakey's body. He dropped his rifle and rushed to her side. He fell on his knees, took her hand, and mouthed words she couldn't hear. Tears coursed down his cheeks. She felt his rough hand touch her bruised eye gently and she saw him look back at Porter's body just before she fainted.

Chapter 36

The Compensation

Billy emerged from the lawyer's office in downtown Jeetersburg and crossed Lighthorse Street carrying a thick packet of documents. His pickup truck was parked on the curb on the other side of the town square. He walked wearily over a brick walkway across the square toward his car. When he reached the fountain at its center, he stopped and sat down on a park bench in the sunlight and set the packet of documents beside him. It was midmorning. The day was warm and Billy had broken a sweat. He removed his hat, ran his hand through his hair, and looked up.

The fountain was a three-tiered stack of copper-colored urns. Water flowed from a ceramic pineapple at the top to cascade over the edges of each successive urn to a pool at the fountain's base. The sound of trickling water was peaceful, but Billy was not at peace.

He turned and looked at the statue of a nameless private in the Confederate infantry that stood behind him in front of the Hall of Deeds and Records. The stone-carved infantryman wore a ragged, tattered uniform. He stood at attention, facing the opposite end of the town square, saluting.

Billy's gaze wandered to the other end of the square to the subject of the infantryman's salute, a statue of General Robert E. Lee in front of the Selk County Courthouse. General Lee stood facing the infantryman with his back arched, one hand inside the breast of his coat, the other hand holding his hat down at his side, his face noble, but sad, and much older than his years.

The sculptor had captured a tortured look in Lee's calcified eyes. Billy had passed the statues hundreds of times over the years without paying much attention, but that day he saw in the general's eyes the great weight of his awful burden. General Lee sent thousands of men to their deaths. He watched them charge the enemy, take the fatal bullet to the gut, the heart, the face, the brain. He heard their cries of pain, their screams of agony. He saw the light go out of their eyes, all of it due to his decisions and under his direction.

"Blakey," Billy whispered.

He sat on the bench for a long time, overcome with guilt. Then he stood, put on his hat, and trudged to his truck. He drove from the square to Dolly Madison Hospital and went to the private room he had secured for Porter. It had been five days since the shooting and he hadn't been able to force himself to make the visit. He felt too ashamed, but Eva said he had to go see him. "None of it's his fault and he loves you." She was right. The boy deserved better than his grandfather's cowardice.

After the shooting, Billy decided that the boy deserved much more, in fact. Billy told Eva what he wanted to do. She agreed. They decided to retain only what they needed to live comfortably: Twin Ridge Farm and a generous portion of the investment portfolio and bank account. Billy met with his lawyer that morning to transfer the title to the old house, the store, and everything else to Porter. He had hoped it would relieve his guilt, but it did not.

Billy stood for a short spell outside the door of the hospital room, taking deep breaths and trying to compose himself. He finally mustered the courage to open the door and step inside. Maureen stood by Porter's bed, holding his hand, her lustrous red hair glistening in the sunlight that poured in through the window. She and Porter turned to Billy, and Billy blanched. "I didn't know you were here," he said to Maureen. "I'll come back later." He turned to leave.

"No! Wait, Grandpa!" Porter said.

Billy turned and looked at him.

Porter's face was bright. "I'm glad you came," he said.

Billy clutched the packet of documents and looked down at the floor, trying to swallow the lump in his throat. The pure joy in Porter's voice broke his heart, but he had to be strong for the boy.

"I'll leave you two alone for a bit," Maureen said. "I'll go get some lunch and come back later." She kissed Porter on the lips and walked past Billy to the door, touching Billy's sleeve as she passed. "Be strong," she whispered. "He's been asking for you."

Billy stared after Maureen. She had risen to the challenge of the tragedy. She was stronger than Billy and most everyone else who tried to help Porter survive the ordeal.

"Thanks for coming, Grandpa."

Billy walked stiffly to Porter's bedside. "Sorry I didn't come earlier, but I didn't have the guts."

"It wasn't your fault."

Billy looked down at the hospital bed sheet, at the place where the sheet lay flat against the bed, at the empty space where Porter's right arm should have been resting. "Some of it's my fault. I raised him. I broke his heart and spirit."

"You did the best you could. You and Grandma tried. He wouldn't listen. You can't blame yourself for what he was."

Billy closed his eyes to hold back the tears. He saw Blakey as a toddler, stepping uncertainly across the lawn, stiff-legged, halting every so often and waving his arms in the air to hold his balance and then leaning forward and coming on again, tippling toward the porch steps where Billy sat with his arms outstretched. Little Blakey giggled and fell into Billy's embrace. Billy saw himself catch the little boy and sweep him up in his arms and hug him and kiss his soft, baby-skin cheek. Billy opened his eyes and rubbed away the tears. "He turned out bad, but he wasn't born that way." Billy's voice quavered.

"I'd be just like him if it wasn't for you."

Billy shook his head and wiped his eyes. He took a deep breath and blew it out. "All right then. All right." He opened a folder and withdrew the sheaf of documents. "The lawyer drew up these papers."

"What are they?"

"Estate planning papers of some sort, legal mumbo-jumbo. The lawyer says we need to sign them today for tax reasons." He handed Porter the pen and held the papers in place for him. "Sign this one down here." Porter curled his tongue and struggled to scribble his signature with his left hand. "And this one here. This one at the top. Good. And this one." When Porter had signed the last page, Billy put the documents back in the folder.

"I don't get it." Porter said. "What do the papers say?"

"It's just some unfinished business, legal matters I should have attended to earlier. I'll explain it to you when they let you out of here, but I'm too strung out to go through it now." Billy swiped his hand over his face and let out another heavy breath. "I've got to go. I have to file these in the Hall of Deeds and Records before they shut down for the day." He hesitated at Porter's side and then touched his right shoulder awkwardly, his eyes blurred by tears. "If I could just go back and live it all again. If I had a second chance with Blakey …"

Porter placed his hand on Billy's hand. "Something good came from this, you know."

"I heard the good news," Billy said. After the shooting, Billy went to see Maureen's father. It took him two hours to convince Zeke to give Porter a chance, only to hear at the end of the conversation that Maureen had already gone to Porter's side against Zeke's advice. "I'm glad you two are back together. You're a good match."

"She's been with me every minute." He squeezed Billy's hand. "She says a one-armed hug from me means more than a two-armed hug from anyone else."

Billy swallowed hard, looked down at his hat, and rolled it in his hands. "Be good to her." He stood at Porter's bedside for a long time, fiddling with his hat. Then he put it on and patted Porter's left arm. "I'll be back tonight, son." He turned to leave.

"Grandpa? Promise me you won't blame yourself. I don't want you feeling bad every time you see me."

Billy looked away. "I'll always be glad to see you, boy."

He walked down the hall to the elevator and descended to the first floor,
where he found room 111 and went inside. There were four beds jammed
into a cramped, stuffy space. A single small window opposite the door faced
a concrete wall and let in very little light. In the first bed to Billy's left, a
middle-aged man was asleep with his mouth open, snoring loudly. In the
bed between him and the window, an ancient, bald, pasty-faced man turned
grayed-out, cataract-blinded eyes toward the sound of Billy's steps.
"Mattie?" he said in a hoarse voice.

"No, sir," Billy said.

The old man waved an emaciated arm and rolled toward the window. A
corpulent old man in a third bed lay with his meaty forearm over his brow,
moaning, "Oh, Lordy … oh, Lordy … oh, Lordy."

The bed to Billy's right had been cranked up to allow Amos to sit up.
"I'm glad you came," Amos said, staring at Billy with wide, watery eyes. A
curtain ran on a track in the ceiling around his bed; Billy pulled it around
the bed in a vain attempt to give them some privacy, but the cloth didn't
shut out the rhythmic snoring or the Oh Lordies.

Billy sat in a chair next to Amos' bed.

The corners of Amos' mouth twitched downward. "I wanted to tell you.
I … I'm sorry."

"You did right, Amos. He gave you no choice."

"But maybe I could have just winged him … shot him in the leg or the
shoulder … I didn't want to kill him. It happened before I—"

"It was the only way to save Jolene. You saved Porter's life, too. The
doctor said you staunched the bleeding with your belt. If you'd dithered
with Blakey, he would have bled to death."

Amos put a shaking hand to his brow. "There had to be another way,
but I couldn't think fast enough. My wits have always been slow." He shook
his head. "He's dead, and I can't take it back. I wish I could, but I can't."

"Amos, listen to me. You did nothing wrong. Blakey tried to kill them
and you saved them."

Amos' bleary red eyes blinked back the tears. "But he was your son,
and I killed him."

Billy looked down at his hat in his lap and fingered the crown of it. "I'm the one who killed Blakey, not you." They were quiet for a long while. Then Billy said, "Doctor Munger says you had a nervous breakdown. I know you never killed a living creature before, but now that you shot one for the right reasons, you have to get past it."

Amos cast his eyes down. "I've had a hard time living with that, but that's not the main problem. I'm a drunk. They're moving me to a rehab center to dry out." He ran his hand through his hair. "Three days clean and sober so far. It ain't much, but it's a start."

Billy stood. "You'll make it. You're tough." He put on his hat. "Who knows? Maybe when you're all the way unpickled, you'll have the good sense to go back home to Jolene." Billy drew back the curtain and went to the door. He stopped there and looked back at Amos, who was staring at the ceiling, his face flushed.

Billy went to the Hall of Deeds and Records and filed the paperwork. It was two in the afternoon when he left, and he was tired. He stood in the entrance between huge Doric columns. The sun shone through tall trees to cast dappled light on the lawn and the fountain in the town square. An oriole was perched on the edge of the fountain's top urn, his orange and black feathers brilliant in the sun. The oriole dipped its beak in the water once, twice, a third time. A second oriole alit beside it. Billy watched them bathe for a while and then walked across the square to his truck parked on the curb. It had been a hard day, but the hardest moment was yet to come.

Chapter 37

The Prayer

Billy drove north on the state road out of Jeetersburg to Fox Run, past his house and the store and a line of ten or twelve little houses. About fifty yards farther along he pulled into a gravel lot and parked under the pine trees in front of Grace Church, a rectangular red-brick building with a white steeple. Behind the church, a cemetery stretched across an open field to the foot of Feather Mountain.

Billy looked at the bundle of daffodils he'd bought at the florist shop in Jeetersburg. He picked them up and breathed in the scent of spring, the end of winter, and a new beginning.

He got out of his truck and looked at the sky. There was a pewter cloud cover. The air was close and muggy, but there was no threat of rain yet. A light breeze rustled the budding leaves of the shade trees bordering the cemetery and blew his gray hair across his face. He swept it back, put on his hat, and walked toward the cemetery gate.

Eva's pickup, the only other vehicle in the lot, was parked beside a wrought iron fence near the gate. The gate creaked when Billy opened it. He walked a path between rows of gray headstones, some of them bearing dates in the 1700s, a few so old the dates had worn off; others were leaning, broken, or lying prone in the tall grass. Two men in work clothes stood way off to Billy's right on the border of the cemetery, leaning against the wrought iron fence and smoking cigarettes. At the far end of the cemetery, at the foot of the mountain, he saw a tent. Standing under it were the preacher and Eva.

Billy took off his hat and wiped sweat from its hatband with a kerchief. He felt dizzy and weak. He stood still for a few moments until his queasiness passed, and then he walked on. The preacher looked up when he reached the tent. His violet eyes were kind and concerned under locks of an unruly black mane that protruded from his black wide-brimmed hat. He took off the hat and held it in both hands in front of his chest. His hair blew wildly in the wind. He tried unsuccessfully to smooth it down. He nodded to Billy. "Mr. Kirby."

"Preacher."

Eva wore a black dress, hat, and veil. She took Billy's arm in both her hands and pressed up against him. "How did it go?"

"He loves me. I don't know why."

"I know why."

Billy shook his head. He looked down at the casket resting at the bottom of the grave. The preacher had done as he wished: dug the grave on the edge of the cemetery, posted no notice of the burial, held no ceremony in the sanctuary, no graveside service. The casket's rich mahogany tones and the brass handles gleamed even in the dark depths of the freshly dug trench. He freed the yellow daffodils from the clasp that bound them together, leaned over the mouth of the grave, and dropped them to spread over the coffin. He stepped back, took off his hat, and wiped tears from his eyes.

The preacher spoke. "Are you sure about all this, Mr. Kirby? I know your son was troubled, but this seems rather harsh."

"It's meant to be honest, Preacher, not harsh."

The preacher hesitated and then said, "I wish you'd allow me to say a prayer for your son before we close the grave. Nothing elaborate, just a short plea for the Lord to have mercy on his soul."

Billy felt Eva's hands tighten on his arm. He was quiet for a long time, staring at the casket. Then he said, "I'll agree to a silent prayer, Preacher."

"As you wish." The preacher bowed his head and closed his eyes. Billy and Eva did not. After a full minute passed, the preacher said, "Amen," and made a cross in the air over the grave with his hand. "Is there anything else

I can do for you, Mr. Kirby?"

"Give us a few minutes here alone, if you please, and have them cover the grave as soon as we leave."

"Yes, sir." The preacher put on his hat and walked a path to the far side of the cemetery to join the two men leaning against the wrought iron fence.

When they were alone, Eva said, "Why the silent prayer?"

"The preacher tried his best with Blakey after he got in trouble. He earned the right to pray for him."

They stood in silence for a long time, staring into the grave. Billy finally said, "How long's it been since you saw your boy?"

"Twenty years."

"You know where he is?"

"Georgia, serving fifteen years for armed robbery and assault."

"Do you blame yourself?"

Eva leaned more heavily into him. "We made mistakes with Franklin, but he made his choices."

"Blakey made his, too, but I put him on the wrong path. I deserve a big part of the blame for what he became."

She put her arm around Billy's shoulder. They stood together over the grave until he took a deep breath and said, "Goodbye, boy." He put on his hat and they followed the path back through the gate to the parking lot.

At his truck, they stood facing one another. Eva pulled the collar of Billy's jacket around him and kissed him on the lips. "Don't look back," she whispered. "Look ahead to happier times." She patted his chest, walked to her truck, and drove away.

Billy looked across the cemetery at the preacher standing under the tent by Blakey's grave. The gravediggers pushed their spades into the mound and began to fill the hole with earth.

Chapter 38

The Marriage

Grace Church could seat a hundred people, and on Easter Sunday, the pews were full a half hour before the wedding. The ushers set up metal folding chairs and people stood along the back wall of the sanctuary. Billy was not surprised that so many people came to his wedding; it was the talk of the county. Even at the expense of part of their Easter Holiday, the good people of Selk County couldn't resist witnessing with their own eyes the spectacle of a filthy-rich old man marrying a down-and-out widow twenty years younger than him.

Billy stood tall at the altar, squared his shoulders, and faced the back of the sanctuary. The preacher's wife banged out the piano chords of "Here Comes the Bride," and Eva appeared in the doorway at the end of the aisle on Toby Vess' arm. There were audible gasps throughout the congregation. She wore a blood-red knit dress and a navy blue bonnet with a wide brim turned down in front. Her friend Gertie Wilson had styled her hair and applied her makeup.

Eva had modeled the outfit for Billy in her bedroom at Twin Ridge Farm the previous day. She looked stunning, but Billy was shocked. The knit dress was tight and clung to her figure. "Aren't brides supposed to wear white?" he had asked tentatively. "A flowing gown with a train? A veil and all?"

"White symbolizes chastity and purity. With what we've been up to the last few weeks, I don't think I qualify."

He looked her up and down. "The gossips will wag their tongues off."

She laughed. "What difference does it make? They're already convinced I'm a gold-bricking slut defrauding a doddering old fool." She spread her arms out and twirled around. "I figure we might as well show em they got us pegged right."

So there she was at the church doors dressed in red and painted like a woman of the evening, and she was the most beautiful creature he'd ever seen. Toby ushered her down the aisle. She nodded to her friends, grinning impishly. When they reached the altar, Toby handed Eva's arm to Billy; the preacher led them through pledges of faithfulness; Porter produced the ring; Billy lifted the rim of Eva's bonnet; and they kissed passionately to seal their vows, accompanied by another chorus of gasps.

An hour later, Billy stood in his back yard, leaning on the split-rail fence, gazing at the pasture that swept down to the barn by Little Bear River. It was a beautiful spring afternoon. The cattle grazed peacefully in the field. Daffodils grew in clumps in the pasture and along the river's banks. His eyes fell on the spot where he and Jolene had spread their blanket in the sun so many years ago, and for once, his heart didn't ache to return to the summer of his life. What lay ahead of him seemed to hold more promise than all the days of his past.

He turned and looked at the garden party. Beds of yellow, blue, and violet pansies bloomed throughout the yard. The little crowd of friends stood among the flowers on the freshly mowed lawn, chatting amiably with one another. Easy laughter floated up from one group and then another. The men's starched white shirts gleamed in the sunlight. Easter bonnets of every color and style bobbed and turned as women smiled and brought crystal to their lips to sip mint juleps.

On the far side of the crowd sitting on the porch steps alone, staring into the distance, was Stogie Morris. The ghosts of Billy's past floated across his mind and dampened his good mood. Eva had said, "Don't look back"; he tried to follow her advice, but his greatest regrets would not die. Blakey,

Stogie, Amos.

Billy had thought he might never see Stogie again, but the old cuss sat in the third row of pews at the wedding dressed in his Sunday suit. He didn't look Billy in the eye throughout the ceremony and he didn't congratulate him or shake his hand afterwards. Stogie would always hate Billy for what he thought he had done to Polly. Their friendship was dead and Billy could never revive it, but Stogie's presence at the wedding signaled that he'd decided they could coexist.

Billy looked down into his crystal glass at his mint julep. There was nothing he could do about Blakey, either. He would carry to his grave an awful burden of guilt and a gaping, ragged hole in his heart.

He wiped tears from his eyes, sighed heavily, and looked at the people laughing and talking. His gaze turned to the forlorn figure of Amos Hukstep, dressed in an ill-fitting mud-turtle-brown suit, staring down at the punch bowl longingly. Billy scanned the crowd for Jolene and saw her sitting beside Toby at a picnic table under the big sweetgum tree.

He looked from one to the other, then set his glass atop a fence post and worked his way through the crowd, through slaps on the back and congratulations. When he reached Amos' side, he clapped him on the shoulder. "I need a favor. Come with me."

Billy pulled Amos through the crowd to the picnic table. When Jolene looked up at them, the sunlight glinted in her blue irises and her eyes sparkled like sapphire, even with the swelling and bruises. Billy smiled to see her. She looked at Amos and then down at the picnic table.

"I need you to do a favor for me and Toby," Billy said to Amos. "Toby was supposed to drive Jolene home, but I need him to drive me and Eva to Jeetersburg. I'd appreciate it if you'd take her home."

Toby covered a crinkly smile with his hand.

"Why can't you drive yourself?" Amos said.

"I can't see good enough. I lost my glasses."

Amos looked at Jolene and his frown softened. "I reckon I can do it if it's all right with Jolene."

"Is that all right with you, Jolene?" Billy asked.

Jolene cast a severe look at Amos. "Are you sober?"

Amos' face flushed. He put his hands in his pockets and looked at the ground. "Nineteen days."

Jolene said nothing for a while, and her contemptuous expression led Billy to fear she might reject the offer. Then she said, "All right, but only if he's sober."

"I'm on the wagon for good," Amos said. He shrugged. "At least, that's my goal."

"All right then, we have a deal," Billy said, rubbing his hands together. To Toby, he said, "I'll come get you when Eva and I are ready to leave." Toby nodded.

Billy turned to find Eva directly behind him, smiling. She took his arm and walked him back to his mint julep on the fence post. He downed the rest of it.

"You don't own a pair of glasses, Mr. Kirby," she said.

"No, ma'am. My vision is perfect."

Chapter 39

The Whippoorwill

As Amos drove her home that evening along Whiskey Road, Jolene watched the steep mountainsides of Saddleback Cove slide by out the window and told herself not to think about him. Not her many years with him, or that day during the blizzard sixty years ago when they first kissed, or the affection she'd heard in his voice when he told Blakey to turn her loose. She told herself to numb her senses and to not look back.

Amos pulled the truck to the side of the road and stopped. She looked out the window. She couldn't see clearly; Blakey's blow had ruined her glasses and she hadn't ordered a new pair yet. She planned to see the world clearly again someday, but she wasn't quite ready.

She squinted out the window at the landscape. It was dusk. The amorphous gray and white blurs of the trailers weren't out there. The scenery was a blur of green clumps in front of a big red structure, a house or a barn or a shed of some sort, beneath a sky of soft blobs of purple and burnt orange and auburn. Jolene widened her eyes and peered at the hazy images. She had no idea where they were or why Amos had stopped there.

"Sunset's pretty," he said.

She stared at a fuzzy orange sun. The horizon was a runny watercolor painting of billowy clouds. "Yes, it is." She saw the reflection of her pale blue eyes in the window. She flattened her hand against the glass beside the image of her eyes.

"He lied."

"What?" she said, closing her eyes and leaning her forehead against the cool glass.

"Billy lied. He don't wear glasses to drive."

Jolene tried not to think about Amos or his words or their meaning. She tried not to care about him or to feel anything for him.

"He was wrong about your eyes, too," Amos said.

She turned to him, alarmed. "What do you mean?"

"He said you had the prettiest eyes in Selk County. It was wrong, what he said, and he knew it."

The air went out of Jolene's lungs and tears welled in her eyes and streamed down her face. She clawed at the door handle until the door mercifully sprang open.

"Wait," Amos said, grabbing her arm. "You don't understand—"

She stumbled out of the truck and staggered down a bank into the midst of the blurred clumps of green, sobbing uncontrollably. Weeds brushed against her legs as she churned toward the colors on the horizon, toward the big red structure and the watercolor sunset behind it. She heard the clank of the truck door slamming behind her. "Jo! Wait!"

She ran as fast as she could away from Amos, his unrelenting refusal to compromise his principles, his ruthless dedication to the truth. He wouldn't even allow her to believe the one lie she still told herself, the only remaining myth that made her life worth living. Jolene sobbed and ran on and on until something sliced her face and clung to her hair. She screamed and fell into the weeds, thrashing on the ground and trying to regain her feet before Amos could overtake her and force her to face all the world's jagged, hurtful points.

He was on her before she could stand. He lifted her to her feet. She slapped at him and tried to pull free, but he wrapped her in a bear hug and wouldn't let her go. She pounded his shoulders with her fists, sobbing and screaming, but he was stronger than she was. Through the din of her cries, she heard his muffled voice, but she fought him until she lost her wind and fell against him.

He held her up while she cried. After a long while, she cried herself out and she leaned against him listlessly. His voice droned on and on, and despite her best efforts, she couldn't block it all out. "Bullitt's apple orchard … old now and broke down because nobody prunes … old man Furman Bullitt died twenty … don't look the way it did all those years ago."

Amos finally fell silent. He held her in his bear hug, supporting all her weight because she had no strength left. After a long stretch of time, he touched her cheek with his chapped, rough hand. "That branch scratched you deep. Are you all right, Jo?"

Her eyes focused on his round, soft face with the sagging flesh and the dumb, blank, plodding look in his eyes, the look of the truth, and her strength came back in a wave of anger and she found her legs and stood on her own.

"Why?" she demanded.

Amos' dull eyes rounded. "What?"

"Why did you have to tell me Billy lied about my eyes? What does it matter to you? Why is it any of your business what he said about my eyes?"

Amos' eyes widened even more. "No … You don't understand what I meant. I'm not good with the words. At least with you … What I meant was Billy's been out of the county, out of the state, too. He's been to North and South Carolina and Tennessee a couple times, unless he lied about that, too. But even if he didn't, he knew better."

Amos' disjointed words and phrases made no sense, but it occurred to her that he hadn't said so many words to her at one time in years. And there was a look on his face she hadn't seen there for so long she couldn't identify it, a look of desperation or urgency, an energy of some sort.

Amos said, "Your eyes are prettier than Billy said. Don't you see?" He stepped back, propped his hands on his hips, and blew out a breath. "He said you have the prettiest eyes in Selk County, but he was wrong and he knew it. They're the prettiest eyes he's seen anywhere. Me, too. I didn't ever say it, though." Amos puffed out his cheeks and looked down at the ground. Sweat drenched his twitching face. "I knew it. I just never said it." He shook his head. "I wish I was good with the words with you, Jo. Seems I could never tell it to you the way I felt it. The feelings were too big and I always choked out."

He put his hands in his pockets and hunched his shoulders. "Billy said I never told you how pretty your eyes are. He said what happened was my fault." He wiped sweat from his forehead and glanced at her, then cast his eyes down at the ground. "In the clinic for drunks, I thought all the time about what he said, and after I dried out good, I finally understood what he meant." Amos shook his head back and forth slowly. "He told the truth for once. It was my fault."

Jolene was surprised. He seemed to be forgiving her. It was a pity, she thought, that it was coming so late. A few months ago, it would have meant so much to her. It would have made such a difference in their lives. She looked around at the clumps of green and wondered why he had chosen this time and place to say these things to her. "Where are we?"

"Bullitt's apple orchard." Amos pointed at one of the green clumps near the big red blur. "We sat on a blanket right there under the apple tree nearest to that barn. Don't you remember?" His face reddened. "It was our first time. In 1907." His voice was husky.

A montage of ancient images of young Amos and his urgent need rolled through her mind. Now Amos' sagging, aged visage was tense and flushed as he stood before her at dusk in front of a spectacular sunset. "I have a blanket. Up there in the truck." He stared at Jolene uneasily. "Maybe we could sit under that tree again." He sighed and shrugged. "It wouldn't be the same. We're old now. I mean I'm old. You're … well … you'll never be …"

Jolene recognized then the desperate expression on Amos' face. Passion was unmistakably etched into his features. Jolene was struck dumb. Amos had ignored her for years. Now suddenly he seemed to want to make love to her.

"Maybe we can bring back the old memories if we sit under that apple tree and, well, you know …"

Jolene stared at Amos for a full ten seconds, speechless. Amos returned her stare anxiously. Then Jolene slapped him hard across the face. His head twisted to one side with the impact of the blow and spittle flew from his mouth. He rubbed his cheek and looked at her with tears in his eyes.

"You froze me out in the cold," she said. "You didn't touch me or talk to me or look my way unless you needed a meal cooked or your clothes washed. Then you found some dusty old notes in my childhood bedroom and you persecuted me mercilessly for a mistake I made when I was too young to know any better. I begged you to forgive me over and over again, but you were too mean and stubborn and coldhearted to do it. Now you come to your senses and you think all you have to do is tell me my eyes are pretty and spread a blanket under an old apple tree and I'll lay down with you and give you my favors. I'm not a light switch you can turn on and off when you feel like it. I'm a person with feelings. I hurt and I cry just like you do, and you've hurt me badly and I've cried too much to dismiss what you've done just because you finally feel like touching me again."

Amos continued to rub his jaw. He looked stunned.

"Why did you stop talking to me in the first place?" Jolene said. "Why did you shut me out of your life?"

He took a deep breath. "I don't know," he said softly.

She scowled at him and shook her finger in his face. "Poppycock! You most certainly do know! You're a stubborn, foolish old man, but you're not so stupid that you don't know your reasons. Tell me why you shut me out and tell me now!"

Amos bowed his head.

"That's it then. I'm through with you!" She grabbed him by the arm and pulled him toward the truck. "Take me home and leave me alone for good. I never want to see you again."

Amos pulled his arm free. "All right, damn it!" He stepped back from her. He looked angry, but as he stared at her, his expression softened. "All right." He turned sideways to her and looked at the sunset, at the ground, and at the barn. He took a deep breath and looked at her. His flushed face reddened even more. "I didn't do very good," he said in a strained voice. He looked down and was quiet for a long time. "We don't have much. It's because of me. I failed at everything I tried to do." He looked off at the sunset. "I let you down. You deserved a lot better. I kept trying to do better, but nothing worked. Time went by and I got old and I knew I would never do any better." He ran his hand over his eyes and then looked at her, his face sagging. "I got so I couldn't look you in the eye … or touch you. I was too ashamed of myself."

Jolene's anger drained away. "All this time I've been living in hell thinking I'd done something to make you unhappy. All you had to do was tell me what was bothering you. We could have talked it out and both of us would have been better off." Her eyes filled with tears. "We've suffered so much because you wouldn't tell me what was in your heart."

Tears filled Amos' eyes, too.

They were quiet for a long time.

Jolene wiped her tears away and looked at the sunset and the red and green blobs that Amos said were the barn and the apple tree. "I don't want to sit under that old apple tree."

Amos hung his head.

"I don't want to live off memories from sixty years ago," she said. "There's only one way to patch up our differences, and it's not what you want us to do under that apple tree. The only way is for us to talk to each other. You have to tell me why you think you failed at everything and I have to tell you why I slept with Billy. We have to talk about how we feel about each other with all that's gone on between us. And if by some miracle we get through this hard time and stay together, we have to talk to each other about our feelings every day and night until one of us dies. Can you do that, Amos?"

He hesitated. "I'm not good at talking about my feelings."

"You're wrong. You're very good at it. The last few minutes prove how good you are."

He looked doubtful. "This is different."

"How is it different?"

Amos toed a tuft of weeds with his boot. "I made myself talk cause you said it's the only way to get back together, but it's hard on me. I can't do it all the time."

"Why?"

Amos opened his mouth to speak and then closed it and turned sideways to her again. He shook his head back and forth slowly. "It's not my way." He swiped his sleeve across his mouth. "I'm sorry, Jo. I just can't do it."

She stared at him sorrowfully. "If you won't share your feelings with me, I don't want you around." She turned and walked back through the orchard and climbed the bank. When she got in the truck, she realized Amos hadn't followed her. She looked out the window. A blurred brown lump stood among the clumps of green. She watched him move to the green clump nearest to the barn and linger there. He stood under the tree for a long time. Then he walked across the orchard and climbed the bank.

He got in the truck, started the engine, and gripped the steering wheel with both hands, but he didn't shift into gear. He sat behind the wheel without moving, staring straight ahead. The engine idled a steady thrum, and the cab vibrated slightly. A car whizzed past them on Whiskey Road and Jolene watched its amorphous black mass disappear around a turn.

Amos stirred and cleared his throat. "My daddy was rough on me. Yelled at me. Beat me."

Jolene looked over at Amos. His knuckles were white from gripping the steering wheel so tightly.

"He never said a kind word to me. Never touched me except to hit me. Made me feel dumb and no-account, like I couldn't do anything right." He let go of the steering wheel and leaned back in the seat. "My momma meant all the world to me. She built me up every time he tore me down." He was quiet for a long time, staring straight ahead. "I loved her." He was silent for another long stretch. Then his chest and shoulders began to tremble. "She proved to be a liar," he said in a hoarse voice, "and it almost killed me." He gripped the steering wheel again. "I kept my feelins inside after that." The muscles of his arms and chest looked as tense as steel bands.

"I didn't know your father beat you. You never told me."

He bowed his head, his chin on his chest. "I never told anyone."

A long silence passed between them. Then Amos said in a reedy voice, "I want to be with you, Jo. I don't want to talk about my feelins, but I'll try to tell you such things if it's the only way."

She looked out her window. The sun had set. From somewhere beyond the orchard, a whippoorwill called, greeting them at last light, their guide into the night.

"It's the only way," she said.

They both gazed at the horizon in the direction of the whippoorwill's call. Then Amos shifted the truck into gear and steered it into the road.

THE END

Acknowledgments

My heartfelt thanks to Meghan Pinson of My Two Cents Editing for her advice and guidance through several major revisions. Without her encouragement I probably would have abandoned this story. She is tactful and yet candid, sensitive to my boundless ego and yet fearless and firm. She has a great gift of being able to tease the highest quality from my work while preserving my style and voice. She's simply the best there is. Thanks to Rhonda Erb, also with My Two Cents Editing, for her careful and thorough work on the final edit. She and Meghan are a winning team and great fun to work with.

Many thanks to Outrider Literary for providing invaluable project management, research, and assistance with completing this book and connecting with readers.

As with *The Closing*, fellow author Pamela Fagan Hutchins reviewed a near-final draft and made suggestions that vastly improved the story. Thanks so much to her, Eric Hutchins, and SkipJack Publishing for their continuing support and encouragement throughout the writing of this book and the publishing process.

Last but not least, thanks to my brother, Larry Oder, and my sister-in-law, Debby. The cover is adapted from a cell phone photograph taken by Debby. Larry suggested, tongue deeply in cheek, that it would make a good cover for *Old Wounds to the Heart*. In the photo, Eugene stands in the fog in late winter in a field in Virginia, nineteen years old, ancient in Angus years, grizzled and wizened by age, heading into what will likely be his last summer. When I saw the photo, it took me a while to get past Larry's joke and realize that I saw Billy staring back at me. Devon Oder then worked hard to enhance the quality of the image, and Hannah Hawker adapted it to the cover. Many thanks to all of you.

About the Author

Ken Oder was born in Virginia in the coastal tidewater area near the York and James Rivers, where military installations during World Wars I and II fueled the growth of urban centers like Norfolk, Hampton, and Newport News. His father worked for the Navy Mine Depot in Yorktown and later as a Hudson dealer until he heard his calling and became the minister at Mount Moriah Methodist Church in 1960. The family moved to White Hall, Virginia, a farm town of about fifty people at the foot of the Blue Ridge Mountains. The mountains and the rural culture were a jarring contrast to the busy coastal plains, but once the shock wore off, Ken came to love it there. He found the mountains and hollows spectacularly beautiful and the people thoughtful, friendly, and quietly courageous. White Hall became Ken's home, and his affection and respect for the area and its people have never left him.

Ken and his wife moved to Los Angeles in 1975, where he practiced law and served as an executive until he retired. They still live near their children and grandchildren in California, but a piece of Ken's heart never left White Hall. That place and time come out in his stories.

Please visit www.kenoder.com and connect with the author on Goodreads for news and new releases.

Fiction from SkipJack Publishing

PAMELA FAGAN HUTCHINS

the Katie & Annalise novels

Saving Grace

Leaving Annalise

Finding Harmony

the Michele novels

Going for Kona

the Emily novels

Heaven to Betsy

Earth to Emily

REBECCA (R.L.) NOLEN

The Dry

Deadly Thyme

KEN ODER

the Whippoorwill Hollow novels

The Closing

Old Wounds to the Heart

ANTHOLOGIES

Tides of Possibility, edited by K.J. Russell

Tides of Impossibility, edited by K.J. Russell and C. Stuart Hardwick

Nonfiction from SkipJack Publishing

HELEN COLIN
My Dream of Freedom: From Holocaust to My Beloved America

PAMELA FAGAN HUTCHINS

The Clark Kent Chronicles:
A Mother's Tale of Life with her ADD & Asperger's Son

Hot Flashes and Half Ironmans:
Middle-Aged Endurance Athletics Meets the Hormonally Challenged

How to Screw Up Your Kids:
Blended Families, Blendered Style

How to Screw Up Your Marriage:
Do-Over Tips for First-Time Failures

Puppalicious and Beyond:
Life Outside the Center of the Universe

What Kind of Loser Indie Publishes,
and How Can I Be One, Too?

Praise for *The Closing*

Book One of Ken Oder's Whippoorwill Hollow novels
Finalist – Foreword Reviews Book of the Year Awards 2014

AN INTRIGUING HISTORICAL LEGAL THRILLER

". . . an intriguing legal thriller that looks deeply at corruption in the jurisprudence system. The recovering alcoholic protagonist is a fascinating lead as he begins to regain his lost life when he accepts the harm he committed to innocent people, his wife, his mother, his mentor and himself. . . . the enjoyable storyline spins from a superb capital case to a more conventional David vs. Goliath thriller, fans will appreciate Ken Oder's strong historical fiction. - *THE MYSTERY GAZETTE*

INTELLIGENT . . . ACHINGLY ROMANTIC

"Ken Oder debuts with an intelligent, atmospheric, and achingly romantic legal thriller. I loved this book, and I can't wait for the next one." – PAMELA FAGAN HUTCHINS, AUTHOR OF THE KATIE & ANNALISE NOVELS

TIMELY AND COMPELLING

"Moments after meeting his client, death-row inmate Kenneth Deatherage, attorney Nate Abbitt explains: *Cases are pending before the United States Supreme Court challenging the constitutionality of the death penalty. There's a nationwide moratorium on executions until the court rules.* Ironically, just days after *The Closing* became available on Amazon, Oklahoma botched the execution of Clayton Lockett, who according to eye-witness accounts, tried to get up and speak after being given the supposedly lethal injection. Although this book is set in 1968 Virginia, the subject matter could hardly be more topical. . . . This is a great summer read. You won't be able to put it down. And whatever side of the issue you are on, *The Closing* should inform your view about capital punishment." - MARLENE MUNOZ, AMAZON REVIEWER

A COMPELLING PAGE-TURNER

"Life in rural Virginia is realistically painted . . . great insight into the corridors of the legal profession . . . tight, solid writing . . . the ending had good punch to it. Looking forward to the next one!" - MOODY, AMAZON REVIEWER

EXCELLENT READ

". . . very true to the rural Virginia location, you truly can feel the humidity, dust and sweat. Highly recommended." - S. HEINECKE, AMAZON REVIEWER

Available in e-book and paperback
www.kenoder.com